The Battles of Rock Harbor– A "Bugging In" tale of the Apocalypse

By J. B. Craig

February 18, 2018

This book is dedicated to my bride, S.L. Craig. Thank you, dear for giving me the space to get this book out of my head, and not mocking me too terribly for it. I love you!

A special thanks to all of you who read and helped edit the "friends and family version" of the book. All you Salmon Silencers and other family members who gave me non-stop grief, but ended up helping make the book better, rock out loud!

Note to Readers – The explosive devices that are created in this book are NOT made with the ingredients mentioned. Yes, I was a combat Engineer, and No, I'm not going to give some 18-year-old kid the real recipe for making bombs. For the demolitions experts out there, you know well enough why I'm not sharing our recipes. Please don't write to me challenging the recipe's. They're vague, and wrong on purpose. Hopefully that won't damage your enjoyment of the rest of the story. Hooaahhh, fellow soldiers and other service members! Thanks for your understanding.

This is a work of fiction. Any similarity to actual persons, living or dead, or actual events, is purely coincidental.

Editorial footnote to readers: For our non-military readers, 'Whooaahhh?' is an Army term for "you feel me? 'Whooaahh!' is the proper response, equivalent to "Hell Yes – I wanna Kill!" If it was the Marine Corps, they would be saying "Ooo-Rah?" and "Ooo-RAH!." Air Force guys ask the same question with "Dude, we cool?" and respond we "Dude, we cool!" I won't get into the Navy, as they picked it up very recently, and it sounds a lot like wanna-be Marines, but without capital letters and punctuation. The Coast Guard are very brave defenders of our coast and may encounter "danger" more days per year than the other branches, but don't have anything like that. God Bless all those branches that serve the USA, and there will always be Inter-service rivalries – that's all this is. It's what service members do when not being shot at by the enemy. As soon as that happens, we are all one fearless killing machine of One Heart and Mind.

The Battles of Rock Harbor– A "Bugging In" tale of the Apocalypse

By J. B. Craig

Chapter 1 – Early April, Not too far in the future

The end of the world as we know it, aka TEOTWAWKI, interrupted a rare fishing hat-trick. That's when one person has 3 rods in the water, and there's a fish on each one. Greg arrived at Rock Harbor around noon on a Monday morning in April. Rock Harbor is a peninsula of land jutting into the Potomac river downstream of Washington, DC, and Northeast of Richmond, VA. In his truck, he had his own fishing kayak. He also had his Bug-Out Bag, a Mauser hunting rifle, 2 low-capacity 9mm pistols, his favorite .40 caliber 1911, an army duffel bag filled with his oldest much worn clothes, assorted fishing gear, and some food, wine and liquor. His plan was to drop off a bunch of this stuff at the family River house and take a week to decompress from his recent heartbreak. He would do that by fishing, writing, drinking and flying his kite. Then he'd go back to Atlanta and deal with the impending divorce, grab the rest of his stuff, and move in to this house for the foreseeable future. The house was vacant except for a few weekends in the summer, when the extended family had a long weekend Luau, or party. His family heritage was half Hawaiian and half Scottish, but he spent much more time with the Hawaiian side. They threw great Luau's, with outstanding food.

According to Google, high tide at Captain's Point was scheduled for around 10 pm and 10am. He fished the evening incoming tide from the dock, and only got a few nibbles in the Harbor. Walking up the 15 stairs from the river to the main level of the house to get a fresh beer made him breathe heavy, another hint that he was out of shape, and needed to work on it. He fished until about midnight with no success, so he went back in the house and drank from the table full of "collective alcohol". Family members who came here would just leave whatever booze they brought on the bar, with beers in the kitchen, and back-up refrigerator downstairs. There was also a stand-up freezer downstairs, mostly filled with ice, and a few frozen foods. The kitchen fridge was just for day-to-day foods. Greg staggered around the house, remembering times with his Grandparents, until he was drunk enough to pass out. It was the first time he ever slept in his Grandparent's bed in the master bedroom. He inherited the house, so he knew that eventually the new master of the property would have to take up residence in the master bedroom. The last thing he thought before losing consciousness was "Nice bed, Pop".

Greg got a few hours of sleep, then had a double screwdriver for breakfast, and went fishing around 9am. He broke a good, relatively healthy (OK, not dead yet) sweat as he rowed the 1975-ish model Aluminum Montgomery Ward's rowboat out the channel of Rock Harbor, into the Nomini River, and steered left (Port, he reminded himself) into the middle of the Potomac River. The harbor was about 20 miles downstream from the 301 bridge that was near Dahlgren Naval Station and was one of the bridges to Southern Maryland. Later today, he would figure out which outboard in the garage worked, and probably mount it (heh, heh, 'mount' he thought to himself), but it was high tide, and he was going to go fishing, even if the new proprietor of the local convenience store where he got bait yesterday told him it was still a few weeks too early for any of the best fish. Greg had a streak of the Scottish stubbornness that his other Grandfather, father and siblings had. Being half Hawaiian and half Scottish gave him a personality that matched his Gemini astrological sign. Tell him that he couldn't do something, and he would work over-time to prove you wrong. He knew that at least the Channel Cat would bite during high tide, it just took patience, and some beers.

Greg paddled out to the junction of the Nomini and Potomac rivers, upstream of the Chesapeake Bay. There are 2 bridges connecting Maryland to Virginia once South of the Washington, DC beltway

Woodrow Wilson Bridge - the aforementioned Route 301 bridge, and the Chesapeake Bay Bridge-tunnel, a 23-mile-long bridge from Virginia Beach to the Delmarva Peninsula (Delaware, Maryland, Virginia) on the Eastern Shore of the Chesapeake Bay. Between the 2 bridges was just a whole lot of beautiful, tidal river and bay. The Potomac joins the Bay at Point Lookout, MD. There, the Bay gets wide. While being mostly known for the Maryland Blue Crab, the Chesapeake Bay estuary is full of wildlife. The tide coming in and out cleans some of the runoff and trash out of the Baltimore-DC corridor, while keeping the Blue Crabs fed with the dense population's runoff crap.

Greg's Hawaiian grandfather bought the 25-year old rowboat that Greg was currently in when it was new. He was following Pop's tradition, with 2 fishing rods rigged for double-bottom-hook fishing. These rods were ideal for catching anything from the small, but mighty tasty white perch, to the much larger Striper (also known as Striped Bass, or Rockfish), but today he figured it would be a catfish or croaker or nothing at all, as it was still too early for either Yellow or White Perch. Greg almost never came home with no fish on the stringer, and today was no exception. On the way out, he trolled a few blood worms in the Nomini channel, and already had a few nice sized croakers (they make that noise when you grab them), and a couple white perch dragging in the wake of the boat. Take that, web sites! Maybe he'd leave a comment on his success later.

Pop, when he was still alive, used to razz Greg, like any Navy man will to an Army Veteran (and vice-versa) about Greg's insistence on using a stringer. Greg didn't like to see the fish suffocate in the 5 Gallon bucket that Pop used and was basically too lazy to change out the water as often as Pop did, to ensure they didn't suffocate. With a stringer, at the end of a long fishing day, every fish on the stringer was still fresh, with the rare exception of the fish that some sea turtle decided to bite in half.

Greg reached the edge of the channel, as indicated by the channel marker, and dropped anchor in about 15 feet of water. He waited for the wind and tide to get him settled in a relatively stable place. He knew from experience that he could do a nice cast, and easily be in over 20 feet of water from this spot. His strategy was to cast one double-bottom rig into the deeper edge of the channel. Another rig would go sideways and hang out at the top edge of the channel. With both rods in place, and the tide running in, he clipped little bells to the tips of them. It's hard to watch 2 rods in different directions anyway, and the bells helped. Finally, Greg pulled out his ultra-light Ugly Stik, with a Mitchell reel, and a #3 Mepps Black Fury spinner, and started casting for top-water fish. This model of Black Fury had caught Greg many nice sized Stripers over the years, but the bigger perch, spot and occasional sea trout would hit it, too.

About 10 minutes later, one of the bells pinged lightly. Greg was confident, based on the light "ting", that it was the subtle kiss of a Channel Catfish or one of its smaller cousins, like the blue or grey cat. They tended to cruise along the bottom of the river, and sniff/eat anything on the bottom of the river. Catfish would circle back if they found something good, and then go over whatever bait was laid down. Catfish were the kind of fish a fisherman had to be patient with. Around the 3rd nibble, they'd gulp down the bait, and it was relatively easy to set the hook and land them. Greg figured he had 1 or 2 more casts with the ultra-light, and on the first cast, he got a hard strike.

"FISH ON", Greg yelled out of habit. Even though nobody was nearby to hear the call, that was drilled into him as a child, when fishing the Salmon River with his Scottish father. If you didn't say that and had a huge Salmon on the line in Upstate New York, you'd very likely have your fishing neighbor cast and tug, as usual, but they'd tug the hook out of the Salmon, making both of you pissed, and the fish relieved. He'd been in a few fights on the river with assholes that knew what they were doing and hooked his fish on purpose.

"I think this is either the world's smallest Striper, or the world's biggest Perch", Greg said to his audience of none. This wasn't unusual for a guy who sang to himself, or just had random conversations with nobody in his head. Greg knew he didn't have a trophy Striper, but did have a decent fish – maybe a sea trout, or a large perch. The hook was set, and the fish was running with the very low drag Greg typically had on his light rods. If nothing else, low drag made little fish feel big, at least for as long as he couldn't see them.

At that point, Greg heard the bell on his channel-rod ring again and reached over with his other hand to set the hook as the rod tried to jump out of the boat. "Now, THAT'S a big cat" he said to his invisible audience, as he clamped the ultra-light between his legs, and let the mystery fish run while he started to dip and pump the reel with the (likely) catfish on it. As he was reeling in the second rod, the third one bent over, and he threw his leg over it as the line screamed out in a third direction. "Hat trick, bitches!", he yelled out loud to nobody but the 3 fish.

Suddenly, it sounded like God was making the biggest bag of microwave popcorn ever. Loud explosions, and bright flashes of light were happening all over both the Maryland and Virginia shorelines. Greg looked at the closest peninsula, Captain's Point, and watched as a transformer on the telephone pole near him exploded. With the way water carried sound, Greg heard the explosions as they moved down both sides of the Potomac, towards Point Lookout in Maryland, and Norfolk in Virginia. "I hope that's not what I think it is," said Greg out loud. He read lots of prepper fiction, and it was starting to sound like a grid-down scenario, potentially with hackers doing what he had read about in several books.

As things started to get quiet, a shadow passed over the boat. A LARGE shadow making the whoop-whoop sound of a ceiling fan out of balance. Greg thought the shadow that passed over him was that Osprey whose nest he came too close to about 20 minutes ago. Osprey are large birds that build their nests in the strangest of places. More specifically, they find a stray piling or channel Marker on the river, and then they bring a whole tree's worth of shrubbery to it, and build a nest. They get pissy whenever Man comes close to their nest. This is even though Man (the species) is the one who put the damn channel Marker in the middle of the river in the first place. They "Peep Peep Peep" in a very "scary" birdie voice, and take off from the nests, circling Man like he is their prey. They are beautiful creatures, especially when flying over Man, showing off their black and white wing feathers They never actually attack Man. Well, Greg had been shat upon by an Osprey, but that's the worst they've ever hit him with. They just put on a show, and then after you keep going where you are going anyway, the fly back to their nests all self-satisfied that they "defended their territory".

Greg was trying to negotiate 3 different levels of fishing "DEFCON One". He grabbed the spinning spool and broke off the line to the catfish who was on the large rod, while giving almost as much attention to the (hopefully) Perch on the ultra-light. He was shifting attention to the ultra-light, because his internal dialog convinced him that a large Perch, or small Striper tastes much better than catfish, and glanced up to show the Osprey what a great fish hunter-God he was, when realized it wasn't an Osprey. Suddenly, Greg's eyes widened when he realized that it looked a lot like someone threw an airplane... Like a United Airlines airplane, through the sky like a Frisbee. The plane's engines were out, and it was, yes, pin-wheeling through the sky....

Of course, that is not how physics works, so the plane was also DROPPING from the sky fast. It was dropping so fast that it exploded into the Potomac river about 200 yards away from Greg.

Greg grabbed the spool, broke off the fish, whatever it was, dropped the rod into the bottom of the boat, and grabbed the oars.

He spun the boat quickly towards the oncoming wave so that the bow was pointed towards the plane. Even with that, the wave hit his rowboat and almost flipped it. The boat got over 45 degrees horizontal, then crashed down into the trough of the wave, only to have secondary wave repeat the process. He held onto the oars, using them as outriggers to keep the boat in the right direction, and vaguely steady. His feet were wedged under the aluminum front bench seat, stabilizing him more. The last bottom rig, and whatever was on it went into the river, with the fish running away with his bottom rig and rod. After several more waves of this chaos passed the boat, Greg put his back into to the oars, and started paddling for wreckage while avoiding fire. "I hope they didn't all die" was all he thought as he paddled harder than he ever had in his life.

His section of river was under the approaches to Dulles and National Airport in DC, and tangentially, Baltimore Washington International (BWI) airport. He heard several more explosions as airplanes coming or going went down. He could only focus on the one right in front of him, even as he mourned for those lost souls, and for what all these explosions meant. It was definitely not just a power grid problem.

On the way to the nearby debris, Greg heard a crash as 2 vehicles of some sort presumably ran into each other back towards the family river house. "I guess they saw those crashes too – and not so much each other", was what he thought, as he kept rowing. "I hope someone calls 911, but I guess I'll have plenty of help shortly, because plane crashes aren't something that go un-noticed for long."

As Greg got to the edge of the debris field, his first thought, between deep breaths, was "Damn, I'm out of shape". His second was "Holy shit – there's nothing left here!" Greg approached, while avoiding patches of flaming water, and saw floating bits of seat-bottom, random carry-on bags, and pieces of aluminum plane, slowly sinking. Then he saw the first body. It was a flight attendant, based on the uniform. She was only somewhat intact, but most assuredly dead, since you can't live very long with your head bashed in and a leg missing. She was already starting to sink, so he paddled on, hoping to help someone.

Greg paddled through the detritus of the plane wreck for almost 20 minutes, seeing nothing resembling a live Human. By the time the fires were going out, he decided to call in the cavalry, because he was surprised at the lack of response. There were no helicopters, there was no Coast Guard, there was NOBODY out there in the middle of the Potomac River as he tried desperately to be of assistance. At this point, Greg dug through his over-the-shoulder tackle bag and took his cell phone out of the Ziploc bag that it was always in when he was on the water. He hit the iPhone button on the front, and the phone didn't light up. He hit it again, figuring that the fingerprint sensor didn't get his ID, because his fingers were sweaty and sooty. Still, nothing. Then he tried the power button on the side, and nothing. "Damn, I thought I had it charged up", he said to himself, while dreading the worst-case scenario. He tried one more time, then put the dead phone away, just about the time someone hailed him.

"Hellooo – Is anyone out there?" he heard from about 50 yards away.

"Yeah, I'm here" said Greg. "Keep talking – are you OK?"

"Well, yeah, I'm fine, I didn't just crash in a plane, how are YOU?" Asked the strange voice.

"Neither did I", he said. "I was just fishing, and then this happened!"

As the 2 boaters rowed towards each other, they continued to talk, and verified that neither one had seen any survivors. Finally, the two would-be rescuers approached each other. Greg in his rowboat, and the other one in a canoe.

"Ah would have been here sooner" said the stranger in his Virginia Drawl, "but mah fishing boat engine wouldn't start. It wouldn't even turn over, and it's never been a problem before. What have you found?"

Greg looked at the skinny old man with white hair sticking out everywhere. He had a bushy beard, a long white ponytail with rubber bands attempting to hold it together, and a white tee shirt on. "I found a dead stewardess, and a few random body parts, but I think most of the folks were strapped in and are down there somewhere."

"Well, Shit", said the old guy in a Virginia drawl. "I guess the Crabs will be eatin' good this week. Hey, do you have a phone? Mine's dead, and I guess we need to call someone, but I'd a figured they'd be here by now."

A creeping feeling started doing the goose-bump walk up Greg's spine. Transformers blowing, plane crashes, boat's not starting, a car wreck and 2 phones both not working. This was not good. This was very, very not good. Greg had prepared for something like this for 20 years, and most of the stuff he prepared was 600 or so miles south, at home with his wife.

"Buddy, I think we got a much bigger problem than a plane crash, or even a power-grid down scenario. Way bigger. Look how that fishing boat is dead in the water. Wouldn't they be here? I don't hear any sirens, and there's no traffic moving on the Maryland shore. I just noticed that."

"Well, yeah", said the wiry old biker (labeled that way by Greg, now that he could see his tattoos by the light of the dying fuel fires). Our power went out just before the plane hit the water. You prolly heard the transformers blow. Maybe this is the power grid collapse that the government has been saying Korea was trying to do to us with that cyber-hacking stuff."

"Sir, you might as well paddle on home. I think something worse than a grid-down scenario happened. If cell phones are down, vehicles with electronic ignition won't work, and the lights are out, we are well and truly fucked! This is either an EMP, or a CME."

"Speak English, Son." Said the white-beard.

"Either we were attacked by a Nuke in the high atmosphere, causing an Electro Magnetic Pulse that's an EMP, or we were unlucky enough to experience another Carrington Event, or Sun Spot gone bad – a Coronal Mass Ejection, the CME. It's what happens when a sunspot gets all big and dark, and then the Sun Pukes a river of hurt out. If our part of Earth is in the way of that, it would be really, really bad. Ions and crazy stuff I don't understand fries anything with a circuit in it. The last one happened in the 1850's, and fried everything electronic in this part of the world. The only thing is that in the 1850's, all that meant was fried telegraph wires, and telegraph operators having a headache if plugged in. Now, EVERYTHING that has a circuit board is done. Everything over a given area, anyway. The size of the area depends on where the EMP went off, or what part of Earth was facing the sun when the solar storm hits. I've been reading about this for years and preparing for it. Want to hear what's crazier than that?"

"I'm not sure I've ever heard anything THAT crazy, so I'm not sure I want to hear something crazier", he said.

"Yeah, neither do I," Greg said. "Everything I prepared for something like this to happen is over 600 miles South, outside of Atlanta with my wife. All I have to deal with this is what's in my bug-out bag. The BOB has all my camping, survival and prepping shit in it. My advice to you is to go home, run the water if you have any pressure, fill up everything you can, and get ready for some dark days. After water, you need the 3 B's. Bullets, Bandages, and Beans."

"Well, I'm pretty good on all 3", said white-beard. "I've heard a little bit about what you're talking about, and I think you're right. You take care of yourself, and if you need anything, I live right over there." He pointed to the vicinity of Beasley Point.

"I'm over in Rock Harbor", said Greg, as he pointed over to the other side of the Nomini river. "Luckily, it's our family's house, and it's only used a few times per year since Pop and Grandma Chambers died. It's way better stocked that the average house, but I'm still fucked, because my wife and son are in Atlanta, and my daughter is in Philly. I don't know what I'm going to do. I'm like a donkey between 2 bales of hay."

"Chief Chambers? Son, I knew the man, and served with him in the Navy. I haven't been to his house, but I've attended some of those soirees in the community center, and we had more than a few drinks together. You might be luckier as you think. That man never threw away anything, and he prepared for a bunch of scenarios. You know he worked for NSA, right?"

"Well, I heard rumors about that," I said. "We only talked man stuff after I did my time in the Army during Desert Storm." Greg said, and started to wonder about what might be at the old family house. This is the house that all family members had said for years that they would go to if anything ever went south, from a Zombie apocalypse to nuclear war. Now he was the only family member there.

"Well, I imagine that's true. Looks like you're right about the shit hitting the fan, and I'm sorry you're away from your family, but you could be in a lot worse shape. I have to go take care of my livestock and the neighbors around me. Take care, and I'll see you around, soldier. Stay strong and watch your back!" said the old-timer. "My name's Les, short for Lester. I always do more with less!" The old man cackled and paddled his canoe away, with his ropy muscles pulling his canoe against the current to get home.

"I'm Greg Creighton," Greg said as he introduced himself, and Les waved over his shoulder. He took one last look around and saw nothing floating around that could be rescued or used, so he put his back into the oars, and started the long row back to the house at Rock. The incoming tide would make this trip a true test of his less-than-combat-ready strength, and the upcoming months would be a true test of his internal fortitude. Who would he go to save? Should he stick with the agreed-upon plan, and wait for the rest of the family to come to Rock?

By the end of the long row home, he was breathing hard, and sweating profusely. He thought along the way, and determined that, for now, he would hold in place, and hope for the best. This decision would be debated in his head many times over the coming months, but he needed to make sure that when family did show up (and he couldn't contemplate the thought of them not showing up), the family homestead would be as safe, and as stocked with food, water and supplies as possible and that he could survive for whomever did make it to the house on the Rivah, as it was pronounced by many Virginians.

After Greg tied off the boat and staggered up to the house, he opened a bottle of wine, poured a tall water glass full, and plopped down into Grandpa's chair, looking over the water and thinking back to how he got into this apocalyptic situation.

Flashback - The Broken Heart Journey

By early April, Greg was going stir crazy after he negotiated a merger that ended up buying out his contract. His wife was in the middle of tax season and came home late to a dinner and a camp fire in the pit. As they sat around the campfire on their mountain cabin property, he expressed his frustration. "Darlin', I'm going bat-shit crazy. I don't know how to handle this unemployment thing! I've re-done the kitchen floors, cabinets, and got carpet put down so we can sell this thing with the kids at college. There's nothing to do but bounce off the walls or go drink at the gun club."

His wife, Leigh, leaned over and gave him a kiss on the cheek. "Honey," she said, "You've worked your butt off for 24 years, you put me through my CPA certification, and we've gotten Maria and Jared most of the way through college. Now we both need to find our own path. I think we're done. You know I'll always love what we've done, and our kids, but I think we're on 2 paths, and so, I want a divorce. Go off, write your book, be what you want to be for the next chapter of your life.

Greg looked at her for a long time. He realized she was right. He probably was done, too. It had been a long time since they had laughed together. So, he took the high road, along with her.

"Well, I have a book in me somewhere, and I need to move some of our stuff closer to where I want to end up, which is near Baltimore somewhere." He said. "I should probably empty out a lot of the stuff from my 'prepper cave', since I'll be moving, and I've upgraded just about everything that I bought when I was young and dumb." He looked up at the moon, and an idea struck him. "Maybe I should take all of my stuff to my Grandparents' house in Rock Harbor. I can stay there indefinitely while we get through this divorce thing. What do you think?"

Leigh got a big smile on her face, and probably not just because he made it easier for her. He also wouldn't be her problem for any longer. She knew, deep in her heart that they were done. He seemed happiest when he was on short vacations between managing his 250 or so staff at the company that he ran the operations for. Over the many years of their marriage, she tried to knock him out of his "bored funks" by doing things like: Learn how to play guitar this year; get your master's degree this year; how about hardwood floors at a 45-degree angle, and other distractions that added value in his mind, and kept her from killing him.

"I think you should do just that. Pack up Bubba the Tundra with all the big bulky things from your shed, including the kayak, and then fill up the passenger seat with as much junk as you can from your prepper closet. Just don't take my Glock!

"Are you sure I should leave you armed?

"Well, you better. You won't be here to protect me any longer. You know I'll always love what we did together, but it's time for us to chase our own dreams."

"Yes, Ma'am. Keep an eye on the boy. His shit isn't straight yet."

"I know. Give Maria my love when you see her next. They're twins, so you know they'll be on the phone in minutes. How about we have lunch with them on Wednesday and tell them at Noon."

"OK, Darlin." Greg stood up and kissed her on top of the head." It's been good, baby. I'll see you around." He needed to get out of here before he lost it, so packed up his most urgent things that night, and drove most of the night, until he found a cheap hotel online in North Carolina.

Over the years, while he was very successful at work, he was less successful at physical fitness. While raising his kids, he changed from a soldier to an old-dude. 25 years after leaving the Army, he was large, and out of shape. Greg had high blood pressure, under control with medicine, but was pushing 290 pounds on his "big-boned" 6'1 frame. He had silvering brown hair, and about a half-dozen tattoos, where they couldn't be seen in work clothes. He hoped this fishing trip would also be the start of another diet and fitness program. When he got in shape, he got more than his fair share of looks, but lately, he'd seen glances, and the "old, fat dude" verdict from too many women in the world, even those that were clearly older than him.

His bad habits were not a good recipe for a long life, but in his defense, he was fighting PTSD from the Gulf War and couldn't sleep well on a normal day. It was his drinking and his PTSD that finally caused his wife to eventually give up, which may have been the reason she started cheating on him. To her credit, she spent time trying to get him out of the La-Z-Boy and off the booze, but he didn't act on her pleas. He understood that he wasn't fully present, so other than his hurt feelings over the affair, it was going to be a mostly amicable divorce. He was not looking forward to telling the kids, though. One of the things he wanted to do while at the river house was to visit his daughter, Maria at college, and break the news to her. His wife Leigh was going to tell their son, Jared, who was attending Georgia Tech. Maria and Jared were twins. While not strictly a "daddy's girl" and "mommy's boy", Maria was slightly closer to Greg and Jared was closer to his mom, Leigh. He could only really connect with his son when fishing, hunting or camping. Otherwise, they bumped heads, and too much time together would naturally devolve into a macho pissing contest. Both his son and daughter were "Alpha's" in their respective peer groups, but for whatever reason, he didn't rub his daughter the wrong way.

He knew he drank too much to help him sleep but was not willing to get into a sleeping pill situation, although he couldn't say why – it just seemed different than drinking. His sleeping problem had been there since he got out of the Army after the firsts Desert Storm. Some said he should get help for his PTSD, but he served with brothers who had it a lot worse. He felt like he would be stealing their VA benefits if he went in and whined about his own bad dreams. He was always a bigger than average guy. Even when he was a soldier, his "fighting weight" was 225. He hoped that this time away from his everyday habits would be the start of a new fitness program, even though he had attempted several, and failed them over the years. A week ago, he started doing push-ups again, and after his first few pathetic attempts, he could do 25-30 in a set, which was encouraging – he hadn't totally lost it. He was starting to get what his wife called the "dog bone" muscle in his triceps, an early first sign that he was moving back towards decent shape.

Just before arriving at the family place, he stopped at the local convenience store, Dubbed "Rock Harbor Mall", as a tongue-in-cheek homage to its tiny size, by the locals many years ago. It had received a face-lift since his last time here, just after Grandma died. Packing up her stuff, and giving it away to various family members and charities was hard on him. At least Grandma packed up Pop's stuff.

Greg grabbed the usual bread, milk, cheese, and other food that he would need as he got the house ready for moving in. The separation with his wife was now legal, and he had to get ready for life in his new home, which was really the old family place. Since she made a lot more money, and worked in downtown Atlanta, he let Leigh keep their property, with the understanding that he would come back to get more of his stuff over the next several weeks.

Getting in the long line at the store, he was starting to regret his decision, as it seemed every construction worker in the area was at the deli counter, ordering food. The good news was that it meant that the food was good, if they were here. A very large Hispanic man turned to look at him and smiled. Greg took the opportunity to start a conversation. "What's the best sandwich here, big guy?" For Greg to call a guy "Big Guy", the guy had to be large, and this man was.

The big guy looked down at Greg, smiled, and said "Hero" and pointed at the sandwich listings.

Greg smiled back. "Perfect. I can eat half now, and half for dinner. Thanks, man!"

"De Nada, Amigo." He was clearly a man of few words, so Greg kept to himself, looking around. The place was much cleaner than the last time he was here. They had put in a covered porch on the front of the store, which used to be the parking lot. Most of the construction workers were sitting outside, eating their sandwiches. The big guy's turn at the counter was up. He asked for 2 Italian Hero's, and when he got them, he handed one to Greg. "Enjoy, Amigo" he smiled at Greg and paid the woman behind the counter. He followed his buddies out to the porch and ate while leaning against one of the porch rails, as all 8 of the seats were taken.

When Greg got to the front, the woman behind the counter looked at him. "Hey Stranger, welcome to Rock Harbor Mall. What else can I get you besides that stuff."

Her smile was genuine, and she clearly knew the locals. "Anything biting yet?" He looked over at the corner rack of fishing gear.

"I'm told not yet, except for the occasional catfish and maybe a croaker in the channels. FYI, Esteban out there bought your Sandwich, so you're OK in my book. Just a fair warning, he likes them spicy, so I made it his way."

"Oh hell, he didn't have to do that! I just asked him what was good here."

"In my place, everything is good. But his 'special hero' is damn good. I make one his way and bring it home for dinner every Thursday... and breakfast every Friday. They hold up well in a fridge or cooler."

"Your place, huh? Under new management, I guess. I haven't been here in 2 years, but I love what you've done with it."

"You know Rock Harbor, huh?   If you haven't been here for a few years, you may not like it so much now. Mr. Essington bought up all of the inland lots, and those are his guys out there. His son, Tripp is officially the developer. They turned the harbor into a bunch of McMansions on quarter-acre lots. Despite the 'Assington', as he is called by many of us, he has influence. Despite that, those guys out there are a good bunch. If you're headed that way, you can save them the walk, which is a few miles, as you know."

"Well, thanks for the info, Ma'am. It's the least I can do to repay the sandwich."

"Don't call me ma'am..."

"Oh? You work for a living?"

She smiled back at him. Looking at the Army tattoos on his arm. "You got it in one, soldier. I see you do, too."

"Well I did, now I'm an almost-divorced and unemployed wanna-be author, but I plan to get back to it, eventually."

"Outstanding. I want a signed copy when you write whatever it is. You better step out there, they're about to walk 2 miles back to work. They get paid by the hour, and Trip doesn't pay them for lunch, so you'll more than make up the price of the sandwich if you give them a ride."

He smiled his thanks to her and did a little salute. "Catch you later. I look forward to talking military stories with you."

Greg called out to the guys, who were starting to walk the way he was going. "Hey, man! Thanks for the sandwich. Let me give you guys a ride. I can probably fit 4 in the cab. He started throwing his bags from the back seat into the truck bed. The rest can fit back there, around the kayak and gear, if the big guy doesn't break my springs."

One of the smaller guys, a dark-skinned guy with ropy muscles coming out of his construction company t-shirt started yelling orders in Spanish. Guys on his crew politely pushed Greg out of the way and started gently piling his bags from the back seat into the truck bed. At that point, based on some internal hierarchy, they took places in the back seat of the truck, and the bed. Esteban, the giant was the last one in, and the guy giving orders got in the passenger seat.

"Muchas Gracias, Amigo. I am Angel (it sounded like An-Hell). We all appreciate the ride."

"Any time, Amigo. My Spanish is no Bueno, but I understand y'all are working on the Rock Harbor peninsula. I'm going there, so it's no problem. Plus, that big guy back there bought my lunch."

"Oh, you have Esteban's special? Es Muy Caliente! I see you have milk in the bag. You will need that. He's from Mexico City. The rest of us are from Honduras. He likes it much spicier than we do. Greg checked out the rearview mirror, to see the 3 guys in the bench seat smiling at each other, and he heard 'Este' and 'Caliente' and 'Hero' several times."

The drive took only a few minutes, with the houses, community center, tennis courts, pool and mansion all tugging at Greg's heart, and memory. Angel pointed Greg at a house under construction. It was on the inside of Seahawk Circle, not far from Greg's family house, but on one of the many inland lots that Greg's grandfather had sold to a developer years ago. Greg recalled wondering when anyone would buy one of the lots. The last time he was home, there was only one house built on the inland lots. It was just across from the boat ramp and had the only inland view of the harbor that the ground floor of a house could have. He recalled it belonging to Mike and Jennifer, a young couple who bought the lot and put in a two-story house, which was rare for the peninsula. Almost every lot that was developed had a rancher on the water. The Historic Rock Harbor Mansion was the only original multi-story house on the Peninsula before Mark and Jennifer built theirs.

As he looked around, every house that was built inland, or in process was a 2-story Tudor wood-and-stone monstrosity. He sighed at the huge houses with almost no lawns, all built tall, to see some of the harbor over the waterfront ranchers.

Greg showed up at the family place, and un-packed what he needed to for the night from his Tundra. He found the hidden key in its normal place and turned on the water at the curb with a wrench from under his back seat. He spent a while un-mothballing the place, like turning on the hot water heater, and running water through every sink. He set the time and wound up his Pop's old Navy "Ship's clock", then he turned the manual hand on the matching brass barometer to the current pressure. His cousins occasionally came here for a fun weekend, and there was a check-in and check-out list that they all usually followed pretty religiously. The Grandparent's estate covered basic things like satellite TV, and Wi-Fi, plus basic utilities. Things had to be turned on, powered up, and some passwords needed to be entered, but it was a pretty routine turn-up process, as the directions were laminated and pinned to the cork board by the phone.

He was really looking forward to a week or 2 of fishing, writing, exercise and drinking. On one hand, he was glad that his wife asked him to leave, on the other, uncertainty caused him anxiety. He was much better in a fight than worrying about the possibility of a fight, for example. The looming unhappiness that they both lived through in the last few years was replaced with sadness, but a little relief, too. He had a clear path to a new life. He was also relieved that the situation forced him to move back into the family house, even though he was pretty sure that the memories of his dead Grandparents would haunt him during his stay. He had so many good memories here. Coming to a mothballed house was going to be painful, but he felt it was time.

What to do first when the SHTF

After drinking his wine, catching his breath, and spending too much time reminiscing about the world before the STHTF, Greg sprang up from the rocker, almost surprised that for a moment he forgot the urgency of the situation. "SHIT! The apocalypse finally comes, and I'm rocking in a chair! First step – Water!" Greg said out loud as he got started on the important business of survival. He sprinted or did an impression of a sprint done by a near-300 lb. fat guy, into the kitchen. He sprayed a paper towel with bleach cleaner and wiped out the double kitchen sinks. He pushed down the sink drain plugs, and started the water running right in between the 2 sinks, hoping to fill both as quickly as possible.

Then, Greg took the spray bottle into the bathroom, and sprayed out and wiped the tub. After it was what the Army would call "field expedient" clean, he plugged the drain hole, and ran that water. He went around the house doing the same thing in every other basin. He knew he had 50 or 60 gallons of water in the hot water heater. He also verified that it, like every other one he was aware of had a drain with a hose coupling in the bottom, he didn't want that to be his only water. He noticed the water pressure was already dropping in the pipes, so took a moment to appreciate how his vaguely-quick thinking may have given him a few weeks more of water in the tub and basins.

There was no time for too much self-appreciation. The clock was ticking. Next, he needed to determine what food there was here at the house. He did NOT open the refrigerator, because he knew that whatever cold was in there would likely be the only cold it got before rotting. He'd have to worry more about the food in there rotting than he would have to worry about what was in it. He recalled from last night that most of the things in the fridge were non-perishable because the house stayed vacant most of the winter. After all, he had to turn on the water at the curb, and the hot water heater when he got here. He did remember the freezer being full of frozen pizzas, hunks of possibly freezer-burned meat, and other things like that.

He started to wonder if maybe he was wrong about TEOTWAWKI, so he grabbed his Tundra keys, and went out to see if it would start. It didn't take long to confirm his worst fears. Not only did the remote not open the door, but when he used the key to unlock it, the cabin light didn't come on. He had to try, so he put the key in the ignition and turned it, to the unsurprising sound of nothing. Yes, it was either an EMP or a CME, and the why's and how's of it didn't really matter, did it? If it was a power grid collapse, something else that he prepped for, the truck would have started and the electronic devices would work. This situation was a step down the Apocalyptic ladder. At least he didn't see any mushroom clouds. Fallout is a very bad thing to try to survive. The Electrical Age of America, and maybe more countries was now a thing of the past, at least in this part of the world. He had no idea how far this thing reached and could only hope that his wife and son in Atlanta, or his daughter in Philadelphia weren't impacted, but he felt that something this big very likely stretched to cover both areas, depending on how high up the Nuke was when it was detonated. If he was at the edge of the impacted area, some things, like boat motors, with very few electronic components SHOULD work.

Nobody really knew what the real impacts of an EMP/CME would be, except the government, which did do some limited tests on EMP's – then gave the results a top-secret security clearance. Greg had heard some chatter on the internet about these studies but didn't really dig into any of it. He thought of himself as a "hobby prepper", spending some money to prepare for the worst, a similar hobby to the one his wife spent money on for lottery tickets. Correction: soon-to-be ex-wife. He'd have to get used to that concept. Once again, he lamented her change of heart towards him. They had regular sex for 24 years of marriage, but something didn't make that enough. He knew his drinking and apathy was a part of it, but figured it might be her corporate drive, in that work was such a big part of her life. She worked 60 hours per week and traveled too much. He figured that had something to do with it, in vague denial about what his role really was.

Having no time to worry about things he couldn't control, he decided to do what he could to deal with the things he could control – making Rock Harbor as safe a harbor for his family as he could. Despite her actions, he would welcome Leigh here if she arrived. He didn't think they'd ever have a romantic relationship again, but they raised kids together, and he owed her at least that.

Greg knew from his time in the Army that those who acted first often were the last ones surviving. Inaction was the only way to guarantee that nothing happened, and he was a man who would rather be moving than not moving at all. Moving in the wrong direction was still movement, and making these mistakes created experience. Make enough mistakes, and that experience creates wisdom. After all the mistakes he had made in his life, Greg laughed internally, he was plenty wise. Hopefully, some of that wisdom would pay off now and in the future.

It was inventory time, and time to do as much as he could to practice the 5 D's of security: Deter, Detect, Defend, Deny, and Delay. To do this, he needed to take inventory of his assets. He knew he had his bug-out bag, BOB, which had all sorts of interesting, state-of-the-art toys in it. He needed to find out what he had at the house that might be useful. Because the house was used by various family members throughout the years, he could see from the time that he walked in that it had lots of party things. There were countless bottles of good booze that had been brought and left in various stages of full. The refrigerator downstairs was where the beer was kept, and had maybe 70 beers made up of a dozen or so varieties. There was one Fisher "Momma Bear" wood stove, which would come in handy on cold nights, and the boat house was full of about 20 different fishing rods for all of the different nieces, nephews, aunts and uncles, most with tackle on them. There were several big tackle boxes, from recent ones to Pop's original tool box, with spinners and lures from his travels around the world in it. Greg remembered the stories Pop told him about the origins of some of them. Pearl Harbor, Japan, Okinawa and other places were where Pop collected fishing lures like some people collected other souvenirs. It would have to get very hungry out for Greg to use any of these treasured mementos.

As Greg prowled the rest of the house that afternoon he saw, under the deck, about a half-dozen crab traps. They had poison ivy vines crawling up them, and through the gaps in the deck. He knew he'd have to clean that up carefully, as he was terribly allergic to Poison Ivy, usually getting a secondary infection from scratching. During this apocalypse, an infection could kill as easily as a bullet.

He also found an old flashlight that worked and inspected deeper into the basement than the fridge that was right by the door. Down there, he saw some remnants of Pop's prepping. As a survivor of the depression, Pop used to keep all kinds of things that others might throw away. There were about 5 cases of Water, drinking labeled in black & white nondescript soda cans from the Anheuser Busch plant about an hour away in Williamsburg, VA. They were pull-tab cans, the kind of tabs that you had to pull all the way of. These were not the kind that modern soda cans have, where you lift a tab, and it bends down the part that the liquid comes out. Greg didn't know if water could go bad, but didn't think so. At worst, it would have to be boiled. He bet that this would be a valuable find in the coming weeks.

Greg found numerous hand tools, rolls of wire and balls of rubber bands. He found containers of all kinds of chemicals, from lock-tite oil to cleaning fluids like ammonia, acetone and bleach. He was covered for refinishing, as there were gallons of polyurethane, paint, deck stain, and other paint supplies. At least 4 cords of seasoned hardwood were piled under the awnings of the garage, and the garage also had plenty of yard-chemicals like round-up, lawn fertilizer, and other things to make the property presentable.

On the shadier side, Greg found several dozen glass canning jars of fruit and other things. They LOOKED fine in their mason jars with bell lids, but he figured he'd have to be pretty hungry to try the cling peaches, tomatoes, or strawberry preserves. Home-canned food didn't come with an "expire by" label. Greg counted these as assets, but didn't know if they were survival food, or poison for bad guys.

Greg also remembered that the basement had a full-sized freezer, where Pop used to store his meat from hunting. While there was no meat in there now, Greg opened it briefly, and saw several dozen 1-gallon milk jugs filled with ice. Pop used to fill them ¾ of the way, and then freeze them so that expansion wouldn't burst them. These, he would throw in a cooler when fishing, or when guests came and needed ice for their coolers. The freezer was pretty full with this ice, and not much else except a few frozen pizzas, lean cuisines, and bait for fishing and the crab traps. This was a great find, in that with the quality freezer in the basement, and full of ice, Greg hoped it would be cold for quite a few days, maybe weeks. He moved several of the gallons of ice to his prized Yeti cooler, which was advertised to keep ice frozen for up to a week. He then moved the frozen food in it to the cooler, and left it sitting next to the freezer. He was curious as to which would stay cold longer, but his money was on the Yeti.

The basement had several types of hand tools, coffee cans full of screws, nails, various oils and paint thinners, and several metal tools that Greg didn't really know what they did. He knew the power tools down there were now just paper weights. What he didn't find were any firearms or ammunition. After food and water, Greg knew that his sparse collection of firearms and very little ammunition would not be a long-term solution. Once again, he kicked himself for leaving all of his prepper toys at home when the

Apocalypse, or at least TEOTWAKI finally hit. It was time to take inventory of his weapons.

Bastard Calibers, and the results

A few years ago, Leigh came up with a term that Greg latched on to. "Bastard Caliber" is what she called some of the ammo rounds that Greg had. While he didn't agree with the term, he did agree that it wasn't very efficient to have his vast (some might say too-large) collection of pistols in .22 Long Rifle, .22 magnum, .32 Auto, .38 Special, .357 Magnum, .40 Smith & Wesson, .44 magnum, .45 ACP and 9mm, all just for hand guns! After all, if he was going to hit the road with his bug out bag (BOB), he wasn't going to effectively carry all those calibers and guns.

When Greg and Leigh first moved to Georgia from Virginia, he stumbled across a gun range near the house. The Governors Gun Club was his neighborhood hang-out for the last few years. They had a huge selection of pistols, rifles, shotguns, and even things like suppressors and fully-auto guns, for those willing to pay for the tax stamp, which is way to shout out to Uncle Sam "I live here with major weaponry, come take it!" While Greg didn't have any tax stamps, or registered firearms (Georgia is good that way), he did have about a dozen pistols, a few rifles, and a Mossberg 500 12 Gauge shotgun that he converted to a "street sweeper" model, with a pistol grip, laser, and other fun attachments like his green-dot laser "zombie gun sight".

Greg decided that it was time to consolidate his gun collection to a few calibers of different utility and spent a year trading 2 guns for 1 higher-quality gun, and getting rid of most of the calibers in his gun room. At the end of the year, he had 2 pistols for each of the 3 of them, and only 2 calibers, plus his "Gucci gun". Greg's daughter, Maria, loved the .22 Ruger that he inherited from his grandfather. It was a 'single-six' Blackhawk revolver that had 2 inter-changeable cylinders - .22 magnum and .22 LR. They both liked the punch of the .22 Magnum for varmints up to about a coyote, and .22LR was cheap plinking load. He also bought Maria a Ruger Mark IV 22-45 in .22LR. This was a target pistol with an inexpensive, but reliable

SpotMark red dot sight. The last time he visited her at college, he dropped off the .22's with her, telling her, over her objections (she was only 19 and it was "illegal") that it was better to have and not need, than need and not have. He had them all packed into a Bug-Out-Bag of her own. One of the common sayings in the gun community is "It's better to be judged by 12 than carried by 6 (i.e. pall bearers). He assured her that if she got attacked, or otherwise needed them, he, or the NRA would help defend her, as long as she used her head and didn't pull them if not needed.

He had tucked the .22's in a camouflage backpack that he filled with various survival things, creating Maria's own bug-out bag, including ammo, pistol cleaning supplies, rain gear, fire starting tools, and some freeze-dried food, among other things. He told her that she should only go into the bag if the shit hit the fan. She had been listening to his apocalyptic talk, mostly involuntarily, as long as she was old enough to understand him, most often rolling her eyes, or mocking him with a "sure dad, why not prepare for Zombies, too!"

His son, Jared shared his love for 9mm's, and was the recipient of a few hand-me-downs which he kept in his Jeep and apartment, despite Greg's protestations that a Jeep with a gun in it was an invitation to a break-in. So far, the boy had been lucky, and his mom's purchase of a vehicle gun safe, with a steel cord connecting it to the seat mount made everyone, even Jared happier.

His son preferred fishing to shooting, but learned long ago, after banging his head against his dad's stubborn Scottish head that it was easier to go with the flow. On one hand, that understanding allowed them to have less "drama" in their relationship. On the other hand, the 2 Creighton Men were a bit more stand-offish, and Jared gravitated to his mom more often than dad. They weren't anything like at odds with each other, they currently just had the peace of 2 Lions, the old one and the young cub that was about to become a man – and didn't want to get eaten by the big lion before that happened.

The main pistol caliber in the house was 9mm, but on several platforms. Greg's every day carry pistol, after much trial and error, was the Sig Sauer P938. A beefed-up version of their famous pocket pistol in .380. Greg didn't feel comfortable with the .380 caliber, as it could be stopped by a drugged-out bad guy with leather and denim, if not shot accurately. 9MM, especially with some good personal defense ammunition was a good balance between cost, recoil, and stopping power. He did like the size, and with the pocket holster that he purchased, it "printed" (i.e. gave the outline in his pocket) like a large mobile phone. While most residents of Georgia understood that about 1 in 4 people was carrying, it was considered bad taste to have a gun imprint, or "print" under your clothes. There were, after all, liberals who might make a fuss. The holster would stick to his pocket, and he could draw from it relatively easily.

Greg's wife Leigh had a Head Down Glock 19 that used to be his. One day, while shooting together, Leigh finished up with a magazine on the 19, looked at it appreciatively, and said "Mine.". Greg tried to point out that it was his baby, and that he would buy her one. She looked at him with that wife look, and said, "Mine – buy yourself a new one." After that day, Leigh had a top-of-the line Glock 19, heavily customized by Head Down, a company in their neighborhood.

Greg replaced his loss with a custom Glock 19 of his own, or Franken-Glock. It had a Venum red dot sight, trigger job, competition barrel and raised sights. The happy gun-toting couple had several interchangeable magazines for the Glocks, including a few 30-round stick-magazines. Unfortunately, this Glock was still in his bedside safe at home. He'd miss his marriage, but the once-bitten, twice-shy side of him said that he'd miss the Glock more.

Rounding out the 9mm collection, Greg had a Ruger LC9 Revolver, which held 5 rounds of 9mm in half-moon clips. Greg bought this

Ruger revolver, as his truck had been broken into by someone in Atlanta looking for guns once already, and he didn't want to have a high-dollar gun stolen if it happened again. Luckily, when the theft happened, Greg's gun was on his hip, but there were several places that Greg frequented that still prohibited firearms, like his old job, so the revolver was often left in his truck.

There are generally 2 kinds of pistol ammunition – semi auto and revolver. Revolvers have hollow cylinders that one drops the rounds into. Because they are hollow, revolver rounds must have "lips" that stick out on the bottom of them. Imagine a straight-sided glass sitting on a saucer... that lip created by the saucer is what stops the round from just sliding through the cylinder and falling on the floor. So, with revolvers, you typically have bullets like the .38 special, 357 magnum, .44 Smith or .44 magnum. These rounds are made for revolvers, and don't work in semi-auto pistols.

Semi-auto pistols have bullets that ARE cylinders, with a notch cut out of the brass, so that they can be ejected. If you were to drop a semi-auto round into a revolver (assuming the caliber was correct, it would slide right through the hole, and out the other side. Common semi-auto calibers are the .380 (versus the revolver .38 special – the diameter of the tube/bullet is the same, but .380 is a lot shorter, and packs less punch). You also have the 9mm, .32 Auto, .40 caliber Smith, .45 Auto, and several other "bastard" calibers for semi-auto pistols. The difference between revolvers and semi-auto is not so much an advantage, but a personal taste.

Revolvers, or "wheel guns" usually have 5 or 6 rounds in a cylinder. Their main advantage is they do not jam. If you pull the trigger, and get a bad round, nothing happens, but you pull the trigger again, and the gun goes "boom". They take more time to reload, because each round has to be loaded into a cylinder, which is often in a lower capacity 5 or 6 round capacity. That process can be sped up with pre-loaded speed loaders, or moon clips.

Semi-auto pistols have become the default military and law enforcement side arm since the early 1940's. They typically have a higher capacity. A Glock 19 holds 15 rounds instead of 6 in a revolver, for example. They're quick to reload, because you can have spare magazines on your belt. So, with 1 Glock 19 and 2 spare magazines, you can essentially dump 45 rounds down-range in the time it would take someone to reload their second 6 rounds in a revolver. BUT – if you get a jam feeding from the magazine, you can't just pull the trigger, it's time for problem solving, and clearing a jam incorrectly in a critical situation can get one killed quickly.

The Ruger 9mm revolver that Greg had was a special kind of crazy. It shot the same 9mm cartridge as his LC9, but because the shells would slide through the cylinder, they had to be clipped into half-moon clips, which mimicked the "lip" on revolver rounds. This means it took even longer to load, and you were effectively stuck with 5 rounds to play with. Greg did have 2 spare half-moon clips. One was loaded with hollow-point ammunition, and another was loaded with a new spinning frangible round that was billed as something that would spin and cut its way through leather, denim, etc. and really put a hurting on the victim with its hydrostatic shock. So, for this pistol, Greg had effectively 15 rounds of various tools, with 5 in each half-moon clip. The half-moon, when loaded, also allowed for a quick reload, although still not as quick as popping out one magazine and slapping another one in.

Greg could not give up his one "Gucci" Pistol. As a treat, he bought himself a Springfield EMP (Extreme Micro Pistol) in .40 caliber Smith & Wesson. This wasn't one of the calibers "in the house", as mentioned above, any longer, as he was bringing it to Rock Harbor. This steel beauty had some weight to it, and was in a 1911 frame, of the famed Colt military frame. The magazine held 8 rounds, with 1 in the chamber. It didn't have the capacity of the Glock, but it was a work of fine craftsmanship. The gun came with a paddle holster, which slid over the belt. It also had a 2-magazine holder that also slipped over the belt. 25 rounds with 3 magazines was a little heavy, and not as compact as some concealed guns, but had the punch of a .40, which was deadlier than a 9mm. He also kept it because each time there was a newsworthy mass shooting, and the subsequent run on guns and ammo, 9mm was bought up, and prices went up. While .40 cal. was a little more expensive, it was a rarer caliber, and was ALWAYS on the shelves, even during the worst of the buy-outs. This beauty had been Greg's everyday carry weapon, when he could have heavy enough clothes to cover the pistol. In summer months, he settled for the Sig P938, which he planned to carry until he got all his gear to the family river farm house. His Glock at home was too bulky for him to carry without a jacket, so was right next to the bedside in the hidden holster behind his bedside table.

Greg was bringing the .40 to leave at Rock Harbor, as it would be his home soon. He also brought his P938 and the revolver in the truck to go with his Mauser. He brought all of his .40 ammunition, which wasn't much – 4 boxes of 50. He didn't bring any more 9mm ammunition for the pistols than he had in them, as there was not a shooting range near the river house.

In rifle calibers, the Creighton family got down to one Ruger 10-22 (also attached to a backpack in his daughter's closet). This came with 3 - 10-round circular magazines of .22 LR. The 2 not loaded fit into slots in the rifle stock. Greg also, bought a 30-round extended magazine for it. These, he loaded with hollow points for his daughter. He also left a few boxes of target-load 22 in her backpack.

In his own home, Greg had an Olympic Arms AR-15 in 5.56mm that Greg traded for at a gun show, because he liked the Army Digital paint job on it. While many don't know this, 5.56 rifles are slightly superior to .223 rifles, from an ammunition perspective, because you CAN run either 5.56MM or .223 caliber rounds though a 5.56, but only an unwise person would do it the other way around. This gave the 5.56 a little more ammunition flexibility than many traditional .223 AR-15's. He also had a great deal on a Smith & Wesson M&P 10 (Military and Police model) in .308 for hunting wild boars. This was basically an AR-15 platform, but with beefed up parts for the heavier round. He purchased several extra magazines for it, and several hundred .308 rounds, also known as 7.62 x 51 – the same round used in many of the weapons he trained on in the army, like the M60 and M240. These rounds could punch through several walls to take out bad guys, and had tremendous stopping power for large game like Deer, Boar and bad guys in leather. Hiding behind anything besides an engine block was not really cover, just concealment. Greg had at least 500 rounds of ammunition for these rifles, stashed safely with several months of freeze-dried food in his "prepper closet" at home.

Finally, Greg had one "bastard caliber" rifle that he just could not part with. It was an 8mm Mauser bolt-action rifle in the 1898 model. This rifle was a war trophy from his grandfather's service in WWII, and although it was in the overly large and expensive 8mm caliber, Greg just loved shooting it (although he couldn't shoot it at the Gun Club, because it would punch holes through the back wall). He upgraded the stock to a modern Sporter stock, and bought a decent Leupold 3-9 magnification hunting scope on it. He brought it to the beach house on his this run, because it was heavy and he couldn't shoot it at the gun club. He wasn't looking forward to the good-byes, because he was a regular, but he figured he'd at least get lots of hugs and free rounds... until this happened.

Despite having these weapons to play with at home, April's apocalypse found Greg in Rock harbor with only the Mauser (and 200 rounds of 1975 Turkish Ammunition that he bought on-line), the "Gucci" EMP .40, the P938 pocket pistol, and the Ruger revolver that he remembered was in the console of his now-useless Toyota Tundra.

In other words, Greg, the Gun Nut who spent so much of his last 20 years collecting guns and survival gear for the end of the world as we know it (TEOTWAWKI), showed up to the dance with his Gucci gun and ammo, plus about 20 rounds of 9mm ammunition, and 200 rounds of Mauser ammunition that had to be loaded 1 round at a time, and into a magazine that held an amazingly low 5 rounds when fully loaded. He also had a huge backpack full of relatively state-of-the-art prepper gear, but he left the vast majority of his Prepper stuff back at home, when he FINALLY might need it. Yeah, Greg realized that he and his generally good Karma just had a parting of the ways.

Since it was approaching "happy hour", Greg sat down for a moment, and had a beer. He needed to reflect on how he got himself in this situation. After all that prepping, he just about wanted to cry over the LACK of supplies he had – especially because if he was at home, he'd be crowing and saying, "I told you so!" to anyone who would listen.

Deter

Rock Harbor was designed as a weekend retreat and retirement community for people from the Washington DC, and Richmond/Fredericksburg VA area. It wasn't a formal "community", so much as plots of land available for people to purchase and develop in a way they saw fit. Greg's grandfather retired from NSA and bought his shore lot, and a group if inland lots extremely inexpensively, as an "investment for the family". No 2 houses on the shoreline were alike, and they were built to the satisfaction of the buyers, and the landscape. Many, like Greg's Grandparent's house, were waterfront properties. When both Pearl-Harbor-survivor Grandparents died, their 4 children decided to keep the property for family use, and Greg was currently the only occupant of this property. As they needed money, some of the children asked to be bought out, and Greg's Mom bought them out. For a while, she was the sole owner, then signed it over to Greg. The condition as that he allowed all of the cousins to use it, as long as they didn't abuse it. Greg's Mom had retired to Arizona and had told her only son that he would inherit it – along with the headaches of managing family visits and maintenance. She had divorced his Scottish Dad years ago, and Greg saw him once per year at the Salmon fishing camp. Greg called his mom from the road, and she encouraged him to move in, since it was his problem, and possibly salvation now. She was relieved about the divorce, as she never really liked Greg's wife. Several of the Hawaiian grandparent's grandkids had lived in this house while they were in a transition, like between jobs or houses.

Because it was the middle of the week in early April (and just barely Spring), Greg knew from driving around the peninsula that most occupants were not in their homes when the shit hit the fan (SHTF). People don't usually go to their beach homes until May or June. Greg's fishing excursion was a pleasant surprise to him, as the fish don't usually start biting until early May, but he could thank Global warming for one thing, if nothing else. He would have to get to the fish on the stringer, but they would be OK for the next few hours, if the disaster going on didn't stop the tides from rising and falling, or more bombs didn't fall. He decided he couldn't worry about shit he couldn't control.

After taking the quick inventory, Greg took the fish off the stringer, and filleted them. He cut the skin off the filets, leaving the skin attached at the tail. This trick was something Pop had taught him at 10 years old, and saved on the mess. It also made it easier to keep the meat together for the traps. He put on gloves, and carefully hacked the poison ivy, and fetched a few crab traps from under the deck. Each trap got a fish carcasses stuffed into the bait hole, with the spiky fins from the fish locking the bait in place. Greg tied each trap to one of the nearby dock pilings with the line tied below the water. At this point, he was less worried about having an un-marked crab trap as he was worried about someone poaching his crabs. He knew he could defend the traps, but didn't want to tempt some hungry stranger into getting shot for something as stupid as poaching a half-dozen crabs.

While doing the relatively mind-numbing task of filleting the perch and croakers, Greg mentally went over the list of his assets on hand.

In addition to the kayak and kite that Greg brought to be left at the beach house, he brought the guns previously discussed. He also brought his Bug-out bag (BOB). Basically, it was full of his survival gear. This gear was the gear he had purchased once he seriously into prepping. He left his older bag at home, in his prepper closet. He was going to empty the closet of all the freeze-dried food and other "prepper" stuff on his next trip home, although he'd probably leave some for his wife and son. Now, they could have it all.

For knives, he had his bench-made switchblade, a very high-quality knife that he always kept in his pocket. He had a 5" fixed-blade Buck knife with a rubber handle and deer gutting hook on the back side. He also had a large Gerber combat knife with a 7" blade, half of which was serrated. The handle had a metal point on the other end, presumably for breaking glass. This knife, which he always kept in the side door of the truck, would be living on his belt from now on, opposite his Springfield .40 holster. There was also a low-end folding knife that he kept with his magnesium fire starting stick in the BOB, as he didn't want to mess up his good blades shaving magnesium flakes from the square. This square also had a flint imbedded in it for igniting the small pile of magnesium shavings quickly, which burned at a very high temperature.

Greg had an Army digi-cam baseball cap, embossed with "Army Veteran", and a "Boonie hat" in the same pattern, sprayed with waterproofing spray. He had a poncho, also in the same pattern – as clashing camouflage patterns was a fashion faux pa that he would not be doing. He was not so well set with cold weather gear, as this trip was supposed to be a trip of 60-degree days, and 45-50 degree nights. He did have a rolled-up set of long johns in the bottom of his BOB, and a polar-fleece pull-over in olive color, with San Francisco embossed on the chest. This was a souvenir of a conference from several years, and he found it in his "gym bag" from the days that he went more regularly. It was a baggy XXL, so it still fit him.

He had many changes of socks, every soldier's best friend. In addition to those in his travel suitcase, he had 3 pair of green Army wool socks were rolled up in the outer pockets of his pack, along with his warm clothes. To go over them, he had a pair of Hi-Tek hiking boots, and a rolled-up army Digi-cam pattern pair of cargo pants.

For food, he had whatever was in the house (and those abandoned ones around him) and about 5 large packs of Mountain House, freeze dried food. This just-add-water food was very lightweight and was packed with calories. Greg recalled flavors like Chicken and Noodles, Chili with rice, and Beef Stroganoff. He snickered, as he thought about the old joke about the Steer Masturbating, or Beef "Strokin'off".

He knew there was one #10 can of some sort of fruit, probably the Emergency Essentials brand of freeze-dried berry blend. This was to have some sort of vitamins in a world where meat from fish, crabs, squirrels, rabbit and maybe a deer would be the main protein staple. Greg also had a few large bags of rice and beans in the bug-out-bag, with his Grandfather's WWII mess kit. He had a big bottle of Men's multi-Vitamins and his blood pressure medicine. Finally, he had a can of prepper bacon in a can! Yes, he would not be entering the apocalypse without one of the major food groups – Bacon. That said, he lamented the loss of the other food group, chocolate.

Other assorted things in the backpack included a life-straw, for drinking water out of mud puddles, if necessary. This was in the bag because as a last resort, as it was tedious. It didn't quite drip out fresh water, but it was very slow. It came with a syringe that screwed in to reverse-clean, or blow out, the impurities that the built-in filter cleaned out. Back at home, Greg had a full-sized Berkey water filtration device. Into the Berkey, any kind of water could be poured in, and over the course of the day, it dripped clean water through the filter into the canister below, which came with a spicket to pour water into a cup or canteen. There were also a handful of water purification tablets in the backpack, to Greg's recollection.

Greg had a portable chain saw in the pack. It had 2 handles and coiled into a something the size of a deck of cards, but he hoped that the chainsaws in the garage would run, since they were pull-start, with no electronics. He also had prepper personal hygiene products, like soap flakes, hand towels that were dried up and shrunk to dime-size circles about a half-inch high, and a travel toothbrush. He didn't think he'd need these since the house was stocked with several family party's worth of leftover soap, shampoo, etc. The linen closet was stocked with more towels than would be normal, except at a summer-time river house.

There were a few smaller things rattling around the bottom of the bag. He saw a sharpening stone, some wire, a whistle compass, and 2 bundles of 550 lb. para cord.

Visiting a Neighbor

Greg cleaned the fish, then rinsed them with a small amount of bottled water and headed toward the fridge to store them. NO – he still did NOT want to open the fridge yet, as he'd be getting the perch cold, at the expense of everything else getting warmer. So, Greg dumped the fillets into a zip-lock bag and walked to the one house in the neighborhood that he knew had someone living in it, based on the now-useless car out front.

Greg knew that the neighbors on the inland side of the loop around Rock were Mike and Jennifer. The last time Greg was here, he was invited to a happy hour at their place. At that time, Mike was a police officer in Fredericksburg, VA, about an hour away, so he had to drive to work, and worked nights. Greg saw the curtains part as he walked across the front yard, so knew someone was home. He walked over and knocked on the door.

He may have soiled his shorts a bit – but would never admit it – when Jennifer opened the door, with a toddler following her. The most important thing he saw was at least a .38 or .357 magnum revolver pointed in his face.

"Whoa, Jennifer. Settle down. It's me, Greg, and I come bearing perch and croaker. I heard little Annie loves those crispy perch fillets, and this is as fresh as it gets." Annie, hearing her name, smiled and reached for Greg, who looked to Jennifer for permission to move. Jennifer pointed the gun at the floor, Greg scooped up baby who had become a 3-year-old since he saw her last, while Jennifer took the perch.

Jennifer started sobbing and said "Mike knew this was going to happen someday. He said the lights could go out, but he didn't say the phones, and the water would go out, and the car wouldn't start! He talked about the power grid going down for a while. That's why we moved here."

"I know, Jennifer – This sucks big time. Mike's a good guy, and he's very likely trying to get home now, but he's got about 60 miles to go, so without a bike, or an old truck, he's going to take a few days, if his police duties allow him to leave at all.   Cities are not going to be fun places to be in a day or two. We're going to have to stay calm, and plan to get through the next week or so safely. Plan on him being asked to keep the peace in Petersburg for a while. But he's a good man, and he'll come home to his girls. Until then, if you must stay here, make sure you're bottled up tight.

"Take care and enjoy the perch. Don't open your freezer until you're ready to cook everything in it. I've got a grill if you don't. While the sun is out, we should see who else is on this peninsula – we're all any of us have for the time being.

"Money is going to be worthless, so if you can manage a few-mile walk to the Rock Harbor Mall, we should probably do it. I always keep a few hundred bucks in my wallet, and if they'll sell us stuff, we should get it while we can. If you can't, I'll get as much as I can carry back." Greg offered

"I can't carry Annie that far, but you can use Mike's mountain bike. I've got a backpack, too." Said Jennifer.

So, Greg found himself riding Mike's mountain bike the few miles to Rock Harbor Mall. As he rode, he saw a few of the neighborhood retirees out on their front porches, and stopped to get their names, and give them his best guess as to what was going on. He didn't have the endurance or the backpack space to offer to buy things for them, but he suspected there wasn't that much non-perishable stuff in a store that was full of coolers for beer, bread, and bait, the more luxurious 3 B's of weekend beach survival.

Shopping at the Post-Apocalyptic Mall

Greg returned to the Mall, intending to take a more thorough inventory of what they had for sale. He recalled the things he purchased, and seeing some dry goods on shelves, some fishing bait and gear, and some expensive necessities, like eggs, milk, oils, etc. He saw that the store was open, so he walked in. The woman behind the counter said "Welcome back. Cash only, and 50% off anything in the fridge. Anything not in the fridge is twice whatever the price tag says, because I have to make up the difference.

He replied "Well, I'm not buying anything in the fridge, so today is your lucky day. I'm looking for enough food to fill up this backpack, and it has to be light, because I have to pedaled it back home." The woman pointed to the dry goods aisle, and he started filling up the backpack with all the beef jerky, Bisquick, dried beans, and Spam that he could fit. The only wet thing he grabbed was a half-gallon of Clorox bleach, because a few drops could help make water safe for drinking. Once the dense stuff was in the bottom, he grabbed 2 loaves of wheat bread, and crammed them into the backpack.

"So, we can do all the math on this, or you can give me a number, and I'll round it up. What do I owe you?"

The woman, who was the owner from the earlier trip, smiled at him and said, "How about an even Hundred Dollars?"

Greg pulled out a folded $100 from the secret compartment of his wallet and handed it over. As someone who was certain that some sort of unrest would happen, he had carried at least 2 $100 bills and 2 half-ounce coins in both gold and silver in the side pocket of his wallet for years. As he shouldered the backpack, he said "I see your fishing gear over there. Do you happen to have any hunting gear here, specifically, ammunition or knives?"

The woman said that she had some ammo, but only in limited calibers, and it would be quadruple the price. Greg asked if she had 9mm, and she said that she did have 2 boxes of 50 rounds. Greg pulled out his second $100 bill, and said "That's about 4 times what I pay for them at my gun club. Fair enough?"

The woman nodded and thanked him for his business.

As Greg left the store, he felt guilty about paying useless money for very valuable goods, so he stuck his head back in the door. "You know, it's going to get really bad here really quickly. Are you sure you're ready for any bad guys that might come along?"

She smiled, and said "As you know, I worked for a living. Second, my other hand has been on my 1911 under the counter the whole time. You looked like a trustworthy type, and you have manners, but I'm ready for those that don't have the same manners. I was a Marine, and I can take care of myself and my store. I do believe that the shit has hit the fan, but this is my store, and I'll serve this community as well as I can for as long as I can."

"Semper Gumbi" Said Greg, laughing out loud. "Always flexible! I was more the Hooaahh of the Army than the OOO-Rah of the Corps, but thanks for your service, back then and now in the community. My cousin did 25 years in the Green Machine, and I respect y'all, even if you are a department of the Navy!" Laughed Greg.

"Yeah, the Men's department" said the lady Marine. Greg laughed at the irony as he was leaving, came back in, and shook her hand.

"My name's Greg, and I'm at your service if you need any help. I'm staying down in Rock Harbor, getting ready for some really dark days. Thanks for the Ammo – I know you know how valuable it will get. What's your name?"

"Most of my friends call me 'Gunny', but until I know you better, you can call me Lorna, or Mrs. Smith, if you choose. Stay safe, soldier!"

"Well, Gunny Smith, I hope we are on the same side of whatever shit hits the fan over the next few days. I know you said only your friends call you that, but we're going to have a serious shortage of military friends on this peninsula. On my ride out here, I counted 4 moms with babies, 6 houses with retired couples, and a majority of empty weekend houses. I didn't go down every cul-de-sac, but it seems like there's a shortage of fighting-age men" he quickly corrected himself, "and women! I don't know how long it's going to take for the bad guys to come to the peninsula, but if you hear them coming, let me know and I'll be here to have your back. I'll do the same if they come by sea first. I've got a good view of the water from Golden Bell point to Beasley Point. I can see the Potomac a bit over the dip in the Captain's Point peninsula, all the way to Maryland, but it's only a few hundred feet of river that I can see."

"You must have some pretty good optics to see Beasley Point from Rock Harbor." Said the Gunny

"Yup, mounted on my 8mm Mauser." She fires slow, but she is a sweet one-shot, one-kill rifle. I'm trusting you enough to tell you that I'm at 21 Seahawk Circle if you need me. If I need you, I'll ring the bell 3 times. It's my Pop's souvenir from Pearl Harbor. You can hear it for quite a few miles, on a quiet day."

"Well Shit, Greg, why didn't you say you were related to the Chief. Of course you can call me Gunny. Losing him was hard on many of us here. I'm glad you're there to keep an eye on their house, and to watch my back! Here", she said, as she handed over 2 more 50-round boxes of 9mm. "This is for a debt that I never got to pay back to the Chief. I'll tell you the story over a bourbon, if he has any left at the house. I recall many 'happy hours' on his back deck. I'll swing by in a few days. Lord knows this store's going to have stuff either rotten or gone by then."

Greg shook hands with his new friend, Gunny. He decided to go another quarter mile or so to the community volunteer fire house. He wanted to see if they had any news. Upon arrival, he saw the doors open, with a couple of volunteers in the station.

"How's it going, folks? Just checking to see if you needed anything." He shouted.

As he pulled up a few more came out. There were 3 men, and one woman. They introduced themselves as Deputy Chief Willy, with Lindsey, Buck, and Shane. These 4 had all had various stories, around hearing car crashes, and wanting to help, but not being able to get any more news, or start the vehicles. The one thing they had in common was that they didn't have anyone at home to worry about, so they came to the fire station. Greg told them that there was plenty of space at the Harbor, for folks willing to work, and they were welcome to stop by, and stay if they wished, as there were numerous empty houses on the peninsula. They said they'd man the station for a while but would consider the offer.

Greg suspected they'd need more able-bodied fighters, both the kind that fought fires, and the kind that fought in a fire-fight. These folks were dedicated to a life of helping the community. He was just planting seeds for now. He shared a round of beef jerky, and pedaled home to Rock Harbor.

Securing the Castle

Greg spent the next day securing the house at Rock Harbor from the most likely threats. Those would, namely, be humans who weren't as nice as those that he had met so far. As he went through the house, he found a closet in the master bathroom that was, awkwardly, Behind the bathroom door. In other words, the only way to open it was to go into the master bath, close the door, then open the narrow door to a larger-than-expected closet. He found a guitar stashed in there, as well as some books and old clothes.

Greg looked up and asked for forgiveness from Grandma, as he emptied out the closet, and tossed her clothes and other supplies that he didn't have a use for in a closet that was more visible. He then started to move his survival supplies into the hidden closet. All of Pops "Water, drinking" from Anheuser Bush were moved from the basement, and the 24-packs were stacked on the floor, along with the other cases of bottled water, soda, beer, and anything else drinkable. Man can typically go for 3 minutes without breathing, 3 days without water, and 3 weeks without food. Water was the most valuable asset that Greg had, besides air, and he was pretty sure that there wouldn't be a shortage of air.

In addition to the water, Greg moved all the canned and non-perishable dry food into the closet. There were several boxes of pasta, cans full of vegetables and fruit preserves, and anything else that was edible and stow able. This also included the jerky from Rock Harbor Mall, and everything else he brought home in his backpack. To his food and water, Greg added most of the case of ammunition for his Mauser. Years ago, Greg had ordered 300 rounds of 8mm on 5-round stripper clips, and in fabric bandoliers, from Turkey. Well, it was from a US company, but it was Turkish surplus ammo. When Greg lived in Virginia, he had a back-yard shooting range, and he ran 10-20 rounds of this ammunition through the Mauser. At that time, despite the age, every round fired, so he was highly confident that most of them would still fire.

He was in the habit of putting desiccant packs from whatever he bought that had them in his ammunition cans. Desiccant packs are those little squares of fabric with beads in them that absorb humidity. Many things that Americans purchase come with them, and they usually just get thrown away. Greg hoarded them, and occasionally would take them to the gun safe and put them in ammunition cans of various caliber ammunition.

Greg took one bandolier of ammunition out of the case. It had 4 pouches with two five-round stripper clips of 8mm in each pocket, or 40 rounds of 8mm ammunition. He removed the stripper clips from the bandolier, because opening it under fire would be unwieldy, and placed them throughout the pockets in his conceal-carry vest, which also had both of his handguns in the inside chest pockets. 5 rounds were always loaded in the Mauser, and another 5-round stripper clip was placed over the hunting strap, where it doubled over itself. Basically, the 5 bullets, in their line, were laced over the shoulder strap in a way that they wouldn't fall off, but could be pulled off and loaded as quickly as a single-shot bolt-action rifle could be loaded, as the scope removed the efficiency of a stripper clip.

Without the scope, Greg would be able to pull the bolt back, set the stripper clip into a notch in the upper receiver, and just push down, or "strip" the rounds off the copper stripper clip. Greg decided that the "reach out and kill someone" efficiency of the scope was more important than the speed of reloading, as the iron sights didn't have the range of a 9X Leupold scope.

Finally, Greg put his BOB in the closet, and removed the doorknob. He replaced it with a lower profile deadbolt from the front door of the house. The reason for this was that Greg then grabbed one of the large floor-to-ceiling artworks that Grandma had brought back from Japan and placed it over the door. While it wouldn't survive an in-depth search, most people who came into the bathroom... even if they closed the door, would not see the hidden closet with his survival goodies in it. He kept enough things in the kitchen cabinets, and pills, etc. in the bathroom vanity to give any potential looters something, without giving up the mother lode.

After the long-term survival supplies were stashed, Greg got to work on building his watch post, or snipers nest. Pop had a ladder hanging from nails into the bottom of his deck, and Greg attached it to the back of the house, such that it sat on the deck, and was at an easy angle for running up to the roof. He secured it with a large nail on each side, so it wouldn't slide sideways in an emergency. Greg found a sheet of plywood in the garage, and set it at the peak of the roof, resting on some cinder blocks that he found under the deck. From this angle, with his back to the harbor, Greg could have a full field of view around the house. This snipers nest was where Greg would keep watch in the evenings. While he had to sleep, he needed to protect the house in the hours where it would be most vulnerable to attack or looting – night time.

On dry days, Greg could bring the padding from the numerous deck chairs up to the roof and could comfortably rest on the plywood with his rifle. On rainy days, he could lay on the pads with his poncho draped over him. Anyone approaching would only, at best, see the lump of his head, but behind him was the chimney, so he hoped that he would be well hidden in this sniper's nest from at least the most vulnerable angles.

Once he had a watch post, and his valuables stashed away, he walked over to Mike and Jennifer's house. Having learned his lesson, he called out as he approached the door. "It's just me, Jennifer. No need to point that cannon at me when I knock.

Jennifer opened the door, and she was nowhere near as confident as his last visit. She looked like she had been crying, and she was in a disheveled state. "Mike hasn't come home yet, and I'm really getting worried, Greg"

"I'm sorry, Darlin'", he drawled in his best Georgia impression. She smiled a bit, because she knew that he was originally from Baltimore, and didn't talk that way. "I don't know any more than you do, Jennifer, but I have an offer for you. It is TOTALLY not what you might think, so please don't shoot me for offering, but you are welcome to move in with me."

He took 3 steps back as her face went through several emotions. First, surprise, then anger, then she reached for her pistol, but didn't actually pull it.

"Woah! I am not trying to work my way into your pants, or anything like that. I am counting on my family showing up, too, and wouldn't want any of that drama around WHEN our spouses show up. Here's what I'm thinking..."

"As the food runs out, bad guys, or just hungry people, will start looking for food. When they come, they may not ask nicely. They are likely to come at night, under the cover of darkness, and they won't knock first. I plan on taking the night watch, but we all need to sleep. Survival will be more likely with 2 of us keeping watch on an alternating schedule than both of us sleeping, and waking up with slit throats."

Jennifer's body language relaxed as the threat of molestation went away. Then her face tensed up as she realized what they were going to be up against in the future. "So, why should I move in with you, and not you move in here?"

"Well, your house is newer, but that also means that the wooden or press-board walls aren't going to be as good against bullets as my brick walls, and I have the harbor to my back. I only need to watch 180 degrees or so, and occasionally listen for an outboard, if any of them work, or oars in the water. You know how well sound travels of the harbor. Most nights, we can hear the people across the water arguing inside their home"

"I would suggest you move over with me, as I have a watch-tower set up – even if you can't see it. Bring anything you need to survive, as I've also got a hidden safe-room, that can hold your valuables, or even you and little Annie if things get really bad. I hope we don't get to that point, but hungry people are desperate people."

"Let me think about it, OK?" She asked. Greg nodded his head. "Mike might be home any minute, and if I was not home, and living with you, that could be bad."

"I know Mike would understand the tactical situation, and the decision, if he didn't shoot me in the first minute!" Greg said as he laughed. "And you would need to leave some note telling him where we are, without strangers knowing. So, no street address, but maybe "Chief's house", for example."

"Oh, depending on what his first impression was, and what he goes through to get here, we're going to need to have more like a 5-second elevator pitch ready. He's very jealous, and you know he's one hell of a shot! I will come over tomorrow morning, and let you know my decision. Until then, I assume you'll be watching at night. I'll take the day shift from the upstairs balcony. It doesn't have as good a view as that nest I saw you building on the roof, but I don't think we need to worry about any of our neighbors behind me – yet."

Greg answered "I agree, and I plan to visit every house on the circle, and out to the entrance to the community today. I've only seen about 8 people on the whole peninsula so far, and don't think there will be more than a few dozen, based on the useless cars in the driveways. And some of those cars don't even mean people. Next door to me, the Jones' have their truck in the driveway, but they keep it here for towing their boat, and aren't here. We may have more vehicles than people on this peninsula."

The Rock Harbor Army

Greg knew that he wanted to get at least 4 hours of sleep before dark. Luckily, he set Pop's old wind-up ship's clock when he arrived, and had religiously wound it every morning, just like Pop used to do. Every 4 hours, at 4, 8 and 12, both am and pm, the clock would strike 8 bells. Then, every half hour, it would strike an additional bell. So, 4pm would be 8 bells, 4:30 would be 1 bell, 5pm would be 2, and so on. He figured he had 8 hours free before needing to catch a nap, then it would be up to the 'Osprey's Nest'. He laughed, as he just named his hide, and it was an appropriate name, with all the Ospreys living on pilings in the Harbor.

Greg knew, from his obsessive prepping, what was coming, but knew he had a long, uphill battle ahead of him. Just based on Jennifer's reaction, people would be in default "civilization mode" and count on the government to fix things, sooner, rather than later. That said, he needed to set expectations as soon as possible, so that the community was ready to defend itself before the bad guys decided to take things. He laughed, knowing how even now, his wife would tell him that he was being paranoid and crazy, and that it wouldn't get that bad, but he KNEW that it would. Dozens, probably hundreds, and maybe even millions of transformers, depending on the scale of this disaster would need to be replaced.

Greg walked from house to house, finding that about 80% of them were not occupied when the lights went out. At each house that there was a resident, Greg needed to give the short version of what he knew happened. No more electricity, probably for years, eat your perishables first, then gather your beans, bullets, and bandages. People took the news in a variety of ways, from shock, to already knowing, and having a plan. At the end of his self-imposed time limit, Greg had made it around Seahawk Circle, the peninsula road that the Grandparents' house was on, and up the road to the community pool house and home owners association building.

The people on the peninsula broke down this way: 8 retired couples, mostly ex-Navy families; 3 widows in their 70's; 5 women who were either single mothers, or home alone while their husbands worked out of town, a few families of farmers who worked some of the nearby fields off-peninsula, 1 man who was working from home, and the crew of 8 carpenters that he gave a ride to. They were building the house on the opposite side of the circle, inland. It turned out that they needed to frame in all of the walls for the electrical and plumbing inspection and were in the house the day the lights went out because their Jefe was telling them that they had to work or get fired. There were more of them, but some of them decided to walk home, as they worked close enough to do so. This remaining group were most of the 8 Hispanic men he met the other day, who decided to shelter in place, as their trucks were dead, and they all lived in a shared apartment the town of Tappahannock, about 20 miles away, with nothing really to go back to. The houses nearby had more food than they had in their apartment, so they decided to wait out the storm. They were very clearly more on-board with the apocalypse than most of the residents. It probably had something to do with their histories. Greg was looking forward to exploring those histories, as they might need each other to survive.

Greg's limited Spanish, and their OK English allowed him to understand them enough to get across the fact that the power probably would not be on for a while. He suggested that they explore the houses around them if they ran out of provisions and promised to get back with them the next day. He didn't know them enough to ask them to help him with watch and didn't want to disclose his supplies at this point. They seemed like nice enough guys, but he wasn't going to risk his life with virtual strangers at this point.

He did list them, in his head, as possible soldiers in what was quickly becoming the Rock Harbor Army, or maybe National Guard. Greg knew that bad days were coming, and he'd need every able-bodied man to keep the residents of the peninsula safe. And more importantly than even that, he needed to have the family home safe, because he couldn't allow himself to believe that his son, girls, and other family members wouldn't make their way to Rock. If... No, WHEN they got there, he was going to have a safe harbor for his loved ones, and he would partner with anyone on the peninsula to make that happen.

Greg's only real problem on his visits were with "Tripp", or William Essington the Third, the investment banker and "landlord" who was working from home that day. His wife was off in Richmond, as she was most weeks. He was the guy who employed the Hondurans, and Este. His father had bought the inner lots from Pop's estate some years ago. His wife came back to the harbor only on weekends, and Tripp was alone. This did not surprise Greg, as Tripp was a "piece of work". Tripp was also the president of the Rock Harbor home owner's association (HOA) and was very suspicious of Greg. He asked Greg what he was doing in the neighborhood. He pointed out that he had never seen him at any of the HOA meetings, and questioned Greg's right to be in the house on the peninsula.

Greg explained that it was the family house, and they paid their HOA dues every year, and kept the yard up to standards. He dropped Chief Chambers' name, but Tripp had moved in after Pop died, so he wasn't impressed, or convinced. Apparently, his daddy made the deal with the estate. Greg pointed out that he was rightfully in the family house, and he wasn't going anywhere. He felt that Tripp might end up being a problem in the long run, but didn't have time for trifling little bureaucrats only 2 days into the apocalypse. He felt a little bad for not giving Tripp the warnings that he gave the others about bullets, Band-Aids and beans, but he figured the officious little prick would either figure it out, or die, either solution, frankly, worked for Greg.

"Well, I don't know if you belong here or not, and I guess the members of the association will have to decide." Said Tripp. "Make sure you're at the monthly meeting tomorrow night at 6pm. The association can decide your fate"

"Tripp, I'll be there, because we need to come together and be ready to defend this peninsula." Greg snarled. "But the only thing deciding my fate will be my survival skills, and how many people I can pull together for the mutual defense of this ground. OUR peninsula." I dare you to try to displace me from my Grandfathers house. Please. You'll be much less of a problem if you try me early. Greg turned on his heel and walked back to the house at 21 Seahawk, to get a few hours of fitful rest before climbing up into his Osprey Nest.

Osprey Nest, Night 1.

The second night in the Osprey Nest was interesting, but not dangerous. Greg had an excellent view of the entire 22-house circle that was Seahawk Circle. He could also see across the harbor to the dozen or so houses there. The road circled the fat end of the peninsula, so the developer could take advantage of selling as many water-front lots as possible.

About half of the inner lots were still un-sold, grassy lots Marked with tattered survey pins. However, Tripp's Dad had some marketing credibility, as they were being built and sold. Several of the residents of the circle who had riding mowers did the community a solid one by cutting the grass in the un-sold lots, to keep the property values up. Because of this situation, Greg had a view across the inner circle of lots and had a decent view of the homes on the other side of the circle.

Greg did notice some activity on the other end of the inner-circle, where his friends in the group of Hispanics had set up camp. They were going to the nearby houses and knocked early in the evening to see if anyone was home. They had several unoccupied houses within a few doors of the one they had set up camp in, and as the night went on, Greg watched them break small windows in covered areas like porches, or pry doors open. He watched through his scope as they came out with bags, presumably containing any salvageable dry goods, and anything else that might aid their survival. They did not get greedy, and salvage from every house, just the ones nearby. Presumably they found enough to stay alive, and Greg didn't begrudge them their booty. He was actually jealous that he didn't get started first, so once the flashlights from the folks across the circle stopped their searching, he took a chance, dropped down the ladder, and did the same to the houses around him, adding substantially to the foodstuffs in his hidden room.

In addition to the food that he collected, he also found various prescription medicines in the medicine cabinets. In 2 homes, he found insulin in the refrigerators, which he moved to the still cold, but not freezing, freezer in the basement. The ice in the bottles was still mostly ice, but each one had water surrounding the large block in the middle. He had a plan for the HOA meeting the next night. His Yeti, as advertised, was still cold, and was winning the ice wars with the freezer. He walked across the circle, and communicated with the contractors about the medicine situation, and his idea. They understood and got to work on the rest of the houses, gathering and storing medication for the meeting tomorrow. Now that it was after midnight, the meeting was, technically, tonight.

Greg finished his self-imposed shift back up on the nest, and all was quiet in the harbor. He did hear some shots from across the Potomac, or possibly across the Nomini river, as sound carries funny across large bodies of water. He didn't know if they were from hunters trying to stock up on fresh meat, suicides, or more nefarious activity, but this night all was quiet in the Rock Harbor community.

At Dawn, Greg announced himself once again to Jennifer's home before approaching. She was awake, and opened the door with a smile, if it was a bit strained. "Annie slept through the night, so I did too. I've been doing an inventory, and our food situation doesn't look so good" she lamented. I'm worried about what we do if this lasts a few more days."

"That's understandable, and normal." Greg reassured her. "Most households in America don't have more than about a week's worth of food in their fridges. We do frequent grocery store trips to pick up supplies every few days. This far out on the peninsula, we may be luckier than most places. Because the grocery store is so far away, and many are only occupied once every few months in the winter, most houses have a decent supply of canned and dry goods."

"How do you know that?" She asked, genuinely curious as to how Greg knew her situation, and that of "most houses".

"Well, last night, I saw the construction guys looking around the vacant buildings, and so I did the same with our neighbors. It's very unlikely they're going to travel here with no cars and electricity, so I helped myself to stuff necessary for survival." The good news is, even though there are several unexplored houses still on the circle, we… and I mean you, me and Annie have probably 2-3 months of food, if we can keep supplementing it with fish and crabs from the river. That's plenty of time to get the garden going, as I also found several packs of seeds in addition to what I have at my place. You remember Grandma loved her garden? Thank God for her safe storage of so many seeds. We'll be in tomatoes forever, because she had a favorite heirloom variety for her pasta. The only problem is most of the other seeds are hybrid, so when we eat them, their seeds will produce very little, if any viable plants next year."

"Next YEAR?!?!" She asked incredulously.

"Well, prepare for the worst, and hope for the best. There were a few packs of heirloom seeds, so we'll have to plant them separately, as I don't know what hybrid cross-pollination will do to the survivability of their seeds. Worst case scenario, we'll have some heirloom corn, tomatoes and beans to harvest, and we can preserve the seeds for next Spring, if we need them. If I remember correctly, there are also several berry bushes along the shoreline that we can harvest for fruit, and those briar patches don't need any upkeep, other than some pruning to make more fruit every year. I'm not sure exactly how that works, but I'm hoping someone at the meeting tonight does. Please be sure to come, as I think I'm going to need some moral support."

Greg continued "You're tagged in, Jennifer. If you can keep an eye out for a few hours, I want to get some shut-eye, then I want to round up our new neighbors and talk tactics for tonight's meeting of the home owner's association. You are welcome to move in next door and keep watch from my "Osprey Nest" on the roof, but I suspect things aren't bad enough yet that you can't just keep an eye out on the approach road. I can't be certain, but I think our construction crew on the other side of the circle is not going to be a problem. On the contrary, they're probably going to be an asset if we can treat them with respect and let them know that we're all in this together. That said, I don't know them that well, and I can't communicate with them so well. My Spanish is terrible."

"Spanish? Well, I took 4 years of Spanish, and an immersion course in Mexico City. When you do your rounds before the meeting, I'll go over with you and chat with them." Jennifer said as she smiled. I'll also have my .357 with me, in case they're not trustworthy. Trust but verify, right?"

"What do I say to a woman with that cannon on her hip, but 'Yes, Ma'am!" Laughed Greg, as he saluted her and went back to the house to get ready for get a few hours of shut-eye. But first – he figured he would binge and have his first post-apocalyptic breakfast.

Catching water and making friends.

Greg made a quick breakfast out of the last of the frozen breakfast links out of the freezer. They were now thawed, but smelled like they probably wouldn't kill him, as they were sealed in plastic. He cooked them well-done on the gas range, just in case. Utility gas was still flowing, if a little weak, so he made the most of it. The oven wasn't working, but the stove-top would cook, if lit by a match. After taking a sniff, he then dumped the rest of the perishables from the fridge and freezer in the remaining crab traps under the deck. These loaded traps he dropped at strategic points around the harbor, tying them to the neighbor's docks – with the strings just below the low-tide line. No sense advertising the food to others!

The one item from the freezer that he didn't throw away was a big hunk of pork shoulder. It was still mostly frozen in the middle, and quite cold on the fatty outside. He seasoned it with various spices from the cabinet, and put it on the Big Green Egg charcoal grill on the back deck, fat side up. Once he got the charcoal to a stable temperature of about 225, he set the exhaust vents to keep the temperature there for up to about 10 hours of slow-and low cooking, then went to sleep.

Greg set the wind-up alarm for 1pm and got several hours of good sleep. When he got up, he went out to the river, and jumped in, with a bar of soap. He had several days of funk going on, so he scrubbed in the brackish water. It wasn't a real shower, but he still felt great, if a bit cold, as it was still April and the water temperature was probably just under 60 degrees. As he got out, it started to rain, and he had an idea. He went to one corner of the house and moved the downspout from the gutters back and forth until they separated at a rivet. Water was flowing pretty well now, and he stood under the downspout to rinse off the brackish water. He was quite pleased with himself and used the soap again on the "stank" parts, like his armpits and crotch. Then his eyes got wide and he said "Oh, Shit – stupid, stupid, stupid!"

Greg was bathing in what could be drinking water. He ran down the stairs to the basement and checked the ever-present heavy duty black plastic yard bag in the corrugated metal trash can. Because the house was not occupied full time, it was up to the visitors to take their trash home, so each family member came to an empty, and clean yard-bag lined corrugated trash can. It held several kitchen trash cans, and was easy to take home to their own trash cans. Greg looked inside and decided "clean enough" and ran up the stairs to where the downspout was still throwing precious drinking water into the dirt. He tucked it under the downspout and ran back downstairs to look around. He found a 5-gallon paint bucket that had been, as always, meticulously cleaned after use by Pop. He Grabbed a hacksaw off the tool shelf and ran to the downspout on the front of the house and made another rain collection bucket. After some more scurrying, all 4 corners of the family home had buckets filling with rain water.

Greg figured that if it rained long enough to overflow the 5-gallon buckets, he would dump them into the 55-gallon galvanized and lined bin, and seal it with the lid, so mosquitos didn't get into it.

Jennifer was next door watching from the upper deck, and when she saw what he was doing, she pointed to her gutters, and ran inside. Greg ran across the road with the hacksaw as she brought 2 kitchen garbage cans out of the house, and they made the same improvised water collection cisterns at her house. While they were running around and making hacksaw noises, one of the construction workers walked over to see what the noise was all about. He looked, yelled "Si, Amigo, gracias!" and ran back to the other side of the circle. The sound of hand saws and Spanish orders being given filled the next half-hour or so. Greg and Jennifer did the same to several of the adjacent houses, until the rain started to die down. "We need to do this to all the houses before the next storm" said Jennifer.

"I think that's covered now" Greg said, as he smiled and pointed at the squad of construction workers running from house to house doing exactly that. They would run into the house, gather whatever trash cans or buckets they could, and cut the downspouts at a height to dump into the containers. I think we'll be good. Let's go over and help.

One of the neighbors who lived at the top of the circle, where it split from the main road, was also running around her house, doing the same, after watching what was going on. Greg ran over, and helped, since he had a hacksaw in his hand. The woman was tall and thin, with skin the color of coffee with just a splash of cream. She smiled, and said "Thanks for the help." While her daughter stood on their front porch watching.

When her house was done, she stood in the rain, and shook Greg's hand. "Thanks, I'm Nellie. That's my baby, Sabrina. I haven't seen you around here before."

Greg said "Pleased to meet you, Nellie, I'm Greg." He then gave a brief review of his history in the area. She told him the story of her husband and her buying the lot and building it about a year ago. Her husband was on a business trip to California, and she was worried sick about him.

Greg did what he could to reassure her, but knew that he was blowing smoke up her proverbial skirt. After some of the usual reassurances, he said, "Nellie, we're neighbors now, and in this together. I look forward to getting to know you and Sabrina better. For now, I gotta go dump buckets of little water into buckets of bigger water. He smiled and started to turn around. Then he gasped, as Nellie hugged him in a surprisingly strong and wet hug and thanked him for his help.

"I feel better knowing you're here, and a good guy. Let me know when and if I can help with anything."

Greg smiled, and did his best, "Aw shucks" look. He tilted an invisible hat (while wishing he had a real one), and said "Thank ya, Thank ya verra much.", in his best Elvis impersonation. Nellie smiled, shook the rain out of her dreadlocks, and went to the porch to gather up Sabrina.

An hour or so later, all the houses on Seahawk Circle had rain collection cisterns under their gutters. For the houses that didn't have gutters, Greg had a plan – for another day. He would get the guys to get some 2x4's, and nail several of them to the roofs without gutters. They would be nailed down in a V-shape, from edge to middle, and the V would catch most of the water, and dump it out at one place. If they had caulk, all the better, because there WOULD be dry spells, and water is life.

One of the construction workers seemed to be in charge, and was barking orders in Spanish, so Greg and Jennifer walked over to him. He remembered his name to be Angel. Greg shook his hand, and Jennifer started speaking in what, to Greg, sounded like fluent Spanish, to his un-trained ear.

"This is Angel", Jennifer pronounced it "An-hel" or something close to that.

Greg inclined his head and said "I remember. Buenos Dias, Angel", as he pointed to himself and said "Yo soy Greg."

"Si, nice to meet you – again, Greg", said Angel in his accent. Greg's best friend, his daughter's God-Father Roberto Campos, was from Mexico, and he was used to (even charmed by) Roberto's family members mispronouncing his name. Whenever Greg heard "Gadeg!" come from Roberto's house next door, he would smile, because mama Campos was most likely calling him over for some delicious delicacy from Mexico City, like Molletes, Haysstacks, or Chilaqulies. Yummy, yummy food. Greg was just as sure his butchering of their names would be understood, without criticism. "Bueno on la agua!"

"He says" started Jennifer.

"I got the gist of it, Jennifer", replied Greg. Then Greg looked at Angel and said "Hablo poquito Espanol, pero entiendo mas." This was Greg's stock answer to anyone speaking Spanish. He understood it to mean "I speak a little Spanish, but understand more."

"Muy Bien, Greg!" Angel said as he smiled. He called over his crew, and introductions were made all around. Most of them had very little English, with Angel being the most fluent. Jennifer and Greg communicated to the group, and Greg asked Jennifer to explain his gestures, because of some of the confusion the group of Hondurans, it turned out, were backing off a bit as Greg flailed the arms of his 6-foot-tall, 300 Lb body around. The largest of the Hondurans turned out to be the only non-Honduran. Esteban of the jalapeno sandwich fame. They called him Este, and he was Angel's nephew from Mexico City. Este didn't say much, but was a giant presence, as he looked to be at least 6'6, and with his bulky frame, probably weighed in at 350 lbs. Despite his size, he moved quietly, and watched everything with an intellect that went beyond language.

Most of the rest of the Hondurans came in at about 5'5, plus-or-minus an inch or two, and they were all very fit, a wiry and strong sort of thin-ness. Greg was getting a very good vibe off this group and did not think there would be any problems. To the contrary, their being on the peninsula may have been one of the best strokes of luck to the community. They were very friendly and tried to communicate as each of their language levels allowed them. In addition to Angel and Este, the rest were named Luis, Jaime, Manuel, Domingo, Carlos and Alberto, who was introduced as "Betto", to Greg's ear.

"Tell them I'm sorry for my flailing, but my dad is deaf, and my first language was Sign Language. When I try to communicate, I use gestures to close the communication gap. For example, if I do this... (Greg mimicked casting a fishing rod), I'm trying to communicate 'fishing'. I don't know the word, but casting a fishing rod crosses all languages."

"Si, Pesce!" yelled Carlos, who pointed at the water, and smiled broadly, before Jennifer had to translate. She communicated the rest of Greg's message, and one of the Hondurans, Manuel, started scuttling backwards, making his hands look like claws, and smiling.

"Si, Amigo. That's a crab."

"Crab?" he asked.

"Si." Greg nodded. Then mimicked pulling a crab open, busting up the claws, and sucking the meat out. "Crabs are Bueno!"

"Si, Muy Bueno Crabs", said Este, and rubbed his belly.

Before this devolved into a sign-language fest, Greg asked Jennifer to tell the men about the HOA meeting this evening, and asked if Angel and any of the others wanted to come to the meeting. He explained that it would be much better to have the community know who was on the peninsula and didn't want any confusion if any of them were found walking the streets by an overly paranoid gun-toting resident. They agreed to meet at 5pm, an hour before the meeting, so that they could talk strategy. Greg also needed them help him carry some things. Greg's head was coming up with a plan that he thought just might make this peninsula a little more secure. The group of Hondurans understood Jennifer and agreed to Angel and his apparent second in command, Carlos, to the meeting.

The Hondurans came to Greg's place, and between English, Spanish and Sign language communicated their appreciation of the view, but especially the smell coming from the Big Green Egg.

Greg said "Carne" and was pleased with himself for remembering the word for "meat".

Carlos said, "Si, Cerdo, Greg, Correcto?"

Greg Said "Yes, I think that's 'Pork', right?" and looked at Angel. Angel nodded and smiled.

Greg went into the house and brought out a few warm beers and a platter. He opened the Green Egg, and pulled out a perfectly cooked Boston Butt, or pork shoulder. The juices were glistening on this huge cut of meat, and the platter was filled to overflowing. As Greg's Spanglish Sign language was mostly understood, Angel finished his beer, and grabbed the platter. Greg asked them to wait a second and ran down to the basement to get one of the old soft-sided coolers. Greg then ran to the house next door, and retrieved the insulin from the freezer, and various non-narcotic medications from his stash. Angel saw what he was doing and sent Carlos off to fetch more of the medicine that they collected in the night.

Greg had an almost-full 90-day prescription of his own blood pressure medicine, and didn't see any matching prescriptions, so everything else went in the outside flap of the soft-sided cooler. He was going to go to the meeting bearing gifts.

On the way to the community center, Greg gathered up Jennifer. He suggested she leave Annie with Angel's men. After a bit of hesitation, Este the Giant picked up Annie, and started making

SpongeBob cartoon noises with her. Angie smiled, despite her trepidation, with Angel's men, who were charmed with her own version of SpongeBob antics. It was clear they all had either their own children, or baby siblings. Greg bet that Annie would be safer here than anywhere else he could think of during this Apocalypse, shy of a hardened nuclear bunker. Several of the men had found guns in the houses, so all were at least armed with side arms. A few had shotguns and rifles. Nellie joined them and asked if Sabrina could play with Este and Annie. She wanted to join the circle community at the meeting. There was no problem there, so they all headed towards the community center on foot.

On the ¼ mile walk to the community center, Greg explained his strategy, and got nods of agreement from Angel and Carlos. Jennifer looked at Greg funny, and said "Remind me to stay on your good side – you're an evil genius."

"Greg laughed – I've never tested out at Genius, but I try not to be evil. I'm sort of a wandering man of many Gods. That said, the best won battles are the ones you don't have to fight. I'm just trying to solve as many problems as I can ahead of time. We'll have plenty of problems that none of us anticipate, but Tripp won't be one of them."

"Man of God, huh?" asked Jennifer, and the Hondurans looked at Greg differently.

"Padre?" asked Angel.

No, just generic clergy. My friends call me Reverend Greg. I've done a few weddings, both straight and lesbian, and I try to help out when people need things like marital advice, and things like that. I like to think of myself as spiritual, but not any particular religion, although I've studied several of them, and appreciate every one that basically says "be good" at the root of it.

The HOA Meeting

Tripp scored the first point of the evening. He had told Greg that the meeting started at 6, but everyone from the community was already there, and it looked like they had been for a while.

"There he is. He does NOT belong here. This is NOT his home. And who are those Mexicans? They Definitely don't belong here." I move that we expel these people from our harbor. Jennifer, you, of course, do belong." smiled Tripp.

The crowd seemed to be leaning Tripp's way, but Greg sensed that many of them were open to a discussion, so he launched into his plan, full speed.

"Folks, Tripp here is right. I have not paid any dues to your association, but my Grandparents did, and their estate still does – well, did until banks stopped being banks. Many of you knew Tony and Evelyn Chambers, and I'm staying in their home – the one my family recently left to me. My family is going to make their way here, and they're going to stay in the house, too. The family trust pays our dues every year, and you've seen many of us at the pool and social events. I'm not here to debate my right to be here. Civilization as we know it is gone. There are no more dues, no more taxes, all we have are the people around us, and nature to feed us. I will help any and all of you who want to work together."

"What are you saying about Civilization?" challenged Tripp.

"Dude, the lights are out, and they're not coming on any time soon. You all heard or saw the transformers explode. Your wells won't pump water, and your prescriptions can't be filled at the pharmacy. Survival, for all of us, is about what we have up here" Greg pointed to his head, and the compassion you have in here" as he pointed to his heart.

"I've spent my life as a prepper. While preppers were often ridiculed, I suspect that they're not now. The damn shame is that just about all of my supplies are over 600 miles south in Marietta, GA – just Northwest of Atlanta. How's that for Irony?" This got a few laughs from the crowd. They still seemed mostly to be siding with Tripp, but Greg had a few friends in the crowd, probably based on their knowing his Grandparents.

That said, I've studied the things that could go wrong, and I have thought long and hard about how to deal with different challenges. I don't think any of us here knows WHY the lights went out, but does it matter here, on this peninsula? Unless any of you have a working radio, debating that is a moot point."

Nobody in the room mentioned having a radio, but Greg felt that he had their attention.

"Here's what I DO know." Greg continued. This here Boston Butt is the last viable thing from my freezer, and I'm here to share it with you. I suggest when you go home you look in your own refrigerators and throw away whatever you have that is going bad – it makes great Crab bait, and nobody wants food poisoning without a hospital. I know most of you on the water have crab traps, right?"

Heads around the room nodded, while some with "water view" lots shook their heads no.

Nellie said, "Look, Y'all. I'm not on the water, so I'll need some help there. That said, I saw Greg and these guys running around capturing rain water at all of the houses on the circle. Y'all can sit here being all defensive and not letting in outsiders, but they're good men, and my family is with them. And not just because I need to borrow some crab traps!" Several community members laughed, and Greg smiled and nodded.

Greg added, "Look, there are enough crab traps in Rock Harbor that we can all eat crabs every day through November, Nellie. In fact, we'll probably get sick of it. Almost all of us have fishing rods, and many of you know the fishing is good, and only going to get better through the Summer. I've got a pile of old spinning-rod lures that I can share with you, so a lack of frozen bait, shrimp, squid, or bloodworms is no big deal. We can catch fish and use parts of them for more bait. My point is that we won't starve in the next few months."

"Then what, smart-ass" challenged Tripp.

"Well, *dumb*-ass", Greg retorted, as some of the residents snorted "we grow food – just like our great-Grandparents did. This is very fertile soil, as any of you who have had some of Grandma's tomatoes know. I know she shared the bounty of her garden with many of you." Several heads nodded. Ethyl, whom he remembered from happy hour with Grandma smiled at Greg and gave him a thumbs-up.

"I have a tiller that is a hand-crank one in my garage, and I bet many of you have various gardening tools that still work, right?" Greg asked.

More heads nodded. One older gentleman said, "I have an old John Deere tractor, and it works, although fuel may be a problem."

"No problem this year" said Greg, "Look at all the cars that don't work. Whether you need gas or diesel, there's enough cars around that we can use it, and I think I have fuel stabilizer in my garage for longer-term fuel issues. There's still lots of undeveloped land on the circle, and I have seeds, as I bet some of you do. You can also find out what your absent neighbors have to help out."

"What?" Yelled Trip. "Are you suggesting we loot our neighbor's houses, you Thug?" Several of the community members looked at

Tripp and nodded. "This is America, and people worked for their property rights. We can't just take their property."

"No, Tripp. Looting is stealing something from someone who needs it. IF, and that's a very big IF, our absent neighbors make the long walk from wherever they live, I'm sure they'd be pleased to know that we 'helped ourselves' to their property IF it helps us, as a community, survive, including what may be in their un-opened freezers now, especially when we offer them food from the community garden that we are going to grow! Freezers full of rotten food won't help anyone, but we can live on what's in those freezers now. They can come here and enjoy the fruits of whatever we grow on their land. I won't stand by if people are looting Jewelry or other valuables that can't help us. Family heirlooms, except guns, are to be left in place for the owners. We can re-evaluate the jewelry and any precious metals if we ever are in a situation where we need them to trade for items of survival. Right now, we're not in that situation."

"What makes you think you can just come in here and start telling us what we're going to do?!?!" screamed Tripp. "You don't even belong here." His face was getting red. You want to take people's guns? That's communist!

"Look, Tripp. Folks, if anyone comes back, they will be entitled to anything that we borrow from their house. If we were to lose the peninsula to the bad guys that, I promise, are coming, and we could have saved their homes from being burned down, I'm pretty sure they wouldn't begrudge our using their guns to defend their community."

"You're talking like it's your community, too. You are not one of us!" Trip was spluttering at the thoughts of his rights being trampled.

"Chill out, buddy. You look like you're going to explode? Do you have high blood pressure? I've got some pills from the empty houses around me. Do we have any diabetics here? I've got some insulin in this cooler here, along with other medicines. I cannot vouch for their expiration dates."

"Oh, Thank God!" yelled one of the residents, named Bill. "I thought I was going to lose my wife Lynn – we're almost out!"

"Thank Greg." Said Jennifer, under her breath. Nellie reached down and held her hand, smiling with her.

Greg smirked, as he, Nellie and Angel were the only 2 to hear her. Angel gave Greg a low-five, subtly.

"Here's the deal, Tripp, and fellow Rock citizens. My leaving the peninsula is not going to happen. It's non-negotiable. Shy of killing me, and prying my cold, dead hands from my OWN firearms", he patted his hip, "I'm going to stay here, and help you survive, and defend whatever we build. I'm not asking for your permission, just your forgiveness for my being here. I will add value to this community, as will my friends, Angel and Carlos, and their friends back on the circle. They got stranded here, just as I did. I hope Nellie and Jennifer can convince you that we're not mad terrorist rapists." The ladies smiled and nodded, staring defiant looks at those that still were unconvinced.

"I mean no disrespect, but there's not a lot of us who can do the heavy lifting that will be required to build our garden and more importantly, defend the community. We can all have a meeting about that in the future. I think we're OK for a few more days, but remember, people all around are going to be hungry, and eventually desperate enough to try to TAKE what we have, at gunpoint probably. Here's what I think we need to focus on now:"

"First – Water. You may not know it, but you've each probably got 50 gallons of water in your hot water heaters. This is drinking water, and your empty neighbor's houses have the same. Use it. Survive. Water is first. We also have gutters, and rain water can be consumed with care. We will help you gather rain water, and I can talk you through the safe way to drink it. I'll ask that you clean your own gutters, if possible, but if not, ask us for help."

"Second – Food. Don't eat anything from your fridge that looks sketchy – it's better used as crab bait. If you have seeds, especially heirloom, please let me know. We'll set up a large hybrid garden on the circle this year, and a smaller heirloom garden upwind. I don't know a lot about this, but I fear cross-pollination of seeds that we can harvest and use year after year."

At the thought of being in this situation next year, some residents were talking among themselves. The thought of the power being out lasting longer than a few days was shifting a few more of the crowd towards Greg. Others could not wrap their heads around the concept and were shifting towards Tripp' side.

Greg continued, "Look, I don't know when or if help is arriving, I'm just thinking ahead, which brings me to my next point – Defense. Do we have any ex-military or LEO (Law Enforcement Officers) in the room?"

About a half-dozen hands went up.

"Any with combat experience or Officers?", Greg asked.

All hands went down, except a few that looked to be Korea or Vietnam soldiers. Bill and Chet stood proud. A guy with a beard put his hand down, but the woman whispering in his ear was animated. Greg filed this away for later.

Are you gentlemen officers, or combat veterans?

Both laughed at the officer question and said that they were both Vietnam Veterans.

"Good, an Officer would have just mucked it up." Greg smiled, to the nods of many of the veterans. "I was a Sergeant in the Army, and unless there's any push-back, or you 2 gents want to run this circus, I'm happy to volunteer to be the chief of security for the island. I've already set up a watch stand, but we need to push our defense out to the choke-point where the community's peninsula entry is. If you want me to run it, I'm going to need you 2 to be my Secretaries of Defense, please.

The 2 Vietnam vets gave Greg a thumbs-up. Chet said, "Not my circus, not my monkeys, but I'm happy to help if you need advice when things go sideways."

Greg joked back at the 2 heroes who earned their respite from leadership. "So, YOU can do KP, and YOU can do latrines, OK?"

Both Veterans laughed, and Chet said, "You'll do fine as Chief. We've got your back. With my diabetes, I won't be much help, and Bill here can barely hear."

Bill said "What?" in an exaggerated way, and then smiled and gave his thumbs up.

"What?" Sputtered Tripp. "You think you can oversee anything here?"

"No, I don't, Tripp. I'm offering to help. If you – no, make that WE, the Rock community, don't want my help, I'll go home to my circle, with my friends here, and we can set up our own defense. THAT is non-negotiable. Seahawk Circle WILL be defended to the death. However, I hope it doesn't come down to that. The more of us we have, the more land we can hold, and the more people we have for guard and support duty. With more land, we can plant larger crops and harvest a greater variety of food. Although I don't expect you to dirty your hands with digging, Tripp."

The heads were nodding, and one of the older military gentlemen in the crowd said "I move that we make Greg our head of security, and that we do all of the things he's said so far. They're all good ideas."

A little over half of the hands in the room went up. Tripp still had a core of supporters. He muttered something about how this was not acceptable at all and stared daggers at the group from the circle.

Greg tried to close the gap between the 2 groups. "Folks, let's start with this. If any of you have friends that you don't want their house salvaged, then YOU get in, and at least take care of the perishables. Then you put a red X on their door, and nobody will salvage their goods. I'd like to talk about this at the next meeting, though. The thought of wasted resources rusting away in an abandoned house really bothers me, but I respect that almost half of you haven't come around to this yet. Maybe the lights will come back on." Greg heard the transformers explode, and knew that this wasn't going to happen, but shifting a whole community's theories of culture and norms was something he did at work for 20 years, through 7 mergers. It was never easy to get the holdouts to change their tune, and could only be done with consistent, supportive leadership. Talking the talk and walking the walk would be critical to make them believe what was coming.

Once again, Nellie helped, with, "Tripp, you need to stop being so uptight, and pull your head out your ass. Greg's talking sense, here. So get with the plan, boss-man, or get the hell out of town! You've always been an asshole, and today is no exception."

Several of the community members smiled, nodded, or flat-out laughed. Trip stormed off with, "This isn't the end of it!"

Greg watched Tripp leave, smiled, and said. "Now, I've got this beautiful pulled pork – anyone have any bread, plates, pickles and things for the picnic? I certainly hope at least one of you has some real Carolina BBQ sauce – the vinegar-based kind, although I don't want to impugn the mustard-based lovers. BBQ sauce is something that everyone gets their own taste for. In my limited experience, vinegar is the best in the world for this stuff."

Bill's wife, Lynn, smiled, and said that she had everything needed to make it homemade. "I won't have any of you eating Carolina BBQ from a grocery store." I'll be back in 30 minutes! Nellie offered to get the kids, and the rest of the construction workers from the peninsula, and they all showed up with kids, smiles, and their own additions to the party, like some bread, refried beans, and a bunch of pickled vegetables.

Residents also left to get supplies and scurried back to their nearby houses for the first picnic of the confederation of the post-Apocalyptic Rock Harbor survivors, although they didn't call it that. The picnic was an amazing bounty of food that was going to go bad anyway in community freezers. People made good calls on freezer food, and nobody ended up sick. Plans were made, as residents talked about their background, and knowledge.

By the end of the night, leaders from among his supporters had emerged, and he knew others would come around. The community had a chief of gardening – Ethyl, Grandma's friend and fellow gardener. She said she knew something about smoking and salting food, to preserve it, and asked if anyone would help. Several of the farmers who lived on the peninsula, but had crops outside, joined her team. They made it clear that they would need manual labor, and protection, but would be happy to bring their crops to the community. They said that their winter wheat was already growing, and that corn had been planted, but soybeans would be following the wheat.

A few other folks joined her team and said they would help gather any remaining meat to be preserved. Greg had not thought of that and was glad that there were wiser people in the room than he was. Preservation of food would mean life through the winter. While Virginia didn't suffer crippling winters, it did have freezing days, and occasionally snow, so having a plan to get through the freeze would be up to Ethyl and her team. Having something other than seafood was also something that pleased Greg. It would be scarce in the days to come.

Ethyl committed her team to gathering Dandelions, for their greens, and Kudzu, an edible invasive weed. While not the tastiest food on the planet, it was edible, and added some vitamins and minerals to the diet, not to mention roughage. She also said that sunflowers could go down now and would be a great addition to the diet in a few months.

Lynn offered to oversee the community laundry. She had some ideas on how to keep clothes clean and create rag-bags of bandages that would be sterile, if they were ever needed.

The Harbor also had a Chief of Fisheries, a retired fisherman named Samuel, who would take charge of the distribution of protein from the river. "Captain Sam" said that he almost had his diesel boat engine figured out and was sure that he'd have a running crab boat in the next few days. The Rock Harbor Association would soon have a Navy!!! Greg pulled Sam aside, and they discussed the wisdom of Marking crab pots versus having them hidden. He also had concerns about showing a power boat on the water, with visibility for miles in every direction.

They disagreed on the verdict, but also agreed that both methods of crabbing would be used. One would increase the harvest, by being able to trap in the middle of the water. The other was the community's chance of defeating poachers and boat thieves – if poaching became a problem. Sam said that he would use the boat, motor and all to harvest those marked in the middle of the river, and he enlisted Carlos to take on the task of harvesting the pier-tied crab pots. With a little translation help from Jennifer, a plan around the crab pots was finalized. Carlos also communicated that he had a few "secret holes" for catching perch and croaker, as he liked to take some time to fish from the river after work was done.

Greg volunteered the 2-person canoe, paddle boat and kayak from his place, along with his one-person fishing kayak (with outriggers) to Captain Sam and his group of fish-slayers. He did reserve the right to take the fishing kayak out at his discretion, as it was one of his favorite toys, and he never came home without fish on the stringer. The navy just got bigger by 4 boats.

Rock Harbor also ended the evening with a Chief of Medicine. He was the shy combat veteran from earlier, a retired army medic, who said that his name was just "Doc". He didn't volunteer for the job, but his wife Kim "volunteered" him. Doc was a quiet man, haunted by his past. He was wounded in Afghanistan saving several soldiers and was a silver star recipient with scars from more than one injury. Greg tried to get more out of him on his service time, but he got quieter than he was already, and mumbled, "I just did my job, like everyone else I had the honor to serve with, both living and dead." That said, he did accept the role, and started gathering and cataloging the medicines.

His wife Kim was an EMT and said that she would round up a few helpers to scavenge the houses for medicine. Greg told her that he had a stash of opiates, that he did not bring, and asked her if she would manage them so that no abuse of these powerful medicines occurred on the peninsula. She agreed and said she would make sure Doc 'prescribed' only as needed.

Greg also told her about his large can of Fish-Mox. This was Amoxicillin for fish that he had in his prepper bag. This was supposed to be the same medicine prescribed by doctors, but could be bought at the local pet store. It just needed to have the dosage managed appropriately. Greg had no idea what that meant, so was glad for Doc and Kim's presence. He just read about it in one of his prepper books, and bought it, to be figured out when needed. Antibiotics would be important in the future, whether the injuries came from cuts, bullets, or an abscessed tooth.

With Doc, Greg knew when to shut up, as he knew the best of the heroes rarely bragged on their service. Doc didn't even raise his hand when Greg asked for combat vets. One thing he learned from his time in the Army during Desert Storm was that those who spoke loudest of their exploits did the least. Heroes don't talk about it, even with each other, unless they went through something together. Those that are that close to don't need to talk about it, because they also lived it. He was just glad that Doc and Kim had volunteered to help, and he bet that they would turn out to be a very important asset in the Rock Army. In Doc's eyes, Greg saw a fellow warrior who saw more than he signed up for, and vowed to try to connect in a quieter setting someday.

Greg worked the crowd and took an informal poll of any firearms the citizens had. He asked for volunteers to be on the security team. He explained that this meant keeping regular watches, 24-7, and by the end of the night, he had about a half-dozen security team members, not counting the Hondurans, with various calibers of ammunition. Most residents had small-caliber handguns, with a few hunting rifles and shotguns. Unfortunately, there was only one semi-automatic rifle, and AR-15 on the island, but Captain Sam volunteered his "ships gun" to the team if he could secure something with a scope, or a shotgun to defend his home and boat.

Greg didn't yet offer up the Mauser, but would if it came down to it. It was his only long-gun, and the AR needed to be at the guard post near the community entry for every shift. Several members of the community knew that their absent neighbors had firearms, and the group agreed to scavenge the rest of the empty houses on the peninsula to find firearms, and to pool any dry goods in the community center the next night, for what would become a recurring community happy-hour of shared bounty, although the bounty was certain to diminish as the days and weeks went on.

Greg pointed out that everyone's primary responsibility was to stay alive, and that they should NOT pool their own personal items, and supplies. There would be no seizure of personal property for those who were present on the island. Those who had prepared better should not have their goods taken by those that didn't, "like that puke Tripp", he added gratuitously. That got a few laughs, and the group also agreed that goods in empty houses were best handled as community property going forward.

Greg and Jennifer had a decision to make about the goods that he had already scavenged, as did the Hondurans. Was that "early bird gets the worm" prepping, and thus not community property? He was not going to decide for anyone else but decided to talk with Jennifer after the meeting. After all, she had her own baby to feed.

Greg also saw, in the eyes of some residents, the lack of hope they had. They put on brave faces, but he noticed that those who went to Doc for the insulin and heart medicine knew that they didn't have a lot of happy hours to attend, without more medicine. With the nearest pharmacy over 30 miles away, and probably already looted, Greg tried to give comfort as he could. He couldn't make new medicine, but he could keep them as comfortable, social, and happy as possible while they had medicine. He felt like he would be giving more than his fair share of last rites in the next few months.

Speaking of last rites. At least 2 members from the community were not present, but accounted for. One man died when the lights went out. Greg suspected that he had a pacemaker that went dead with all other electronics. Another woman died, and her husband had buried her, and was mourning. Dead was dead, and debating the reasons didn't add any value. Greg was going to make a point to visit both the widow and widower tomorrow, to send his condolences, and get them caught up with the community teams. Maybe they'd want to help. Sometimes grief needed an outlet in the form of work, and sometimes it needed someone to talk to about the big picture, spiritually speaking.

Greg was, technically, clergy. He had some friends who wanted to be married by him, and so he sent off for his certificate. While not specifically a religious man, he was very spiritual. After his time in the Desert, he had studied several religions looking for peace, and decided that there were good things to say about many of them. He understood that each religion did good and bad things in its name and understood that they all had similar roots. He was comfortable in the cardinal rule – do unto others – regardless of the religion that it came from. An "eye for an eye" was, to him, just an interpretation of the same principle. Some of his friends back in Georgia called him "Reverend Greg", and most knew that he tried his best to be a good man, although every man is a sinner. If asked, he would say that he was agnostic, leaning towards Taoism. Something powerful started the universes, but he had the humility to not ever be able to understand what IT was. He just tried to do the right thing, when possible.

Greg also knew that he had just under 3 months to get his blood pressure under control. He hoped that a mostly seafood and Kudzu diet would force him to lose weight and get that blood pressure down naturally. He tried it about a year ago as part of his survival and prepper studies. The Kudzu wasn't tasty, and the texture was like cardboard on the larger leaves. That said, it was roughage, and had some vitamin content making it worth the chewing – in a pinch. He wondered if they could make "greens" out of kudzu, like mustard or turnip greens were made more edible. The roots were supposed to be starchy, and could be dried and pounded out flat, creating a semi-flour type substance that could be used to coat and fry fish, for example.

He also knew that a very limited amount of alcohol on the island meant he wouldn't be working on his "beer belly", which would help, although he had worries about what a lack of alcohol might do to a man who drank steadily since leaving the Army. His PTSD was going to come back and bite him at bedtime when he ran out of alcohol. Getting to sleep at night would be a problem for another day. Today was about surviving tomorrow.

Finally, Jennifer was nominated to be the Chief of education, as there were a handful of children on the Peninsula. She was thrilled to have more playmates for her daughter. Kim offered to help her when first aid wasn't needed. Jennifer offered up her home to be day care for the children, and various citizens offered to teach whatever knowledge they had, from gardening to knot-tying to Math, from Kim, who had a knack for it.

The only awkward part of the evening was when Jennifer mentioned that she would be moving into the guest room in Greg's house. Carlos tried to high-five Greg, but he was waved off. There was some talk among those that knew that she was married to Mike, the police officer, but Greg and Jennifer assured them that it was not like that. They were both expecting their spouses to show up any day now. They explained that until a security rotation was set up, and defenses could be built, every house, or group of houses should consider defensive watches. Bill and Chet noted that neither of them really slept for more than a few hours any longer and would alternate guard duty at the community entry. Bill said, "if you hear gunshots, come running with more guns." He really didn't seem very stressed about the duty.

Regarding people showing up, Chief Willy and his band of firefighters showed up that evening and were encouraged to move into a few houses by the community center. They brought their own stash of food and equipment, including a wagon with an old hand-powered water pump. This could be used for pulling water from the harbor to wherever they needed to put out fires. They also were offered some of the BBQ feast, which they enjoyed very much. The Harbor now had its own fire department.

Teaching the Hondurans, and the defense team Sign Language.

The next day brought more scavenging of the local houses, and dropping off the goods to Ethyl, who had taken over the community center as the community food bank. Greg intended to talk about that scavenging and food storage situation, because the center was located at the front of the community, closest to any threats coming from the mainland. On the other side, it had a huge propane tank and working industrial ovens, since they were installed when the center was built. Greg thought the supplies should be cached in a more non-descript house, hopefully located farthest from potential threats, but considered that threats could come by sea, so decided not to create debate in the group without a strong solution in his pocket. In his years as a non-profit executive, his one rule around problem solving was that if his team brought him a problem, they had to bring at least 2 solutions, and one recommendation. He might not take the recommendation, but he would talk about theirs, and then tell them what he thought the solution might be, for consideration.

The community members who came to the center for meals, planned for 6am and 6pm every day seemed to gradually embrace the scavenging of food a bit more than at the first meeting. Greg had a clear majority of people on his side on that topic. Closed freezers in vacant houses, especially those with lots of ice, or larger cuts of meat yielded another day's worth of bounty for a community BBQ, planned for the evening. True to her word, Ethyl had a smokehouse sent up to preserve the rest of the cuts of meat. She salted others that she thought would be better preserved that way, based on the knowledge gained from her own grandmother, who raised her in the ways of the old world.

At the meeting that night, each Chief briefed on progress, and most of the community joined at least one team. Some, because of their skill set, joined a few. Greg focused on security, and arranged that the veterans, and most of the Hondurans, Nellie, the firefighters and some of the residents would be on his team, even if some were on other teams. They decided that training would start tomorrow morning, but tonight's watch list was set up, with two guards at the entrance to the community, one across the harbor overlooking the Potomac, and one on the peninsula's tip, in the Osprey's nest. The second guard needed to be young and fit, as they would act as a runner. They didn't have a good communication solution at this time, other than running and banging on doors, but Greg was thinking through a better way to get the word of danger out to the Rock Army. There was a ships bell, a souvenir from Pop's time in Pearl Harbor, hanging on the back deck, and another one across the harbor attached to a piling on a dock going into the Potomac. He suspected there were more around this mostly-retired naval community. He could send an alarm if there was an attack by sea, but needed to come up with something for the front guards.

Tripp was conspicuously absent that evening, but Greg noticed that many from the community who were hesitant last night were more involved, helping and joining teams. It seemed that another day with no electricity drove the point home. Several weapons, presumably scavenged by some, were brought to the center and distributed to the security team. Greg made sure that people were not giving up their own home defense weapons, as he suggested that each house should have one weapon per person. The few houses that didn't have one were "issued" one of the lower rate of fire, short-range weapons, like revolvers or pump shot guns. Giving unarmed citizens weapons shifted a few more to Greg's team. He just asked that if they heard one of the bells ringing repeatedly, that they would show up at the community center for instructions, if able.

Samuel reported that he got his boat running, and crossed the Potomac, only to find that friends of his over there reported the same situation. No lights, no power, no military or police presence to speak of, and scattered gunshots, which mostly ended up being suicides among the elderly or sick.

The night was uneventful, and the "Army", along with those issued new weapons, met at Greg's house to receive some initial training at dawn. The morning was spent ensuring that the army of 16, plus a handful of non-gun owners understood the functionality of the weapons available to the team. Because half of his Army were Hondurans, Greg decided that sign language would be easier to communicate than teaching Spanish to the English-speakers, or vice versa. Greg's dad was deaf, and he saw many advantages to the Army language being sign language, but he joked that it didn't work so well over the radio.

He started with teaching numbers. In American Sign Language, or ASL, all numbers up to 100 could be communicated with one hand, and 2 motions. Numbers from 1 to 19 could be communicated with one hand and one motion. The first number that was not normal to hearing people was 3. To most Americans, communicating the number 3 consisted of putting your pinkie to thumb with the 3 middle fingers up, creating 3 digits. The problem is that configuration is the number 6. To sign the number 3, the pinky and ring finger go down, with the thumb sticking out, along with the next 2 fingers.

4 and 5 are normal, but 6 is putting the pinky to thumb (a traditional American "3"). 7 is putting the ring finger to thumb. 8 and 9 are the next 2 fingers on the hand. So pinky to thumb equals 6, ring finger is 7, middle finger to thumb is 8, index is nine, and a thumb straight up over a closed fist, and wiggling is 10.

The teens are similar, with 11 being the 1 (index finger) extending and retracting, like the universal "come here" sign, but with the back of the hand to the person you needed to communicate the number to. 12 is 2 fingers, pointing up and down, with the back of the hand out. 13 is the thumb, index and middle finger (the number 3 in ASL), but with the non-thumb fingers pointing up and down. 14 through 19 are the same. Sign the number, then wiggle the fingers up and down.

Greg continued to explain how to count to 100, which was mostly lather, rinse, repeat, but doing 2 numbers. 23 would be the 2, then the 3, 99 would be the 9 (it looks like "OK"), and then doing it again. Greg knew that if over 99 enemies came at the Rock Army, they would be overwhelmed, as traditional military calculations for a successful defense were based on 3 to 1. For every 3 attackers, 1 defender, on average, could hold a well-defended position.

Greg spent the rest of the day teaching the signs for enemy infantry (guys walking with guns), flanking (either you are being hit from the side, or you are doing the flanking), heavy weapons like machine guns and "technicals" (heavy weapons on a pick-up truck) and armor, which he hoped he would not have his army face.

He then taught structural sign language, like houses, roads, trees, water, boats and other things that he could see in the community. By the end of the day, with quizzes throughout, Greg felt like the Army could effectively communicate what they saw silently. One of the advantages of ASL is that you could talk across a crowded and large room and talk to your partner without noise or distance (to at least 30 feet or more, depending on eyesight and the sign) interfering with the communication. The down-side is that it doesn't work so well in the dark.

Greg's wife Leigh had a favorite sign: "home", all fingertip closed together, and touched to the cheek, like "the place where you get kissed on the cheek." Leigh would sign "home" to Greg when they were at a party, and she wanted to go home without being the one to decide that "it's time to go". Greg was usually pretty good at giving excuses for going home, and usually ended it with an allusion to something subtly veiled in sex-talk, which Leigh would never do.

Greg asked about bells, and the guys said that they knew of at least 5 around the peninsula. They had clearly been scavenging and knew the area. The team agreed to move one to the entrance of the community, and one on the deck of the Honduran's home, as it had a good view of the water on the other side of the tennis-racquet shape peninsula. They agreed to use them sparingly, as their presence would be communicated across several bodies of water. One ring would indicate approaching people of unknown danger. 2 would be a group approaching. 3 would mean several armed individuals approaching, and a continuous ring would mean an attack. With the placement of these bells, they could guard against approach from both the Nomini and Potomac, within Rock harbor, as well as a frontal assault from the mainland, or up the handle of the tennis racquet.

As the training went on, Angel clearly established himself as Greg's second-in-command. His English was good enough, and he reminded Greg of every First Sergeant Greg ever served under. His 5'2" frame would puff up when he needed someone to pay attention. He got loud and intimidating when one of their "Privates" needed to listen better, or behaved in a way that deserved a little discipline. One trick he had was cussing them out in Spanish, then saying something like "Do you understand me, Private?!" The Army didn't have enough bullets to do target practice, but they did do some dry-firing, with coins on the round-barrel weapons. Those soldiers who jerked the trigger, instead of squeezing, would have the coin fall off. The first time any of these soldiers fired any of the rifles might be while in combat, under stress. The muscle memory of drilling with a slow, deliberate stroke of the trigger would come in handy. This exercise would happen every day until all of the Rock Army Soldiers could easily load, aim and dry-fire their long guns.

Pistol training, especially with square-framed guns was not effective with the coin. Greg and a few other experienced shooters would stand behind the shooter, to see if they were nearly on target.

Then they would, after being sure the weapon wasn't loaded, would stand on the pointy-end of the gun, and see if the view down the barrel was about right. Until one stands on the other end of a barrel, and sees how big a 9mm, or a .45 beast's aperture was they couldn't really understand what might be thrown at them.

While it broke the first rule of firearm safety – namely, don't point your pistol at anything you don't intend to shoot and/or kill, it was a learning experience for the leaders of the Rock Army. Angel pointed out that after the first time he looked at someone pointing a pistol at him, and after his butt un-clenched, he thought the privates in the Army should experience it.

Angel pointed out that if the instructors could tell if a pistol was aimed at them correctly, it might help the privates understand whether they needed to duck, or not. If someone was randomly pointing a gun over a stump, the soldier on the other side would know if they were about to get shot, or if they could take careful aim when the aggressor was brave enough to lift their head. There were several flaws in this theory, but Greg and Angel agreed that knowing what a weapon pointing at their soldiers felt like, so that the first time it was pointed at them, they didn't clench up, like Angel did the first time.

The last part of the day was spent on when a pistol was OK to use, and when it was a waste of time. It was explained that most of these soldiers wouldn't need to fire a pistol, unless needing to give cover-fire, as it would only be effective at 15-20 yards maximum, for good shots. In most sudden combat situations, a sidearm was just a tool to use to get to your rifle, if the rifle is not being carried. Rifles are often piled up or stashed by a door, and pistols could throw enough lead to keep the attacker's head down and assist the shooter to get to the rifle.

Pistols also are decent in structure clearing situations, where the rapid fire of the pistol, combined with the short barrel for slicing off angles of a corner, would help keep the pistol-wielder safe. Approaching a corner was trained into the Army. You would keep your pistol back from the corner, and have the pistol, and your one shooting eye slice, or "pie" around the corner. It was much safer than just jumping out from the corner and opening your whole body to incoming fire aimed at your center of mass. It was also a much better tactic to help one surprise a guard in a hallway, for example.

Doc showed up, and quietly helped several guys who didn't have the right grip, sight picture, etc., but never picked up a weapon himself. Greg caught up with Doc at the end of the day and asked if he could have the honor of sharing one of his few remaining cigars with Doc on the back deck at sunset. Doc accepted the invitation, and Kim came with him bearing a potatoes au gratin made with some Velveeta and the last of their root vegetables, or at least those not confiscated by Ethyl for planting in the gardens.

While Kim and Jennifer hung out in the house, watching Annie and Sabrina play in the front-yard sandbox, Doc and Greg went to the back deck to visit. Greg brought out 2 Padron cigars, and a mostly-empty bottle of good Bourbon. About that time, Nellie came around the house, and looked at the men sitting in lounge chairs. She said, "Is this a boy's club, or can a fellow veteran sit down and have a cigar, too?"

Greg and Doc both looked at her in surprise, to look at her beautiful smile. "Yeah, grunts, I'm one of you. 4 years overseas, 2nd Armored division, but I was a Rear Echelon Poge. That doesn't mean I didn't see my share of the shit in Afghanistan. They tried to blow me up plenty of times."

Doc stood up. "Then take this seat! Greg, you got another smoke?"

"Well, it's my last one, but for a fellow brother... um, sister in green, I guess we should make a party of it."

The 3 veterans sat on the deck, watching the sun go down. Greg and Nellie talked about the units they served with, while all three smoked nice cigars. Finally, both Greg and Nellie looked at Doc, and said, "Your turn."

Doc was always a quiet man, but among fellow Army veterans, he found his voice. "I was deployed to Iraq and Afghanistan twice. I got blown up once in each country. This is from my second Iraq deployment." He pointed to his neck and shoulder, where the stitches could clearly be seen going under his t-shirt. "After that, they kicked me out. I never shot at another man, and don't plan to, but I'm here for you guys. I didn't forget any of my training. I just don't talk much. Do you have any bourbon, Greg."

"As a matter of fact, Doc, I have about 3 doubles left of some of my favorite. There's no time like the present." Greg went in, and when he returned, Nellie had her arm around Doc's neck, and was whispering something into his ear. There were tears flowing down both of their faces." Greg stood in front of them both, handed them each a healthy double of bourbon, and stood at attention.

"Brother and sister, God bless the USA. Join me in a toast to all the bravest that we could, and could not save, and those that, most certainly, will need saving. We all know that they're the real heroes. Thank you for your service, and let's do everything we can to save more than we lose in the months to follow. Not many here know what is coming, but I'm glad to have you on my side."

Nellie gave both men a hug, and Doc just nodded his head. When Jennifer and Kim came out the back deck, all 3 of the former soldiers had tears in their eyes, and were puffing on the cigars, and sipping the whiskey that was packaged with a wax stopper.

"Well, y'all are just a barrel of fun, aren't ya?" She smiled, without laughing, and Kim walked behind Doc and Greg, putting a hand on each of their shoulders.

"Chow time, Rocks!" Move your ass! She smiled, as she escorted them all into the house, to sit down for a nice meal at the dining room table. Nobody asked about the conversation at the dock, but Greg knew that bonds were formed, and that he could trust these two with his life, and the lives of those he loved.

May – A Late Planting

Late April, and most of May was occupied with gardening, and guarding. Greg did get the family tiller fired up and had the section of the circle that Ethyl pointed out tilled out and ready for planting in a few days. The farmers in the community griped that the planting was late, and Ethyl looked at them in her special way, which shut them up. Ethyl selected another empty plot that would typically be up-wind, or West, and a smaller, heirloom garden was planted. After consulting with the local farmers, who did this for a living, they agreed that cross-pollination with the hybrid seeds couldn't help the efficacy of the heirloom strands, which were descendants of durable plants whose seeds could be stored over winter, and planted the next year. Hybrid seeds had a very low reliability for future years, but did make bigger, and more pleasant fruit and vegetables to the eye, but not necessarily the palate.

Ethyl mentioned that the farmer's winter wheat fields just outside the community would provide flour, provided they could work out a trading system. The farmers, to a man and woman, agreed that having a team to help defend their families was a fair trade for all of their produce, as long as everyone ate. Grinding it would be a challenge, but she and her team would figure that out when the time came. Usually, the farmers would just have the fields harvested, and driven away on trucks, in exchange for cash.

Inside the large glass windows on the front of the community center, Ethyl rigged up a set of growing tables so that the community could get some fresh sprouts, supplementing their bland food with some necessary vitamins. She made a point of saving and drying the seeds from most of the foods that she served. She would dry the seeds, and see what grew into edible sprouts, or could be planted. This was met with moderate success, resulting in various types of sprouts that were edible and nutritious very early in the growing season. Vitamins would hopefully not be a problem for the community.

One of Greg's favorite things to do was to take Annie to the gardens and have her "help" him with weeding the rows of plants. She was taught to not touch certain types of green coming from the ground, and occasionally did get some weeds, but it usually ended up with the two of them making mud pies, and little castles in the mud. They had a very vivid fantasy world, with little princesses, and ogres. Greg was pretty good as a mimic, so he would make all kinds of voices, and Annie giggled a lot. He was really falling in love with this little, good-natured girl. Whenever Esteban was not on duty, he would come over and do really good TV impressions, like Shrek, Scooby Doo and SpongeBob, among many others. While he didn't speak much, when he did, he was on-point and hilarious. It was hard not to love the big guy.

Greg did the exact same thing in his garden at home 15-20 years ago when his daughter Maria was Annie's age. His son Jared didn't like the make-believe in the garden, but would run through the woods creating his own fake "Army fights." When he was old enough to participate in his dad's paintball fights with Army buddies, Jared was in heaven. He took to stalking and hiding in ambush like a champ. He knew that his dad was a soldier, even though Greg didn't often talk about his time in the service. One day, if Jared joined the military like he had been threatening to do, Greg MIGHT tell his son about his own time in, and the dangers of it. He secretly hoped his son would find a woman, or career. The only stipulation that he had for his son and military service was that he got his degree first. While he couldn't require it (as much as he could with a "man" over 18), he told his son that he could decide to enlist as an E4 or be an officer, but the degree was a deal breaker. Because Greg tried to let his kids make their own mistakes after giving some "mild guidance", both of the twins rarely heard "deal breaker", so knew when something was important. Greg's "deal breaker" speech was much like when their mom used their full names, so the kids usually paid attention. Since his son seemed to enjoy Georgia Tech, they didn't bump heads over this "requirement" too often. He also had at least one girlfriend there at school, and maybe he'd miss the whole Military thing, despite his threat of ROTC enrollment, which Greg suspected was just his way of messing with Dad.

These adventures in the garden with Annie were occasionally bittersweet, as it reminded Greg that his kids were out there somewhere, in the highly-populated Washington-Baltimore-Philadelphia corridor, and Atlanta. He had to count on both of their common sense and physical strength to keep themselves alive. Maria was always into sports, from soccer to fencing to ice hockey, so her strength and endurance wouldn't be a limiting factor to her survival. He was even more confident of his son's ability to live, as he had picked up some of his Dad's prepper traits, including building a Bug-out Bag of his own, mostly with Dad's cast offs. These cast-offs were perfectly fine, but giving them to Jared was an excuse for Greg to buy higher-quality toys for his own bag.

Jennifer

Jennifer woke up early, after doing her night shift in the Osprey Nest. She looked in Annie's Bunk, to find an empty bed, with Annie missing. This wasn't the first time Greg had let her sleep, while taking Annie, so Jennifer stretched out, got a glass of water. She quietly padded across the street to her house and went up to the balcony. She took a seat, quietly, in the shade while she watched Greg play with Annie in the community Garden.

Because her house was in the center of the circle, she had a commanding view of the community garden. It had 4 of Ethyl's crew in there, weeding and watering, but she only had eyes for Greg and Annie. They were playing make-believe along a row of corn that was about knee high. Greg was pretending to defend each corn stalk, while Annie pretended to be invading the "castle".

"Oh, no you don't you scoundrel! I will protect this corn with my life." Greg said in a deep voice.

"No, my corn!" squeaked Annie, who wound up a pretend catapult, and threw soil at the castle.

"AAAAhhhhh, Incoming!!! We know they won't hurt the corn, so hide behind it!" Greg finger-walked his defender behind the corn stalk, and then said, in his best French accent, "I Fart in your general direction. You stink of elderberries!"

Annie laughed out loud, probably at the fart reference, and not so much the Monty Python quote. "YOU stink of elkerberries!"

"Oh, do you want a piece of me? You can't handle a piece of me!" Greg pointed at the tot.

"I WANT A PIECE OF ME!" she wailed, then moved towards Greg.

Greg laughed, and fell back into a puddle of mud. Annie took the opportunity to launch herself at him, and they both got muddy, as a tickle-fight took place. Even the over-worked kitchen crew took a moment to laugh. A few threw mud pies at the wrestlers. Jennifer smiled to herself, and her feelings for Greg grew by quite a bit as she watched what he must have been like as a Dad.

"He'll more than do, in a bind." She said to herself out loud, then had to take some time to process that she may have just said a little more of a good-bye to Mike.

After an afternoon of "weeding", Greg brought Annie home, to a mom who pretended to be shocked at the amount of dirt Annie had packed into every crevasse. "Greg, you know that we can't just drop her in a tub, right?"

"Yeah. I figured I'd put on her swimmies, float around the harbor, and then you could rinse her off with some rain water."

"YAY, Swimmies!" Annie had voted.

"But what about the Sea Nettles?" Asked a concerned Jennifer.

"Well, they better stay clear, or Annie might dress them up!" Greg laughed at Jennifer's frown. "Seriously, hot momma, I'll keep them clear, and she's going to get stung at some point. It's not like they're Portuguese Men-o-war. Worst case, she cries, and you rescue her."

Jennifer spent the next 15 minutes or so watching Greg wade around the pier, with Annie in swimmies. He made a big deal about defending from the invading swarm of Sea Nettles. He even picked up a few and threw them at the dock where Jennifer was sitting, smiling with a big hat on, and even bigger smile. He was careful not to hit her, nor did he make a big deal about the stings on his hand from his bravado.

When they were done, because Annie's lips were blue, and she was shivering but smiling, Greg handed up Annie to Jennifer, and then swam a few laps of the harbor. This feat of cardio was not lost on either Jennifer or Greg. She watched him swim, and realized that he had probably lost 40 or 50 lbs since the day they met. The meals at the community center were healthy, but no more calories than needed for survival. The bigger citizens were losing weight, and the smaller ones were putting on muscle. Jennifer took Annie to the bath tub, and rinsed her off with a gallon or so of lukewarm rain water, and used some Johnsons baby shampoo to clean her hair, and the rest of her.

"Mommy, Greg is funny! I like him."

"I like him too, snuggle-bug. I think we'll keep him." Jennifer said, unable to keep herself from walking to the glass, and watching his muscles as he swam laps of Rock Harbor.

When Greg swam back to the stairs on the dock, she met him with a rare treat – a cool-ish beer that she had tied to a string, soaking in the harbor, in the shade. She also had a gallon of cool-ish rain water, which she handed to him, to rinse off with.

"Don't bring that stinky harbor water into the house, Greg. You did good today. Rinse off and we can go to dinner at the community center."

Training

Training the following week was a string of banner days for the team. The Rock Army had gathered up enough bullets that Greg felt they could spare 3 rounds each, to practice shooting, and to zero in any weapons that weren't dialed in. With bullets being so precious, each shot was a long, slow practice round of shooting, with the other members of the army cheering, or jeering, and sights being dialed in to the point that every member of the defense force felt they could at least hit a paper plate at 50 yards with a rifle, and 25 yards with a pistol.

Greg was pleased at the accuracy of his Army. Unsurprisingly, he was once again one of the worst shots in his group. The problem was that he had too many bad habits, from years of shooting as a child in Upstate NY. He qualified well enough with weapons in the army, but only ever shot expert with the M-16 rifle. Pistol qualification for him always ended up with the lowest ranking, Marksman.

Greg and Angel debated the wisdom of having everyone on a 12-hour shift of either day or night. Greg's experience in the Army was to have a consistent shift, so that the internal timer could get used to the circadian rhythm of a new "normal" work day. Angel pushed for rotating shifts, so that people could work the night-shift, but not always. Timing shift changes at the 2 meals served in the center was a no-brainer. The men agreed with most of the citizens being on weekly 12-hour shifts, with staggered days to do half-shifts and swap out the day and night crew. The exception was that Greg insisted on being on night shift at the peninsula, just as Angel agreed that day shift at the gate was his right. Both men knew that they were each working more like 16 to 20 hours on any given day, with sleep being a luxury that neither overused.

After more discussion with the larger group, they ended up with a protocol where every week, half of the defenders would have one day where they worked 6 hours, then took a break for 12, and then took up the second half of the opposite shift. In this way, people would rotate who they worked with, and also build a sense of comradery with the whole unit, not just "their shift." This meant that every person had 2 weeks of day, and 2 weeks of night, but the timing of the shift changes meant that they would all get to know each other.

May was a tough month, in that a few of the elders who had specific medical needs started to die off. A few killed themselves before succumbing to the symptoms of not having heart, diabetes, or liver medicine. Others found living without air conditioning too hard, and had various ailments, so they shot or hung themselves. Usually, they'd leave a note for the community, on where their good stuff was. Often, sadly, they'd have dug their own grave ahead of time. Sadly, Greg knew when something like this was coming, as the elders would stop showing up for meals a day or 2 in advance, most likely so they could save the food for the survivors. Everyone who did this was given the respect of a burial in the growing community cemetery, across the street from the community center in an empty lot.

Esteban and Manuel often went "outside the wire" salvaging for things and talking to the neighbors out there. Much of the larger peninsula between the Nomini and the mainland was farm land. They came back one day with some interesting news.

"Jefe, the good news is that there are about 4 more farming families in the 3 miles around us. The better news is that there are about 10 farmsteads. We found a few with dead farmers in them. They killed themselves. Before they do that, they planted crops. We will be OK on food, if we can harvest their crops of corn, winter wheat, and soybeans. The farmers out there say they can't harvest what they have without the tractors, and nobody to sell the food to. Some even rented combines when the crop was ready. Now it's going to be hand-picking, but I told them we have the people. I also tell them that we have defenses and houses here if it gets too bad. We have friends most of the way to Montross, and about halfway to Warsaw, with plenty of food for everyone over the winter.

"Your friend Gunny says hello. Her store is now empty, but some of the families go there to trade, and we can trade there too. She say 1 bushel of crabs for 10 bullets or 10 eggs. I traded the last 20 bullets for that .32 auto we found for 20 eggs. Then I throw in the pistol and she gave me a live pollo! I give the eggs to Ethyl for dinner, and Este is keeping the chicken as a pet, since he found the .32.

"I will give all of the eggs to Ethyl, Jefe." Said Esteban, guiltily, "But I had chickens when I was a Niño, and always loved feeding them. I can find food for the chicken in the fields outside."

Greg's deaf parent gave him a gift – the gift of calling BS. He could usually smell a lie like a fart in a car. He saw Manuel's eyes dart up and to the left when he talked about the eggs. "10 bullets for 10 eggs, huh? So you traded 20 bullets for 20 eggs, is what you're telling me. Is that right, Este?" Greg looked at Esteban, who couldn't meet his eyes. Greg looked back at Manuel. "Is that right?"

Manuel looked at Greg and couldn't keep up the charade. "OK, Jefe. OK. It was 20 bullets for 2 dozen eggs. But Este and me – we haven't had any eggs for a long time. She hard-boiled 4 for us, and offered us old bay to sprinkle on them. We each eat two. Scavenging is hard work, Jefe," Manuel blushed, in shame. Este hung his head and walked away. Manuel added, "I think she like me, Jefe. She did not offer Old Bay to anyone else. I was being friendly eating those eggs." Manuel smiled, with a twinkle in his eye. I did this off shift, Amigo.

"You've been working hard, Manuel. You too, Este. Don't sweat it. You get to take some of what you find, that's the rules of salvage.

But there's no need to lie to me, Hermano. We all have to eat. Especially that big one over there!" Esteban laughed out loud and smiled at Greg. The guys learned a valuable lesson that day – Don't B.S. Greg, and they wouldn't get called out. Greg had established a little more loyalty on this day.

Hidden Treasures

One day in May, Greg was digging further into the recesses of the Grandparents house on Seahawk Circle after sleeping a beautiful 6 whole hours. He was digging into a fairly empty closet in the back-left corner of the bedroom. It had very little in it. A few jackets and fishing shirts, along with some too-small shoes that he would bring to the community center for someone who fit a size 10. He also went through the hallway pantry, looking for canned food, as he wanted to eat something, anything, without the eyes of the community on him. He found a can of spaghetti O's, and a packet of microwave mac & cheese tucked in at the back of the top shelf. While he didn't have a microwave, he had a meal.

"Hey Jennifer, how about dinner at home tonight? I bet Annie could be convinced to eat some Spaghetti-O's?"

"Pisketti!!!!" Yelled Annie from the living room.

"I guess that's a yes, Greg. Where'd you find that?", asked Jennifer.

"Top shelf. I needed to get the step-ladder. It's a little expired, but who's counting during the apocalypse. I'll go see if Ethyl has any stuff to go with it. She'll understand our wanting to have some time alone with Annie."

A few hours later, they had cooked a decent dinner consisting of perch fillets in Mac & Cheese sauce, spaghetti-O's that went mostly to Annie, some Kudzu and baby lettuce in an olive oil, vinegar and dried herb dressing, and one warm Coke, split 3 ways, along with some boiled rain water.

"I can't believe you found this on the top shelf. I've looked in that closet a dozen times."

"Tall man strong and creative!" Greg blustered

Jennifer laughed, then added "I wonder what else is in this house. Any other surprises?"

"Well, Pop did work for NSA. I'm sure he had lots of secrets. The family always talked about treasures that nobody could find after Pop died. Even Grandma didn't know where he kept things like his guns and gold, even though she knew he had both. I suspect the aunts and uncles each thought someone else 'acquired them' but were too nice to ask. None of them are like that, though. I bet he's got a stash somewhere… ", Greg trailed off.

"Jen. Follow me, like physically and metaphorically. I have an idea." They got up from the table, set Annie on the floor of the living room to play with her coloring book – the last one they got from the "school" library.

"Follow this thinking. See THAT wall - the one behind the wood stove?"

"Uh, Yeah. It's right in front of me!" She sounded sarcastic, but when he looked at her, she was smiling her 10,000-watt smile.

"OK – This closet where I found the food is part of that wall, right?"

"Still not blonde, Greg. Keep talking."

Greg laughed out loud, and swatted her on the ass. "That's for being a smart ass. Now… come into my bedroom."

"Pervert – You have your room, and I have mine, remember?"

"Yeah, just come on in here for a second. We'll leave the door open if you need it, although you'd probably kick my ass if I made a move. So, come in here and look in THAT closet. I was going through it today and wondered why it wasn't just a rectangle. See that cut-in? I thought it was for cleaning the stove or something, but the stove clean-out is in the cellar."

"Yep, I see it. Still have no idea why we're in your room, other than the obvious reason – and the answer is still NO, even if you are getting cute as you lose weight!"

"Stay with me, horny woman. THIS wall, at the back of the closet, is the other side of the fireplace stone wall, right?"

"Yeah, I guess so. Makes sense. What's your point?"

"My point is, the closet is 2 feet deep and 2 feet wide. The hallway one is the same. That means that 6 feet of space behind the bed, times 2 feet deep, and 10 feet high, are unaccounted for. That's 120 cubic feet of storage area. You could put a lot of stuff in that much space. I'm hoping that Pop's history with hunger during the depression, and the NSA sneaky stuff he did at work may help us out. Let's get a pry-bar or some hammers.

As Greg stood looking at the wall, the first thing he did was move the bed away from the wall, hoping for something behind the headboard. No luck there. Before Greg started banging on the wall, he wanted to respect the family, and take down the pictures over the bed.

The solution came to Greg when he tried to remove the pictures. They were in frames nailed to the wall. The frames weren't hanging on nails or screws, they were nailed into the paneling behind them. They were access panels!

Greg and Jennifer used a pry bar and hammer to lift the picture frame/trim off of the wall, and it took the picture and paneling behind it with it. In a few minutes, they were looking at 2 holes in the wall, about 6 feet up, and almost 2 feet square.

"I'm going to get a candle," said Jennifer, who ran out of the room. Greg got on the step stool and looked into the holes. He could see the brick of the fireplace vent filling the space between the holes, but he could also see hints of treasures between the fireplace.

The next few awkward minutes were spent with Jennifer standing next to Greg, holding a flaming candle next to his face while he looked around at the gifts from Pop. They settled on a short boat-hook from the shed and pulled out everything back there. Lying on the bed was Greg's "inheritance" from Pop.

First, there was a German-era Browning 12 gauge semi-automatic. This "Goose gun" was a long-barreled 12 Ga that, once loaded was just "pull the trigger" fast. It wasn't a pump, or a lever action, but a fast-shooter. Greg tried to load it, and it only took 3 rounds in the tube, which didn't make sense to Greg. He removed the cap on the tube, and the loading spring popped out, with a plug. Pop had a hunting plug in, because in many areas, 3 shots are all you are allowed. "Well, we don't have to worry about Game wardens!" Greg shouted, as he tossed the plug, and was able to load 6 rounds of buck-shot into the tube, chamber one, and then add 1 more, for a total capacity of 7 rounds of 2 ¾ inch 12-gauge heaven. The peninsula just added very formidable stopping power to its Army!

Pop had 2 ammo cans full of 12 Ga. One was buckshot, and one was full of slugs. Both were magnum shells, with the expanded brass on the bottom to deliver more punch. While only good out to about 50 yards with buck shot accuracy, the slug put the range out to more like 100 yards.

There was another weapon, farther down in the wall. It looked like a short-barreled rifle, or SBR. When Greg hooked it, and pulled it up, he found that it was, technically, a pistol. It was a CZ Scorpion 9mm pistol with a "wrist stabilizer" where a rifle's stock would be. This was a work-around to SBR laws, in that it was made to wrap around a forearm, and be shot one-handed, but could be shouldered, even if some said that it was illegal to do so, because shouldering it made it an SBR. This theory was silly, because holding a hammer head to ones shoulder doesn't make it a rifle stock. That said, it was a nice close-quarters weapon. It came with a sling, and a 30-round magazine, shooting the same 9mm ammo that Greg's Glock 19 did.

Looking back in the hole, Greg hooked an old Crown Royal bag. This was the big, half-gallon bottle bag. He pulled it up, and it was heavy. It had about 100 loose rounds of 9mm in it, and another loaded 30-round magazine, with 2 more loaded 20-round magazines for the Scorpion. He smiled at Ginger. "This is our new home-defense weapon!" It stays with us, whenever we are near Annie. It will throw 30 rounds pretty accurately, and can hang from our shoulders, easily staying out of the way. It's not as easy to carry as, say, my .40, but holds a lot more, so we'll keep it here in the house. If we ever get cornered, it'll allow us to blast someone through these thin doors."

There was another, lighter ammo can in the storage space. This had various silver "proof sets" of coins, from the 50's to the early 70's, when quarters and dimes were still made of silver. This container also had several rolls of Morgan silver dollars, and even a half-dozen gold-ounces in either American Eagle or Canadian Maple leaf. These would come in handy for trading in the future. The several thousand dollars in cash rolled up wouldn't be so useful now, but might be at some point in the future.

"I remember Pop being all fired up about the Y2K bug back in the late 90's. I was working in computers at the time, and I made a fortune doing consulting for a few dozen firms that didn't have an IT guy, but worried about their systems crashing, and possible grid-down talk. This could be from those days. Because he was alive during the depression, he saved everything, and said that he'd never go through hunger like he felt in the 1930's."

Jen picked up a few flags, and asked "What are these for?"

"Those are Semaphore flags. For signing letters between ships at large distances. I don't know how it works, but it's all about arm position. A Navy buddy of mine was a signalman, and was so good, he could spell and read almost as quickly as typing."

"Well," Smiled Jen, "here's a quick chart on how to do it! I don't know what we'll do with one set of flags, but we should list it among our assets." She winked at Greg and her reference to one of their favorite movies, the Princess Bride.

Later, Greg sat on the back deck, cleaning and checking the Browning. Jen was off at her old house, now the community school, teaching math to the kids. The mindlessness of cleaning the gun allowed Greg to remember all the times he would ask Leigh, and make Maria and Jared help with cleaning guns after they went to the range. When Greg shot alone, he didn't always clean the guns after each shooting. A pistol like his Glock, safe and sound in the holster mounted behind his bedside table at home could easily fire 500 or more rounds between cleanings. After all, their advertising line of "Glock, Perfection" was not far from the truth. They fired every time you pulled the trigger, unless you put in crappy ammo, and even then, they fired almost every time unless you tricked them out with competition triggers, which Greg always did.

That said, Greg wanted to instill in his girls, son, and any other guests he brought to the gun club, the practice of shooting, then cleaning. It also created a familiarity with how the guns worked mechanically, while also getting users familiar with how to easily break-down and re-assemble the weapons. Despite some initial push-back, once they were sitting around a table with a protective towel over it, they had some pretty good times cleaning barrels with CLP (Clean, Lubricate, Protect) oil and giving each other crap about how their own gun was cleaner than Greg's. He missed his son and those girls, and missed the non-stop ribbing they gave each

114

other, all in fun and love. Truth be told, his son always got the guns the cleanest. His Engineering training, and attention to detail meant that he was also the family gunsmith, since he would experiment and take them apart farther than what "field maintenance" called for.

He remembered how Maria rolled her eyes when he brought home the Ruger Mark IV 22-45 Lite semi-auto target pistol, with a Site-Mark red dot. Her first words were "That looks a lot harder to clean than my revolver, Dad." She rolled her eyes and grumbled about another gun until he took her to the range, and she first used the red-dot sight on it. After that, she never complained about the cleaning, even though it was a lot tougher, and more necessary to keep clean than her Blackhawk revolver. He hoped she was keeping her guns clean now, and hoped his wife and son would come down the driveway any day. His daughter lived closer to the extended family in Maryland, so she would show up with an army of cousins, Aunts and Uncles first – he hoped. He knew it was a long shot, but he had to keep his hope alive.

June

About 2 months into the end of the world, Greg woke up to one bell from across the harbor. Greg looked across the harbor, and saw 2 men talking on the sand bar, with who could only be Esteban covering from the trees. It looked like someone was handing one of Greg's guards a weapon, so it was indeed just a 1-ring alert. About 5 minutes later, Greg was geared up and headed out when Angel knocked on Greg's door. Greg had been on guard duty the night before and had heard more than the usual shooting sounds coming across the water. He wasn't sure where it came from, but knew that someone had a really bad night. The residents still alive in Rock Harbor were about done listening to the single, or 2 gunshots of those that decided to end their own lives, rather than die from lack of medicine, or food.

At the door Greg saw Angel, who was in charge for the first shift, with Les, the "biker" from the first night at the airplane crash in his canoe on day one. Les looked less than at his best. His leather vest was dirty with either mud or dried blood, (it turned out to be both) and his shoulders were slumped. He looked the opposite of the confident, self-sufficient biker that he did when they were surveying the plane wreck.

"Greg, I didn't know what house y'all lived in, but I remember you from E-Day. That's what we folks in Beasley Point call the day that the EMP happened, or the day we lost electricity. I'm glad to see that you're doing OK, and you've got a pretty darn good security perimeter here in Rock. I wish we had done the same in Beasley Point. Those assholes from the Homeowners association didn't do anything but divide us. Some wanted us to all share food, others hoarded, and nobody got their shit together for mutual defense. Now most of those idiots are dead, and ... my wife was killed." He paused to wipe a few tears from his face, then continued, "Can I come in? If you had a drink of anything, I'd appreciate it – it was a long night." The bloody wound over his ear made that pretty clear.

Angel looked at Greg while carrying a strange hunting rifle over his shoulder. "Greg, this man gave up his gun with no complaint. I don't like to take it but you know rules, Jefe. If you cool, I give it back, OK? If he shoot you with it, then maybe we get more time off." He laughed. "If you trust him, then I give it back, OK? Then he can keep you safe – because you shoot for shit, Amigo!", Angel smiled as he said it. This was based on the few rounds of ammunition the community was able to spare for the Guard's target practice the previous month. It's true, Greg was not a great shot. That's one reason he joined the Combat Engineers in the army. Close is good enough in horse shoes, and more importantly, demolitions!

"Angel – Go back to making frijoles or something, amigo..." Greg smiled, sure that Angel knew he was kidding, as all soldiers do with each other. "Giving a Piss" was a world-wide phenomenon among veterans of different branches, or just guys in bars in general. Appreciation was expressed by how hard a time you gave your friend. "We've got this. Gracias, Angel, por bringing my visitor. I've got him from here. Come on in, Les. Let's go out on the back deck. I have a bottle of Pappy that I've been saving, and this is a rare, if sad occasion."

Les took a seat on one of the plastic recliners that Greg had found in a nearby house. He looked longingly across the Nomini to his own community, and Greg could see some signs of smoke coming from the area, miles away. Greg poured 2 fingers of Pappy Van Winkle from a freshly cracked bottle. Not even his thirst would have made him crack it shy of an emergency.

"Over there," Les pointed at the smoke column about 4 houses from the point. "That's where I lost her. Those assholes from the HOA wouldn't get their shit together, and so I was keeping watch by the entrance to the community by myself. I heard motorcycles coming and was behind a picnic table that I turned on its side. I had my trusty M1 Garand with me. It served me in Korea and continues to be one hell of a gun.

"The sound of the motorcycles masked whoever came up behind me and bashed me on the side of my head. That's the sum total of my memory of the battle. For whatever reason, I'm guessing that they thought I was dead or they left me for later and joined their brothers. Lesson 1, Greg – They send scouts ahead on foot, and this one was quiet to sneak up on me. He was close enough that he could rush me when the motorcycles came in.

"Anyway, I woke up, and ran along the shore to my back yard. I heard lots of screaming from other areas. The assholes just shot my wife, looted my liquor cabinet and bathroom cabinet of any drugs that they liked. I found her there, with a hole in her head, laying on the floor in her night-dress. I am proud to say she went down fighting, because there was a perforated, dead Meth-Head in the doorway. I say Meth-Head because he was skeleton-skinny, had those nasty black teeth and scabs on his arms – it could be heroin, crack or other drugs, but I'm just painting a picture of the attackers. There were .45 shell casings on the floor near my wife, and my Colt 1911 wasn't in the bedside drawer. Those sick tweaker fucks weren't as kind to the younger women.

"I saw what they were doing from my upstairs guest room window. They would take turns with the women on the front lawns, often with their husbands tied to the trees, being forced to watch. When they got bored, or the women went catatonic, they'd shoot both of the couple, and move to another group. I emptied my M1 on a few of them, and I think I killed everyone that I sent a bullet to, but the rest of them came out of the houses like cockroaches and zeroed in on where I was. So, I ran." Tears ran down Les's face as he told Greg the story.

"There's no shame in living to fight another day, Les. Here. A toast to the heroism of your wife. She went down fighting. God bless her, and God bless you killing those animals."

"I don't know if God has anything to do with it, Greg. I'm starting to wonder. Anyway, I ran out the back door, and jumped in the water, hiding under my dock. It was high tide, so they couldn't see me from the side, but I had breathing room between the dock stringers. They made a fuss, and I heard the leader call for someone. He asked where the gate guard was, and upon visiting my position, they saw that I wasn't there. The leader shot that scout in the guts, right there in my back yard, and threw him in the water about 12 feet from me. It took the guy a long time to drown, and he saw me just before he went. I almost felt sorry for him.

"The water is still pretty cold, but I waited there, under that dock, until night fell. I held that Garand on my shoulder the whole time. I heard the motorcycles fire up, and heard a few women scream. The bad guys drove off with their loot, and I assume they went back to their home base. When things settled down, I gathered up a few things from the house, including an ammo can full of .30-06. Then I buried my wife in her rose garden. After that I paddled my ass over to Captain's point in my canoe. I ran into Angel there, guarding the entrance to the harbor by road. He was very polite, despite being approached from inside the wire by an armed guy. Then I saw this Giant of a dude following me, with his gun on me. Did you know that big guy can move so quietly?"

"Yeah, Esteban is a freak of nature. I often call him Shrek, for his ability to own the forest. I'm glad he's on our side."

"Yeah, Me too!" Les agreed. "He doesn't talk much, he just asked me politely to hand my gun over and put my hands up while he searched me. Then he handed me off to Angel and disappeared into the pine forest. I mean, how does someone that big disappear into a bunch of trees?"

Defend

Over the next few days the security team all heard about the fall of Les's community. They spent more time coming up with strategies for how to defend against the same.

First, they agreed that 2 men needed to be on point at all times, with a scout like Este wandering the forest on both sides of the community entrance. They needed to be able to see each other and communicate with sign language.

Next, they needed to be able to defend against an attack from dozens of bikers. Greg had some solutions to that problem.

Back in his Army days, Greg was trained in land mine warfare. Specifically, he spent 5 weeks after his 8 weeks of BASIC training learning how to emplace obstacles to deter the enemy from advancing and kill those that did. Those obstacles might be tank ditches, concertina wire fences, or mine fields. One of his instructors went off-curriculum and spent half a day talking about how to improvise mines and explosives when you're not issued an Army-Grade anti-personnel or anti-tank mine. The instructor did this because for the first time in his career, he was preparing troops to go to an actual war, as Saddam Hussein had invaded Kuwait, and was building heavy defenses at the borders of Saudi Arabia and Kuwait, in addition to the borders that were already defended against Iran.

The most basic, and that means least-lethal, anti-personnel mine is called a "toe popper". It has a purpose, and that purpose is NOT to kill the victim. The military version of these are small, racquet-ball sized mines that are flat, with a pressure plate on the top. When stepped on, they do what the name says – pop off toes. The purpose of these is to make it so that 1, or even 2 able-bodied soldiers must remove themselves from battle and drag a wounded soldier off. If the mine killed the victim, then the healthy soldiers would just move on. In this way, a mine field, which should always be guarded by soldiers on over watch, has removed 3 bad guys out of the immediate fight, instead of one.

Mine fields are not the answer to stop an invading enemy. They are there to slow them down and bunch them up, so that they can be picked off by artillery, snipers, and other concentrated fire. This reasoning means that it's sometimes smarter to "surface lay" land mines. Vehicles coming can see them and must stop. It also means that not all of them need to be live mines, just the first few that blow up an advancing army.

After getting together most of the residents of Rock peninsula at one of the HOA committee meetings, and having Les tell his story, Greg convinced them that they needed to defend the peninsula with obstacles. The first thing the group did was round up a few working chain saws, and they cut the trees at the community entrance, a natural choke-point, in such a way that they fell, and overlapped over the one road into Rock Harbor. The trees were notched, and "persuaded" to fall at a 45-degree angle away from the peninsula, towards any bad guys driving towards Rock. The trees were not cut off at the stump, just cut about 3/4 of the way through, and then felled into the road in front of and behind the masonry community gates. This obstacle was not only a vehicle stopper, but couldn't be dragged away, as the trees were still attached at the stump.

Consecutive pine trees (the predominant species in Rock) were cut on each side of the road, and farther back from the first few. This created a thatched-tree defense, which would stop any vehicle up to a bulldozer, or a tank. If tanks were employed against the citizens of Rock, they'd have bigger problems than staying in place and defending. Survival would be job one, and the navy would be their means of evacuation.

Greg surveyed the fallen tree obstacle and was very pleased with the way it looked. He asked a few of the neighbors to round up several of the ever-present "pricker bushes" (Greg's Upstate NY term for anything that had thorns on it). He recognized a few as probably Hawthorns, but others weren't straight thorns. Others were curved back towards the stem, and really a pain to get un-tangled from. He didn't know what they really were, other the perfect supplement to the obstacle they were building. Neighbors gathered them from around the harbor, with more than a few curses and bloody arms, despite the gloves. They brought those thorny nightmares to the tree obstacle. Greg had had clothes, crashed kites, and feet savaged by these beasts, so he knew that they would be very effective in slowing down anyone who decided to sneak OVER the tree obstacle. He had the residents put them well into the forest around the obstacle, so that it could not be bypassed easily.

Next, Greg found the most obvious paths around the thorny tree nightmare. This would be the most obvious approach to anyone who wanted to march infantry, or a walking group of bad guys onto the peninsula. Greg asked some of the younger kids to get some plastic bottles and other weatherproof items, and decorate them with "BEWARE", Skeletons, and other scary warnings to anyone attempting to come through. This deer path would be the one heavily-guarded path onto the peninsula, and anyone trying to approach through without an escort would be in for a painful surprise. On the other hand, he didn't want his wife or daughter to travel hundreds of miles, only to be blown up by his "toys". As he put the warning signs out, he was sure to put his initials on them with a Sharpie.

Greg pulled out his backpack, and loaded his field expedient toe poppers, very carefully, and one at a time. These consisted of a length of copper pipe he cut into 2-3-inch sections. Onto the bottom of each one, he soldered rigged a firing pin as his instructors had taught him. Over these firing pins, Greg placed any sort of spring he could find that would hold the weight of a 12-gauge shell (preferably buckshot, but he had assorted ammo from the community, and beggars could not be choosers). A lot of click pens lost their utility that day, as he raided all of the small springs from them.

Into these tubes, Greg GENTLY slid the 12-gauge rounds onto the spring, such that it would rest over the thumb tack/firing pin. He then dug small holes in various places around the path around the obstacle, and just as gently put anything waterproof he could over the improvised toe popper. Often, this would be a PVC cap that buck shot could go through, but rain water could not. Then he would place a few leaves over the whole thing, such that uninvited guests would step on the hidden shell, push it down on the firing pin, and be down a few toes (if lucky) and eviscerated if not so lucky. He marked each one with a particular type of quartz rock, agreed upon by the security team to be both innocuous and, for those looking, conspicuous.

On the harbor side of the paths, Greg made sure that the kids made VERY SCARY signs, letting all of the residents know that these were not paths that they should walk upon. This was also made clear during the now-weekly happy-hour meetings, as well as the more informal shift-change meals, at 6pm and 6am.

In the back of the V-shaped road obstacle, Greg was able to round up a tree stand from one of the farm fields outside of the harbor. This was someone's covered deer stand, and was anchored at the far back side of the V. Up close, the trees had fallen in such a way that one could sit on a lower tree near the front of the V and be covered by the trees in front of them. This gave them a forward observer, who could see the front of the mined alley, and over-watch in the rear of the defensive formation.

The plan was to have at least two guards on duty always, with one high and low, plus a roving scout that would double as a runner after they scouted a threat. Greg needed to come up with some system of calling in the other able-bodied men and women in the harbor to come to the defense pretty quickly. The front guard's job was to stop anyone from going on the paths, by warning them to stop. If they did not listen, it was up to the toe poppers to further deter the invaders while the rest of the community got into position in their firing holes set back from the trees.

Building Obstacles

For a week after the road obstacles were built, the gunshots at night were more and more frequent. Most often, it was the lonely sound of one bullet – either a hunter, or more likely someone who didn't want to live in TEOTWAWKI any longer. A few nights, though, there were barrages of different calibers echoing over the water. People out there were getting more desperate and were willing to take supplies by force.

Greg was checking out the security team one morning, when one of the toe poppers went off. Greg and the security detachment carefully negotiated the mined lane, only to find a deer crumpled in the woods a few yards from the toe popper. Greg put the deer out of its misery, gutted it, took the heart and liver, and carried the rest of the viscera to a nearby crab trap staging area. He and Este carried the gutted deer to Ethyl, who kissed Greg, and said venison was on the night's menu!

That night, venison steaks with greens and some canned corn were a wonderful meal. Greg told all shooters that they should take these targets of opportunity, even if on guard duty. Protein that wasn't from the harbor was getting rare, and Venison really hit the spot. They worked out an all-clear signal after a hunting kill, which was to bang 2 sticks together, 3 times, as sort of an "all clear" signal, which could be repeated until all citizens would know that meat might be on the menu. Greg laughed, knowing that he or Jennifer would literally be ringing the dinner "bell". He laughed at the Pavlov's dog reference, as it would be likely that more than a few citizens would be salivating at the 3 knocks, when they happened. The community knew that those bells would be too loud and didn't want to confuse their "incoming bad guys" signal with "incoming venison" signal.

After his arrival, Les had moved in next door to Greg, and joined Samuel's Navy, harvesting food from the bay for the community.

He also volunteered to rotate on and off watch, as needed, with his trusty M1 Garand being more than enough to either stop a Meth-Head biker or a deer.

July

Rain had come and gone several times this Spring. Now that Summer was here, it was less frequent, but the community had unearthed the filled-in Rock Harbor Mansion's well from the late 1800's. With some digging, they found a supply of fresh, if muddy water. They would have to eventually dig it deeper, so that the water coming out wasn't so silty, but it was good to know that there was a plan B.

After an uneventful night on guard duty, Greg was sitting in his favorite chair, overlooking the dock and harbor after he returned from breakfast. He was amazed that, to the fish and birds, nothing had changed. He watched a blue heron wading in the water, eating mouthfuls of minnows. In another part of the harbor, a school of minnows was being hunted by something below the surface, causing them to make patterns on the otherwise glassy surface of the harbor as hundreds of them at a time jumped free of the water, trying to evade whatever was chasing them. Greg figured it was a big perch or a small striper. He watched its progress by the furor it was creating with the minnows. It swam back-and-forth around the dock, creating beautiful patterns on the surface.

Not able to contain himself, Greg, who should have been sleeping now, grabbed his spinning reel, and wandered down to the dock. Knowing where the fish was going based on the minnow action was helpful. He cast his black fury in front of the carnage, and jerked the tip of the rod while slowly reeling in. To entertain himself, as he often did, he started talking to himself. This time it was his bad impression of the groundskeeper in that old movie about golf. He had one half of his mouth shut, like he had a stroke, and said, "Here, fishy fishy. I'm just a harmless little wounded minnow, swimming along in front of you. Pay no attention to the line coming out of my face. Here, fishy-fishy."

He tried to cast about 3 times in front of the flurry of minnow movement and couldn't convince the predator to take the bait. On the fourth cast, he was sure that it had passed him up again when the fish struck the spinner right at the dock... and then decided to weave between the pilings as it streamed out his line.

As the line got farther from the rod tip, the rod couldn't do its job, and absorb the bursts of speed. Fishing rods allow good fishermen to catch a 30 lb fish with 10 lb line, if they use the physics of the rod to absorb the fast bursts of speed from the much larger fish. Greg knew that the fish would break off if he didn't do something radical. "Shit. Well, here goes!" Greg jumped into the harbor and walked his rod around the 2 pilings under the dock, scraping himself on some tiny mussels living on the pilings. The mud between his toes was squishy, and sucked at his feet, but he got clear from the tangle, and stood in chest-deep water with his rod high over his head. Whatever it was, the beast was running toward the sand bar and inlet. Now that he had the fulcrum and tension afforded by the rod tip, he was able to do some serious fishing.

Greg was pumping and pulling in the rod tip, while walking into deeper water, because the fish was now trying to tie itself up on the dock of Les's adopted house. He had his rod high up over his head as the water was getting to neck height. He stepped on several questionable obstacles under water, and at least one old crab trap poked him in the leg. Soon, he was in over his head, and floating on his back, reeling in the fish, which wasn't giving him any breaks. Greg kicked his feet, holding his breath so that he mostly floated, trying to bring himself and the fish to shore. He was making decent progress, as he saw that the line on his spool was gaining in size. He finally landed himself back in water shallow enough to stand in. By now, he was at the other neighbor's house. He knew this because his head hit the bottom of their dock, as he was focused on getting the fish in. Because the neighbors had built stairs down to the surface, for their old Labrador who couldn't help but go swimming at every opportunity, he was able to walk backwards up the stairs as the fish got close. A last effort with the rod tip, and Greg reached down to grab the tail of a Striped Bass, well over 2 feet long, and tossed it up on the overgrown grass of the neighbor's yard.

Greg caught his breath, which would have been harder months ago, and bent over to grab the striper by its gills. Standing up out of the tall grass, he looked around, like any fisherman does after a good fight with a "Did anyone see that?" expression on his face. Up on his porch, Jen had her hands on her curvy hips, and was smiling at him. When they locked eyes, she clapped her hands and said, "My Hero! That was right out of 'A river runs through it!' Color me impressed, but I bet you stink now."

Greg smiled, looked at the fish, and said, "Nope. He's the one that smells like fish. I just smell like Testosterone!" As he was standing in the neighbor's yard, he heard and saw the sound of the water delivery team making its rounds on the circle. He carried the fish towards them.

In the last few weeks, the community gathered up all of the propane tanks in the community and had a couple of outdoor gas stoves made for frying turkeys, or boiling crabs. Ethel would have her team of helpers go from house to house and gather the rain water from cisterns in a big plastic fertilizer sprayer on a trailer that was rigged to be towed behind the tractor. Also on the trailer were 5 gallon buckets of clean water. Ethyl's team would filter the rainwater, and then bring it to a rolling boil, adding a few drops of bleach to each container. These would be dropped off at the homes where residents lived, much like a milk delivery in the past.

When dry-spells happened, the well was a source of water that required much hauling and filtering, but they had a back-up water plan. One day, they'd have to send people down into the well to clear out the years of silt and settling, but for now, water was not an issue, as long as the rain water was conserved.

As Greg was walking towards the water tractor coming, he held the fish up, triumphantly, and Ethyl clapped her hands appreciatively.

"Good morning, Gunga Din's", Greg said and smiled. "I come bearing gifts." Most of the group laughed back at him, and Greg saw Ethyl explain to the younger ones his reference to the storied water bearer in the English battles in India. Greg walked out to the tractor with the empty 5-gallon bucket by the front porch, and picked up a fresh one, saving the team the trip. "Ethyl, my contribution to dinner is this fish, who made me swim to get him. Please save Jen a tender piece with some crab-meat stuffing if you can spare it."

Both of them laughed, as crab was something that they never had a lack of.

"Nice Job, Greg. I'll do better than that. The asparagus is coming up, and I'm thinking something with crab, asparagus, and a little hollandaise sauce. We have enough to give everybody a little if Sam can catch one this nice, or at least some perch. Don't you worry, Jen will be able to bask in your glory, oh great fisher God!"

Greg smiled at the ribbing he was taking, but put the fish in his empty bucket, and handed it to one of Ethyl's helpers. She was one of the farmer's daughters. Now that all of the crops were in, and the main farming job was to "watch the crops grow", the had a larger population, which would be that way for a month or so. Then, the plan was to have all but the guard shift go help the harvest. The influence of the Rock Harbor community was growing outside of the borders of the harbor.

He carried the full bucket back to the cistern he built in the house, on top of the refrigerator to let gravity feed water through a garden hose to the sink area. He got on Grandma's ancient, but still sturdy, step ladder, removed the plastic cover, and topped off his "plumbing."

For toilets, everyone in the community agreed that they would scoop their own water out of the harbor, and just fill the big tanks on the back of their toilets. This saved potable water, yet allowed residents to use modern plumbing, and flush it when done. Because some trips to the harbor were farther, or more uphill, Greg reminded them in one of their meetings of Pop's old saying from his life on the family Pineapple farm in Hawaii: "If it's yellow, let it mellow. If it's brown, flush it down." Greg foresaw a time when septic tanks would be filled, but hopefully with limited flushing, and the bacteria in the harbor water, that wouldn't be for a while. With an abundance of empty homes, that was a problem he would worry about at a much later date, as every home had at least one toilet and a septic system.

As Greg was finishing up his morning constitutional, and flushing per the old saying, he heard Angel knocking on his door. "Greg, I have report for you — Mucho importante!"

Greg had the spare bucket of harbor water by the side of the toilet and swished his hands in it for a quick cleaning of sorts and made a note to come back and fill the toilet tank later. He headed out to the porch, where Jennifer was standing with Angel.

"Que Pasa, Amigo?" asked Greg, in deference to the language that they were developing among the groups on the peninsula.

"This morning, dawn. One, how you say?" (he mimicked a motorcycle noise, and put his hands up in the air, like on handlebars).

"Si, motorcycle — good sign language, Angel! But muy malo — bad news, right?"

"Si, he drives up to the trees, and looks through, um, eye glasses?"

"You mean binoculars? Greg stepped inside and pulled out the pair that the Grandparents kept on the porch to look across the water.

"Si! Yes – Binoculars. He sees our tower, and then he, ah." Angel looked at Jennifer and pointed to his middle finger instead of lowering the other 4 fingers. "Lo Ciento, senora."

"He flipped our guard tower off?!?!" burst out Jennifer.

"Si. He saw our tower and, how you say, 'flipped us off'. Then he ride away back West. "

Greg was thinking about how they just got scouted by a potential enemy. "I think I just figured who's behind most of that shooting the last few nights. It has been getting closer, hence the few farmers that moved inside the perimeter. Hopefully his middle finger was out of frustration at seeing our defenses. Maybe the wolf will pick easier sheep to eat."

"What is wolf, Greg?"

Seeing as how they weren't likely to be attacked during daytime, Greg shifted into professorial mode. Greg looked back through his limited knowledge of Spanish, but Jennifer saved his butt once again.

"Lobo, Angel."

Greg explained, and Jennifer translated as necessary. "Angel, I have a sheepdog patch on my Bug-out-bag. There are 3 types of people in a situation like this. Wolves take what they want. They are the criminals, rapists, druggies, murderers, and apparently, these bikers."

"Sheep are the defenseless ones: our children, the elderly, sick, those that can't, or won't fight for what they believe. That's not meant to sound disrespectful, or treat them as stupid, but Tripp is a sheep, also. They're the ones that need protecting for whatever reason."

And Sheepdogs – that's us. We protect the herd, even if we must lose a fight to the wolves. Wolves cannot be allowed to bully the sheep. If left un-checked by sheepdogs, the wolves will take over everything, and everyone.

"Now, I've known a bunch of great bikers – Look at Les, Doc and Kim. I don't want us to assume that anyone on a motorcycle is a threat, but today shows us that some may be dangerous."

Jennifer snorted – "YOU, the nonprofit tree-hugger prepper knew a bunch of bikers, did you?"

"Yeah, Jen. My daughter's godfather, Carlos was a biker. I attended his biker wedding and made a lot of good friends. I also picked a fight once, with the biggest biker ever, and he bought me a beer."

"OK, I'll bite." Said Jennifer.

"Just a few weeks before this apocalypse happened, I took my nephew to St. Augustine. We wanted to find something to eat, and I Googled 'St. Augustine best food'. I sure am going to miss Google. I hope it's not gone forever." He paused to think about a world without Google. Jennifer translated as necessary for Angel.

"Anyway", he continued, "The online review gave the place right next door 5 stars for food, BUT there were a few comments that said they didn't like tourists. It was a local joint. We went over anyway, since we wouldn't have to drive after a few beers. My nephew and I walk in, and the place is packed – with lots of leather-clad riders. The bar was full, and there was a wait for tables – at 9:30pm! So I knew the food was good."

"The biggest, hairiest biker I ever saw – he had to be 6'6, and 350 lbs., turns around when his buddies look my way, and it gets a little quieter in the bar. I had on an Army tank top, and was with a young man who was fair of hair and skin, and only about 125 lbs."

"This biker walks up to me and says 'Son, this here is a local's bar only – and we're all Navy, as he points to the group of bikers behind him. I figured they'd been riding together all day, and now they were clearly enjoying the March Madness, and beers."

"My nephew took a few steps back toward the exit, but I walked up to the big dude, and I said to him 'Well, I doubt this is a Navy Bar. There's not enough drinks with umbrellas in them, big guy. That, and none of you have hit on my nephew yet."

"No, you did not!" laughed Jennifer in her trademark guffaw. "You're still alive."

"God's-honest truth, Jen. Things got really, really quiet for about 10 seconds, then the big guy laughed out loud, and his buddies laughed with him. The guy patted me on the back, said 'welcome' and walked back to his buddies. One of the older guys in the group told the 2 bikers sitting on stools next to him to stand up, and they did. He gestured us over and pointed to the 2 bar stools."

He said to me, "That took balls, son. Luckily, I'm also Army, and I know the 2 of us have more balls than all of these Nancy's." The guys with him laughed, and I realized there wouldn't be a bar fight tonight. "You're drinking on me tonight."

Jennifer had translated the story to Angel, who laughed, looked at Greg and said "Si, I always say you Loco, Greg."

With a little bit of levity out of the way, Greg asked Angel to call together the rest of the sheepdogs. It was time to turn up the defenses. The wolves might be coming back – any night.

Scavenging

As the defensive plan was fleshed out, and the patrols picked up in range and intensity, those off-shift continued to get more creative in their scavenging of houses. More than one had hidden closets like Greg built, or goodies stashed in crawl-spaces.

One of the treasures found on the peninsula was a mint-condition Remington R-25 found in one of the absent neighbor's hidden gun closet. This rifle was based on the AR-15 platform, but instead of being in a 5.56mm, AKA .223 caliber, it was in a larger, more powerful .308 caliber. In the Army, Greg knew guns of this caliber as Main Battle Rifle's (MBR's). .308 caliber, also known as 7.62 x 51mm NATO is the same caliber as the M14 rifle used by the Marines in Vietnam (see Full Metal Jacket) before they switched to the M-16. It was also used in the Army M-60 machine gun that Greg carried at times during his time in service, as well as the M&P 10 "boar rifle" he had at home. This versatile caliber was also used by its younger brother, the newer M240 belt-fed gun. It was good to punch through up to 3/8ths inch of steel and keep going. This treasure came with about 100 rounds of boxed hollow point hunting ammunition, and another 200 or so rounds of "green-tip" armor piercing rounds.

When the find was brought to Greg's attention, he immediately moved it to the lower position at the barricade. With the bipod stand, Leupold scope, and 20 round magazines in semi-automatic, it was the peninsula's most potent defensive weapon. He felt that it needed to be lower than the tree stand, because a lucky shot would take out the peninsula's only tower. While Greg would prefer something like the "Ma Deuce" he trained on (i.e a .50 caliber M-2 Machine gun), he would take the .308 in semi-auto. While the round didn't have quite the punch of his 8mm Mauser, being able to pull the trigger and empty a 20-round magazine on assorted targets in under 10 seconds was a definite plus. Since the ammunition that was found with it was "green tip", or armor piercing ammunition, only a very stout tree, or an engine block would create cover. Everything else anyone was hiding behind would only be concealment. Concealment kept you hidden, but not safe, as bullets go through concealment. Think of concealment like hiding in a bush, and cover hiding in a bunker.

Carlos came to the command center and showed what he found while scavenging houses inside the perimeter, but out on Captain Point. Rock Harbor was really "The Rock Harbor & Captain Point association (RHCP). Captain Point was a second community, accessed through a road alongside the club house. There were only 2 people in residence on the Captain Point when the lights went out: Ethyl and Drew. There were probably 10 houses on Captain Point, and while they had been scavenged for food and medicine, digging deeper into them was something that Carlos was doing. He would go into the rafters in the basement, check for fake walls, and do a very thorough job making sure no survival things were unknown. Carlos was a tremendous asset to the community, as he worked a full night shift, and only slept about 5 hours, maximum, on any given day. He was very unselfish, as anything that he found, he brought to the community center for Ethyl to distribute, or to guard shift or other groups, as appropriate.

During the shift change one day, Carlos brought back his latest find: an ammunition can inside of a cardboard lined galvanized trash can. When he opened it, he turned on one of a set of 2-way radios, and both shifts exclaimed in delight when they heard the squelch of a walkie-talkie radio.

"Fuck me running!" exclaimed Greg, before he remembered those around him. "Someone built a Faraday cage! I thought I was the only prepper on this peninsula. Carlos – that house needs to be dug through like no other house. This person knew what they were doing."

Jennifer translated the main idea of what Greg said, then put her hands on her hips, and said "Spill it" to Greg.

"Faraday cages are made to suppress EMP's. A microwave is a Faraday cage, as it doesn't let the microwaves cook your head when you stand in front of it, right? What Carlos found was an improvised faraday cage made by someone as paranoid as I am. Layers of steel and insulating material were thought to maybe keep electronics intact. I have one at home with a world-band radio, and a few walkies in it, along with a tablet with the full library of "Mother Earth News" loaded on it and a solar charger with a USB plug. Lotta good it's doing me here." Greg frowned at all of his wasted effort.

"Greg, you have to keep believing that Leigh, Jared and any friends down there are using everything you stashed away. They have a lot farther to go than you did, since you were here. Stop beating yourself up. Your faraday cage might just save their lives." Jennifer put her hand on Greg's shoulder, and looked very sincere. "You can't give up hope. I know – I'm living this with you. Jared, and maybe Leigh will get here, just like Mike will."

Angel had a shocked look on his face and blurted. "You two really aren't..." he trailed off. "Never mind – not my problema. What's in the box, Carlos?"

Carlos pulled out a Red Cross crank-and-solar charged radio. In addition to that and the 4 Midland GMRS radios, a folding Goal Zero Nomad 7 solar charging array, with attachments to charge the AA radio batteries, and a set of 6 spare batteries." He was smiling, and looked at Greg – "Bueno, No, Jefe?"

"Fucking-A Bueno, Carlos. Bueno Trabajo, Amigo!" Jennifer laughed at Greg getting the words basically right, but not exactly. Carlos and the other Hondurans were used to his totally trying, and failing to connect with proper grammar, diction and verb tense.

Greg heard them laughing and said, "OK – Sign Language!" and gave Carlos a thumbs-up.

The shift leads should keep this cranked up and check all bands at least twice per shift. Try different times each day, at the top of whatever hour you want. I don't know if there's a government out there, but if they are, they MAY be able to broadcast on one of these bands – probably AM, because it travels a longer distance.

The group smiled at the possibility of news from the outside world. Greg checked the charge on the radios. They were down, but not dead. "Day shift, keep the charger with the spare batteries in the sun all day, please." Greg requested. Angel – I'm taking one radio for the Osprey nest. The day and night security captains each get one. The last one goes to the community center. Captain's point can ring the bell if there's a problem, and we can relay that via radio. We'll replace the batteries every day-to-night shift change alternating which radio has to wait a day, since we have radios needing 8 batteries, and only 4 can re-charge at a time. We'll talk on Channel 7.11. Easy to remember, and not a usual channel that the bad guys would guess. When I get home for the night, I'll do a radio check. "Night Hawk" is the call sign for night-shift. "Phoenix" will be day shift leader. "Osprey" will be my place, and our fallback position. Crab Cake will be Ethel's community center. We all good?"

Gunny

Gunny woke up to the sounds of a gun battle, and her chicken coop going bonkers. She lived in a house behind Rock Hall Mall and had the chicken pen in a clearing in the forest between her house and the store. She liked fresh eggs, and sometimes sold them at the store, to locals.

The next community out-peninsula appeared to be taking pretty heavy fire. So, she did what Gunny's have done since the rank was invented, she suited up in some dark clothes, put on a boonie hat, and grabbed her M-14, chambered 7.62 x 51 NATO, the same ammo as the R-25 at the front of Rock Harbor. With that ammo, she had plenty of stopping power. Gunny was issued the M-16 A-2 when she was a Marine, but after years of competitive shooting, she decided that the M-14 was the gun for her. The increased reliability, and the greater stopping power made it her "home defense" weapon of choice.

Gunny moved quietly along the well-worn path to the next community inland. She had a few friends there that she visited, bearing gifts of fresh eggs when she had a surplus. The community had plenty of retired Navy, and a few "former Marines". People had often made the mistake of asking Gunny if she was an ex-Marine, and after a proper scolding, she'd explain "Once a Marine, always a Marine" and that she was just in mothballs until they needed her get her out so she could kill some more.

As Gunny approached the community, she saw that things were not good. Several homes were burning, as the attackers, who were riding motorcycles, decided that houses that shot back were easiest dealt with by throwing Molotov cocktails. Once the house was burning, they would take up positions behind trees, and wait for the occupants to come outside, then shoot them, unless the occupant happened to be a younger woman. Those women would be raped, often right there on the front yard.

With all the gunshots going on across the community, Gunny took the opportunity to explode the brains of some of the attackers who made the mistake of not having back-up nearby. She didn't want to give her position away, or be followed home, but she killed several of the worst offenders, before the lawn rape could begin. Stunned and confused women would run to the wood line where the shots came from, and Gunny would tell them to stay low, and wait for instructions.

By the end of the night, the community was occupied by about 40 bad guys, and all of the inhabitants were either dead, enslaved, or with Gunny. Gunny had an idea on how to get help for these women, and to get a little revenge. She knew where she'd be going in the morning, and she would bring these 3 traumatized ladies with her. Unfortunately, she heard her best friend die screaming in the house fire, rather than leave her house. Revenge would be hers.

– The shower

Being the chief of security, Greg somehow was moved to day watch, as he delegated the shift assignments to Angel. His Security team wanted him resting most nights, and he didn't really have veto power. He suspected that they thought he had something romantic going with the local "School Marm", Jennifer, but that was far from the truth. Greg suspected he was getting the worst of both worlds. He had a live-in woman, who gave him almost as much grief as his wife did when he was misbehaving, but he was still sleeping in a separate room, with no romantic involvement. There was a deep growing friendship between them, and he would take that over loneliness and despair. Every day, he decided to head North to get his daughter, or South to get Jared – and at least check on Leigh. Then he argued with himself, and decided to stay one more day, because passing them on the road was a high risk, and he couldn't bear what would happen if they made it all the way to their family retreat, only to not find him there, especially since they all knew he was staying in Rock Hall on the day the lights went out.

Annie was sleeping in, as usual, when Jennifer knocked on Greg's door at dawn. "Come in – this better be good." Grumbled Greg, who peeked out from under his covers. Being the OCD guy that he was, he couldn't leave the night-shift guys alone, and often spent several hours every night out with the night-shift troops. He'd help them with whatever chore there was, make some jokes, try to learn more Spanish, and otherwise try to lead. He didn't want to be in a situation where he could anticipate what the day shift would do in an emergency, and not know the night shift at all, although the rotating schedule was integrating the teams nicely. Both 12-hour shifts often just passed at the gate, gave a few-minute briefing, then went to sleep. He wanted to know ALL his sheep dogs, and how they would react when given orders under the stress of combat.

"It's going to be good — for me." smiled Jennifer, wearing a skimpy summer robe. It was almost translucent white cotton, hanging just below her behind. She had it knotted around the waist, but the cut of the robe went down below her breasts, so Greg got a view of some very astounding cleavage. She was showing entirely too much of her very shapely legs for Greg to NOT have dirty thoughts.

Greg gulped, and started to respond down below. "Um, Jen, I can't... Um, what are you doing?"

"Shut up, before you put your OTHER foot in your mouth. I need a favor, and I don't need you for the kind of favor I can imagine you're thinking about based on the layout of your sheets down there. Dream on, soldier boy!" She smiled coyly. "I heated up some water from the big rain last night. The smaller cisterns were going to over-flow, so I took advantage of our plentiful water situation. I want — no, I NEED a shower. I need you to be a good boy and keep your eyes closed and pour water over the shower curtain when I tell you to. It's all ready to go in the bathroom."

Embarrassed at the first thought that came to his mind, Greg nodded, and then backpedaled. He said "Sorry, you woke me up from a dream of my wife. I'll be there in a minute."

Jen was a VERY decent looking woman. She had curves in all the right places. She had a small waist and breasts just a little too large for what one would expect on her frame — not that he was complaining! Watching her walk away in that robe gave Greg dirty thoughts that he needed to push down, but her hips flared out to a very nice behind, and as she turned the corner, he could at least see the bottom of her ass cheeks. He'd always appreciated a good ass and was even told on more than one occasion he had a "Fine Scottish Ass".

That said, it was time to be a grown-up, and help a friend, not have fantasies about her. So, with his libido suppressed, he hoped, Greg took a shot out of the flask he kept by his bed for wake-up. He was rationing the booze that he salvaged to 2 shots per day. One in the morning, and one at night.

Greg turned the corner just in time to see Jennifer's fantastic ass go into the shower curtain that she closed behind her. "OK, you can come in now!" she yelled.

Embarrassed, but a little excited to have fouled up his orders, Greg paused a second, then said "I'm here. I see the water. I see you lowered the shower curtain – good plan."

"I wanted you to be able to dump water over – but keep your eyes to yourself, Mister!" The vixen actually giggled, knowing that she was torturing him. "Go ahead and pour about half the water over the shower.

Greg leaned forward and poured a few gallons of water over the middle of the shower curtain. She was anticipating it towards the front, where water usually comes from, but he poured it over the center of the shower curtain. She moved quickly over to the middle, rubbing Greg accidentally with her very nice breasts through the curtain in the process. "Sorry" she said, and sounded like she meant it. "Hold off while I wash my hair and soap up." Greg set the heavy bucket on the lid of the tub, pushing in the shower curtain inward a bit with the top of the bucket. Between the closeness of the curtain and the suds Jennifer were rubbing all over her hair and body, the curtain stuck to her a little more than Greg was comfortable with, yet he didn't move the bucket. He didn't peek around the curtain, even though he was tempted, knowing that her eyes were probably closed, but the thought occurred to him. He did, however, keep his eyes open as different parts of her body were sticking to the translucent, but not transparent shower curtain with soapy bubbles.

"I may need a shower after this, too – a cold one!" He mumbled to himself.

"I'll pour the water for you next!" she laughed. He was embarrassed that he heard her.

"I said that out loud? Sorry!" He admitted in embarrassment.

"No worries. I have urges too – I'm just not as, um, Male about them as you are. I'm sorry to ask you to do this, but I was getting pretty ripe, and this is heaven! I'm ready to be rinsed off, please pour slowly – there are suds everywhere."

"I know." Greg said in his head ONLY this time. He poured slowly, trying to get as much water in the shower as possible, but water did run down the bucket and down his arms. "I guess I'm getting my shower right now, too. We need to rig a better system. At least a half-gallon is on me!"

"Let's do that", said Jennifer. "I don't want to torture you like this again. You can leave now, Mister. I'm done with you." Greg walked back to his room and pulled on his jeans, which were a little easier to pull on most days - with his new apocalypse diet. He was down about 30 lbs already. Today, though, they were a little more difficult to pull on, for other reasons. He was glad SHE couldn't see him sticking to the curtain through the gym shorts he slept in – he hoped.

As he percolated a cup of ever-diminishing salvaged coffee on the ever-diminishing salvaged propane for the grill burner in the back yard, he heard voices in the front yard. He thought again about taking an off-shift on a scavenging run tonight – outside of the barricade and mines. They needed to stock up while there might still be salvage out there.

On one hand, it was good having a team that cared enough for him to keep him on daytime hours. Morning coffee was a pleasure, but also missed the night shift. He liked going to bed at 6am after a night of watching the stars. Unfortunately, the security team wanted him awake during daylight hours, when the residents were up and about, so he could be political. By now, just about everyone but Greg acknowledged that Angel really ran the show. Greg was evolving into the equivalent of a military officer, even though he had no desire to do so.

"Hey Jefe!", yelled Manuel, "You got visitor! She says her name is Gunny!"

"Outstanding!" Greg yelled. He walked out to the porch, his t-shirt and gym shorts still wet from the shower. Jennifer stepped out behind him, in her robe, drying her hair and looking inquisitively at Greg, Manuel and Gunny.

"Ahoy, Gunny! Glad to see you! I'm glad you finally took me up on the invitation. What's up?" asked Greg. "This is Jennifer. Jennifer, Gunny runs Rock Hall Mall."

"Ran it. It's burned to the ground now. I see the apocalypse isn't treating you too terribly." smiled Gunny knowingly, while looking at Jennifer. "Y'all got running water."

"Nice to meet you, Gunny." Said Jennifer. "Well, we rigged up a one-Greg-power shower system. It's not working as well as I hoped, but he'll do."

"Gunny, we're not, like... um." Greg sputtered.

"No time, Greg. Not my circus, not my monkeys. Things are going to shit out on the road into Rock Harbor. You have less than a week to be ready for about 40 bad dudes, unless someone drops a bomb on them. They're savaging the communities one at a time from

Beasley Point and around the Nomini River coast. They're sticking to the waterfront neighborhoods. More money means better loot, and better-looking trophy wives, I guess. They took the one next to me last night. They're killing the men and using the women until they're done with them. I can't even talk about what happens to the poor kids."

"What did you Recon, Gunny?"

"The local biker gang with various bullshit pistols and shotguns, but their leader won't let them retreat. He kills them if they move backwards. I got there too late last night. I saw the leader shoot a "deserter" in the gut, and he laughed while he bled out. You need at least 20 fighters in foxholes, and as many things that go boom as you can. I'd suggest pulling them into your kill zone, then doing what a kill zone is best for. You built a pretty good one out there, for a Soldier." She smiled as the usual inter-service jibe was exchanged.

I also brought 3 women from the community by me. They are traumatized, as they all lost their men, and are being taken care of by your corpsmen, Doc and, um, Kim?

Greg sighed, then said "Those are my medics, Gunny. Unfortunately, I have maybe 12 women and old guys in addition to these Hondurans and 4 of our local firefighters. Some of the Hondurans fought in Guerilla wars in Central America, so they're good fighters. Now, the rest of our folks are smart, and can shoot, but only a few others have been in combat – in VIETNAM. I'd love to have stuff that blows up, because most of my security team will tell you that I'm a lousy shot, but I can blow shit up, given the right chemicals and incentive." We already have toe poppers throughout logical flanking areas.

Gunny smiled, and said "Well, you might like what I have in the wagon back in the wood line."

"Oh, you brought presents?!?! Do they go BOOM?" Greg smiled.

"Well, they need your 'special touch', but I think I have everything you need to make things go boom. I've got fertilizer from the farm store, and enough Diesel to make it happen. I also brought some hydrogen peroxide and other chemicals in case you can do some crazy shit with that."

"Damn, shit's going south fast, isn't it Gunny?" Please feel free to join the community – pick a house – more than one if you need, for your refugees. I suggest one between Les, who fled Beasley Point when their community got shot up, and the Honduran's places over there. This circle is the end of the peninsula, or our Alamo, if necessary. We are facing what they did on Tarawa, is what you're saying, then, right?" asked Greg.

"Is that like TEOTWAWKI, IED and FUBAR?" asked Jennifer.

Greg smiled, and Jennifer returned her 1,000-watt smile. He replied. "I know I have a lot of military acronyms, but that's not one. It's an island chain in the Pacific where, in WWII, the US and our Allies hit our first serious Japanese defense. The Japanese lost the battle, but fought to the last man. They were trapped and determined. Most of the 4,500 Japanese died, because surrender was never an option for them. But several thousand allies died taking them out."

"Manuel, take Gunny to, um, el Primo casa that's not occupado." Greg tried in his best Spanish pidgin.

Manuel looked a little confused, and Gunny surprised everyone by popping off with perfect Spanish, explaining the plan. Manuel smiled enthusiastically and started to lead the way. Gunny followed and said to the group over her shoulder "I'll pick out a hooch or 2, then we can go gather the toys I brought. I don't want to blow it up in your minefield – which I can't wait to see, by the way! We've got a lot of work to do!"

The Rock army of sheep dogs just got another Non-Commissioned Officer (NCO) to help run it.

Building the defenses.

Greg rolled a wheelbarrow full of supplies from his house out to the checkpoint. He had several coffee cans full of rusty nails, courtesy of Pop and his depression-era mentality of "save everything – you never know when you need it." In it, he also had two of Grandma's old pressure cookers, some lengths of copper and iron pipe, and a bag of fireworks that Greg found, presumably left over from a July 4th party when the family popped them off at the end of the dock. Finally, he had various wires and lightbulbs in a small box, along with the Red cross radio. Greg had some very deadly toys to teach the team how to build.

Jennifer followed behind with a fabric grocery bag in each hand that had most of the ingredients that were used in the movie Terminator, when Kyle Reese improvised pipe bombs with fuses out of corn syrup, plumbing pipe and other household ingredients. Greg gathered up Ethyl and some of her helpers, as he figured they'd be best at following his "recipes". They set up in the kitchen in the clubhouse.

While Greg and the kitchen crew very gently cooked up some improvised explosive devices (IED's), Manuel escorted Gunny back to the security team, and introductions were made all around. With Gunny's command of Spanish, she was able to tell the story of what she saw to both the English and Spanish speakers. The looks on her audience's faces was enough that Greg understood her to be getting the story out.

Gunny, Manuel and Angel walked over to Greg, who could free himself up with Ethyl running the show. Ethel said she got the chemistry of it and would not need him until it was time to talk about fuses or other ways of detonating the IED's. They had Gunny's cart of explosives, retrieved from the other side of the wood line, and rolled through the concealed "safe" path in. The path through the woods was marked only with various stones, known only to the security team.

Gunny said "I see where your minefield Markers start. Excellent use of the landscape features to funnel our soon-to-be victims into a kill zone. I wouldn't advertise it, but I understand your concern for civilian casualties. We need to think about what happens when some of them get through – they've got the numbers to break through this." She then translated her words to the guys. Les, Nellie, Jennifer and Chet all joined the group, as did all of the security team that was not at the forward observation point or in the tree stand.

Tripp also ambled up and hung out on the periphery of the group. It was one of his first appearances in about a week. He would occasionally show up for one of the community meetings, eating as much as he could, and staring daggers at Greg. Today, he wasn't causing a scene, and it seemed, to Greg, that like all able-bodied men fighters would be needed.

"Tripp, do you have a gun you can shoot?" asked Greg. "We're going to need everyone we can to repel some bad guys in a few days."

"Well, duh, I wouldn't have spent $5,500 on my skeet & trap gun if I couldn't shoot it." Retorted Tripp.

"Great, buddy" Said Greg. "What do you have, a 12 or 20 gauge? 2 shots? That'll be helpful."

"20 gauge – the bullets are cheaper. And yes, 2 shots, it's an over-under gun Holland and Holland – outstanding for blowing up clay pigeons. Not like you'd know that."

Greg laughed inside at the thought of spending $5,500 on a "Gucci gun", and then skimping on the ammunition. 20 Gauge shells, although the number is bigger, are really a smaller, less powerful round than the more popular hunting round of 12 gauge. 12 Gauge is the diameter of a gun that will hold a lead sphere weighing $1/12^{th}$ of a pound. 20 Gauge is a smaller diameter cylinder that can hold a lead sphere weighing $1/20^{th}$ of a pound. While shot guns don't shoot perfect spheres of lead any longer, the labeling of the cylinders still describes the diameter.

Because Tripp was a skeet and trap shooter, Greg figured he would have fairly useless (in a battle) "bird shot". This is great for shooting birds, but a slug, or lump of lead the diameter of the barrel, would be much better for taking down a leather-clad meth-head. Tripp's gun would only piss off a biker if hit him the leather. Thinking it would be better to have a motivated man on the line, Greg said out loud "Excellent – Bring slugs if you have them. We'll work you into the security rotation."

"I haven't agreed to anything yet. Nobody shoots slugs at clay pigeons, idiot. Besides, why would I get myself killed defending you people?"

"Shut up, Tripp." Said Jennifer. "This is about us all staying alive. They're not going to save you just because you don't fight them. In fact, they'll probably butt-rape you like they'll rape the rest of the women. Don't be a bitch, Tripp."

The color drained from Tripp's face, but he shut up. Gunny guffawed, and immediately dismissed Trip as any sort of asset. She was thinking he was just the first 3 letters of the word asset. She changed the topic, saying "Greg, you know the layout better than I do, but if it were me, I'd lay down some foxholes with overlapping fields of fire on both sides of the road."

"Yeah, Gunny, that's what I was thinking about a first line of defense. I was thinking 2-man teams, with v-shaped fields of fire, overlapping. It stops the shots from coming straight into them. The down-side," Greg explained for the civilians, "is obviously losing someone covering your front. I don't know that we have enough bodies to cover gaps. We're probably stuck with straight-on defensive positions."

Greg continued: "My only concern is what we should do if we fall back. We have those drainage ditches on both sides of the road. They're almost always full of run-off water, and the slogging will be tough, but it's probably better cover than just running away. If we stagger the foxholes so that they're pointing towards the tree obstacle and woods, those closest to the fighting will be closest to the drainage ditches. Those farther back would have to move farther to the ditches to retreat, if necessary, but they will be farther from the bad guys.

"I can also work some IED's in strategic locations so that if we must fall back to the circle, we'll have lots of boom and smoke covering our retreat. I'm still a little worried about my plan for detonating them. I'd love to have a tank ditch, or moat to slow them down.

Chet ambled over as Greg was talking, and said, "I can help you there. I think my fellow Vietnam vet, Bill, has a 'turning plow' attachment that we can use on the tractor. It won't be bull-dozer fast, but will be a LOT faster than digging. With a dozen shovels, we can build your ditch and wall.

"Why didn't you list that as a list of our assets?" Greg laughed, remembering the quote from the Princess Bride movie. Surprisingly, Este, the quiet, gentle giant from Mexico City, laughed out loud.

"Princess Bride – Muy Bueno!", he laughed and explained the joke to his buddies, who smiled politely. Greg knew that Este spoke English, but he rarely did so. He was determined to try to get more out of him... If they lived that long.

A turning plow is an attachment to a tractor that could be set to turn the soil, to one side, or both. It digs and throws dirt. The team set it to turn the soil to the left, and it created a small pile of dirt. The tractor would do a big, looping turn, then run through the furrow again. After a while, the pile of dirt was too high for the tractor do drop the plow any deeper, and the guys started digging, Throwing the soft, freshly turned dirt onto a pile, and digging a ditch out. The cool thing about dirt is if you move it from a hole to a hill, every foot you dig down, makes a 2 foot gap, like the gap between the trough and crest of a 1 foot wave is 2 feet. After a while, the team got down to hard dirt. Chet and Este rigged a sideways attachment for the plow, so that they could run the tractor along the ditch, and still drop the plow in to break up the soil. This needed something like an old-fashioned plow horse in front of it pulling so that there was not too much stress on the sideways arm. Este hitched himself up a rig, and pulled while the tractor did most of the cutting.

By the end of the day, the Rock Harbor Army had a defensive wall that was 40 feet long and 3 feet high, with a water-filled ditch another 3-feet deep in front of it. They accomplished this by simply tying their ditch into the drainage ditches running parallel to the road. When the water poured in, the team cheered. Some, including Greg jumped into the mud, and sprayed water on each other. Their new obstacle stretched from the drainage ditches by the road to the wood line in front of the clubhouse. With this improvised wall, the defenders could kneel, and shoot from cover, but the attackers would have to scale 6 feet of dirt to get over it, while being muddy. The road was an obvious weakness – so Greg placed his new toys there. He hoped any bad guys would funnel to the that choke point, as he placed home-made claymores on both front sides of the wall, buried in the dirt, with fuses behind the wall. If they were lucky enough to have the bikers come through together, there would be something like 8,000 lbs of shredded biker and leather to clean up.

Along the wall, each fighter dug with assorted shovels, piling up dirt into even-higher fighting positions on either side to avoid stray shots from their flank, and making a position for them and their night-shift buddy. When the night shift showed up, they were amazed at the work that was accomplished. Imminent death is an extreme motivator to get stuff done. The night shift took up the shovels, with orders to improve the fighting positions. They were also given a task that involved the tractor. They were to build another surprise for any unwanted visitors.

After a day of moving dirt (Jennifer was making explosives with Ethel while one of the other "school marms" took care of the kids on the circle), Greg was filthy. "Jennifer, I think it's my turn for that shower. Cold works for me. I just don't want to climb into my sheets like this."

"Absolutely, Jefe". She smiled. "I'll just put Annie down. Have a well-deserved cocktail on the deck. I'll come get you when I'm ready.

Greg poured a double-shot of Makers Mike, a drink that he liked but rationed, as it was quickly diminishing. Today, they built a freaking obstacle that any combat Engineer would be proud of. Their defensive posture just went up by quite a bit. He worried that it still wouldn't be good enough to stop 40 bad guys, but that tractor, and the non-stop diggers seriously improved their odds.

Greg heard the sliding glass doors open. Luckily, they had a cooler-than-average day this July. All that digging would have sucked in the worst heat of a Virginia coastal summer. Jennifer placed her hand on Greg's shoulder. "Nice work today, Jefe. Now, don't get all heated up, but it's time for your shower, and I'm not tall enough to dump that bucket, especially after I watched you spill half of my warm water. Despite your comment earlier, you deserve a warm shower, so I heated up some water to a little north of Tepid."

"I was going to jump in the harbor. I should be Good." Greg turned around, to see Jennifer in a stunning stars-and-stripes bikini. "Um, that's hot! You told me not to get my hopes up."

"Well, I'm not going to dump warm water on you in the shower naked, you pervert!" She smiled. "I" (she stressed the word) "will have my eyes closed the whole time. I promise. Come on, Hero. You did good work today. I actually feel a lot safer today than I did yesterday – and It's all to your credit. That said, you behave yourself, Greg. I saw how much you loved the shower this morning, and we're not doing anything in your dirty little mind, even if it was in mine, too. It's been a long time, and a woman has needs too."

At her urging, Greg followed Jennifer into the bathroom. She turned around and looked out the window. "Strip down and get in, Jefe."

Greg did, and turned his front towards the shower head. He heard Jennifer get in behind him. "Nice ass," she said, "IF I was in the Market for some ass."

"Thanks, said Greg. I got that from the Scottish side of the family." As a bucket of tepid, as promised, water was dumped over his head. To Greg, it was a few gallons worth of precious water, but it felt fantastic.

"You wash your front, I'll wash your back where you won't be able to get. There's a pretty gross sweat and dirt line down the center of your back. No hanky-panky!"

Greg was treated to a very nice, platonic back-scrub from one of the hottest women he knew. He had no control over what he was feeling on the front. Another 1/2 gallons of water was poured over him, and Jennifer stepped out of the shower. He heard her filling the smaller bucket back up from the 5-gallon outside the tub.

"My work here is done. Take your time 'finishing up', cowboy. Do you want me to hang a towel on your towel rack there?" She giggled. "I'll be in my room doing the same. Thanks again for everything you're doing. You know I love you in our own weird way."

Greg did indeed 'finish up' and used the last bucket of water to rinse himself one more time to wash any other detritus down the drain. On his way back to his room, he heard Jen 'finishing up' herself.

"Good night, Beautiful. Thanks for the mammaries." He laughed, as he walked past her room. She made certain quiet noises herself, since her daughter was in the room. Greg hit the sheets and slept better than he had in weeks.

Mike's Return

Greg woke up to an unfamiliar sound – the squelch of a radio. "Jefe – Jefe – Big problemo.

Greg picked up the radio. In the excitement of last night, he forgot to do a radio check. "Angel, you have to say 'over' when you are done talking. Did you pick up any news on the radio, over?"

"Greg, you have a big problem. This man here says he is Jennifer's husband. He has 3 police with him. He is not easy to stop. I don't want to shoot him, because I know his face. He's no lying."

Greg's heart dropped into his gut. Somewhere in his subconscious, he had given up on both spouses actually making it, but he needed to man up, and do the right thing. "Delay him, Angel. I need 10 minutes."

"Si Jefe, Diez Minutes. I will warn about the mines, and escort slowly. You will have worse day than me, Jefe."

"Cayate, Angel." (Shut up). "It's not like that. Over."

"Si, Jefe. Good Luck, Amigo."

"Angel, if you can have them leave weapons, promise we will give them back, maybe we all live. Do what you can, por favor. And remember to say 'Over', OK."

"OK, Jefe. Encima."

"I assume Encima means 'Over', Angel. We'll talk about this later, if we all live."

"Si, Jefe. Encima."

Greg threw the walkie on the bed and ran into Jennifer's room. She was asleep, and her breast was not quite as tucked into his over-sized, v-neck t-shirt as it should be. He took a quick moment to admire the swell, and the edge of her nipple peeking out. No man can resist looking at a breast for at least a little bit before getting the job done. He picked up Annie and started changing her 'diaper'. They were down to cloth scraps, but thanks to the kitchen and laundry crew, they were clean, and cut to fit. The safety pins were a God-send thanks to Pop's basement of stuff.

"Jennifer. Wake up. Shut Up. Listen up. Mike is at the gate. He's here in 10 minutes. You tell me how to play it. I've got Annie."

Annie heard her dad's name and said "DADDY!"

"Yes Annie, Daddy's home!" Greg said with a reassuring smile. "Jen, I think we just play this straight. He's a cop and can smell B.S. like a fart in a car. The TRUE story is that I never touched you in any sorta way. That's our TRUE story."

"Oh, My." Whimpered Jennifer. "He's here! Thank God. And he's going to kill us."

"No, stick to the truth. If he doesn't believe you, then that's on him. He'll be here un-armed, if Angel is as good as I think he is."

Jennifer got dressed, and walked out to the top of the circle, carrying Annie. "DADDY!", Annie cried when she saw him walking down the road with 3 men in regulation, but disheveled State Police uniforms behind him. Mike ran to his daughter. Angel and half of the night shift were following, carrying the M-4's, or AR-15 type rifles the police brought.

Mike ran to his wife and baby and sobbed when they all embraced. Greg cried from the porch, both because at least Jennifer got her husband back, and a little bit (if he was honest with himself) in regret for being alone with only the bottle again. He did what his drill sergeant used to say, and 'sucked it up, buttercup'. He joined the crowd outside Jennifer and Mike's home, and Jennifer made tear-soaked introductions to all of the men.

"Jennifer. We have to get out of here." Mike said with vehemence in his voice. "Bad things are coming. "

"We know, Mike. The bikers are coming, and we've got surprises for them." She said proudly. "You saw our obstacles, right? Greg designed them we all built them."

Mike looked at his wife for a moment, like "who are you?". Then he regained his bearings and said. I have an escort out of here. We need to take all civilians that can walk, ride or bike to the FEMA camp at Dahlgren Navy Base. We have two Deuce-and-a-half Trucks outside the obstacle. There are Marine and Army National Guards at the trucks waiting on us. I don't like them being alone for too long. What's that obstacle talk all about?"

"That's my doing, Mike.", said Greg. "The bad guys need to be slowed down, because they outnumber our shooters by something like 4 to 1. We could really use the help, if you guys can stay. They're coming soon. Possibly tonight."

"Greg – You're Tony's grandson, right? I thought I saw your truck out front, but I didn't recognize the Georgia tags."

"That's where I live... Well, lived. I'm hoping for most of my family to come here from Atlanta, and my daughter Maria from Philadelphia."

"Good Luck, buddy." He replied cryptically. It took me weeks to get here from Fredericksburg, by way of Dahlgren, where we were all ordered to report. It's not a nice place out there."

"Are the roads that bad, Mike? What's the news from the world? What happened?"

"The roads are full of stalled cars. Communities have been clearing them manually in many towns, but the open road is still full of obstacles. You'll be glad to know with the trucks we brought, we cleared at least one lane all the way from here to the 301 bridge. We understand the Maryland National Guard and Police teams are doing the same thing across the river, but they're having a much tougher time, since DC and Baltimore are lost, and the violence has spilled out everywhere.

"The news from the world isn't good. Rumor is it's the North Koreans, but it could be any nuclear country. Anyway, on EMP day, nuclear weapons were smuggled into the ports of New York and Los Angeles. They were small yield, but the result is the same. America's 2 largest ports, one per coast are nuclear holes filled with radioactive water. Los Angeles took a lot of the fallout, but the NY fallout pretty much went out over the ocean, although there are now a lot fewer Islander fans, since Long Island got it pretty hard.

"Near the same time as the port bombs, 4 mini-sub-launched Nukes were sent up on rockets, to detonate high up in the atmosphere. The good news is there's no fallout from them way up there. The bad news is the lights went out. A ship in the Gulf shot one over Houston, taking out all of the Southeast. One was off of San Francisco Bay, another was off the shore from Baltimore, and the last one shot theirs from the Arctic circle, covering all of Canada and the Northern USA. North America is effectively lights-out."

"Who did it?" Greg asked.

"Unknown. As I said, speculation, based on the size of the nukes, is North Korea. That said, they've been pretty broke-dick on their nuclear program, and the Subs could have been the Russians. We just don't know enough, and our technical limitations are severely curtailed with the EMP's.

"I heard that some of the mountain communities, specifically in the valleys, escaped the full effects of the EMP, in that their vehicles and electronic devices work. But they're attached to the same grid as everyone else, so they also lost their electricity. The EMP's electrons, or whatever, traveled across all power lines, and they're all connected, frying everything attached to any North American grid. Transformers everywhere are blown, and a few cities burned because of the fires. Many more burned because of the people.

"There are rumors of some Nuclear Plants having problems, because not all of their back-up generator shielding worked as planned, but most of them were able to do emergency, manual shut-downs. I also heard of one melting down up North, like in New Hampshire or Vermont, maybe?"

"Add to that a smuggled Nuke at Atlanta's Hartsfield Jackson International Airport – the world's busiest. They had been publicly criticized numerous times for lapses in security, and smuggled weapons. There was even a gun smuggling operation that was broken up there. One test showed that over 90% of guns and fake explosives associated with a random security test got through security. Well, a weapon got smuggled in. Again, not a huge yield one, but the world's busiest airport has been reduced to radioactive crater. Most of downtown Atlanta is gone, too. The suburbs got some of the fallout, but the prevailing winds pushed most of it East."

As Greg was listening, Jennifer saw the color drain out of his face, as he slowly fell to his knees with his head down. "No, No, Not Atlanta,"

"Greg, where is your home in relation to the blast?", asked Jennifer, patting his shoulders.

We are northwest of the city in Marietta, but only 25 miles as the bird flies from the airport. Mike, what's the definition of 'small yield'?", asked an Anguished Greg.

"I have no idea, Greg. I heard bigger than Nagasaki, but not what the US could do to, say Moscow with the multiple warheads on our ICBM's. I'm sorry to give you the bad news. Word in the camp is that LA, New York and Atlanta are burning – and not just from the bombs. Several other cities, those not bombed, are also burning. Any real population center is suffering big time food riots and the bad guys banding together. There aren't enough sheepdogs in the cities to band together against the bad guys. The locals in these highly-populated cities are fleeing the bomb area and taking what they can, trying to get away from Radiation."

Greg lost a little bit more hope for his son, and Leigh. He thought, no... hoped that she was far enough away. Georgia Tech is even closer to the airport, and the hope of ever seeing his son Jared faded a little more. He knew the house was prepared, and his wife could shoot. He also knew that several good friends had said that they would come to Greg's forest retreat if the SHTF. He didn't know if they would move TOWARDS a bomb to do so, as most lived farther out.

I'm sorry, but that's all I know about anything not in the immediate Dahlgren zone, Greg. Then he looked at Jennifer and said "Go get your essentials, we're Oscar Mike." Oscar Mike is OM, or military speak for 'On the Move'. Jennifer looked from Mike to Greg, then walked towards the house she'd been sleeping in to get her things.

"What the fuck is this?" yelled Mike. "Are you fucking my wife?" He yelled this as he moved towards Greg. Angel tried to slow him, but he threw him off, and kept coming, fast and angry.

"Mike, I swear to you I never touched..." Greg was able to get that much out while standing back up, just as Mike hit him with a haymaker and knocked him flat. Greg's first instinct was to punch Mike in the balls as he was getting up. Greg had been in his share of fights in the Army and knew that the only fair fight is one you won. Then, he got his anger under control, and took a deep breath.

"Through his diminished eyesight, Greg saw a melee happening as the 3 troopers started swinging at the armed, but disciplined guard rotation. It ended up with a lot of yelling and pointed guns, but no deaths.

"Mike, STOP!", yelled Jennifer as Annie was somehow sitting on the ground, balling, after being knocked over by rumbling troopers and sheepdogs. Greg was sitting up, shaking his head, and saw Jennifer pulling him into Grandma's house. Greg followed, while Angel spoke to Angie in his Spanish baby talk. Annie was OK, and Angel had her smiling and babbling broken Spanish in no time. The rest seemed a bit calmer on the road. While Greg hoped nobody would get hurt, he was glad that his guards had the weapons.

Mike, Greg, Annie and Jennifer went into the house, with Mike throwing death-glances at Greg. Jen walked Mike through the house. "This is where Annie and I stay, Mike. THAT..." she pointed across the hall, "is where Greg has slept every day, and I have slept HERE." We did this because this house is safer, and the Osprey nest is on the roof."

"The Osprey Nest?" Mike sputtered. "What the fuck does that have to do with..."

"SHUT UP, MIKE!" Jennifer yelled in a voice that Greg was glad he hadn't had to hear so far – because that sounded like the voice of someone who was in a relationship, and really pissed off. It was a lot like the 'FINE!' voice Greg heard from Leigh when he was being a bone-head. He was thinking about everything that did NOT happen, and glad she never had an excuse to use that voice with him. He was shifting his world-view, once again, and was coming to terms with the change in group dynamics.

"Greg, show Mike the Osprey nest while I get my things." Ordered Jennifer.

Greg said, "I understand why you would think what you did, but nothing happened. Let me show you why we're here, and why your house is not occupied.

Mike nodded and followed Greg out the back deck, clearly restraining himself and giving Jennifer the benefit of the doubt. Greg pointed at the ladder, and said, "Osprey Nest" and climbed up, across the roof, and pointed to the sniper's platform. "It's only 180 degrees to cover, cutting in half the threats to this house, me, and the girls." I swear to you, I never touched her in that way... ever. Here, take this." Greg would stand by his statement, even if he couldn't exactly say the same for Jennifer not touching him. He figured that wouldn't help the situation, and Jennifer could tell Mike what she wanted to when they had more time together. Hopefully when Mike was far away from Greg.

Greg handed Mike his main sidearm, handle first. It was his prized Springfield .40 cal EMP on a 1911 frame and said "Shoot me if you don't believe me. I knew it would look bad, so I had my guys take your weapons until we could talk. Jen and I are just good friends. No, I think of your girls as my family, but not like you're thinking. Keep the gun until you leave. You decide, you kill me if you want. I'm still waiting for my wife, son and daughter, but every day when I wake up, I look down that barrel and think about pulling the trigger, so death by you would be one solution, and not a terrible one at this point."

Mike said "You called her Jen. That's my pet word for her." His grip tightened on the gun, and he pointed it closer towards Greg. Greg saw Angel point his rifle more towards the confrontation on the roof. Things could get messy quickly in this situation.

"Yes, you stubborn, jealous asshole. We shared a house for the last 2 months without any support from OUR SPOUSES! She asked me to call her that, because we're close. I helped take care of Annie, and she's learning Spanish and gardening! However, I never touched Jennifer in passion! I never did anything but try to be a good guy. Shut up and pull the trigger, or BACK THE FUCK OFF! Look at this from our perspectives. What would you do? Leave a woman and child in a more vulnerable house? Let them be raped, killed, or taken? Shoot me, you fucking idiot, or LET IT GO!"

Greg closed his eyes, more than 50% certain that he saw his last daylight. Then he felt the gun poke him in the chest, around the heart region. He was sure this was the end. He could not see, but he was sure that Angel was aiming down on Mike, and he waved off in his direction.

Mike said "The handle is against your chest, man. Take your fucking gun back. I'm sorry – I've been crazy. I trust Jennifer – I've been worried about her every day. Worried sick. I don't know what's come over me. It's been months of nightmares thinking about what could have happened to my girls. You don't know what I've seen. This is actually a better situation than I ever imagined. Thank you, Man, and I'm sorry about hitting you. How about you calm your guys down, because 2 have guns on my partners, and the rest are pointing my own rifles at me."

Greg was relieved, but almost regretted the loss of the oblivion he could have rested in if Mike had killed him. "That's OK, you hit like a Navy Puke." Then he laughed and laughed until tears streamed down his eyes.

Mike said, "I was an Air Force MP before joining the cops."

"Well, you hit pretty hard for the Chair Force, then." Greg laughed again, trying to catch his breath.

Both men on the roof waved off their men with signs that said: "All Clear - Everything OK". Angel and his squad returned the firearms to the Troopers, even if they looked a little worried about doing so.

"How did Angel get you guys to give up your rifles? I know that's one of the main rules in both the service and law enforcement."

"Well, he's pretty convincing. He had half of his guard shift give up their weapons to my guards by the truck. Then said he wouldn't let us through the minefield without giving up ours. He said Jennifer and Annie were OK, and he spoke like he knew them, so I was motivated to see them and convinced my guys to trust me. I'm glad we didn't have them 5 minutes ago." Admitted Mike.

"Yeah, me too. Angel took them on my orders. I don't know you all that well, and I hoped for some discipline and understanding, but I also know how first-hand how I would feel if I was showing up to find MY wife in some relationship with another man. Mine cheated on me in Atlanta, and I wanted to kill the guy. On the other hand, I would take her being alive over any situation than dead, as I now fear mine is. She always said she'd eat a bullet when we discussed life without electricity. A nuke in our backyard and riots leaving the city is not helping my assessment of the situation."

"Well, I'm truly sorry for you, Greg. You're a smart leader, based on your handling of this situation and the defenses you've put in. I think you'll need them, but I hope for the best for you." Mike paused, and visibly relaxed. He looked Greg in the eye, and stuck out his hand, again trying to hand back Greg's pistol, and offering the same hand for a handshake. "I'm sorry I hit you. Get your stuff, we're headed to the FEMA camp and safety."

"We'll talk about that at the community center." Greg picked up the radio clipped to this belt and looked at Angel to get eye contact. He also knew he had 2 other groups listening. "Angel, all clear. Get those troopers some hot food and send runners to pull together the community. Enema." Then he laughed out loud, and told Mike, who had a confused look that Encima was Spanish for "over" and it was a pun he just made up. Greg laughed again as he sat down on the Osprey Nest to collect his thoughts and emotions. "Go to your girls, Man. I've got over watch." He chuckled to himself again, because nobody could be within sight, with the barrier ¼ mile or so away, so he just kept laughing at the irony, sadness, and relief of the situation. He also couldn't do much from his sniper's nest with no Mauser – it was just inside the door by the ladder, safe and dry. Life would be different without Jennifer, but there would be a lot less sexual tension in the house, if nothing else.

Greg needed a few minutes to stop his hands from shaking, and he didn't think it was from a lack of his morning shot. Then, he pulled himself together, descended the ladder and followed the larger group to the community center.

Do I Stay or Do I Go?

Greg was only a few minutes behind the guards and troopers, but arrived to chaos at the center. The first thing he saw were highly agitated Hondurans, who were vehemently protesting going to any Federal detention center, FEMA camp, or not. Gunny was translating as quickly as she could, attempting to calm them down. She was also making it clear that there was no way she was leaving the peninsula to go to a FEMA camp. "I served in the Corps, and I don't trust those Homeland guys to get anything right! I'm taking my chances here."

Others in the community were excited about getting some help from the government. These people were generally those who had medical issues, and medicine running out. They were anxiously looking toward their homes, wanting to go get their personal articles, as the troopers were instructing.

"Listen up, folks!" Greg yelled. "Nobody is going to be forced to go to a FEMA camp. This is still America, and we have the right to stay in our homes. I'm staying, because my son and girls are headed here. That said, any of you who want to go, please go gather your things, and may God go with you. It's been a pleasure, and an honor seeing how we all worked together.

The radio on Mike's belt went off, and he listened into his earbuds. "Well, get your weapons back and help hold the trucks!" he yelled. Then he looked at Greg and said, "Meth head and biker gang coming in fast." As this sunk in, Greg heard the big guns, presumably on top of the Trucks starting to fire, and small arms fire in return. This was all happening on the other side of the obstacle.

"Everyone to your fighting position or your fallback position, now!!!" The community had drilled for this, and everyone dispersed quickly, but with a purpose. Non-combat troops, including children, the medical team and the kitchen team retreated down the peninsula to the circle, where the 'Alamo' plan had been prepared. Les was in charge of that detachment.

Both shifts of security - those not out with the trucks, anyway, reported to fighting positions on the berm, and Greg directed the troopers to the firing positions not filled by those guards with the trucks. An explosion occurred in front of the obstacle. It was large enough that Greg assumed at least one of the trucks had blown up. That was the first heavy weapon's shot of the battle of Rock Harbor. It sounded to Greg like a LAW Rocket or an RPG. Someone got a good shot off.

As the sheep dogs got into position, the first toe popper was tripped on the access path. The problem is that it only popped a tire on the first motorcycle to trip the mine, not a toe. Several more mines went off, as motorcycles started to pour out of the path. On the back of the lead motorcycle to emerge from the gap was Tripp, pointing the way through the last of the obstacles.

"That son of a bitch!" Yelled Greg and fired his pistol at Tripp. Unfortunately, hitting a moving target, with a compact pistol at that distance was not an easy task. In the excitement to settle the FEMA issue, Greg left his Mauser at the bottom of the ladder up to the Osprey nest. The single-shots of most of the defenders from their bolt-action rifles and pistols mixed with the sound of the 2 peninsula semi-auto rifles and the 3-round bursts of the troopers. Gunny's M-14 was barking, and Angel was firing the Browning 12 Ga, one or both were having success knocking bikers off their motorcycles. Carlos, on duty in the tower was the first Sheepdog shot and fell to the ground 15 feet below, twisted in an unnatural way. Este was the guard at the front with the .308 turned from the road, apparently out of forward targets, and started shooting at the motorcycles behind him. The .308 in Esteban's hands looked more like a toy rifle, but it whatever it hit, like the motorcycle gas tank carrying a biker with a shotgun, blew up, throwing the rider over the handlebars, on fire. Este's shots were low and disciplined enough that any missed thunked into the berm, so there were no friendly-fire casualties from his shooting.

As the first few bikes approached the gap between the walls, Greg fired his improvised claymores, by plugging in and cranking the hand-charger on the Red Cross Radio in his fighting position. He had spliced a USB cable into a flashlight bulb, was able to generate the power to ignite his primer. While probably not the use that the Red Cross had intended, the hand crank and solar charger kept it charged enough to start the explosion. Several pounds of nails and other scrap metal spewed from the front corner of both berms at an overlapping 45-degree angle. The effect was an instant shredding of a half-dozen motorcycles, and those riding them. The attackers were lifted backwards and flew in bloody chunks. Greg's ears, as well as those in a large diameter around him were immediately ringing. He didn't have ear plugs, and didn't prepare for the overpressure, as trained. Luckily, the berm deflected much of the blast up and out towards the bad guys.

"Damn, they worked!" yelled Greg with a relieved smile, even if he couldn't hear himself. The relief was short-lived, as more bikers came through the gap. At the pre-arranged signal that was the big boom, Chet, who had the tractor fired up behind the meeting house, drove forward, pulling the telephone line that was scavenged at about chest-height across the gap, and anchored to a telephone pole on the other side. The next few bikers who hit the wire were removed from their machines, almost beheaded. The bikers behind them dropped their bikes, and got behind them, returning fire towards the shooting positions.

Gunny low-walked to Greg, and yelled "Sorry about my Recon, there's more than 40 in here now, but only about 20 left alive. Nice work! I guess they recruited more!"

Greg looked over and saw Nellie rocking and rolling with her shot gun. Every time she pulled the trigger, a biker fell. She screamed,

"You are NOT getting my baby, mother fuckers!" Then she'd pump the 12 Gauge, and down another one, reloading from the shooting bag she carried around her waist. At all of 120 lbs., he was surprised that the 12 Gauge wasn't hurting her, but adrenaline is a powerful pain killer.

"Yeah, and I have to believe the big guns rocking and rolling out there on those trucks took out a few!"

Greg watched Esteban take a hit to the upper body, and drop behind his log, out of the fight. There went their heaviest artillery – both the gun and the man. Chet came running around the corner of the house, shooting his revolver. He also brought more than a few of the pipe bombs that the Kitchen team cooked up. Demolitions, plan B. He was lighting them with his last cigar, saved for this event, and throwing them into clusters of bikers. After the booms, it looked like another 10 or so bikers were down, but so were at least 3 of the defenders, including the trooper to Greg's left. He had a hole in his eye and was flat on his back. Greg picked up his M-4, and a few magazines from his cargo pockets. Greg emptied the M-4 over the berm and reloaded.

Gunny yelled "We're out-gunned, we have to fall back to the Alamo!"

Greg agreed, and gave the signal to fall back. The remaining troopers new to the group were pulled from the wall and into the ditch back to the circle. Greg, Angel and Chet were holding the berm, but the bikers were advancing. There were too many. Greg yelled "You guys fall back, I'll cover you as long as I can", and asked Chet for the last of the pipe bombs.

"No sir, you've got a job to do back there. You protect our people! Give me that M-4. I will hold them off – it beats dying of Diabetes. You guys run!" Chet snatched the M-4 from Greg, and Angel snatched Greg from the wall.

"Run Jefe – don't make me carry you! You're prettier than when I met you, but still have me by 25 kilos!"

Greg took one last glance at Chet, who nodded back sagely. He knew he could hold them for a while, but he was not likely leaving this alive. Greg and Angel ran down the middle of the road towards the circle. The ditch would take too long. A few bikers got shots off that pinged off of the asphalt around them, and then there were a few more explosions from Chet's pipe bombs. After that, Chet sprayed the M-4 in bursts, as the retreat continued. Greg heard a silence as Chet switched magazines – to his last one. He looked back, and saw bikers creeping around the edge of the berm. He fired his pistol at them until it emptied, and Angel did the same with the Browning 12 Ga. They ducked back around, buying Chet a little more time.

Greg and Angel put their heads down and ran, getting back to the circle just as others were. The rest of the soggy defenders had climbed out of the ditch as soon as they felt far enough out of range. Greg yelled "You know what to do, everyone", and the groups dispersed to the various houses on the fringe of the circle, where supplies, ammunition, and civilians with guns were waiting. Greg yelled "Good luck" to Angel and grabbed his Mauser on the way up to the Osprey nest.

There was no more noise coming from the berm. After about a minute, Greg heard motorcycles start. He guessed they had successfully removed the power line obstacle, and he made a note to create more of this type of obstacle – if he lived through the next few minutes. Then about a dozen motorcycles roared down main street, and into Seahawk Circle. The angry bikers started circling the block looking for victims. They hollered and shot their guns into the air, a waste of ammunition. Greg looked through his scope and aimed at the person who looked to be in charge. This bald, tattoo-headed guy was leading the group, and had Tripp, the traitor, on the back of his bike shouting into the leader's ear and pointing at Greg's house. Greg aimed for the leader, squeezed the trigger, and missed – hitting Tripp and knocking him off the bike. He had failed to lead his shot enough to account for the motorcycle's motion, but it was certainly not a missed opportunity.

At Greg's first shot, various shotguns, pistols and hunting rifles around the circle started pouring fire into the bikers. In the first 30 seconds, half of the bikers were down, and the leader was shot in the shoulder. He managed to keep from wrecking his bike, but he was obviously in pain, as he cursed and looked around for an outlet to his anger. He and his men could not find a target to concentrate on and were being ripped apart from all angles. The leader revved his bike up, continued around the circle to where it started, and headed back out of the Alamo at top speed.

Greg breathed a sigh of relief, as it seemed like today would not be his last day on earth. While the bikers were leaving, Greg heard a few scattered booms from someone, presumably his toe poppers, or the remaining guards by the trucks. Finally, their sound died down as the Motorcycles roared off, leaving their wounded bikers and broken motorcycles behind. The first battle of Rock Harbor was a victory for the residents, if you could call the loss of even one citizen a victory. The ringing from the improvised claymore, and all the shooting without ear protection was starting to die down, and thing started to slow down for Greg, as he just took deep breaths, and tried to get the Adrenaline from the last few minutes out of his bloodstream and willed his hands to stop shaking. To him, it felt like every pore on his body had opened up. He was covered with a cold sweat, almost as if he'd been pushed into the cold water of the harbor. Then he realized how thirsty he was.

Greg looked out as Doc, followed by Kim, exited their designated house on the circle. Doc ran hunched over towards the nearest victim of the violence. It happened to be Tripp. Greg saw Doc stop at Tripp, and frantically open his med kit. At the realization that

Tripp was alive, Greg stood up and ran back to the ladder, which he almost slid down like he was in a movie, but he twisted his ankle when he hit the ground faster than he thought he would. So much for being an action hero, he thought.

After pulling himself out of the crumpled Greg-puddle that he had become, he limped on a hurt ankle to where Doc was administering first-aid to Tripp. When Greg got there, he saw what damage from an 8mm Mauser looks like, and it wasn't pretty. Tripp was breathing in ragged breaths, with his eyes wide and panicked. He locked gazes with Greg, as Greg moved closer.

"Doc, go see if any of our troops at the barrier survived." Ordered Greg, who was sick to his stomach with the carnage he passed on the circle. "I've seen wounds like this, and can take care of it." Greg looked to Kim, and nodded, as she gathered Doc up from the ground.

Kim said "Look, Doc! That bike there is almost like your old one. Let's grab it and get to the front area quicker!"

Doc looked at the bike, then at Greg. "Keep pressure on this, Greg." He got up, and, with Kim, managed to get a bike from a fallen biker up and started. They roared off up Main Street towards the main battle zone, with their first aid backpacks bouncing on their backs.

Cleaning Up.

Greg was holding down the field dressing on Tripp long enough to see Doc and Kim get out of view. Then, he lifted it up, as Tripp panicked and tried to pull it back to his chest wound.

"You won't be needing that, Ass Hat." Greg then took out his Bench Made switchblade and flicked it open. I'm going to do you one favor, and make it quick, instead of watching you bleed out – which is my first choice, traitor! He thrust the knife into Tripp's quickly widening eye and gave it a twist as Tripp convulsed and was still. Greg stood up, and walked to the other bikers on the ground, in various states of dead – or soon to be. He repeated the same end for the second one when Mike ran up to him and threw him backwards.

"Stop! You're killing these men in cold blood! They might have valuable information!" he yelled, as he stood over Greg's next victim.

Just as Greg was about to reply, a pistol shot rang out nearby. Both men instinctively ducked and looked for the source of the danger. 30 feet away, Jennifer was holstering her .357, and below her was a biker doing the last-dance twitch, with a puddle where his forehead used to be. "That's the last here, Greg. Let's go clean up the field out front." Like Jennifer, Gunny had clearly done the same as Greg did with her knife, as she was kneeling next to Jennifer, wiping her blade on the biker's jeans, with a dead man at her knees.

"Mike," said Gunny, "You haven't seen what these animals did to the communities they've come through. None of these Fucks live through the afternoon. But you have a good idea about interrogating them. I don't want to end them in front of Doc. If we need intel on where they're staying, or what they're thinking, maybe one will spill the beans in the fruitless hope for survival. If they don't tell, we can still listen for the motorcycles, and look for the Turkey Buzzards circling."

"Why do you think they hit us during daylight?" asked Jennifer. The shock of her last kill was starting to get to her, as the color drained from her face. She took 2 more steps, then threw up into the grass. Greg got to her first and held her shoulders as she sobbed at the realization that she just killed a man in relatively cold blood. Mike was approaching quickly.

Greg replied with "It's OK, Jen. Tripp clearly told them about our defenses, and that night-time was not going to be an advantage. I saw him pointing as the first bike emerged from land mine alley. A lot more got through because of that ass-hat. Then Greg looked at Mike. "I'd kill him slower this time, now that I realize how he betrayed us. Let's go take care of OUR living and find out what happened out front."

Nellie walked up to the group and asked, "What does a dislocated shoulder feel like?", then dropped to her knees and cried. While she served in some pretty ugly situations overseas, this was her first time in shooting combat. Jen dropped to her knees next to Nellie, and they both cried, and held each other now that the killing was done. They spoke quietly to each other, and Greg left them to their consolation, headed to the barrier.

3 more soldiers, and the attack.

As the Rock Harbor Sheep Dog's got back to the berm, Greg's eyes were drawn to Chet's body. He had a semi-circle of dead bikers around him, with his cigar still clenched between his teeth. He went down swinging. "Reverend Greg" walked over to Chet and closed his eyes. He then recited Psalm 23:4 over Chet, as he knew that Chet was a Christian. "Yeah, though I walk through the valley of the shadow of death, I will fear no evil, for thou art with me, thy rod and thy staff they comfort me." Then Greg took the cigar, re-lit it, and thanked his friend for his sacrifice by doing him the honor of not wasting a fabulous Opus X cigar. He cried as he surveyed the field of battle, and all of the wasted life.

"Over here, Stat!" Yelled Doc. Greg Looked over to see him standing among the logs where Este went down. I need 4 strong bodies to move Este, Now! Greg could see him applying a field dressing on what he hoped was Este's lower shoulder, and not his lung area. A shoulder wound isn't always simply through-and-through, as large arteries and veins move through there. That said, it usually beats a collapsed lung. Given that Este was shot early in the battle, Greg was encouraged that Doc was still working on him and wanted to move him.

Greg directed a few of the survivors over to help Doc. He grabbed Kim and her medical bag and said "From what I heard after the bikers left, there were survivors out front. They might need medical attention. Gunny! Interrogate the prisoners away from Doc!" Gunny gave a thumbs-up, and Greg knew that was covered.

Kim, in all her tattooed glory smiled at Greg, pointed at her Harley, and said "Get on, you get to ride bitch, Jefe! I'll get you there quick, I know the way around the mines." She fired up the bike, Greg got on, and held on for dear life as Kim not only navigated around the mines, but also around a few crashed bikes with flat tires. The toe poppers didn't kill any bikers on the path, so Greg assumed they either were killed in the battle of the berm, or ran back the way they came.

To keep himself distracted from the mad dash through the minefield, he yelled to Kim, "If you can both ride, I assume you had bikes here. Why not ride them around?"

Kim yelled back over her shoulder, "Doc used his military retirement bonus to buy us NEW bikes. I told him I was happy with my old Harley Softail, but he said I deserved a new bike. Both of ours were full of all kinds of electronics, and we had no spare parts. I'm glad to have the bikes the assholes left! The Sheepdogs will have a cavalry once we get a bunch of them fixed up. There will be no shortage of spare parts." she indicated with her chin, as they passed the last crashed bike on the trail.

Greg did not think, until now, about the fact that bikers were coming out of the path, into the kill-zone of the trucks. "STOP!" he yelled, and Kim did. Quickly. They both almost went over the handlebars, but she was strong, and evidently a good biker.

"I thought about what you just did, at just about the same time!" Friendly fire would suck, especially if it was me!

Greg laughed. Kim dropped the kickstand while Greg yelled out "Sheep Dogs coming out! Hold your fire! Greg and Kim ran out towards the trucks, followed closely by the barrel of an M-2 .50 caliber machine gun on a truck that was otherwise trashed and an M-240 on an un-harmed, if slightly scorched Deuce and a half truck.

"Any casualties?" Kim yelled as she un-strapped her pack.

"No, Hefe. Tres Muerte, Dios mio!" said Jaime, the Honduran with the least English.

Bill clarified, because a death is a casualty, "Nope no wounded, but 3 Killed in Action, sadly. They are all the soldiers that came with Mike."

Kim quickly checked vital signs. 2 of the soldiers in the deuce were clearly dead. One of the soldiers from the other truck said "They had an RPG in the wood line. He popped out as the bikers were coming and killed my men. One got a lucky shot on my 240 gunner, so early on we just had side arms, but I jumped up on the 240, and we were able to turn them. Your Sheep dogs, as they call themselves, fought well, even though their weapons are crap. I've given them the M-4's from my dead guys, along with the LBE's."

Greg knew from his time in the Army that LBE's were Load Bearing Equipment. Shoulder straps attached to a belt, like suspenders, with various things attached to them. He looked over at Luis, Bill and Jaime, who all had LBE's bulging with magazines, a flashlight, and a pistol, probably the Beretta P92, from the look of it. Parts of the equipment were bloody but functioning.

Kim verified that all of the presumed dead had no vital signs and said "You don't need me here. I'm going back to help Doc. See you later! She trotted back to the bike, and Greg heard her roar back through the woods.

Greg introduced himself to the soldier that took over the M240 and seemed to be in charge. "Sergeant Greg Creighton, inactive. I served active duty 90-93, then 5 years in the Guard. I got out with the same E-6 stripes you wear."

"Staff Sergeant Tony Long, they call me Tiger. You serve in the first Desert Storm?"

"Affirmative, 12 Bravo, Combat Engineer, although I heard the MOS changed since the I served. We can catch up later. My condolences for your troops. I'm also clergy. I'd be honored to give last rites and can check their dog tags if you think that's appropriate. In days like these, I know you have body bags, and I can have my men help."

Tony said, solemnly, "Thank you, Sergeant Creighton. You do the last rites as you feel appropriate. I don't know much about that God stuff, and I didn't know these men all that well. We have been throwing together mixed units of Law Enforcement and Military since the fall, and we're always shorthanded. No troops in the back, just a driver, TC (Truck/Tank commander) in the passenger seat, and gunner in my "troop carriers' here." I think my men would want to do the body bag detail, but we'll yell if we need help. Thanks again."

Greg gave last rites as appropriate. One of the soldier was Jewish, and he struggled to remember the words. He placed the soldier's hands over his own eyes and did his best to remember the English translation of the rites. He had no chance of remembering the original language. "Hear, Oh Israel, our lord is our God, and our God is one."

After giving each soldier what he hoped they might want said over their bodies. Greg asked Jaime in his best Spanglish to stay behind, help them with bodies, then escort any who wanted through the minefield.

"Si Jefe, no problema." Nodded Jaime. Greg gathered up the rest of his Sheepdogs and they went back to the area of the battle of the berm. As they walked back, they lifted and pushed the 3 motorcycles, on flat front tires, through the field, to eliminate any telltales of where the mines might be. Greg would have to remind one of his guys to re-load the toe-poppers for the next assault that he was sure would come eventually. The biker leader had more intel on the community and their defensive tricks and didn't seem like the kind of guy to forgive being shot. He would have to recruit a bigger Army now, though, since his was almost wiped out. Greg remembered about a half-dozen leaving, but didn't know how many left.

"Bill about how many bikes and personnel got away?"

"There's no 'about' about it", smiled Bill. "7 motorcycles, one that probably won't get far, based on the oil that it was burning. They had 4 riding 'bitch', so 11 fuck-puddles, and 6.5 bikes. Do you think they'll be back?"

"If not them, some other scumbags will come and try to take our stuff.

The FEMA Departure

Over the rest of the day, and early evening, body bags were loaded with soldiers, Chet and Carlos were buried on their homesteads, and the bikers were fed to the crabs, near the usual crab trap spots. Greg tied cinder blocks to their waists, and dumped them off the deepest docks, with a quick 'prayer' of "better you than us, puss bag."

Gunny secured the location of their camp, and they got, through reliable reports, amid shrieks, that there were 4 guards left behind to guard their prisoners. Gunny finished them all off, much to Mike's chagrin. Kim had a better understanding of what these guys were up to, as she and Gunny had grown close in the past few days.

Esteban the Giant was secure in his bed, with a positive prognosis from both Doc and Kim. The motorcycles were pushed up to the parking lot of the community center, in various states of repair, with 3 that Doc got working in a few minutes. Kim claimed the Harley Softail, and Doc took the Panhead, with a Sportster, the smallest working motorcycle, reserved for "cavalry lessons".

The survivors all got together for an impromptu dinner at the center. Ethyl and her team did a great job, and the Soldiers brought almost all the rations they had in both trucks. These MRE gifts were saved, because of their shelf life.

Tony brought Greg one of the best presents ever! He gave Greg the M-2 .50 caliber machine gun off the wrecked truck, along with 4 ammo cans worth of .50 caliber, or just under 400 rounds of Armor Piercing ammo total. He also gave the spare tripod mount from the back of the truck.

"One thing we have plenty of is guns and ammo at the FEMA camp. I'm writing in my report that this thing blew up with the Truck, but it only has a few dings, and my armorer/driver says that it's serviceable. I also included a spare barrel on the table over there. You guys are going to need it more than we will. The .240 on top of my truck is my preferred weapon. Not as much punch, but a higher fire rate, and more than only 100 rounds per box!"

Greg, who would have blown Tony right now – if he was Navy – gave him a 3-slap 'bro-hug'. "Sergeant, this is going to really help. I'm not putting it in the tower, though, after what we learned today." With the range on this puppy, I'm probably going to put it on a balcony of the Mansion over there, and I'll be able to defend from a distance, as well as cover a retreat better than today's half-assed plan."

"Don't beat yourself up, Greg. You guys lost 3, and they lost over 40. That's pretty in-credi-fucking-bull! You saved a lot of lives today with your things that go Boom!"

Greg reflected on that, but still shed a tear for 2 lost friends, and the trooper who died defending the community.

"Hey brother," said Tony. "You can still come back to base with us. But I already heard tht asking that is like pissing in the wind. That said, those of us on this detail are only bringing back one M4 and a load-out of ammo, with the truck. Minimal rations and water will get us back, as long as we practice the 2 means 1, and 1 means none' philosophy on rations, and fuel. Help yourself to anything else we leave on the truck for you. Speaking of which, Private Jones and I are going to rotate out our guys on watch at the truck. This is goodbye. We're Oscar Mike at dawn. Be well, and may we meet again, brother!"

Again, tears welled up in Greg's eyes, not just for the gift of supplies, but for the brotherhood soon to be lost. All he could get out around the emotion was "Hooo-ahhh, brother!"

As Tony and Private Jones 'hugged it out' with others around the community center, Greg moseyed over to the table with Mike, Annie and Jennifer huddled in a corner, in some sort of disagreement. They saw him approach, and Jen smiled, while Mike looked angry, but not as angry as Greg might expect.

"Hey Greg, Join us." Came from Mike, surprisingly. Dinner that night was yellow perch stuffed with the crab meat. There was a salad of the ever-present Kudzu, leaf lettuce and baby spinach, with green onions mixed up with a vinaigrette. One of the condiments that the kitchen crew had plenty of were salad dressings. Between the unopened store-bought ones around the community and non-perishable things like vinegar and oil, they had many months' worth, thanks to the salvage team. The salad vegetables didn't last longer than the week after the lights went out, so the first salad of the season was a nice treat. Before today, the peninsula only had Kudzu, sprouts, the occasional small serving of vegetables from cans, and vitamins (also in large supply in a retirement community). After the day's adventure, everyone had a hearty appetite

Greg joined them, gave Annie a peck on the head, and shook Mike's hand. "Without those M-4's today, we would have lost a lot more of us, if not all of us. Thank you, Mike."

Jennifer replied with "That's why he's going to leave his and the other troopers guns, aren't you, Mike?" She looked to her husband.

"Yeah, Greg. They both got destroyed or looted in the attack, I'm not sure – at least that's what my report will say. The road out was already cleared of most threats, so I suspect we'll get back safely with the 240 on the Deuce and a half and the soldiers rifles and side-arms. We'll clearly keep our own side arms, but we did happen to use all but a full magazine of our ammunition in addition to one in the pipe. The rest of the ammo that we, um, officially 'used' is over there in that ammo can. It's .40 caliber, and I remember that you have a one of those, so use them wisely. Also, the gear from my deputy is piled over there. He won't be needing it any longer."

"Mike, that's a lot. Thank you so much, man." Greg was again overwhelmed with the generosity he saw today. I'm also leaving 2 of our 2-way radios. I know you have a set of 4 walkies, but these are police band, and you can monitor them for any news that reaches this far. You won't get a good signal from Dahlgren, but if any friendlies are in the area, I'll let them know of this outpost, and they'll announce themselves, and come bearing gifts, if possible. The batteries are also rechargeable. I should go gather up my guys, and those that are going back with us and make sure we have a plan for the morning. I'll take Annie home, and leave you and Jennifer to say goodbye." Mike rose and shook Greg's hand again. "You did a hell of a job saving my girls today. You're a good man. I'm sorry that we got off to such an ugly start. With a girl like Jen, it's hard not to be jealous." He touched her shoulder and walked away to be in charge again."

Jennifer and Greg were alone at the table, and Greg knew that his tears for the day were not done. "Jennifer, I'm so glad for you to have your husband back. I hope to have my family with me someday soon. Go be happy. Thanks for the mammaries!" He laughed at their old joke. Everyone went back to their places for a good night's sleep, except for those on watch.

Jennifer

When Jennifer and Mike got back to their house, Mike took some time to play with Annie, and get her tired out before bedtime. Jennifer looked across at the light in Greg's home. She saw him climb the ladder to the Osprey Nest and look around in his Mauser Scope. When his scope crossed the window she was watching from, he waved a sad, defeated smile.

Mike came up behind her and hugged her. "He keeps watch like that every night?"

"He does it after his 12-hour day-shift. I swear, he's in shepherd mode all the time. I think he sleeps about 4 hours per night, if that. I promise, Mike. He's a good man, and he never put his hands on me like you're worried about."

Mike told Jennifer that they should go to bed, and they went to the bedroom they shared before the lights went out. Mike made noises like it would be good to get some loving tonight, but Jennifer told him that with the deaths today, and killing her first man, the last thing on her mind was having sex. Mike huffed and puffed but went to bed without making an issue out of it.

The next morning, many of the citizens of the peninsula, as well as those from Dahlgren met outside the mined lane. All 3 of the ladies that Gunny rescued from their community opted to go to Dahlgren.

Greg spun Annie around, and then handed the giggling toddler off to Este, who threw her high while using his Shrek voice to entertain her. This was her new favorite game.

When Greg hugged Jennifer, she confided to him, "I don't think this FEMA camp is a good idea, but Mike says they have supplies, and after yesterday, I like the idea of a very secure facility. I'm going to miss you more than you'll ever know, and you know I love you in our own weird way. She could not keep talking, so she just grabbed him in a hug that expressed her emotion and kissed him right on the lips in front of everyone. There was no tongue action, but still, Greg felt a little stirring. This would likely be his last sight of Jennifer, and what a sight she was!"

"You're doing the right thing, Jen. Love you too. I'll miss you and Annie more than you'll ever know. Stay armed, stay safe and take care of the princess. If the shit hits the fan again, we now have radios. Keep checking, and if in range, I'll bring a QRF to get you, and whoever is with you." Quick Reaction Forces, or QRF's are just groups of warriors on "stand by", ready to quickly react with force to whatever the problem is.

Greg had kind words, hugs, and handshakes with those few of the community who were leaving. Those with medical conditions and a lot of the single moms with kids all took up Mikes offer of the FEMA Camp. Ethyl's kitchen team would be cut in half, but she was not going to leave her home. The fire department team, now fully trained sheepdogs and other retired couples in relatively good health decided to stay. His Sheepdogs didn't lose a single defender, other than those lost yesterday in the battle. A few of the younger retirees who were on other teams wanted to be cross-trained to join the 'dogs. They saw from the defense of the Alamo that knowing how to shoot would be required to survive, even if their every-day job wasn't on the security team.

The security forces were now much better armed after scavenging the biker's weapons, and the gifts from the soldiers and the police. By the time the group heading to FEMA left, every one of the original sheepdogs had at least one semi-automatic weapon to carry. Greg's error of not having his Mauser with him meant fewer dead guys earlier. From now on, every guard would carry their semi-auto AR-15's, or 3-round burst M-4's with them all day, and into bed, if necessary. They each also had 4 full magazines, and a decent sized pile of spare .556 for them.

The group that left for Dahlgren FEMA checked in until they got out of the range of the radios. They got to the main road, Route 3, headed towards 301, the highway to Dahlgren. Jennifer kept watch, with her pistol, and the road to Dahlgren was indeed clear.

Upon arrival at Dahlgren, Jennifer and the rest of the civilians were checked in, and then driven to the "family area" of the base. This area was just a few Quonset huts, lined with bunk beds. Family units would hang up blankets for some semblance of privacy, but there was never any quiet. Family disputes, people playing cards, and other conversations filled the huts with noise. Despite Mike's constant attempts at intimacy, there was never an opportunity, or, at least, Jennifer didn't feel that the opportunities were right.

The Mansion

With the number of residents down to 27, Greg had a proposal for the next meeting. One week after the group left for the FEMA camp at Dahlgren, Greg pitched it at the community center.

"Folks, Thanks for coming together. And thank you for staying here with me. It's an honor to be in the community with you." He started his pitch. "What I remember most about the battle was the long run down the main road to our circle. Disengaging from the berm needs to be a smarter, better covered route, where we don't have to slog through the drainage ditch." At that, several heads nodded. That terrified slog through a quarter mile of ditch was still giving some of them nightmares.

"Our 'Alamo Defense' is going to be a lot easier if everyone is working is in one place." Greg paused for a minute to let this sink in. "I think we should move into the Rock Mansion. It's not occupied, and those of us that have scavenged it know that it's built for survival without electricity, since it was built in the late 1700's. It seems to me that it has enough room for everyone, as long as we don't need too much space."

The thought of leaving their homes and supplies created some conversation. Greg could tell that everyone was not up for his idea.

"Look, I'm not going to make anyone do anything. I'm just going to tell you what I'm going to do, and why. Here's my thinking:

"First, the mansion is set up for year-round living without electricity. They have breezeways for the summer heat, and fireplaces everywhere for the winter. Winter will be here eventually and trying to heat every house is much less efficient than heating one house. Body heat also helps."

"Next, it's a lot closer to the defensive berm, and we could do the same sort of defense that we did on the circle, without everyone on duty running the long way with no cover. It has windows all around, but couldn't be flanked, as its right on the longest peninsula in the harbor.

"Third, there are enough bedrooms, or at least rooms, that all family units could have privacy. There's also a kitchen that was built for cooking with firewood. We WILL run out of propane. Not this week, but this month. We need to think about heating water, and cooking everything else. Yes, we can salvage more, and having 3 working bikes help, but we can't really drag a wagon full of propane on the back of any of those bikes."

"Finally, with the loss of many of our friends, it's fewer and farther-between each inhabited house. We can be ambushed at night, since we don't have any night-vision. Being close to one another in a problem will exponentially increase the value of individual weapons, especially if we have pre-determined fields of fire. Including hidden kill zones, rigged up with my boom-toys."

"Whether or not you agree, I'll be moving in, and setting up the .50 on the balcony, as I think it's the best defensive position to back up the berm, and it was given to me as a present." Greg smiled, as he knew it was a community toy, but hoped they'd give him some slack. "Are there any objections to my moving, whether or not you are coming yourselves?"

No hands went up, so Greg was set to move into one of the nicer rooms of the mansion, namely, that one with the balcony and Ma Deuce!

Ok then. I'll not ask the rest of you if you're behind the rest of my plan. Just eat well tonight, I hear crab is on the menu again!" This got groans from most of the crowd. "Let's talk about it next week."

Greg saw Manuel and Gunny huddled into a corner, with the other Hondurans listening in and nodding. Luis was holding Marcy's hand. She was one of the women whose husband went to work in DC and never came home. It appeared that some relationships were forming, despite marital status. Greg just smiled at them, remembering the old song about 'If you can't be with the one you love, love the one you're with'. He smiled at Luis and gave a smile to Marcy – who nodded a sad, understanding smile back at him.

Gunny and Manuel declared that they would be moving into the mansion, and only needing one room. The crowd just smiled.

Finally, Angel stood up, and stated to the crowd, "Jefe, we move in tomorrow. You tell us your room, and we move in around you. Bueno idea, amigo!" Gunny nodded her appreciation and sign-off, so now both of Greg's NCO's would be no more than a few rooms or bunks away. The top floor of the Rock Mansion was a bunk-room that was built like a series of berths on a sailing ship, as it was indeed crafted by ship-builders who came from England, and slaves in later years. The captain's room, unknown to Greg, was the room with the balcony, as would be guessed.

Greg nodded his thanks, but told the rest of the community, "no need to rush your decisions, folks. The Mansion could just be the command center of the security team, but we'll be there to defend any of you, regardless of circumstance.

By the end of the week, all of the full-time security team were moved into decent rooms of the mansion, except Bill, who wanted to stay at home. Greg made it clear that if families came, the single soldiers would have to move upstairs, and there was no push-back. This was because Esteban, who was mostly healed by this time, took 2 bunks, after cutting the divider wall between them and shifting the mattresses to fit his bulk. He declared that he would be dragging any of them up, if they needed to be relocated, but did enjoy the empty space to himself for now. Greg felt better knowing that Este had the bunk, or bunks, by the window facing the tree barrier, and he never left his .308 more than 2 feet from him. He set up a sniping perch by dragging a table to the window, and a well-built chair to it. Even when off shift, Este often covered the road and mine-path from this perch. He was not unaffected by the battle, and it seemed to Greg that he was determined to not be shot again, if he could avoid it. His sniping skills were clearly the best of the group, now that the group had a little bit of ammunition to practice a little more. The government came through for them on ammo!

The gate-facing balcony was dubbed "The Eagle's Nest". It was set up on the corner of the mansion porch, above the main entrance, and was fortified with 2 sheets of thick plywood, one on each side making a U with the window access behind. The team pulled up about 50 gallons of sand from the beach and hauled it up a rope to be poured between the 2 the plywood frames. Ma Deuce, the .50 caliber machine gun, was emplaced up there, with someone trained on her ready to punch holes through everything less than an armored vehicle at the 150 yards that it was to the breach in the berm. Greg would rotate the 'dogs through that perch, because it was a very cushy "gig". Those here would be on the balcony, with a rigged rain-cover, and sitting in a comfortable firing position almost as comfortable as Este's perch.

With Samuel's backup fish provider, Carlos, killed in the battle, it turned out that Greg was the most experienced fly and spin-fisherman on the peninsula. The fishing team was reconstituted, at the expense of the security team. Greg and Sam now spent their days doing things that they WISHED they could spend their days doing before the lights went out – fishing and crabbing. Greg insisted they move to night patrol, too, with only a few hours in between for sleep. There were gaps in the guard station schedule, and Greg compensated for that by pushing a scout farther out, with the police radio. The other one was in the Eagles nest, with over watch, who also had a walkie. Greg kept a walkie on the boat, with Gunny and Angel having the others. Luis learned quickly how to use a spinning rod and was enlisted to fish with Sam when Greg had other duties. Protein was going to be at a premium as the store-bought food was quickly running out.

Greg and Sam went out about 2 hours from high tide – at "zero-dark-thirty", about 2 hours before sunrise. Greg had the opportunity to walk the guard posts, have some fun dropping Princess Bride quotes with Este, and otherwise keep himself busy. Without Jennifer and Annie there, he had plenty of spare time to create a cohesive unit bonded by shared experiences.

This part of the river had the most aggressive fish action from about 2 hours before high tide until 2 hours after high tide. Sam explained that it was a good general rule, but the tide chart showed when there would be higher highs and lower lows, and how the moon impacted that. The state of the moon and how much it illuminated the water was another factor. Greg realized that, despite his knowledge of fishing, he had a lot to learn from Samuel, the Fish King.

Their boat bumped against one of the not-so-rare bodies floating in the river. Samuel said "Greg, this one is a skinny one. Grab 2 of those red bricks in the bow and pass them back."

"I was going to ask you about that. You don't need ballast on a crab boat, right?"

"Nope, but you'll see what I need them for." Samuel said as he pulled a length of 550 para-cord out of his cargo pocket. He tied a fisherman's knot, aka a noose, out of it, and pulled the free end through the holes in the bricks. He looped the noose around the body and looked at Greg. "Care to say a few words."

Greg nodded. "Lord, we don't know this man's religion, but it is my hope that he did more positive things than negative things in his life and has found his way to his version of heaven. May we all one day understand what you're thinking, letting this happen to your world. I know we probably caused it ourselves, but you sure are testing us. In his God's name, we pray you take him home. Amen."

"Strange prayer, Greg." Said Sam, who tossed the bricks into the water. The body went more under-water, but still bobbed around a bit. "Here's why I carry this machete."

Sam stabbed the body in the swollen part of its gut, and noxious gas spewed out. Greg threw up over the bow. "Oh, God. What the fuck, Sam?"

Sam laughed a rattling croaking laugh. "Most times, the floaters are floating because of gas in the lungs or gut. I'm just helping him settle to his final resting place – down with the crabs. It's the great circle of life. Hakuna Matata, Greg. That's my prayer.

"Wow, done this much, old man?"

"Sadly, at least once per day. You see all those bricks, right? A big guy like you might be a 4-stone drop, even if I cut out the gas that you seem to be so full of." Sam laughed out loud, and motored a few hundred yards farther out. "It may seem gross, but between the crabs and other bottom-feeders, they're cleaning up the mess that we men made, and the fishing is the best it's been in years!"

Sam always brought back enough fish to at least get each community member a few ounces of meat. Greg thought he had a lesson or 2 to teach the old fisherman, though. "Sam, are we doing bottom rigs, spinning, or flies?"

"Today, I think we each run a couple of double-bottom rigs. The croaker have been pretty hot lately." Sam motored them out to the first deep channel, and they cast their rods in 4 directions. On the edge of the channel in both directions, deep in the channel, and out on the flats. These "probing casts" would let the men know what was happening where on this day.

Within about 20 minutes, they had several croakers, who were running the channel, so most of the rods were in the channel. These large fish "croaked" when brought into the boat. Greg didn't know the exact science of it, but Sam said it had something to do with vibrating their swim bladder. Neither knew if it was a warning, or mating call, but it was what every one of them did when pulled into a boat. The bigger ones would vibrate the hull with their croaks.

Sam was visibly distracted by Greg's inattention to the 4 rods. While Greg didn't lose a single croaker, Sam did occasionally have to set a hook while holding a "Fish On" between his legs or in a rod holder. Greg had lived the 2-fish lifestyle, and knew Sam was not too bad off. Whenever Sam set a second hook, Greg would set his ultra-light rod down and grab a rod from Sam. Nobody would starve for Greg's folly, but the tide, moon, and action he saw from some bait fish had him intrigued. He had been here before and was hoping that the déjà vu was telling him something.

Greg's Mitchell Ultra-Lite casting rod was his baby. It was rigged up with only 4 lb. line, and a #3 Mepps Aglia Black Fury. Sam had sniffed at the large spinner bait on such a light line. "You know, you hook a fish that takes that, you're not going to land him, right. I'd go with a #2, it's a smaller bait for smaller fish. You'll catch lots of yellow and white perch with the #2."

"I don't want lots of small perch – I burn almost as much calories cleaning them as I get from the tiny fillet's. Trust me, old timer. This old dog has a few new tricks, if the stars align."

Between catching mostly croaker, some spot, and some perch on the bottom rigs, they also landed a few smaller catfish. The buckets were filling up nicely, and the crab traps would have fresh bait.

Between bottom-fish hook-ups, Greg kept casting that #3 Black fury. He was hunting around the channel Markers, then would switch to the other side and try to hit the shoreline. After several casts, he got his first hit. The rod bent, and the reel started to unwind quickly. Greg set the hook and yelled "Fish On".

"Don't play with it, Greg, tighten up that drag!"

"The drag is where it needs to be with this line, Sam. This is my play rod, not my meat rod. Let me have a little fun. Hang on." Greg pumped the rod and reeled it in. The fish ran, and Greg pumped and reeled. After about 5 minutes, which any fisherman knows feels like an hour, he reeled in the grand-daddy of all yellow perch. This was about 15" long, and fat with tasty meat. It wasn't what Greg was going for, but it was the "Fish of the day", or FOD, even though it wasn't as big as some of the catfish.

"Nice fish. Probably 2-2 ¼ lbs." said Sam grudgingly. I've caught bigger, but that's pretty good.

"High praise, indeed, Sam." Greg smiled and dropped the perch in the bucket. He had had the same stringer vs. bucket debate with Sam in the dining hall many times. "Too slow – keeps you from fishing." It was Sam's boat, so Greg dropped the perch in a bucket, but it was an empty bucket that he filled with fresh water. He wanted that Perch alive and kicking when he filleted it. Fresh Yellow Perch was good eating.

A few more bottom rigs landed a few more fish, and the tide had changed. Greg was still casting back-and-forth between the shoreline and deep-water channel Marker. Just as the false-dawn was brightening the sky, Greg got a hit on the Aglia. And the rod did scream this time. This was not a perch!

"Fish On – Holy Shit! Get the lines, Sam, start the engines, we're going for a ride. The fish had already stripped of half of the line as it ran for deep-water. Sam pulled in the lines, grudgingly, and growled out a "I wasn't quite done yet."

Greg kept the rod tip way up, with his arm up in the air, and the rod taking most of the tension. Sam started the engine and started following the fish without needing direction. Greg was grateful to have a seasoned fisherman with him. They chased the fish, as Greg reeled and pumped, trying to recover some line. He saw that he could see the glitter of the spool starting to show under the line.

"I'm about out, but he's slowing down. You got any more speed in this thing?"

"It's a crab boat, knuckle-head!" Sam cackled. Greg was reminded of his father, who used to call him that. For a few minutes, the weight of the leadership and defense of Rock Harbor was forgotten in the chase for a fish. He smiled with the sheer joy of simply fighting a beautiful fish. What looked like a striper jumped out of the water about 80 yards away, and both men laughed out loud.

"Crank up the drag, Greg!" Shouted Sam

"Shut up, Old Timer, and steer."

Sam Cackled again!

"OK, it's starting to tire. Greg reeled and pumped, and the line moved away from 'between E and Oh-Shit' and started to fill the spool again. The fish was tiring, and they were almost in the middle of the Potomac river.

"I hope we have enough Gas to get back, Captain Ahab!" shouted Greg over his shoulder.

"You land the fish, I'll drive the boat!"

Greg pumped and reeled. Sam cut the engine. "You got it from here, bubba."

All was going well until the fish got within 10 feet of the boat and saw it. The fish got another burst and ran out some line – but not most of it. Greg pumped and reeled, adrenaline making the night breeze cool his sweat. He didn't notice, because Adrenaline is a fun drug that way.

Greg slowed down the fish and brought it back to the boat. This time, it was turning sideways on top of the water, still twitching its tail, but exhausted. He was at the point that many good fishermen know as 'I've got it if I don't screw up!'

"Now you can crank up the drag, Son. It's going to get light soon. We need to evac."

"OK. You're the boss, but tweaking the drag mid-fish always burns me. I don't want people on both sides of the Potomac seeing that we have a motor boat, either." Greg turned up the drag a bit, and the fish came towards the boat. When it was 2 feet from the hull, it made one last run away from the boat, and SNAP."

Sam had anticipated it and was behind it with his long-handled net.

"Look what I caught, Sonny!" Cackled Sam. "Shame you lost the FOD!!! Wait until I hand this baby to Ethyl! I'm eating good tonight."

"Thanks for the save, Sam! I told you about the drag."

"I knew that, I just wanted to be sure you knew it. You changed your philosophy under duress. Don't ever do that. You have good instincts and shouldn't doubt them." Sam scolded. "Hell of a fish though. Good thing I saved this lure, because I'm keeping it. Mepps Aglia Black Fury #3. Thanks for the tip!"

"Not like you'd catch anything with those meat-hooks you call fishing rods. Sure, they make it easy to land, but the ultra-lite with a heavy spinner lets you really get it out there, and you need light line, because the big fish got big by being smart – and line shy. They see the heavy lines on the water and won't take the bait.

Sam reached under his seat, took out a 2-piece ultra-light and had it ready to go in about 5 seconds. On the end was a Mepps Aglia #3, but not the Black Fury model! "The only credit I'm giving you is for fishing with a black fury at dawn. I figured out the rest of this game myself years ago, Son. Don't let your head get too swollen!"

The fish in the net was, to Sam's estimation, about a 35 lb Striped Bass. Enough to feed most of the community one of the rare treats of the river, the Striper. "You're almost 20 lbs from the state record, so don't get all cocky... But on a 4 lb line? Nice job, son. I'd fish with you any time."

"I'd have never landed it from my rowboat. Thanks for the assist – both of 'em!"

"I usually catch them with the bottom rigs, and much heavier line, but damn, son... that was a Hoot! My hands are shaking from the adrenaline. You know, you're not as dumb as you look, numb nuts. Now switch out the water on these buckets, while I drive your ass home.

Greg spent the 10-minute ride home dumping water out of the buckets with a bailing tool and refilling it with fresh, aerated river water. The tool was the top half of a Clorox bottle, with the lid screwed on, but the bottom of the bottle cut off. It had a handle and could scoop over a half-gallon at a time, easily. "Well sure, old goat, if you have someone to refresh the water, the buckets aren't so stupid."

"Why do you think I need to fish with a first mate?"

Greg looked over his shoulder, as they approached the Mansion dock, and flipped off the old sea dog. "You don't suck too bad, old man. Thanks for the memories."

"That night, at the community dinner, Rockfish with mixed garden herbs and stuffed with jumbo lump crab was on the menu. Sam asked the ladies to make bread with the dwindling supplies. With olive oil that hadn't turned yet, and spices for dipping the bread in, it was probably the best meal Greg ever ate, and the food wasn't even the best part."

"I told the damned fool that 4 lbs. was too light, and if I hadn't been there with the net, he would have lost our dinner!" Sam regaled the crowd with "his version" of the fight, but never mentioned that Greg increased his tension. To his credit, Greg never mentioned Sam's 2-piece ultra-light that he kept hidden under his bench seat. He thought of Carlos, and his death in the first attack. He bet that Carlos knew about Sam's "dirty little secret." Looking at Sam, he locked eyes, and would almost bet that Sam knew what he was thinking.

Like most older brothers, or fathers, Sam spent the evening roasting Greg, but the pride in his eyes was apparent. Greg thought back to his mom who lived right on the in Arizona. She was pretty sick, and he doubted She'd have made it without air conditioning. Since she was a good shooter, and kept a Glock 19 in her house, he figured she'd either be safe, or go out blaze of glory if there was rioting in her area. She was on many medications, including insulin and couldn't walk a mile without having a heart attack, on a good day.

He had subconsciously blocked out that part of his family. He would miss her and mourned her tonight. However, he also gained something else tonight – more family.

He had no idea of his Father's situation in Vermont, but he knew that he would be able to survive in his cabin, as he was a classic prepper, and prided himself on "living off the land". It was fun to visit him at Salmon fishing every year, but his Dad took coolers full of fish home, while Greg practiced catch and release with the Salmon. He didn't like the taste, and Great Lakes Salmon wasn't exactly prized seafood. He tried to visit his father a few times at the cabin, but his did seemed pretty uncomfortable having guests in his cozy little 450 square foot log cabin. Greg could count on his dad to bring some good Venison, and occasionally bigger game to the River every year. He loved his Dad but could only take him in small doses.

Greg took the razzing and hoots at Dinner with a sense of satisfaction that he hadn't felt in a long time. They were treating him like one of the group, without any regard for "Rank", whatever that was in this community. They were coming together as a new family, and it brought a tear to Greg's eye to think about all his family that he knew, or suspected were lost. Greg looked at the ancient Scottish "Tree of Life" that he had tattooed on his arm. It symbolized life everlasting, with leaves falling to the ground, only to turn into fertilizer, growing new leaves in the Spring. He didn't know if that was the official Scottish interpretation, but it was his, and Tattoos were not about what others think. They were intensely personal.

Greg recalled the first tattoo he ever got, at 45 years old. A few days after her birthday, his daughter came up to him with all the moxy she could gather and said "Dad, I'm 18. I'm getting a tattoo, and there's nothing you can do to stop me."

"Reeeeeaaaaaaalllly?" he asked, with a sarcastic Jim Carrey voice.

"Yes, I'm a grown up, and you can't stop me."

"You're right, Maria. I can't. But can I pay for both of us to get our first together?"

After her jaw came up off the floor, and she thought about what his angle might be, she said, "Um, I guess." She told him how she researched the safest, cleanest, highest rated tattoo parlors in Marietta, and he believed her, because she was prepared for a long argument.

"Look, Kiddo. When I was 17, after my Mom told me no to some stupid request, I told her 'I can't wait until I'm 18, so I can get out of here!' Her reply to me was 'I don't care how old you are, get the fuck out!'. I'm not going to get into a pissing contest with you, and I've always wanted a tattoo. I just didn't know what was worth it. A tat with my daughter would be an epic story, and worth it, so can we go now?" He asked to her surprise and shock.

"No, we need to make an appointment!"

"OK, book it any time except during these few times when I have meetings. I'll leave work for this, absolutely. How much were you going to spend?"

"Um, I saved up $150. I have some ideas in mind."

"OK, Maria. You go first and keep your $150. Your budget is $300, because I don't want your first tattoo to be a piece of shit."

"Daddy, I love you!"

Greg looked back to this day, where he got "Daddy" instead of "DAAAAADDD". Possibly for the last time ever. He had tears in his eyes and a smile on his face.

"You OK, Jefe?" Angel elbowed him, but had a look of concern on his face.

"Just thinking about Mi Hija, Manito" (Spanish slang for my daughter, and little brother). "I won't be OK until she is here with me. But don't worry, I'll live. He said as he caressed the Makai fish hook tattoo on his arm. His daughter got a similar tribal version of a fish, as she wanted to both respect her name, and the man who gave it to her – Greg the fisherman.

Greg's leadership lesson on the day of the tattoo was that there are sometimes when you can fight and lose. Or you can think outside the box, seize the opportunity, and create a win, and a damn good story, out of an imminent loss. All it takes is ceding some power, without letting your ego get in the way. Oh, and buying your daughter shit that she had saved up for will always make you a little more bearable.

Greg tuned back into Samuel, still telling his fishing story, at Greg's expense. Greg had to admit that Sam made it funnier than real life. Greg remembered a saying of his Uncle, another old Scottish sea dog: "Never let the truth get in the way of a funny story." The crowd was digging it, and everyone got several good laughs in.

These were his people, his clan, his family. He vowed at this table that he would die to keep them safe, if necessary. That said, he thought of the famous quote by Patton: "The object of war is not to die for your country, but to make the other bastard die for his."

Fresh Meat

After moving into the mansion, Greg eventually un-packed his Bug out bag from the house at Rock. While un-packing into all the cubby holes and built-in cabinets of his "Captain's Chamber", Greg finally got to the bottom of the bag. Down there, among things like spare batteries and some more 550 lb. test "para" cord (to keep parachutes from dropping guys), he found a steel snare. This snare was a length of twisted steel with a plate on one end. That plate had a hole in it that could accommodate a nail or most screws. On the other end, it had a noose, with a piece of hardware on it that only tightened, without opposable thumbs to loosen it up. It might have been called a "cam", but he wasn't sure. In Georgia, they were illegal to use for game hunting. He had honestly forgot even purchasing it.

Now that no game warden was going to write tickets, snaring game was on the table. Greg was ready to test out the snare. The problem was that he bought it one day when he had an urge to learn how, and the DVD that came with the set of snares, along with most of the snares in the set for larger game (i.e. medium game like turkeys and coyotes, and large game like wild boars and deer) were back home in Atlanta, with the DVD on how to use them. Greg had read a few articles on how to snare, and how to create traps that would pull the snare tight, like the bent-over tree with pins attached to the snare. But he feared that putting it into practice and being successful would not be an early win.

At the next meeting in the club-house, Greg brought the snare, with the intent of getting some of the community thinking about meat not coming from the harbor. Most people here were ready for red meat, even if that was squirrel, rabbit or anything else they could catch. The thought of a nice, meat stew made Greg's mouth water, so he brought the snare, to show what he had, talk about the concept at a high-level, and HOPE that someone in the community knew how to use one.

Several in the community had heard of, or used snares in the past, and by the end of the week, there were snares in every garden. The trick with a snare is to set the loop along a known, or suspected trail for the prey. Squirrels walk along the tops of fences, and along fallen trees. Rabbits run along walls and will tend to eat certain plants. The prey would catch their necks in the noose, and then run, tightening it. It wasn't a particularly nice way to go, but the people needed meat. Well, "needed" is a strong word. The vegetarians and pescatarians didn't care for the snare concept, but there weren't many of them left.

Greg was not going to live through the summer with fish, crabs, Kudzu and garden vegetables, if he could help it. It beat starvation, but just barely. He was discussing this with Gunny, when she said "I guess I could move my chicken coop here."

"Your what?!?!" He spluttered.

"I've been walking back to the Mall every day or 2. When I can't make it, Manuel goes for me. Out back, in the woods, I have a chicken coop with about a dozen birds. I've been giving Ethyl the eggs to work into our dinners. You know you can't make that pasta that we had without eggs, right?"

"I figured it was Barilla or some other store brand!"

"Nope, we ran out of that a while ago. We never have enough eggs for like, eggs for everyone for breakfast, but with all the empty houses, we've got plenty of flour, which stores well. Kudzu roots can also be dried and pounded into flour for frying the fish. The eggs in the refrigerators were gone by the end of the first week after the lights went out. My point is, we could move the flock here, let a few eggs hatch, and maybe one day have some fresh chicken from those that won't lay any longer. The farms around here can also help us out, although my last few trips on recon didn't show a lot of them alive. I've grown my chicken coop population, because they won't be needing them. She frowned. Too bad there's no dairy farms around here. Beef and milk would be good.

July - Jennifer – The fall of Dahlgren.

Jennifer settled into the routine of Dahlgren quickly. She kept herself busy between volunteering to run a school for the kids during the day. At night, she walked the perimeter of the family area until she was too tired to walk any longer.

Mike was increasingly busy with off-base duties. These included doing recon in nearby neighborhoods to ascertain their food and defensive needs. At this point, FEMA was not forcing relocations, despite some stories. If people wanted to defend their homes, then not only were they guaranteed that right, but they would be less of a drain on the limited resources of the government. With most of the transportation infrastructure down, the government's capacity to ship supplies over any distance was severely diminished. That said, soldiers and other government personnel were encouraged to relocate their families to Dahlgren, where there was a minimum, but survivable standard for food and living quarters. It was by no means comfortable, but it was survivable, and most families pitched in to make it a little more private, and as comfortable as living ins something like a Red Cross shelter could be.

Mike wasn't around much most days, as he was out rounding up draftees. Jen had heard the government was playing the selective service card, and drafting kids from 18 to their late-20's. At least one computer survived the apocalypse, and they had lists of recruits to enlist. They were trained and bunked on the opposite side of the base from the families, who were near a back gate, near the aviation complex. When Mike was around, he grumbled a lot about the Department of Homeland Security (DHS) guys who "led" each outing, with their lists of draftees' names and addresses. He pointed out that while they did better in residential areas, they were lucky if 1 in 10 of these draftees were still living at the address they registered under. Of those that they could find, many shot at the "legitimate government" and, if they didn't die in the battle, were summarily executed for "treason" by the DHS.

For those that did go, many families begged for an exemption, as the draftee was the only able-bodied man to defend the home. They cried that the DHS was giving them a death sentence. In these cases, DHS explained that the needs of the government outweighed the needs of the few. Mike and other less-brutal members of the team would often give the family a case of MRE's, or other rations that might help them in the short term, even if it was just prolonging the inevitable.

More and more DHS personnel were flown in, as the leaders of the country, hidden in their bunkers, found that even at 1 in 10, this part of the world was recruiting more troops than the more populated areas. Because of that, the DHS troops were going out with more and more raw recruits, who were even more brutal in their recruiting. Jennifer noticed more and more hollow-eyed recruits, more tattoos and bad teeth, and more general nastiness around the base when she left the family area for the inevitable errands necessary for survival.

The draft teams brought in progressively scarier "draftees". Many were pretty clearly those released from prison by DHS, gang members and bikers, who seemed to enjoy the duty. They got trained, and got their M-4's. Pretty soon, the base was full of young recruits outnumbering the career military and law enforcement by about 10 to 1.

On her last run to get some fruit for the mess hall that she volunteered in, Jennifer was surrounded by a handful of these recruits, and was afraid that things were going to get ugly. As the first one made a grab for her arm, she yelled, and a group of 3 Marines who were original Dahlgren staff, based on their uniforms, turned the corner behind the supply tent. They ordered the recruits to stand down. She noticed the scabs on her attacker's arms, his nasty teeth, and prison tattoos, including 2 tear drops tattooed under his eye

"Who the fuck are you?" yelled the recruit with his hand still holding Jennifer, who tried unsuccessfully to pull away.

"My name is Corporal Semper Fi, Motherfucker. Hands off, or die here and now."

The 6 punks made a move on the 3 Marines, and in under 1 minute, all 6 recruits were down, with various broken bones, or unconscious and at least 1 with a crushed skull.

"Ma'am. You should get back to your area. We'll clean up this mess." Said one of the Marine saviors. Jennifer kissed him on the cheek and went back to the family area with her cans of fruit cocktail."

That night, Mike came home, and looked more tired and depressed than usual.

"What's up, Babe?", asked Jennifer.

"Those DHS Pukes. I don't know who is really in charge any longer, but they seem to be running the show everywhere I look. They rounded up 3 Marines for the "cold-blooded murder" of a new recruit and had all 3 of them executed without a trial. They insisted that they were defending a civilian, but it was the word of 5 against 3, and the DHS has been doing everything to reduce the strength of the military since they took over. The Base commander is livid, but they keep waving their orders from the White House in his face. Marines, Soldiers and us Law Enforcement guys think that there's a breaking point coming soon."

"Mike, I think I was that civilian. Look at my arm." Mike looked and saw the bruising on her arm. "Those men saved me. They were heroes. 3 of them took out 6 of the recruits, in, like, seconds. Oh my God. They're dead?"

Mike looked at Jennifer in shock. "Are you OK?" Jennifer nodded. "I need you to come with me. We need to go find Top Garza. He needs to hear this."

Jennifer was taken to the senior NCO in this area of the base. First Sergeant Garza listened, showing no emotion other than grinding his teeth together. "We need to go to the base commander. I'm going to gather up some of my troops, and we'll get some revenge for this bullshit." Garza gathered up a dozen or so veteran mixed-service troops from the family area, and they made their way across the base to the HQ building.

Halfway there, they were stopped by a platoon of skinny, tattooed recruits who were guarding the entrance to HQ. They were told that they were not authorized entry.

"Fuck authorization private. Do you see this diamond in my chevrons? I'm THE First Sergeant. Make way or I'll kick your ass into next year."

"I don't recognize your authority, Sir."

"SIR! You incompetent fuck. Do I look like I don't work for a living? I'm not an officer. Now move your ass." Top Garza shoved the recruit back about 8 feet, and the recruit ran into another guard, whose rifle went off, hitting the soldier next to Jennifer in the abdomen. She screamed and immediately attended to his wound as the 2 groups devolved into a bloody battle. The recruits, once again, fared poorly. The entrance was cleared, with dozens of recruits lying dead or dying."

Top Garza surveyed the carnage, amazed at how quickly things were going sideways. About half of his group was wounded, with a few dead, compared to all 30 or so of the DHS Recruits being down and out of action. Top looked up, and his eyes got wide. "Gather our wounded and fall back to the family area, NOW!

The rest of one company of recruits were emerging from barracks around the HQ building, and they were all armed to the teeth. Firefights in the Headquarters building, as indicated by flashes in the windows, indicated that this was a coordinated attack, and that Top's group was just the spark, or just plain unlucky.

Several members of the true military had heard the commotion on base, and were rallying around Top Garza, whom they all knew and respected. Garza got on the military channel, and rallied more troops back to the motor pool.

"Fall back Men. Defend the Family area and motor pool. Gather loyal soldiers and Marines. Spread the word!"

Thus, the battle of Dahlgren began. Jennifer took care of wounded soldiers as they conducted a bounding retreat, giving much more than they got to the relatively un-trained bad guys. Unfortunately, they were outnumbered about 10 to 1, and out-gunned.

After about an hour, all surviving family members, and the remaining patriots were backed into the motor pool garage and armory, near the back entrance of the base when the artillery started to drop into the vehicles outside. The idiots at DHS were dropping rounds right into their own troops without regard for their safety. Garza was shouting out defensive orders, as well as ordering supplies to be loaded into 3 of the 5-ton trucks that were repaired or awaiting regular Primary Maintenance, Checks and Services (PMCS) in the garage. He had a large number of the seriously wounded in the rear truck. The civilians were in the middle truck, and the forward truck was full of most of the fighters, using the ring-mounted Mark 13 grenade launcher to throw 25mm grenades into the attacking recruits as the troops shot over the top of the truck bed. Grenades flew, and the DHS recruits died in large numbers, but they never stopped coming.

Top grabbed Jennifer by the arm and walked her to the middle truck. Jennifer put her daughter on the floor of the passenger side and told her to keep her head down as she climbed up.

"This guy on your peninsula, you said he was an Engineer?"

"Yes, he said he 'blew shit up' when he was in the army. He used to say that he was trained to build bridges, dams and forts, and then blow them up."

"Good I have some presents for him." Top grabbed a corporal who was walking wounded and ordered him to grab a few bodies to grab some supplies. Jennifer didn't understand what he was asking for, but the Corporal and his detail came back with a several crates and a few heavy tubes. They also had several backpacks bulging with something. All of these were handed up to the wounded and civilians in the back of the middle 5-ton. The longer tube was thrown behind the seat of the truck

"Alright men. Listen up! We need to get Oscar Mike now. I need covering fire at the front door – reload that Mark 13. Sergeant Jones is in charge. I'm covering our retreat. He headed to the back of the building, where Jennifer saw Mike leaning against the wall, holding onto some package. She saw Top and Mike arguing, and Mike pointed at the truck. It was then that Jennifer saw all the blood in Mike's lap. She jumped down and ran towards them.

"The hell you are!", said Garza to Mike. Just then a stray round hit Garza, and he spun around. He ended up leaning against Jennifer, who held him up, as he was not a large man, and he was mostly supporting his own weight.

"Jennifer, Top, I'm done." Mike lifted up the satchel that he had compressed against his chest, and they both saw that he was indeed done. He took 2 shots to the left of his chest, and blood was coming out of his mouth. "Top, you get my girls to safety. She knows the way, and you know how to lead these men. I can blow the fuel bladders with this charge, if you go quick."

"No, Mike!" She moved towards him.

"Yes, Jen. Leave now, before I don't have the strength to do this."

Garza dragged Jennifer, sobbing to the middle 5-ton. He ordered Jones into the gunner's hatch and blew the horn. The front 5-ton moved out of the garage, spraying the Mark 13. Defenders ran in all directions. Then a lucky Artillery round hit the front truck, and it blew up, killing or maiming all aboard. Garza swerved, and got around the burning vehicle and screaming men who were blown free. As the 5-ton behind Garza followed his path, the Artillery hit almost the same spot, flipping the 5 ton on its side. Garza looked behind and saw that most of the wounded were thrown from the bed.

Top steered towards the back gate, with Jones spraying the M-240 on top at anything that was a threat. Jones got shot and dropped down into the cab. Top blew through the gate, scattering defenders, and headed down the road. As the defenders were searching through the motor pool for vehicles to give chase, Mike evidently did what he said he would. He blew the satchel charge he was holding, which ignited nearby fuel trucks. The explosions and shrapnel from the fuel trucks touched off an explosion of the jet fuel bladders in the aviation area creating something that, to Jennifer, looked like a nuclear bomb going off in the rear-view mirror.

Most, if not all the vehicles and aircraft from Dahlgren were destroyed that night, putting a serious dent in the strength of the

DHS division in Virginia. She hoped that no survivors knew that a 5-ton full of survivors to spread word of this had escaped. She eventually got Annie quiet, and then sobbed for the loss of her husband, and all those brave defenders who saved this one truck full of families and wounded. Through the night, she steered Top to the entrance to Rock Harbor.

August – Jennifer returns with some folks from the FEMA Camp.

The days since Jen left were spent with Doc and Kim teaching the group how to ride motorcycles, and with Greg improving the defenses. The first battle taught the Rock Harbor group where their weaknesses were, and Greg got creative with new types of obstacles and demolitions.

Running out of alcohol (except the opened bottle of Pappy) didn't turn out to be that big a deal at all. Greg was down to 225 lbs., his fighting weight in the Army, and was feeling good. He still had an urge to have a drink at happy hour, but his weaning off by only having 2 per day seemed to be one way to do it.

"Jefe – big truck coming down approach road." Esteban called on the radio from the lookout in the steel reinforced bed of the destroyed Deuce-and-a-half.

"Reinforcements coming your way.", replied Greg. The day shift got on their Harleys and negotiated the mine road while the night shift was called up by Angel, who was holding the fort by the berm-gap detonators. After much planning and debating the best defense, the day shift's job would be to get near the head of the minefield and lay their bikes across the path (not on a mine) in such a way that any invaders would have to go over the bikes, or onto version 2 of the community land mines – the leg exploder. There had been some improvements in the community defense systems. Gunny manned, or "womaned" the .50 caliber in the Eagle's nest.

Greg got on his Harley, and roared to the first defensive bike, and gathered up his troops to approach the road.

Coming in was an Army 5-ton dump truck. It had twice the capacity of the deuce-and-a-half trucks, hence the name. It also had a much larger and taller footprint, since it carried twice as much cargo.

Hanging out the passenger window and waving with her hands out, was Jennifer. "Hold your fire, Sheepdogs! Hold your fire! Friendly's incoming, and am I glad to see you still here!" Jennifer yelled, with tears dripping off her cheeks.

Greg gave the 'Clear, but not ALL clear' sign that meant "safeties on, but rifles in the general direction of the possible danger." The truck came to a stop. The sheepdogs complied, and circled the front of the truck, with Este coming down from the Deuce to check the back of the 5 ton. He looked up into the bed – possibly the only one of the dogs that could do so without stepping on the bumper. Then he shook his head and came around the back of the truck.

"It looks clear, Jefe. You might not like it, though!" Este shook his head and held position at the rear.

Jennifer dropped out of the passenger seat, and ran to Greg, hugging him. Her tears were still falling. Annie stuck her head out of the cab and yelled "Hi Greg!"

"Hi Annie!" Greg nodded and smiled she had grown in the last 2 months. He then turned to Jen and said "What's up – is there trouble coming?"

Jennifer replied, "Yes, but no time soon. They're busy raiding Dahlgren. It all fell. So much blood! We got away out a back gate. Many brave men gave their lives for us." Here, her breath hitched. "Including Mike!" Then she sobbed and fell into Greg's arm. Greg felt her resolve stiffen, and she said, "We have wounded that need help. We also have women, children, and all the supplies we could carry."

Greg knew that a 5 ton could carry a lot of supplies. He got on the radio and called all able bodies to come out and help. He asked the guards who laid down the Harleys to clear a path through the field with the police tape they had salvaged.

"All of you who are mobile, please follow these gentlemen through the path that they lay with the yellow tape. Stay on the path – there are mines, and you've been through enough. 6 women and 4 walking children got out of the truck, 2 were carrying babies. After the back of the truck emptied out, Este gave Greg a boost into the bed to look around. There were 4 soldiers in various states of wounded. They looked like non-life-threatening injuries, but they were not going to be moving. Doc and Kim roared up in their bikes, and were directed to the bed of the truck, where they commenced triage.

Jen said, "Greg, organize the stretcher bearers. There are military stretchers rolled up right THERE", as she pointed to a group of them. Greg started barking orders from the top of the truck, while giving words of comfort to those men not with Kim or Doc.

An unknown man came around the driver's side of the truck, followed closely by Este. Greg looked down, and saw a man with a bloody arm, but in good shape otherwise. "And you are?"

"First Sergeant Emilio Garza" – You can call me "Top". My men pushed me into the truck to evacuate the civilians – against my will. Unfortunately, they were also well trained, and I had no choice. My men died to save me, and these civilians and wounded." Top's words were bitter, and angry.

"Staff Sergeant, no longer active, Greg Creighton. Thank you for your sacrifice, and for bringing these civilians to safety, for however long that lasts. It looks like your men are being taken care of. Can you give me a high-level view of what the supplies you brought are?"

Top looked at his troops, being carried on stretchers to the field-hospital on the harbor and nodded in satisfaction. "Your troops are disciplined, and your medics are squared away. I think we're going to get along just fine, Sergeant Creighton."

"I hope so, Top. I've got a strong, small group of well-disciplined civilians, with one Marine Gunny and a retired Vietnam Vet. They keep treating me like an officer, so I sure could use your help getting them straight on the rank thing."

"Well, you know a Gunnery Sergeant, at E-7, already outranks your E-6, so it looks like rank is going to be a fluid thing. For now, I'll treat you like the Lieutenant in charge, since this is your fire base, and we'll re-evaluate. On supplies, we've got the 3-B's. Beans, Bullets and bandages. There's a several cases of MRE's that were pre-loaded, along with the handful of small-arms that we could carry to the truck. Based on what Jennifer told me about your skill-set, I was able to pack a few surprises for those bastards if they show back up, although I didn't plan on being here to have the pleasure of using them to get some revenge. Can you get some men to carry these 4 crates, specifically, in first? Oh, wait."

Top looked at Esteban and started barking orders in Spanish. He slid 2 of the crates to the edge, almost without effort, slung his .308 and threw a crate over each solider. After the reality of the situation hit him, the looked at Greg and asked, "OK Jefe?"

"Si Este, I'll see you at the community center. Round up the non-wounded, unless Doc and Kim need helpers. Standard guard shift otherwise. We don't know what's coming. Call in our Navy and get the Galley crew cooking." Greg threw a crate over his shoulder, and Top grabbed the last weapons crate. Greg wondered how strong Este was, because he was going to need to take a break on the walk back.

"That big guy has the Mortar Rounds. I'll send back my team to get the plates and tube. You and I get to carry the Recoilless Rifle rounds."

Greg danced he Snoopy dance up and down. "Tell me you have a 90MM, Top, Please!!!!   These crates say that's what's in them!"

Top winked and gave a thumbs-up.

"Bill, keep watch from up here. If you see anyone coming, fire off a shot. It doesn't look like you have a radio."

"Si, Jefe", smiled Bill. I got this. Send back some runners with a radio, and to get the rest of the supplies. I'll stay on this station until end-of shift. Please get me up to speed at shift-change."

"You got it. Hooaah, Bill."

Top and Bill both said Hooah and smiled at each other.

"Follow the tape, Top. Everywhere else is a combination of toe poppers and leg blowers."

"Leg Blowers?" asked Top.

"Top, I was a 12-B in the first Desert Storm. I don't have any actual claymores, bouncing betties and other AP (Anti-Personnel) mines that they trained me on. Think of the leg blowers as bouncing betties that don't bounce. They'll kill a man, unlike a toe popper. In our first battle, we learned that toe poppers don't do well against Harleys, although they do serve to disable the bikes. "

Top looked at Greg, and his respect meter went up another notch. "You led the battle that Mike told us about?"

"I don't know about led it, Top. I fought in it, same as everyone else. I didn't die, but I lost 3 good men. I don't know if I'd call that leading. We all fought, we won, they ran."

"Yeah, you led it. Nice job, Soldier!" I heard you killed over 40 and only lost 3. Don't beat yourself up too hard – that's a rare ratio there. Nothing to be ashamed of. A good defense can be expected to kill 3 to 1, if you need a comparison. Hooaaah!" and here Gunny smiled, "Jefe."

"Well, we killed about 10 of them after the battle, mostly us veterans with our blades. I didn't want my rookies to have the rough dreams that I have."

"Greg, in this world, you kill them, or they come back stronger. You did the right thing."

"That means a lot, Top. Let's go to the Mess Hall, get you patched up, and debrief. Our back is covered by one of my best, if Bill doesn't have to run!" Greg laughed. "He's pushing 70, but he was at the Da Nang, and spent months in Cambodia, even though he was "never there". He's the real deal."

Homecomings and bad news.

The residents and off-duty Sheepdogs were all in the mess hall, and heard a horrific tale of betrayal, subterfuge, and massacre, as told by Top.

First came a story of the Presidents Selective Service call-up. Calls had gone out to all State FEMA camps. Most were on military bases, and groups of National Guard, Active Duty and Law Enforcement were led by A Department of Homeland Security (DHS) leader. The went into the more populated areas, and the DHS leader took them to the addresses of anyone 18-30 years old, drafting them on the spot. Refusal to be drafted was treason. The other choice was execution.

These young men were brought to Dahlgren for an abbreviated BASIC training and were sent out with more teams with DHS leaders to recruit more. Uncle Sam was short on bodies, due to the outage, and the crimes happening all over the country. Uncle Sam DID have plenty of bullets and firearms, especially the M-4 that most were issued. The families and regular military somehow ended up billeted in a section of the base reserved for supplies, the families of the original Guard Units, and Law Enforcement families.

In that same area of the base there was also a small helicopter air-base and maintenance shed. Some of the Army's helicopters were either EMP proof, or repaired, and they ferried supplies and DHS Personnel from the Military and FEMA caches throughout the country. Top didn't see too many fixed wing aircraft still flying, but heard there were some out West.

The president had been evacuated to one of the Nuclear Proof strongholds and was running the country from there. About 1/3rd of the senators were stored away in various areas, but because there was a congressional recess at the time of the EMP, many were un-accounted for.

What nobody on the base except the bad guys knew was that many, if not most, of the draftees that were picked up later in the "draft" were plants from various local gangs. A few nights ago, top told him about the "Spark" of his confrontation at the HQ gate, and they turned their M-4's on all of their non-gang recruits, as well as the regular military and law enforcement. With the barracks free of any "good guys", they proceeded to storm the base, including opening the gate for access by the other motorcycle riders. The base fought back, led by Top's quick thinking, and there were many lost on both sides, but the Guard and Law Enforcement were pushed back. The rallied around their families, and fell back, taking way better than 3-to-1 due to their superior training, but they didn't have much better weaponry than the bikers.

In a last desperate attempt to save their families, they loaded as many supplies as they could easily, and got their surviving family members in the truck. Top's remaining soldiers forced him into the truck, and sent them out the back gate, giving as much covering fire as they could. His last radio transmission was from his Mike, telling him that he was one of the last, and they were about to end it – for the guard. Then a huge fireball filled the corner of base where the last of the survivors were. Top saw it in the mirror, and for one of the first times in many years, shed a tear for his men, who gave all. That fireball turned into a second, and third, with numerous secondary explosions. Top listed the names of his surviving troops and vouched for the skills of all of them. They were mostly Rangers with a SWAT team member. Army Ranger Sgt. Jones, Marine Corporal Baker, PFC Newman (another Ranger) and Police Corporal Simmons were going to be an asset to the community, if they recovered.

Top told the group, but mostly Greg that 1 of the crates carried high-explosive (HE) Mortar rounds, the other had flares, and assorted other types of charges. He said that his guys could run a mortar without a problem. In the back of the truck was the tube, plates and aiming devices. The other 2 crates were rounds for the 90 MM recoilless rifle, which Top left behind the seat in the Deuce, under the stewardship of Bill.

The 90 MM, or Ninety-Mike-Mike was, basically, a bazooka. It was a tube that you loaded from the rear, and the back-blast shooting out of the back of the tube was supposed to counter the projectile coming out of the front, making it recoil-less. Greg had trained with the 90MM in the Army and couldn't have been happier. This was better than the Ma-Deuce. It had a much slower rate of fire, and was best used if 2 people manned it, one shooter and one loader. So, there was much less lead going down-range, but there was a much bigger, high-explosive BOOM. Top brought one crate each of High Explosive (HE) and Anti-Personnel Flechettes. The second type was made for turning men into shredded men-burgers.

The backpacks that Jennifer saw loaded into the truck ended up having a variety of anti-personnel mines, including, joy of joys, Actual Claymore AP mines with blasting caps and detonators.

The last present that Top brought was a world-band, or HAM radio, along with enough wire to rig a decent antenna. They would be able to hear news of the world with this thing.

All in all, the Rock Army just acquired some tremendous fighting assets. Unfortunately, it sounded like the bikers had recruited a lot of new bad guys. He hoped most of them were taken in the explosion that Mike give his life to make happen in Dahlgren.

Expanding the Sheepdog Army

The selfless soldiers at Dahlgren were seasoned and battle tested. They were smart enough to load not only bad-ass soldiers, but those that they knew could still defend the civilians, and who would make it with moderate medical treatment. Over the course of the next few days, Top made sure the truck was emptied of the rest of the supplies, and then he worked with Greg, Gunny, and Angel to set up the best defense possible.

Several of the women had lost their husbands in Dahlgren and wanted to be trained to "get some" back from the bad guys. Jennifer was one of those women. She had asked Greg if she could have a room near his in the Mansion and she and Annie were put right next door, at the insistence of Este, who had become Greg's bodyguard, whether he wanted him or not. Este himself moved all the personal items out of the room next to Greg's, even though Angel protested at being moved forcibly. Este explained to Angel that he had a nice, spacious corner for him on the 3rd floor, and Angel moved there without any more complaint. Este was a gentle giant, but when he set his mind to something, he was un-stoppable.

Top had a conversation with Greg about the 90MM, and after quizzing him, was convinced that Greg should run the 90MM. Nobody else on the peninsula except Top and the 3 Rangers had worked with one. Top and Greg also agreed that the front of the peninsula was heavily fortified, and they needed some heavy artillery at the rear. Jennifer insisted that she be trained as a loader, and Greg and Jennifer spent a few days drilling with practice rounds, until Greg and Top was comfortable that Jennifer had it covered. She was now a 90MM loader. She still carried her .357 revolver, and Greg insisted that she get trained up on the Mauser, because once the 30MM was loaded, she could snipe from their position.

Top wanted his Rangers to run the Mortar, with a radio so he could walk in the rounds from a forward spotter, who would be the Marine. The third ranger was paired with Angel and trained him on how to call in mortar fire from a position near the approach road. They had a highly-camouflaged deer trail so they could pull back from the road, and view the battle from a sniper hide near the front of the berm. This way, if the bikers got through the trail, they would have fire called in on them from behind them, while being sniped at the same time.

Este's self-declared firing position was from the third-floor window. After a loud and long argument in Spanish, Top agreed that Este had a "good idea" and let that be his fighting position. Nobody had said no to Este yet, when had an idea, and was persistent about it.

The last Ranger, Sergeant Jones, was made the other team lead, opposite Gunny. Top, Gunny and Sgt. Jones had a lot of inter-service trash-talk, and grudgingly, agreed that Gunny knew her shit. She wasn't a Ranger, so took the day-shift lead, with Sgt. Jones taking the night-shift lead.

One of the women who came in the 5-ton wanted to contribute but had never used a gun. She had, however fished her whole life, especially with her husband, a deputy sheriff from Fredericksburg. She wanted to stay true to his memory and contribute to the community. With this pronouncement, Greg was pulled from the fishing crew, and was back on security rotation, almost exclusively stationed in the Osprey nest.

Somehow, despite his best efforts, Greg was relegated to "the officer" role by all of the Enlisted men. He was given his "bazooka", and was consulted on his demolition designs. He was clearly among better tactical soldiers, but still had valuable input on strategic issues, especially obstacles and position placement.

The Brain Trust

One day, when the leadership group, consisting of Gunny, Angel, Top, Sgt. Jones met in Greg's original house, below the Osprey nest. Joining them were the Chiefs of the respective teams: Mess hall Ethel, Doc, Greg's ever-present shadow, Este, and Sam. Jennifer also showed up, and when questioned why she was there, pointed down the hall and said, "That's my bedroom, this is my house too." Top knew that voice and shut up.

"Sheepdogs, we're getting chatter on the radios, which means that the wolves are close. The last time they came, they had a scout with an RPG. I don't want to lose 3 'dogs to a clean shot, so I say we use the 5-ton as bait. We need dummies or something, with some fake guns, so they think we're using the same tactic. Maybe they'll give themselves up."

Jennifer spoke up with, "I found a dress-making mannequin on a salvage run. Lord knows we have enough camouflage in the group. I'll take Greg's Boonie hat and rig up a machine gun out of a broomstick and some scraps. I think I can make it look realistic."

Greg looked at Jen, with admiration in his eyes. "Sweet! Except you can't have my boonie hat. Assuming you can find another hat, I'm good with this plan. Any objections?"

Greg, this isn't a democracy. You make a decision, and I'll talk to you off-line if I think you're being stupid. That's how commanders and senior NCO's do this."

"Top, I remember, and respect this, but we have non-military experts who may have good ideas. I'd like to hear them. How about – speak up if you have strong concerns, otherwise, we'll go with it unless Top, Bill, Manuel, Angel or Gunny pulls me aside. I spent 25 years in the corporate world, and it took me a while to learn about group-think.

"When I used to be in the corporate board room, I watched some CEO's come into a large group of staff, and say what the problem is, and what they thought we should do about it. Starting out that way makes everyone 'group think' along the path that has already been inserted into their thinking process. By the time I was a senior leader, I learned that I got a whole lot more from my team if I walked in and said 'Here's our agenda of things to discuss and problems to resolve.' Other than calling a close and signing off on a resolution, I didn't speak on an agenda item until the team had brainstormed through it, and debated the best solutions. Near the end of the discussion, I'd point out lessons I learned painfully around an issue like the one in question, then we'd gain consensus on a solution. Rarely did I have to decide – because the right answer often showed itself with enough discussion, and people smarter than I almost always had better ideas."

Greg saw Top have a bit of a concern on his face with all this squishy talk of 'discussion and consensus'. He said to Top. "Gunny has been here since day 1 and lived all we have. I know you out-rank her, but she's got the Marine perspective. Angel lived through more guerilla war than, I dare say, any of us, in Central America, or at least a different kind of warfare. None of us are current military, so we can go around the chain-of-command in favor of brainstorming an answer. They've all fought these bikers on this land, so please give me the benefit of the doubt on this one."

Top was trying to hold his tongue, then thought about it. He smiled and said "Yes, Sir Jefe."

"So, we have a decoy, unless anyone can think of a place to stash the 5-ton and use the Deuce as a decoy." Asked Greg.

"Si, Jefe," said Este. "There is a barn about half mile down road. 5 ton will be safe. No reason to blow that baby up. The truck will be safe. My new Ranger buddies are teaching me fun, um booby traps." He snickered at the way English idioms sometimes turned out.

"Outstanding, yelled Top! Greg, you just proved your point in less than 2 minutes. That 5-ton will be an asset if we can save it. We can pretty-up the Deuce-and-a-half, move it a bit, and make it look like a legit target. We can swap out some of the good rear tires for the blown front ones. Maybe we even rig a real rifle to pop off a few rounds remotely, to draw their fire?"

Greg smiled and high-fived Top. "That's teamwork and thinking outside the box team. Now we have a decoy and over-watch. The clothesline worked well, at low cost last time, how about we rig a few more biker-chokers?"

"I'm on it, Jefe." Esteban smiled at having a way to set up a few biker-killing trip wires. "Maybe they lie sideways off of path when bikers get close, like our snares. Tripwire bends tree, and noose tightens. Muy Bueno, Jefe. I'll also find, ha ha, 'volunteers' to fix up the truck."

Greg got up, and tried to hug Este, but he was too big around. "You are one sick giant, Shrek", joked Greg, referring to the guy's large size and kind heart – when he wasn't slaying dragons.

Este said "I'm like an onion, Jefe." Referring to the Shrek movie. I'll leave you safe with this team and go rig some death quicker than Iocane powder. They won't smell this coming, either!"

"Another Princess Bride quote, Esteban? I'm going to have to get you a working DVD player. I have your Christmas present in mind." Joked Greg.

Este did his Andre the Giant laugh from the same movie and walked out to set up snares to kill the bad guys.

"Let's talk heavy weapons", said Top. "We have Andre the Giant there on the 3ʳᵈ floor with the .308. Someone on the .50 cal. in the Eagles Nest. Our support team will be in the circle, farthest from danger. Greg and Jennifer will be in the Eagles nest with the 90MM." We're getting low on .308, so let's put the 240 in the Mortar nest, so they can defend our only artillery, but only in a pinch. I think we have 1 belt left, plus assorted stray rounds from Este's gun.

"What the fuck is that!?!?" yelled Greg. I'm out front, with my men.

"No, Jefe, you are the fuck not!" Said Top. Jennifer, Gunny and Angel all conveyed the message in various words, almost at the same time.

Sergeant Jones said, "As the uninvolved third party, let me tell you why, Sergeant Creighton: First, we need someone conducting the battle with 2 radios, long and short-range. That means in the rear. Second, you know the 90MM, and we need some heavy weapons back here in case they break through. Third, they might come from the harbor. They tried a frontal assault, and they are likely to try to flank us next time. If it were me, I'd flank the last killing zone. We're going to have support team members in water-facing windows. They'll know if they need to shift to circle attack formation. Jennifer is going to have to be not only loading, but watching the harbor behind us. It's likely they'll send something up our ass, and the 90MM will take out almost any boat they have, especially with the sand bar limiting the size of the boat. We have some flares for the mortar, so if you hear anything, you can call for some light, and then light-em-up!

Greg just looked at Jones, then at Jennifer. She nodded, and then said, "We'll need one of the M-4's. The Mauser is good at a distance, but too slow for multiple targets."

"Wow, Jen, I was just thinking that!" Greg was surprised at Jen's increase in battle tactic skills. He guessed that being in a fortified compound with bad guys all around sped up one's learning curve.

"We already discussed that." Said Sgt. Jones. You'll have an M4, along with 6 magazines. We've also set up a river-facing bunker near the boat ramp. You'll have to move your ladder to the side of the house, so you can disengage and move to the position if you start drawing fire. The view of the boat ramp isn't so good from the nest, so you'll have to drop down and run to the bunker, which is also protected from the view of any attackers on the boat ramp. I was able to improvise a crater charge and some honest-to-goodness claymores from my backpack around the boat ramp. That's their most obvious ingress point, because of the concrete slope. What they don't know is that concrete makes excellent shrapnel when there's an upside down crater charge buried in it. You think you can remember how to use an old-fashioned Claymore detonator, after that bull-shit radio-crank detonator you rigged?" Jones smiled sarcastically. "I heard the story. But seriously – nicely done, Jefe. Remember to yell 'Fire in the hole this time', and plug your ears, Hooaaahhh?"

"Hooaahh" Responded Greg with a smile.

The community boat ramp was 2 houses down from the Osprey nest. A quick slide down the ladder and sprint across a front yard could put Greg and Jennifer in a fortified bunker with a view of ramp and sand-bar at the mouth of the harbor. They didn't know what was coming, but having options was a beautiful thing.

"This plan was not just thrown together. It sounds like most of you already discussed it.", said Greg, confused.

"You don't think the NCO's first get-together would include the officer, did you?" Top said, smiling his Cheshire grin.

Let me run this by the group. The Chinese General, Sun Tzu, once said something like, "When you surround an Army, leave an outlet free. Do not press a desperate fool too hard." His thinking was that desperate men fight to the death, but those with a way out might retreat. "That may work in conventional war, but I think we made a mistake. We did that once, and it looks like we'll have to fight them again. If we had cut off the head when they were down to 6 bad guys, we might not be in this position – and Dahlgren might still be there. He looked at Jen apologetically.

"That was NOT your fault, Greg. Stop beating yourself up over that." She walked over and hugged him from behind. She may even have tweaked his nipple, although it was subtle.

Greg continued, with a smile, "These guys aren't going to retreat if they're winning, so we need a plan to cut them off when we're winning again. Any ideas?"

Sgt. Baker smiled and replied "I've got this covered. Do we have any civilians who can drive a 5-ton?" Discussion of his plan followed, with many smiles around the table. When this plan was nailed down, Greg circled back around to his last question.

"OK, so Jen and I are on the roof? You mentioned flares for the mortars. What's the plan on their deployment?"

Top said, "We'll have that back behind the brick house halfway between the community center, and the circle. We've already dug the pit and reinforced it with hardwood. They'll have a 2-man fire team, with over-watch from Este on the front, and you from the rear. Do NOT let them get flanked!" Radio discipline would be necessary to drop accurate mortar fire. Now Greg understood more why he was in the Osprey nest with both types of radios.

While the military vets were adept at calling in artillery, most of the Sheepdogs didn't know how to call it in, so the team discussed several pre-spotted artillery targets. They labeled them with easy-to-remember nicknames. This way, anyone with a radio could call in a target by nickname, versus an 8-digit latitude and longitude, so the first target would be at least close, and could be adjusted with distance and directional guidance.

"What's your fire station, Top?" asked Greg.

"In the ditches with the bitches." Smiled top. No offense, ladies. "I'll be holding the line at the berm and directing fire. We have a strategic retreat plan if there are too many, thanks to Este covering our ass. We rigged up a few detonator toys for Este and Gunny in the Nest. With the .50 covering from over-watch, we'll be able to disengage and regroup in the Mansion, where the civilians who can't shoot will be. If the Mansion gets hot, we have an escape route along the shore to the circle."

"If you hear the mansion go, Sir, that means that you'll be covering a strategic retreat. Stay frosty." Greg nodded at Top, sincere in his conviction not to lose any more people, if possible.

Top continued: "I've had PFC Newman working with the galley crew cooking up some improvised Napalm, in case the berm or mansion falls. We don't want fire like that out here unless the Shit has truly and desperately hit the fan. If the berm falls, they'll all be in hell, and we'll cook the Bastardos. Those that don't burn will remember it and be a little jumpy. Remember, most of these guys are raw recruits. They'll wilt in the heat.

"If the mansion falls, it will fall in a shit-storm of trouble for the attackers. The escape route along the water should be safe, and we've got some civilian escorts set near the water in case anything goes wrong. The path requires some crouching and crawling under docks, but we'll be covered and concealed all the way to the house next to the Osprey Nest at your old place, Greg. I figure nobody will be able to get close to there with you on, um, "bazooka", not to mention Jennifer's magic sheer force of will stopping bullets. She's made it this far through the big shit, and is unscathed. That's magic." Top laughed out loud, while Jennifer gave him 'the look'.

"Corporal Baker has been scouting with one of the PRC backpack radios that we brought with us. Doc is in the 5-ton monitoring and can relay info on the walkie. We'll know when they're coming. Baker has some surprises with him to slow them down, so we can be pretty sure he's back in the mortar pit before we need him. If not, I have a plan B."

Greg laughed. "Doc can't be in the truck. I understand he's there now, but we'll go with our civilian, and a little radio training. Well, y'all have already made the plan. What the hell are we here to discuss?"

Top said, with a straight face. "To get the officer's approval!" The group laughed. "But seriously, Greg. You had a few excellent strategic ideas that we haven't thought of. They may make the difference. We're a team, and we've got your back. Whooaahh?"

"Whooaahh, Gunny!"

Mourning together

That night, Greg was awakened by a body in the bed, climbing up his own body. He pulled his .40 from under the pillow and was greeted by Jen's voice, saying, "Relax, Greg." I don't know what else to do. I lost my husband, and I have this deep, deep need to hold him, or someone. If I promise to stay clothed, will you hold me, please?"

Greg looked up at Jen in her t-shirt and underwear, "Um, yeah." His voice was husky. "I'm not sure I can be a gentleman, but I'll try. I've felt the same way since I heard about Atlanta being Nuked."

"I feel like the worst wife ever," Jen sobbed quietly into his chest. "We never got the privacy at the barracks in Dahlgren to have sex. I haven't made love since before this STUPID thing happened. Now, it's too late, and I want to go back, and hold him, but he's dead. You're the only one I trust to not tell stories." At that confession, she fell on Greg and sobbed into his shoulder.

Greg spent every day trying to hold it together, so he could relate to Jen's situation. Most nights, he fell asleep crying into a pillow, wishing desperately that the pillow would hold him back. He whispered to Jennifer that he could use a good hug, too. He admitted, "I've not had anyone to hold, and some nights I sob into the pillow. Losing someone you love is the most crushing thing I've ever experienced. The only thing that's worse is not knowing."

Jennifer lay on top of Greg's chest, and wrapped her arms around him in a death grip. She also happened to be straddling his waist. After they both sobbed for a while, and some of the worst of the emotional loss was out, she was still on top of him panting.

"Um, Jen, I'm sorry. You should probably go."

"I feel you under me, and that's exactly what I need to feel. To feel some passion. We are BOTH keeping our clothes on, mister, as I'm a widow, but I still need to be held. Just hold me and follow my lead. I think we'll both enjoy this, and you will not say a word about it, ever."

Jen started rocking on top of Greg's under-armour boxer briefs. A few moans escaped her lips. Greg could feel her wetness through both sets of underwear, and damn-it, was enjoying this. He could feel Jennifer's labia open up and add lubrication to the whole deal. She kissed his forehead and said "shhhhh". She started moving forward and back. "You're just a sex toy, and I am too... let me know if I'm going too fast.

"Um... OK." Greg gasped out. He was growing beyond the bounds of his boxer briefs, and she didn't happen to care, as she stroked him with her powerful inner-thigh muscles. "I need a little 'me time', Greg. That's all this is. Hold me, please."

Greg held Jennifer and whispered in her ear that it would be OK, as she rocked, and climaxed on top of the tip of his cock, which had peeked out from the boxer-briefs. He also came, quietly, and knew that he'd need a fresh t-shirt, as this one needed to go in the laundry, along with her underwear. All of this was done without raising voices above more than a whimper. She shuddered one last time, and rolled off him, onto her side. He spooned her, kissing her neck, and his arm just happened to fall over the front of her. When he tried to move it from her breast, she reached up and moved it back. Then she reached back and put her hand on his cock. "Thank you, lover" was what he thought he heard her whisper, before her breath calmed down, and she started to doze.

As they both lay there, sated, she eventually rolled over, brushing his chest with her breasts. She kissed Greg's forehead, and said "time to go check on Annie. Thank you for holding me. I needed this more than you'll know. I feel human for the first time in a long time. It's like you hit my reset button. You're a good guy, Greg. I'd follow you anywhere."

He said "How about the shower? That's been good to us."

In your dreams, lover boy. "There's no warm water, and I told you, it's just a little exercise. Behave yourself."

He pulled her back on the bed by the back of her t-shirt, turned her around and kissed her. The kiss lasted a long time. "You know, I could call what you just did to me sexual assault. But I won't. Thank you, beautiful. I won't push, but you know I want more, if you ever do."

She kissed back, and put her tongue into his mouth. He finally got to find out what she tasted like. Her lips, and her passion were smooth, firm, and knowing. He could feel her body getting more pliable. "I'm sure it will be one day soon, big guy. But not today. Thank you, and you know I still love you. I just have stuff to work out in my own head."

"Can I at least have your panties as a souvenir?" He smiled.

She slapped his cheek, but playfully, and walked to the door. Her ass was as fine as ever.

"Kill me now, Lord", He said, and she giggled.

After Jennifer went back to her room with Annie, Greg rested, and fought with his conflicting thoughts. After about 30 minutes, he got up, with a surprising spring in his step, and spent the next few hours bullshitting with the night crew. Several of them were wondering about his jokes, and the spring in his step, but nobody wanted to ask, or get an answer. They knew that he wasn't getting laid, because they all totally knew when Gunny and Manuel were getting busy. Sound carried on the post-apocalyptic quiet nights in Rock

Harbor, especially with all of the windows open, and only screened over, in the August heat.

Date night.

Greg knew that canning and preserving the garden vegetables, like tomatoes, would be an important exercise to get through the winter, but they had a long way to go before winter survival became an issue. That said, they'd have to prepare long before it arrived. Late Summer brought a bounty of fresh food. On offer tonight were crabs, as usual, with some perch. They were done up in a nice seafood soup, which Ethyl called Cioppino. There was tomato, basil from the herb garden, some potatoes and onions, which were just starting to be readily available, and the inevitable Kudzu filler.

Ethyl splurged and had fried chicken from a few of the butchered chickens that had stopped laying. Everyone only got one small piece, and the breasts had to be cut in half, pounded flat and fried with a kudzu flour, to have enough for everyone. Greg and Jennifer were both on day shifts, so were getting off after a day of patrolling. There was increased activity from the Montross area. Gunshots meant the approach of more bad guys. Greg worried every day that their preparations would not be enough, but the toys brought from the Dahlgren group would help in making mass-casualties (of any invaders) more likely.

Greg and Jennifer sat down, facing each other. Next to them were the peninsula "lovebirds", Gunny and Manuel. They were conversing with others around them, but occasionally would speak in lowered-voice Spanish to one another. A few times, Jennifer looked at Greg like "did you hear that."

Gunny, while being 100% Marine, was at least 200% woman. She wasn't a "swoon if you whisper in my ear" kind of woman, but her love for Manuel was clear, and she showed it. She was never a woman who would paint her nails, but since she and Manuel got together, and eventually moved in together, she just seemed more

– Greg couldn't put a word to it – but she seemed to exude more sexuality when he was around.

Nobody would dare ask her about the change, or they'd be arm-barred, and whimpering for mercy in the dirt. If you were to ask her, she'd say she "dabbled" in Mixed Martial Arts, but Greg had seen her during their guard workouts, and she was quick, slippery, and deadly, much like a King Cobra might be. Yes, Greg knew snakes weren't really slippery, but the term fit for Gunny.

After Dinner, Jennifer asked Greg if she could "tour the perimeter" with him. As they carefully navigated the mine alley, she reached out and grabbed his hand. He turned to face her, and she looked into his eyes. "I never said Thank You for bringing us back in and moving us in next to you. I will always appreciate it, but I have to admit, I don't like living in the Mansion as much as I did when we lived under the Osprey Nest. The other night was a gift, too."

"I'm still trying to figure the other night out, Jen. Not complaining, for sure. I needed to be held as much as you did. I didn't face my loss and have needed to be held for a while. The mansion is a little cramped, and when we're on the same shift as Gunny and Manuel, it can get a little, um, loud." Greg laughed.

"Agreed. With no air conditioning, and screened windows open for a breeze, there's not a lot of secrets in the mansion. I wanted to go on this walk for many reasons, but that's another one. They're going to head back to the room and get busy. Did you hear that talk?!?!"

"I heard Spanish, but mine is not optimized for bedroom talk... yet." He looked away from Jennifer, embarrassed. "Um, I mean, you know... I learn a little more every day, but Este doesn't usually whisper sweet nothings in my ear."

Jennifer made a very un-lady-like snort, and laughed loud enough that the guard in the Deuce-and-a-half called out "Jennifer, You OK?"

"Just walking the path, Bill! No problem", she yelled out. Then she turned to Greg. "Maybe I'll teach you some more Spanish, then." She winked at Greg. "Like I was saying, I wanted to Thank you, but I wanted to spend some time talking through some stuff with you. I knew before today that Mike is gone, but it took a while for me to accept it. The other night helped."

"That night was torture, and re-birth, if that makes any sense. How is Annie doing?"

"She's 3 years old. She cries sometimes, but remember how she never really asked for Mike when we were under the Osprey Nest?" Greg nodded. "She saw him even less at Dahlgren. She's with Regina tonight. I asked a favor, and she's babysitting all evening, if necessary. Don't give me that look, mister! I've got a lot to get off my chest." At his eyes roving down to that part of her anatomy, she smiled, and said, "Zip it, I'm up here, pervert!" She pointed to her eyes. "Let's check out the circle defenses."

Jennifer let go of Greg's hand when they exited the path, and they separated and chatted with the fire team around the tree stand, making their way past the rest of the residents leaving the community center. They could see the kitchen crew inside cleaning up, and Greg waved at Ethyl, and blew her a kiss. She turned around, and shook her 80-year old behind at him, and Jennifer squealed in delight.

"Let's check out the view from the balcony on the Osprey the Nest. Make sure no bad guys are coming." Greg informed Jen that the team had stored the 90MM in the hidden closet, with 2 crates of assorted charges. The trade-off between security and response time was mitigated by the scouts they had deployed.

The Adirondack chairs under the Osprey Nest were still on the deck, facing the sand-bar, and the gorgeous sunset. The colors were more brilliant these days. Some said it was because of the lack of electric lights dimming the horizon. Greg privately worried that it was because of more ash particles in the air, from the nuclear detonations in Atlanta and NYC, or melting down power plants. He remembered reading a quote that said something like "Nuclear blasts are great for beautiful sunsets." So far, people who knew better than him (i.e. the Rangers) said that there was no danger from radiation, and this far after the detonations, he felt good about the prospects.

Greg and Jennifer sat down and enjoyed the sunset for a while. "So, what were Gunny and Manuel talking about?"

"He was veiling his words, because there were folks around them, but at one point he asked her how long dogs in heat are stuck together."

"Wow! Romantic! Greg laughed, but understood the nature of the proposal. "That was a pretty good line, for the right woman. After all, we are Sheepdogs!"

Jennifer slapped him on the hand but laughed at his joke. "Seriously, I just wanted to spend time with you, and this is a beautiful view. I miss this place, and I miss the 2 of us with our joking and flirtations. Is there any chance we can move back here?"

"We can do anything you want, but it's a security issue that we should discuss. I would raise eyebrows, but I don't care what they think at this point."

"Why don't you care now? Blue balls? Just kidding!" She blushed. "I don't know what came over me."

"Well, that too – but after last night, it's not terminal!" he shot back, smiling. "The 'came over you' was just gratuitous on your part, but for the record, I was under you. What I'm saying is that Atlanta got nuked months ago, and you heard about the unrest. Leigh is likely dead, was divorcing me anyway, and if she's alive, she's probably with her new man. If she decided to come here, she's got a snowballs chance of getting here. I've also come to terms with the fact that my daughter probably won't be here, but if she showed up, that's a different equation than what we're discussing. My baby boy was at Georgia Tech, close to the airport. I hope he went quickly, but if anyone could figure out a way to survive, Jared, my junior prepper would. If, that is, we're discussing what I think we are! I know it's only been about 5 months, but 5 months in the apocalypse, when you can die any day is a lifetime, and I can't mourn any more. I'll always miss them all, and there's a snowball's chance that Leigh will show up here, but I'll deal with that when and if the time comes. Even if she gets here, we're good. She chose not to stick with me. And there's plenty of houses that aren't this one to move into. We had a great life together, but I'm not holding on to it. Getting your heart broken that way sucks, and I'm not going to lean into it again."

"Your face is getting red, Greg. Calm down. I just need to talk through this. I KNOW my husband is gone. I saw the fireball. I'm worried about what you'll go through if we do this. I'm telling you that I want to do this, but I don't want to pressure you. I love you first for who you are, and what you've done for us so far. I also know that I'd like to get to know you a lot... better." I'm tired of hearing Gunny and Manuel do what they are, knowing that we could do the same – but I don't want to do it there."

"I don't want to be too forward, but we've been working hard, and I haven't had a shower in weeks. I saved up some water and would like to enjoy a shower with you again, but without, um, so much in between us." Jennifer was now the one to blush, as she looked at him.

Greg jumped out of his chair, and said "I'll fire up the propane, Jen!"

"There isn't any more propane here. It's been scavenged. It's tepid, clear rain water. But I made sure the towels on the rack and the sheets on the bed were clean. We can warm up after."

Because it was Summer in Virginia, the water in the bucket turned out to be a not-unpleasant lukewarm temperature. Greg put in a few drops of bleach, so that no nasties congregated in them afterwards.

"Aye Aye, Gorgeous", Greg said, as his eyes soaked up her body. He was, once again, not thinking about any kind of leadership or defense strategies. She had lost some weight since he saw her through the curtain months ago. Some of it was in her breasts, as he recalled, but she was solidly built, with a hint of her ribs showing under those beautiful B/C-cups. He was never going to be able to look at a woman and guess her size, but his Dirty old Sea Dog, Uncle Brian used to say 'More than a handful, and you'll sprain your tongue." Hers were the perfect size to his eyes.

She walked in the door, and started dropping her clothes on the floor, much to his delight. First, he got a prime view of her ass. Maybe she was exaggerating or not, but he was mesmerized by the way each butt cheek moved up and down separately as she walked. Then she turned around, and wiggled her finger to wave him into the bathroom. Gone were the days of the "Brazilian" bikini wax, and that was fine, to Greg's way of thinking. He'd never been with a red head, and he was mesmerized by her hair down below. She was indeed a natural Ginger. Tonight was theirs, and he was not going to waste a minute of their time together.

At first it was awkward, as the tub was narrow, and the shower curtain stuck to them. Trying to fool around standing up in a narrow shower is more difficult than some might think, but others around the world know this very well. It sounds good on paper, but the physics and geometry of it is difficult in a standard-sized tub. They finally found a good position, where she was standing on a few washcloths on the lip of the tub (so she didn't slip) and leaned against the wall on a towel. Greg was able to kiss her, and they were able to have a very fast and furious first session. While it wouldn't be at the top of Greg's list for the longest, it rivaled his honeymoon for the hottest. Lots of gasping, and panting, and nibbling, as they climaxed together, within a few minutes. It had been months since Greg had real sex, and he was just thinking of this as a warm-up, stretching session. Luckily, the other night took some of the edge off, and he was able to hold his own, and wait for her. There was much more to come if she would allow him several hours.

"Get out, Mister!" She finally panted after catching her breath. "I'm going to do a quick scrub-up. I'll be in bed, scrubbed fresh and clean in 3 minutes. How about we use that last gallon to rinse off. I'll give you a splash, then clean up and be in your bed in a few minutes for round 2."

Greg would always remember their first time together in the shower. That said, when Jennifer walked into the bedroom, naked and unafraid, Greg put his finger to his head, and said "Click – that's a picture that I will play over and over, including on my death bed."

Jen crawled across the bed on all fours, and the way that she dragged her breasts over his legs, balls, and chest really made the kiss worth waiting for. The kiss lasted, and lasted, and then she giggled and asked, "Round 2?"

"Yep, but round 2 is all about you." Greg whispered. "We're going to expand all 5 senses tonight. The sun is finally down, but I don't want you cheating. Lay on your back, please. Put your hands up over your head." He straddled her and lay a pillow over her hands. Then he placed a clean t-shirt from the drawer over her eyes.

"You've had enough visual for a while, and I'm not quite done looking at you. Just imagine that you are blindfolded and tied up. If you're not comfortable with it, you'll actually be neither and can get out of it. You can pull either off at any time, but try to trust me."

"I do. I do. She moaned. Me likey." As he started moving his fingers on her body. They weren't long tickles. They were short, fingertip brushes in unexpected places. An inch of fingernail on her inner thigh, a tongue across her belly button, the stroke of his thumb on her armpit. Each one got some sort of twitchy reaction from her."

"More, she groaned, as her back arched."

"Actually, no more..." He said, and she stiffened. "No more words for this exercise. I want to get to know your body, and the best way is non-verbal communication. My parents wereboth deaf, and I was raised in the deaf community, so I want to teach you MY language. You can use your body to communicate, or your moans, but you cannot speak English... Or Spanish he quickly corrected, as she started to open her mouth."

For the next half-hour, Greg explored Jen's body. Fingertip by fingertip. Caress by caress. He used his lips on her nipples, he used his tongue on her belly and thighs. He licked the bottom of her feet and kissed her on the neck. There was probably not a square centimeter of her body that he didn't caress, pinch, lick, or otherwise enjoy before that half-hour was over. He came up several times for long, deep kisses, knowing that his manhood was tickling her inner thighs. Several times, she tried to shift her body to envelop him.

"Not yet, baby. We have several months of angst to wear off. I know you also got yours in the shower, so I'm going to take my time for round 2." Greg kissed her, and bit her bottom lip gently, then he moved his face lower, slowly. He kissed both breasts, both on the nipples and under them, where he saw Jen was clearly still passing the "pencil test." She could put a pencil under them, stand up, and it would, indeed, fall out. This was not for lack of breasts, but her muscle tone was incredible."

As he moved his lips lower, and kissed her on her pubic mound, she arched up off the bed, with only her ankles and shoulders on it, and tried to push herself into his face.

"Yes, it's time for that, he mumbled huskily, as he used the tip of his tongue to probe her glistening, and ready lips, apart. He gently circled, and maybe signed a few letters of bad words with the tip of his tongue, until he located her clit, swelled and wanting some attention."

As her moaning got more guttural, and her bottom lifted off the be, begging for more contact, as her back arched, he placed 2 fingers under his chin, and slowly inserted them into her, fingertips up, and caressed the rough spot of flesh that he was pretty sure was her G-spot, as it is with many women. She made all kinds of interesting noises, groans, moans and screams as bucked her hips as she built to an explosion. She was moving her hips into his face so hard that he had to be careful and put his lips over his teeth, so he didn't accidently bite her. It took about one more minute for her to arch her back and climax, filling his beard with lovely Jennifer juice. She shuddered, as he rode her back down to the bed, keeping his tongue on her clit, teasing her. "Stop! Stop.", she sighed and shuddered, "I need to breathe." She moaned.

Greg Crawled up her body, and tried to kiss her, wondering if she would return the kiss, which she did, hungrily! He rolled her on her side and spooned up to her. He whispered in her ear, "I lasted longer in the shower than you did, and I haven't been laid in months!"

Jennifer giggled. "Nobody has ever done that in that way. The sensory override almost had me exploding when you were just touching my body. Once you moved down between my legs, I was already most of the way there. Let me catch my breath, and I want to ride you. I can feel you're already starting to get back in the saddle. That was AWESOME!"

"You make it easy to want to go again, beautiful." He whispered in her ear, then nibbled on her ear lobe.

Greg took the next few minutes to feel her ass against his manhood and reached around to play with her belly and nipples, while telling her how beautiful she was in her ear. "I've watched you, and tried to behave, but being here – I never knew how hot you were. I want to do this a lot, if you're willing."

"Willing? I'm able, cowboy!" she said as she shoved him onto his back with her behind, spun around, and sat up on his waist. Then she kissed him, slid OVER and past his manhood, and said "So, we have touch, feel, sound and... yep," she sniffed his lips and fingers), "smell covered. You got your taste. It's my turn, she said as she took him into her mouth, slowly, and deliberately moved down his shaft. She was really good at doing her part there, but after a few minutes, Greg pulled her up to him.

"Enough, if I'm going to be inside you, I want to be inside you down there. I don't want to just take from you. Let's share the pleasure."

"I was enjoying that, for the record." She scolded. But since you're such a gentleman cowboy, I think you need a cowgirl. She slid up his leg, flexing her inner thighs around his. Then, she got on her knees, lifted her hips off the bed, reached down, and grabbed Greg. "You hold onto whatever you need to so that I don't fall off!" She laughed that throaty laugh that he really was getting crazier about, although her giggle was sexy, too. Then, she grabbed Greg's hands, and put them on her breasts.

The next 40 minutes, plus or minus, were some of the slowest, sensual minutes of his life. Greg looked up at her body, mostly hidden by the dark, but his night vision was tuned in, and the curtains and screen facing the bay were open. Jennifer proceeded to slowly rise and fall on Greg. She would slide almost all the way off, until Greg was afraid that he would pop out. Then she would moan, and slide back down around his strawberry tip, wiggling herself as Greg tried to contain himself, literally. When she felt him starting to cum, she would stop moving, lean forward, and French kiss him, telling him that she wanted him to stay in her longer. When he had control again, she would squeeze her muscles down there, and then start stroking again. When they both finally came together, she fell on his sweaty chest, and whispered, in almost English, "More shower, as shoon ash I can feel my legshhh."

Jen and Greg slept for an hour or so. Then he opened his eyes when Jen grabbed his handle. "You go get some more rain water, cowboy. I need a rinse-off for round 3."

"Round 3 for me, darlin'." He said in his best cowboy accent. "You're at least on 4, if you're not lying."

"She looked him in the eyes, and kissed him deeply. Her tongue was gentle, yet probing, and he responded. "Cowboy, I need to wash up for my number 6!"

Greg looked at her said, "I wasn't keeping count, too busy enjoying myself, but a couple of those were the quiet kind, I guess."

"Indeed. The 'deep ones' ones can get loud, as you heard, but I just shudder and moan a bit for the first kind. After we shower up, I want you to get one more. The view from behind isn't as good, but those are the deepest ones." She looked down. "I see you have one more in the chamber, cowboy."

"We've already had all 4 kinds of orgasm, not just the first 2." Greg smiled, because it was his best racy conversational line – in the right setting. He always had at least one woman at a party that was among the kind of friends you could talk this way to, who would hear him and say what Jen was about to…

"FOUR Kinds! There aren't 4 kinds of orgasm, you liar!" She smiled and grabbed his ass.

"Yes there are. Sadly, some women go through life without ever having any – alone or with a partner. Many only know the first kind. Only the rare diamond gets to have all 4 – especially in one night."

"Not if they're with you!" She said, stroking his manly ego. She was sure that he knew she was teasing, OK, mocking him.

"True Story." he said with a straight face. "First is the kind you got from my tongue – clitoral. Most women who have ever had one, by themselves, with a toy, or with a partner know that one very well. You named the second type – the 'deep one'. That's where I find your g-spot. Yours, by the way is the rough patch on the top, inside, just under your belly button." Jennifer blushed.

"OK, Casanova. What's number 3?"

He smiled. You had those, too… Multiple, where you get both kinds in the same session. You admitted to that one, cowgirl. Before you burst from anticipation, the fourth is 'simultaneous'. I promise, we checked that box at least twice. First in the shower, based on your feedback."

"That's cheating!" She giggled and slapped him on the ass again.

"I hear there's a fifth, but I'm not into anal." Greg said with a serious expression.

Just to see the look on his face, she said, "Not yet you aren't." Yes, the look of confusion, surprise, and then genuine laugher was worth it, even if she probably wasn't either."

By the end of the night, Greg really could write a story about the virtues of Jen's fine ass versus her front. It's not that he wanted to rule on which was better, but he did come to appreciate all the angles that she had to offer. They got about 3 more hours of sleep before it was time for the day shift. Greg decided that being in charge had to have some benefits, and he grabbed a few more gallons of water, and they had a morning shower, with stroking and kissing, but neither was dying for more sex. Their hips and parts were a bit sore.

"Let's go waddle to breakfast, Cowboy." If I knew you had those tricks, I might not have waited so long.

"Jen, at least half of those tricks we made up together last night. MY desire to not disappoint you was what kept me going."

"Disappointment absent, cowboy." Then Jen smacked his ass, hard. "Now GET UP, SOLDIER! It's time to save the world."

"No pressure." Greg then returned the favor and left a hand-print on her fine behind. Not a dark red one, but something to remember. They had slapped and pinched throughout the night, so he knew she was Ok with it, but she still made a little "Meep" sound. They both cleaned up, dried off, went to the mansion to wake up Annie, geared up, and went back to breakfast and the front lines.

"I sure hope I don't die any time soon, but If I do, I'll replay last night before the lights go out." Greg said, as they held hands and walked out of the circle, under the view of a smiling few who were out and about early.

"Don't you die, cowboy. I want to get to know more of you. Oh, by the way, we're moving out of the Mansion. I don't want your soldiers to mutiny after having to listen to us like we were last night."

"Yes, Ma'am. I'll fix up Annie's room when I am off-shift. Is it safe to assume you'll be staying with me?" He looked her way, worried.

"That's the only way I'll move in with you." She paused and looked into his eyes. "I love you. I think I have since Mike took me away. I've dreamed of us. Is that bad?"

"Not for me, sugar. I'm thinking I was in the neighborhood, myself. I'm falling hard right now, cowgirl." He admitted shyly, as they walked into the breakfast hall, holding hands.

"Well it's about fucking time, Amigo!" cheered Angel, as the whole community made lewd comments or gave a round of applause. Even Annie was cheering, although she didn't know why, exactly. Her mom was smiling for the first time in a long time, and that was enough for her.

Gunny walked over, hugged Jennifer, and yelled "Ooooh-Rah". The rest of the soldiers in the compound gave their own version of the response – "Hoooaaahhh!" Only Top had a pensive look on his face.

New friends

At breakfast the next day, Top and Greg were in a corner, having a conversation. "Look Top, the 'dogs got together without me and assigned Jennifer and me to the rear. How far do you want us to run when stuff goes down? Another thing - For the sake of Morale and all that is holy, please, please move Gunny and Manuel down there, or at least out of the mansion. People need to sleep! And it can't be healthy for the single ones!"

"I've heard some complaints from the single soldiers, Jefe. I think you're right. You may not have noticed, but several couples have formed. You'll never guess who Esteban has a thing for."

"Based on his size, I hope it's the 5 Ton, for everyone's sake! The tail gate may not survive, and I hope they give tetanus shots in Mexico City!"

"If you were to say the fire truck, you'd be close." Said Top. "It's Lindsey the firefighter, but she and Shane have been keeping their relationship on the down-low. Esteban took her rejection like a man, and I don't think we need to worry about any friction, but the poor guy is disappointed. I pity the fool that shows up with aggression in their mind. He'll crush them, just out of sexual tension."

Both men laughed at the joke. "It's a shame she doesn't have a thing for him, he's such a good guy. He'll find love one day. Give him a break if he's a little crestfallen. He's asked to be on 5-ton duty for a while. I think it's so he can either gather his thoughts, or cry alone. Maybe he's toking it up a little, since we're out of booze. Hopefully he'll find some peace before the shit hits the fan again. We both know that we need Esteban to be sharp and focused when the next wave comes."

Top looked at Greg with a shocked look on his face. "Smoking weed?!?!" My soldiers aren't druggies!"

"He's not a soldier, Top, but I was just joking about it out in the shed. He's too disciplined to smoke while on guard duty. That doesn't mean he won't when he's off duty, though. We all deal with this situation in our own ways. I don't know the answer, but keep in mind that we're desperate enough that we've rigged the mansion to blow, worst case. Trade that off with an attack from the rear as another possibility, and death is all around us. If someone burns a little "happy grass" when they're off duty, I'm good with it. Don't tell me there aren't a few cannabis crops growing out here. Hell, I've had a toke with some of the residents!" The look on Top's face was incredulous. Greg tried to calm him down.

"It's the fucking apocalypse, brother. DEA isn't going to swoop down on us, and how harmful can an occasional toke be. Pot has only killed 7 people in the history of the world: One person ate themselves to death. 4 friends got the giggles after a particularly funny joke and laughed themselves to death. The last, lucky 2 fucked themselves to death."

Top laughed, nodded, and said "Whatever floats your boat. None for me, thanks. The shit they grow here is brown-weed. Now, that stuff I had in Taiwan... I'd do that again!" Top laughed at the look on Greg's face. "Yeah. Close your mouth. This old dog has seen the world!"

"You move where you want to, and I'll have a talk with Manuel and Gunny. I think you're right there, and having 2 strong and deadly couples anchoring the circle won't be the worst thing in the world. You clearly don't care if people are talking. I have your back on this, as long as you don't lose your razors edge with your druggie habits, or that woman keeping you up at night!"

"Come on, Top. How many hours of sleep does a man need?"

"The Army issued us 5 hours a night, so get at least that much, or I'll be on your ass, Sir."

Greg noted that this "Sir" thing was starting to get out of hand. Somehow, Jefe was different, after all he was the Chief of Security. As a non-commissioned officer in the Army, he didn't like the moniker. Top saw his face, and to help cushion the blow, he smiled and said, "Well, you don't work for a living any more. Hence, you're an officer. That said, at least you're at least a Mustang, and they don't suck too bad." At the look on Greg's face, Top slapped him on the back, and walked away guffawing. Mustang officers are those that rise through the enlisted ranks, then go to Officer Candidate School (OCS). All else being equal, they garner more respect from the enlisted ranks, and tend to treat their men a little better, having had to live the life of guard duty and Kitchen Patrol (KP) that comes with being a junior enlisted man. Leadership lesson: Humility breeds empathy.

Just then, the radio squawked. Barn Owl here. 3 men walking down the road. They're Armed, but not sneaking. They see the truck, and all 3 just put their rifles up over their heads in a T, with fingers off the trigger.

Greg clicked on the radio. "OK, Este. Keep an eye behind them, in case they're scouts. Top and I will be at the trail head. Break. Bill, you're at the truck, right?"

"Roger, plus one. We see them."

"Glad you're there, Bill. Stop them, but don't be too aggressive. Glad you're on duty, brother."

The radio clicked twice, acknowledging the order.

Top and Greg ran towards the front. Without any orders, a handful of men and women streamed out of the mansion behind them, and followed silently, armed and ready for action. In 2 minutes, they were at the trailhead, and saw Bill chatting with a trio of men. One was Caucasian, one looked Hispanic, and one was clearly African American. The Black man was standing in front and led his men in moving their weapons from the overhead T to the ground. Bill's rifle was pointed up, and 'Betto had his on his hip, pointed up. The 3 men startled when Greg cleared his throat. They turned around and had more than a half-dozen men behind them, rifles pointed at the road.

Greg walked forward. "Hi gentlemen, I'm Greg, and these are the Sheepdogs."

The black man walked forward with his hand outstretched, and a huge smile on his face. "I'm Leo. We come from Tappahannock, down the road. We wanted to introduce ourselves to our neighbors holding our Northern front. We've heard a lot about you."

"Nice to meet you, Leo. We haven't ventured that far from here. Would you like to come in and have some refreshments? Are you OK with leaving your weapons with my men in the truck? We'll return them."

"No problem, Greg. We did our homework. We know you're good people. Several of the outlying farmers are friends and family of me and my friends here. We'd be happy to join your group for some snacks. I'd say it's a long walk from Montross, but we left our 4-wheelers a mile or so back. We didn't want to intimidate."

"I saw you with your rifles over your head in a T. That's very non-threatening, and really settled down my guys, including the first one who saw you."

"Yeah, it's not foolproof, but that's our signal for an un-threatening friend in our town. We also have a flashing light signal, letting us know a friend is coming. It's not very original, but it works."

"What, like Shave and a haircut, two bits." Greg laughed, joking with Leo.

Leo looked surprised. "Yeah, man. You got it in one. Maybe we need to change our code, guys!" The other 2 men with Leo laughed. Greg laughed with them.

The group went back to the community center, and the visitors had their plates filled with filling, if bland breakfast. The leaders of both groups got down to business.

Greg said, "So, Leo, what's up in your part of the world?"

"Well Greg, we're holding the Route 360 bridge on your southern flank, effectively cutting off access to the peninsula by vehicles. We've lost our share, as I understand you have, too." Both men looked at each other and shared the sadness of leaders who have lost team members.

"Thanks for that, Leo. We were barely able to hold our own little community, I can't imagine what you're going through."

Well, Greg, we have a much larger population, and most are good folks willing to fight for freedom. That said, we heard you decimated that gang that was chewing us up a few months ago. We also hear that they're reconstituting the gang, and we haven't heard the end of them, but you punched them right in the nuts, and we appreciate your buying us all some time."

Top said, "We won't be letting any of those fuckers get away next time. If they pick a fight with us, they're all dead!"

Pete nodded. "Understood, Top. These guys are pigs. We need to slaughter them. The problem is that we don't know where their HQ is. We think some are the bad guys across the river in Tappahannock, but we also hear of others up the peninsula, and random reports of more south of y'all, down by Cabin Point. We don't know if they're all the same group, or just multiple groups of thugs."

Jen asked, "What if they're the same group, and just moving around a lot? They all had motorcycles the last time we fought them? I think there are ways to get around the bridge you hold."

"Well, Ma'am, our smartest people think the same thing. We don't hear the bikes moving, but they could have some boats or other river transport, and that would work. We're here to give you the heads up on that, because we think they have some version of a Navy. We also just wanted to touch base with you, as there are so few good guys, and safe communities out here."

Greg said, "You're probably too far away for us to keep in touch by radio, but you can count on our support if you send runners. We know your signals and won't gun anyone down if they use your code. Heck, we don't gun anyone down unless they are hostiles."

"Same with us, Greg. We want you to know that we think we need to band together when possible. 'Hang together or surely hang separately', right?"

"Agreed, Pete. We've got your back. These guys need to be wiped out and made an example of. There are still good people like us all around, or at least I have to hope so." Greg Paused. "Do you have more than hope on that?"

Pete smiled. "Yep. There are some pockets of civilized folks across the Potomac, and between us and Richmond. The closer you get to the cities, the less likely it is you'll find survivors. I can't speak for anything west of 95, South of the James, or North of Waldorf, but these waterfront communities are holding their own."

Greg smiled, and reached for Jennifer's hand. "Then there's still hope for all those of us that have people out there." Jennifer smiled a sad smile, and Greg Squeezed her hand.

The rest of the evening was spent telling stories and laughing with the new neighbors to their South. The 3 men from Tappahannock bedded down in a corner of the community center and were escorted out at dawn to head home and pass the news to their community.

Precursor

Greg got a call on the radio just after dawn the next day. Este was calling in an intruder.

"Jefe. One woman, limping. Curvy, brown skinned Amazon beauty. Sorry, TMI, boss. What you want me to do?"

"She could be a mole, or a diversion, Este. Keep your eyes out. Let her get to the Deuce stand. You stay in the 5-Ton barn. Watch outbound, buddy, OVER." Greg emphasized the word.

With all the civilians on the net, 'Over' had pretty much gone the way of the military time. No longer was it '14 hundred hours'. It was "air force time", or 2pm again on the radio. The military guys gave up, as it communicated the necessary information.

The woman finally made her way the last quarter mile to the Deuce and looked at it as if confused why there was an Army Truck in the middle of the road. "Help! I need help! You... Boy... come down here. Help me out. I can't walk no more."

Este continued to watch the road, but it was just about shift change. His relief came and tagged him in with no issue coming from the general direction of their potential threat – Inland. Este walked back to the Deuce, where a woman was chewing out Bill.

"Look Bruddah, Dey come and kill my Ohana. Dose men da kine bad. Watch youself. Hey, you got any food?"

Este came down the road as Greg came out of the mine trail. They met Bill and the new guest at the trailhead. Este had his rifle in low ready and was trying to understand the newcomer.

Greg had a good look at the newcomer. She was about 6 feet tall, and a strong, but bulky 275 lbs., after all these days of hunger. Greg wasn't judging, as he arrived here at 6'1 and 300 lbs. She had brown skin but wasn't Hispanic or Black. As he was half-Hawaiian himself from his Grandparents, both Pearl Harbor survivors, he trusted his gut and took a shot.

"Aloha, Seestah. What's up?" (Hello, sister.)

The woman smiled and said "Aloha" and started spouting off in a Pidgin that was more Hawaiian than English.

"Jefe, what's she saying?" Asked Este, as he checked out the only woman that could near his size, with a smile. It was clear to both Greg and Este that this woman's attitude meant that wasn't an immediate threat, but she would very likely have some intel. Greg also knew that pissing her off would be a huge mistake, as he married into a family of Hawaiian women. Be nice, you live. Be not nice, and life sucks. She also commanded respect, as many Hawaiian women do, even without trying.

"She's Hawaiian, Este. Let's get her inside and find out what she knows." Based on her Muumuu, or sun-dress, in Hawaiian, she wasn't packing any guns or explosives, as there was no place to hide them. "What's your name, Seestah?"

I'm Leilani, I was staying at my Bruddah's house because I needed to leave my husband in Hawai'i. Kimo – that' my brother – lived halfway between Montross and here. He had a nice little house way up on the Nomini River. They killed him and took his wife. One man tried to tie me up, and he..." Here she shuddered, and a tear rolled down her face. "Failed. Permanently."

"That's OK, Leilani, you follow me, OK. Be careful – we have landmines on this path. You just step where I do. My name's Este, and those bad men have tried to take us before. They gave me this scar." At that, he lifted up his shirt and showed her his bullet wound. Greg was surprised to see that he also had been growing a

6-pack under there. The originally pudgy Esteban was looking more like the wrestling and movie star "The Rock" than the "Shrek" that he was originally associated with. Then he looked down sadly. "We killed all of them but 6. I'm sorry we didn't get them all. Trust me, we won't make that mistake again."

She took a minute to gather her will, and possibly to check out Este's physique, then nodded her head, and followed Este down the path. As they exited landmine row, she saw the community and smiled. "Look at those dandelions! I hope you have the dandelion wine."

"Dandelion wine?" Greg and Este said in Unison.

"Oh, I make you some. It is Ono!" Upon seeing their confusion, she clarified with "Good, tasty. I'll show you soon. Hey, you got something to eat? I'm hungry."

"Take her to the community center, Esteban. There should still be some breakfast to be had, since Ethyl keeps some snacks for those going off-duty. Based on their location, it sounds like we have a day or 2 to get ready for these sick fucks."

"Si Jefe. I'll take care of her and find a place that she wants to stay in." Greg walked ahead of them, let Esther know that they had a guest, and grabbed a breakfast wrap to go. Now that they had harvested much of the winter wheat from the surrounding farms, flat-bread and tortillas were often the delivery mechanism for the rest of the meal. Esther did occasionally break out the sourbread, as she had her tricks for keeping the last of the original yeast going, but a lack of plentiful sugar only occasional milk in trade meant that leavened bread was rare treat. That said, she had friends among the local community, and was always trading for something. Her skills at putting together a good meal were, by now, legendary.

The community decided that survival was better than personal property in the last month or so, and were willing to use jewelry from their own, or salvaged houses to get those things necessary to trade for essentials.

Greg went back to the Osprey nest, spending the day keeping guard of the water approach, and watching Jennifer play with the kids in the "schoolyard" across the street. Annie would occasionally call out to Greg and show him some acrobatic trick, like a semi-cartwheel or a trick on the trampoline. That little girl was really growing on him, but still occasionally would do something that Maria or Jared did at that age and create a twinge of sorrow.

After an uneventful guard shift, Greg returned to the mess hall to find Leilani ordering around everyone except Ethyl, who was smiling at Leilani's leadership style in the kitchen, and seemed glad to have a second-in-command. Doc had bandaged up Leilani's foot, and pronounced her OK, with just abrasions from walking so far without any footwear. One of the laundry team produced some men's flip flops big enough to fit her feet.

Greg liked to preserve the Hawaiian traditions in his family. His daughter's name was changed to Maria Kai at one year old, as the tradition was for the matriarch to get to know the baby, then give them a Hawaiian middle name once they were a year old. He knew that a Hawaiian woman in the kitchen was someone to respect, and fear. The food situation was about to get a lot more interesting. Ethyl was an excellent cook and bringing in a whole new culture's choices of food would be amazing.

Greg sat down next to Jennifer, who immediately said "You HAVE to try these oysters. What Leilani did with them is fabulous! The salad has a flavor I've never tasted, either. She actually made Kudzo tasty, instead of just edible!" Annie endorsed her mom's opinion of the food, with a smile and thumbs up! Her face was smeared with whatever this Ginger-flavored dressing was called.

"Where'd she get ginger, Jennifer?"

"Powdered, maybe? I don't care, as long as she keeps it up!"

Ethyl came over, and put her hands on Greg's shoulders, massaging them a bit. Then she leaned forward, kissed him on top of the head, and said "Bless you, son. Thanks for the help." Before Greg could even turn around and respond, Ethyl was walking back into the kitchen, shouting orders for the dishwashers to get moving, as they were all just standing around watching the tropical storm that was Leilani.

Este moved Leilani into the house next to Greg and Jennifer. Les had moved out some time ago, and into the mansion. Greg didn't know if it was to hear the community "porn radio" that was Gunny and Manuel, or if he was just lonely. He did like to take his turn on the Ma Deuce in the Eagle's nest, but even then, his M-1 never left his side.

Leilani said that the mansion was too crowded, and she wanted to have quick access to the dock at that house, which did indeed stick out farthest in to the Harbor. She asked about some fishing gear, which Greg provided from the family boat house. Properly armed for fishing, she promised more culinary delights. She was disappointed that there wasn't squid or octopus in the harbor, but Greg told her that the Skate, or Rays could be caught, and their wing meat was a lot like calamari.

"I'm a little worried about a stranger not being supervised." Greg whispered to Jennifer once they were lying in bed, after another amazing night of some more vigorous exercise between them. "My gut tells me we can trust her, but trusting the community to an unsupervised stranger?"

"I trust her, too. A woman's intuition is rarely wrong. Don't worry, though, I'll keep an eye on her when I can. Jen got up, stretched, and Greg was treated to her sexy silhouette against the screen sliding door. She walked over and looked out. "Right now, she's got 3 fishing rods in the water. She's dancing some hula or something at the end of the dock. It's beautiful. I think we're good."

Curious, Greg got up and walked to the screen. Mostly, he wanted to put his hands on Jen's body again, but he also wanted to see what was going on. "I've seen that dance at the Hawaiian State Society Luau. I don't remember what it's for, but they did it every year. It could be mourning, or a fishing dance, or whatever, but damn, she's graceful. Well smack my ass and call me stupid – that brings back memories."

Jen moved as fast as a cat and was behind him. She smacked his ass, and whispered in his ear, "Take me again, Stupid."

Greg could take orders as well as give them. The hour, though not hours tonight – Greg remembered Top's warning – passed in happiness. She proposed, through the positioning of her body – words weren't necessary – a new position that they hadn't tried. This ended up with both on their side. To open herself to him, she lifted her top leg, with her knee up and hooked around his knees, as he was behind her. He liked this position, as his hand was under her waist, and the free one on top could find interesting places on the front of her to caress, tickle, and otherwise massage. Once again, all '4 types of orgasm' were achieved, even if not 6 times. Then he slept a few hours. Getting out of bed, with Jen there, covered only partially by a sheet in this summertime heat, was one of the more difficult things he ever had to do. But he was a leader, and duty called.

Convo on the dock

Greg stretched, and got up. Time to spend some free time in the Osprey nest. He walked to the window and looked around, and saw Leilani still fishing. He got dressed in Gym shorts and an Army t-shirt, then walked out on the dock. At the sound of the sliding screen door, she startled, and looked his way. "It's just me", he whispered. He opened a rain cistern in the corner and splashed water on his face. "I have some bottled water inside; do you want a drink?"

"No, your sweet friend Esteban made sure I had some supplies. Sound like you had a good night so far. You with dat pretty girl from dinner? You know sound travels far on the water here."

Greg blushed, "Yes, I'm lucky enough that Jennifer loves me. Her daughter Annie does too."

"*Her* daughter?"

"Yes, her husband died and my ex-wife and kids are probably dead. While she's not my ex-wife yet, she and my son Jared were in Atlanta, which was Nuked. My daughter, Maria Kai, is in Philadelphia. I can't say "was" because I have hope that she'll get here. That home," he pointed at the Osprey Nest, is the Chambers Family Ohana home. This is where we are all supposed to come if bad things happen, and they haven't got here yet."

The quick surprise on her face was replaced by a smile. "Chambers. Yes, I know the name. My brother always talked about Tony and Evelyn, and I even knew some of the family back on the big island. Adam was her brother, no? I look forward to joining your Ohana, too – some day, if you think it's OK. Mine is all gone." She said sadly. "I look forward to meeting Jared and Maria Kai. Then we won't be the only ones here with Hawaiian blood in our veins." She smiled brightly at Greg, and he saw that she seemed CERTAIN that she would meet Maria Kai one day. Tears flowed freely from his eyes.

Looking to change the subject, Greg changed the subject. "Any luck fishing? I usually don't have much luck this close to the docks – especially at low tide."

"Yeah, not much luck for me either. I only got 1 bucket full of catfish, she frowned. I tried calling them, but they are Haole fish. They don't speak Hawaiian" She laughed.

"One buck...!" Greg spluttered. "One bucket of fish? It's low tide! I need to introduce you to Sam."

"Oh, yes, I met Samuel. I'm going fishing with him at high tide. He says that's the best fishing. I can't wait for high tide! Only shy catfish in here at low tide."

"Please, Leilani, be gentle with him. You caught many fish at low tide. He will say that's not possible. Try not to break him! You called the fish Haole. My Grandma used to call me Haole Greg, or the 'white Greg', because of my Scottish background. Are you saying the fish are white?"

"No, the fish just don't speak Hawaiian," she laughed. "You don't either... or barely. Kimo was my brother, and he could talk Pidgin. I think he would like you anyway, though. You have a hero's heart. Kimo died well, like a hero – and he made it so I could get away. He took many with him." A tear rolling down her cheek caught the moonlight.

"A good death is all the rest of us can hope for. I hope to give my enemies bad deaths, and when my time comes, meet whoever is our maker with pride." Said Greg.

"Me too. I gave a man bad death day before yesterday. He shit himself. Good riddance.", Leilani cried quietly.

"I'm going to go up on the Osprey Nest to keep watch. If you need me, just toss a pebble from the landscaping up on the roof."

I think I can sleep now, Greg. Thank you for the talk. She moved the fish, head down, into a bucket she made with holes in with a kitchen knife. She half-submerged it in the water, tied to the dock so that the fish were under water, but the top was at the high tide line. They thrashed a little, but couldn't get out. If you still up in a few hours, lift the bucket up a few inches for me. If not, I think they still Ok. Catfish are hard to kill. I will drop 'em off at kitchen before breakfast. Good night, Gregory. Then, Leilani embraced him in a hug that almost, he would never admit if she did, squeezed the breath out of him. Then she bent down and kissed him on the forehead, probably the only woman on the peninsula tall enough to do that, and went up the stairs to sleep in her new home.

Greg watched her go. He saw the classic Hawaiian beauty in her. Este was already smitten. Greg wondered how long it would take for Este to realize it. That said, Leilani would very likely tell Este, as the Hawaiian society was Matriarchal. Women didn't typically wait for a shy guy to make a move. Greg recalled that, although only a little Hawaiian ran in his wife's blood, Leigh's twin sister *proposed to him for Leigh*. Sitting on that very table there under the ladder, Greg recalled, as he walked to the ladder, Leigh's twin, Sabrina had pulled out her appointment book and asked "So, when's the wedding?"

On the way home, Leigh and Greg were silent for a long time. Finally, Greg said "I guess we're getting married. Let's pick a date!" Leigh let out a deep breath, grabbed Greg's hand, and said. Let's not. Let's just elope when the time feels right. They did just that and were very happily married for most of 24 years when the lights went out. She didn't make fun of him for his crazy prepper stuff, and he didn't mind her compulsive sweepstakes entries. After all, she had won many trips and other valuable prizes. His hobby only proved valuable at the time of the lights going out, and he didn't even have the supplies when he needed them! At least he hoped Leigh and Jared knew, if only briefly, that he was right about TEOTWAWKI. Best case, the supplies he left at home helped them survive for as long as she wanted to. She always said she just needed one bullet if the lights go out. She didn't want to live in a world without hot baths and air conditioning.

Greg climbed the ladder with the 90MM in his hand, and the Mauser over his shoulder. He was going to settle in on the lawn chair cushion for another night of over-watch. He did a quick radio check, to which Top replied "Go back to bed, Sir, that's an order."

Greg replied, "You're not the boss of me – I'm good, Top." Angel clicked in long enough to laugh out loud. Then, seeing the stars, and no threat of rain, Greg dragged up a crate of ammo for the 90MM and covered it anyway, with a plastic garbage bag. This crate was a hand-mixed bag of high-explosive and anti-personnel flechette rounds, He had another one just like it tucked into the secret closet. Flechettes, or anti-personnel steel darts, which had tail-fins just like dart-board darts, but were made of steel or tungsten, would shred all people in the circle of destruction with metal slivers. The high explosive rounds, or HE, were made as shaped-charge bunker busters, and would be fatal against any vehicles shy of Armored Personnel Carriers and Tanks. Combat Engineers were issued 90MM's into the early 1990's, when he was active duty, as field-expedient bunker busters. It's easier, and less fatal, to shoot an HE round into a bunker than to sneak up to it with a satchel charge, for sure. Many soldiers, from Normandy to present day died trying to throw a satchel charge into a machine gun nest or bunker. The weapon was retired for several years, until they were brought out of mothballs for the wars in Afghanistan and Iraq. The reloadable nature of the weapon made it more efficient than the AT-4, one-shot Anti-Tank weapon, and the LAW rocket, or

Light Anti-Tank Weapon. They still were not built to take out armor of any significance, but they would breach the hell out of a house, wreck a truck, destroy a bunker if shot through the shooting port. This flexibility accounted for its resurrection as the perfect tool for those wars.

Greg kept watch for a few hours, through the "witching hours" of Midnight through 3, when most sneak attacks would happen. He got a couple more hours of sleep, even though he had to resist temptation when he crawled in with Jen, and she snuggled her fine ass up against his waist. They had plenty of time for more of the early-evening antics they had earlier – he hoped. So, he draped his arm over her side, conveniently settling it on the perfect handful of breast, and slept well for a few hours.

It's said that when Einstein was in full-creative mode, he had several cat-naps per day. He then woke up to bursts of creativity. What's not said is that every 3rd or 4th day, he would sleep for 11 hours straight, catching up on REM sleep. Greg slept way past wake-up and shift change, and nobody bothered to give him any crap. Even Esther had some leftover breakfast for him. She smiled as she gave it to him, and said, "You're a good boy."

Leadership lesson: The troops talk, there are no secrets in a war.

The Scout

It was mid-morning, after Annie and the rest of the kids were fed. Because it was Sunday, there was no school. Greg asked Annie if she wanted to play a new game. One of the salvagers had found a set of Polly Pocket miniature toys in one of the houses, and Greg appropriated it from the pile of toys in the school.

"What game, Greg?" asked Annie.

"Well, it's called Polly Pocket, but it's really about Bug, the super-hero fairy bug."

"Super hero fairy bug?" Annie looked skeptical, until Greg pulled the little bug with wings from his back pocket.

"Annie, this is 'Bug'. He's Polly's friend. And this little girl," he produced a little Polly Pocket doll, "Is Polly." He reached into a cargo pocket and pulled out another half-dozen little toys. "These are her friends. See that little house over there? That's their village."

For the next few hours, Greg and Annie played make-believe with the little characters, creating a fantasy world of monsters, good guys and super-bugs. Greg did the same thing years ago with his daughter, Maria. He slipped right back into the land of make-believe, glad to be relieved of the burden of leadership for a few hours. His son preferred playing jet fighter, and dropping bombs on targets, but make believe was what most of their childhood was about.

The next afternoon, Greg got another radio call from Este. "Jefe. One man. Marpat (Marine Pattern camouflage), walking down the road with M-4 and a big tube underneath. Walking with weapon shouldered, and hands up. What you want me to do? Over"

"That's an M-203 rifle with 25 MM grenade launcher, I hope. What's your gut say? Over"

"He's Bueno, Jefe. He walks like a hero."

"This is Top. I'm taking 2 Sheepdogs with me on bikes. We'll meet you at the trailhead, Sir. Este, stay covered, that 25 MM will hurt even you, Over."

"I'm Oscar Mike." Greg got on the Harley Sportster in his front yard. After some wobbly training, they assigned the bike to him. He protested that he was too big, but Doc said, "You can do the least damage with it, and it will carry your 200-plus lbs. pretty well, as long as it's not a road trip." He smiled and winked at Greg.

Greg grabbed the Osprey Nest's M-4 and roared off with it over his shoulder. He saw Jen climb into the Eagles Nest and take up a guard position with the Mauser. "That is so hot," he thought to himself. Annie was in the community schoolyard, introducing her friends to Polly and Bug, and they would see her at dinner.

At the head of the Trail, Top was smiling and talking with the stereotypical Bad-ass Marine. His back was straight, he had confidence and a steely glance. Angel had his weapon, and the Marine looked like he could care less. His look was pure predator, or sheepdog. It was up to Greg and Top to find out.

Greg walked up and stopped next to Top. Top looked the man up and down and said "I know you."

Yes, you do, Top. "Staff Sergeant Robert Pulaski. You might know me as 'Ski'. Marine Recon out of, and I stress the "out", Dahlgren – nobody wants to be in there these days. I worked with the big gun team. I came back to Dahlgren to a shit-storm, and I've been shadowing the pukes that did it. They're not far away. I expect them to hit you tonight. All I want is the leader of the meth-heads. He got my brother hooked, and dead. I'm going to tear his spine out with my teeth!"

Top looked over at Greg. "He's Legit, Jefe." Then he looked at Ski and said – "Greg here is our leader. He's a combat Engineer, and is our unofficial officer, despite how much he bitches about it. He's smart, for an officer." All 3 men laughed, and Este walked up, confused at the banter."

"Este – Back in position until relieved. We'll brief at dinner."

"Si, Jefe. Tell Leilani to save me a seat."

The 3 warrior leaders and their guest made their way back to the community center. Ski didn't want to ride "bitch, or on the back seat, so he just ran behind the bikes. He kept up, while carrying his M203. He was clearly in Marine Recon shape. His backpack rattled, too. It wasn't a full 60 lb. Ruck, but it was clear that he had some toys beyond the .203 rounds on the bandolier across his chest.

Over a decent meal, "The first real food I've had in weeks", said Ski, he brought the team up to speed on what was coming, and it wasn't pretty.

Prelude to war

Manuel took the early part of the night watch on the Osprey Nest, at Greg's request, and Jennifer joined the group at the community center. Greg was checking on the night-shift going on duty and telling them to be on full alert. He asked Bill to take the 5-Ton and be their first responder. Bill had also briefed on how to trigger the "Sun Tzu" solution, if needed.

After giving orders, Greg walked back into the center, and joined the command group, consisting of Jennifer, Top, Gunny, Angel, Ethyl, Sam, Doc, Kim, Les and the soldiers from Dahlgren. Some had been on night-shift, but they'd tagged in day-shifters or reserve forces to cover for them for the time being. It appeared introductions had been made. Este and Leilani loitered nearby, listening in and standing really close together, but not touching. The rest of the group conversation was about getting Ski caught up.

Greg sat down and dug in to tonight's dinner. "Leilani this is NOT a Salmon Log. I know this, but damn, it sure tastes like it. How did you make Grandma's secret recipe?"

"Well, you know da kine, Jefe." She smiled when Este smiled at her use of Spanish. "I found some condensed milk, and we had lots of fish to blend for flavah, bruddah. Then I used..." She paused, with a look of disgust on her face, "MRE Cheese."

"This is fantastic, Leilani. Thank you for the memory of my family. If we go today, we had an amazing meal." Eyes looked at Greg, like 'what the fuck'. "But, our goal is to send these sorry Meth-heads to their graves with no last meal. Time to talk about how we are gonna FUCK THEM UP!"

The crowd cheered. As it died down, Greg looked to Ski and asked, "What's up against us?"

"Well, Sir, he said with no hesitation. We have a mixed gang of Bikers, Meth heads, prisoners and gang bangers, not that they're mutually exclusive. They were recruited by a guy named 'Phoenix'. The word from the guys I caught and, um, interrogated, is that he was the one that led the first attack here. You guys messed his shit up, and he's got an axe to grind. He pulled together all of the local gangs, and then masterminded the mutiny at Dahlgren."

"I was out on recon and got back too late. I followed those fucks to their next few camps. They had you in mind, Greg. They've taken all resources, and people along Route 3, and 202. I've been following, and 'interrogating' any of their stragglers. This guy is a tattoo-headed guy with a left arm that doesn't work so well. He blames you, and he's coming for you.

Doc interrupted, "Interrogate, huh? Waterboarding, or what?"

Greg tensed up, as he figured Doc would have a problem with torture. He waited for Ski to Respond.

"Yeah, man." Ski smiled and continued. "Sticking my K-Bar in their chests, millimeter by millimeter. Going towards their heart. They all talk, eventually. If they don't their buddy does when he sees them explode blood like something out of that movie about aliens."

"Well Ok, then, as long as they're not suffering prolonged agony." Smiled Doc.

"Nope, doesn't last long at all. They talk quite quickly, or not at all. Amazing what a K-Bar headed to your heart will make you say. Once I know they're done talking, it's quick."

Doc gave a thumb's up. Greg, surprised as hell, said "Doc, what the fuck? I thought you had taken a Hippocratic oath or something, brother."

"Nope. I took the same oath you did, Greg. To protect against all enemies, foreign and domestic. If I'm not ordered to save the enemy's ass, why the fuck would I? I can't stand to see them suffer from their wounds long term. Once they're turned over to me for care by the chain of command, I must take care of the fucks, but you have a cure for that, don't you, Ski?"

"Well, that will make clean-up easier this time, eh, Gunny?"

"Oooh-Rah, Jefe!" She smiled, and Top looked around, wondering what just happened.

The blood rushed out of Jennifer's face, and she looked like she was going to be sick, remembering her first execution of a biker. She took a few deep breaths, then grabbed Greg's hand, and nodded into his face. He kissed her on the lips, and the briefing continued.

Phoenix's second-in-command, if you can call him that, is a guy named Whip. This fuck pulled my brother into his crew and didn't even bother to bury him when he OD'd on Meth & Heroin. They left my little brother in the dirt, in his own Puke. This was just before the lights went out, and I've made it my hobby to get this fuck-puddle. Unfortunately, he's super-paranoid, and always has a dozen of his 'Rangers' around him."

The Rangers around the table started to call bullshit, but Ski held up his hand. "I know, brothers. They're big, gym-rats with Mac-10's, Uzi's and other pussy weapons. They try intimidation, and if that doesn't work, its "spray and pray". That said, I'm going to take this fuck out. That's all I ask. I have a backpack full of fun toys, but I'm going out after him with my Beretta, canteen and my K-Bar. Greg, you and Top can inventory the toys I brought. I think you'll find a good use for them."

Ski went on to tell the team of the enemy's disposition. He noted that they had about 200 "Infantry". These were the remaining recruits from Dahlgren. They had M-4's, M-16s, and civilian AR-15's, but were extremely light on ammunition. He estimated about 60 rounds each, as the last act of the heroes of Dahlgren was to blow up most of the spare ammunition in the ammo dump. He said that he knew what load they were carrying, because their magazines were in his backpack, and the community was welcome to it.

Ski pointed out that, while the infantry only had 2 magazines each, the cavalry, which consisted of 30 Harleys and other bikes, had plenty of ammunition. Whip and his dozen 'Rangers' had a lot more firepower, including some grenades and at least 2 RPG's. Ski wasn't sure about the group dynamics, but his gut told him that there were some power struggles going on, with each of the leaders informally commanding about half of their infantry.

The reason for a few extra days of respite became obvious. An army can only move at the speed of its slowest members, or foot soldiers.

Ski continued, "For now, I haven't eaten in 2 days, so thanks for this meal, ladies. Before that, it was limited rations, and I'm about tired of MRE's. I scavenged whatever toys I thought might be useful in killing the most pukes, and Kudzu isn't the worst food ever..." he paused. "OK, it is." Ethyl brought him his second plate of salmon log, and he sucked it down like it was his last meal, scooping up the leftover with Johnny Cakes, or buckwheat pancakes harvested and ground from the local fields fall harvest.

Hell on Earth

After dinner, the day shift brought plates of food, and full canteens to their partners on night-shift. All locations would be manned at double-strength until Ski could call in a scouting report on the enemy's disposition. Ski left with PFC Newman, who didn't talk much about his motivations, other than to say "Those fuckers aren't Rangers. Watch me prove it!"

Ski dropped off one of his 2 throat-mic radios with Top, who added it to his gear with an ease that told Greg that he was familiar with the device.

Greg and Jen were in the Osprey Nest, with Annie asleep below. They didn't have the luxury of fooling around tonight, but they still took the time to occasionally kiss each other, or just caress. As long as they were watching, they were fine.

Leilani was on the dock, fishing again. Esteban was in his overlook, high up in the Mansion. Gunny was on the balcony with Ma Deuce. Bill was on the 5-ton, and Jaime had the front of the log barrier. Top had Angel, Cpl. Simmons, and just about everyone else, except the mortar team of Jones and Baker on the berm. Les was watching the other side of the peninsula, in case they came up the Nomini. This was less likely, as the shore approach was full of nasty thorn bushes, poison ivy, steep slopes, and nasty fallen pine trees. Greg had spent years scouting land-approaches to the water on that side of the peninsula, so he didn't have to row around, and he never found one.

The Radio crackled to life. A whispered voice said "Sheepdogs, this is Ski-dog. 100 plus infantry advancing through the forest, approaching mine path. No sign of cavalry. ETA 10 minutes. Over"

Top, who knew his radio discipline, double-clicked twice, meaning "received"

Les, who did not have a radio, came running over to the Osprey Nest, and climbed up. "Greg, I saw several full boats, rafts, and a sailboat coming from up the Nomini. They couldn't find a good landing, so they're going around Golden Bell Point. They're probably approaching the boat ramp."

Greg got on the radio. "Top 'dawg, we have multiple landing craft turning the point, and headed to the boat ramp. Lesser evil," Greg made up a call sign for Les, "Headed to crater lake." Off the net, he said "Get Leilani off the dock, and into the house. Tell her to keep her head down. Jen nodded and headed down the ladder, but returned quickly as he saw Leilani headed into his house, presumably to protect Annie.

"Copy, Jefe. Tiene Cuidado. All stations copy?"

"Eagles Nest, copy." Gunny's voice. "Lover Boy in place upstairs." Greg smiled at Gunny's reference to Esteban.

"Truck stop, copy. Standing by for Sun Tzu." Bill checked in.

"Deep throat, Five-by-five." The mortar crew was listening and ready.

"Momma Kass, all pigeons safe." Most of the reserve team had been pulled back to Seahawk Circle, with Esther in charge.

As the moon was waning, Greg heard the boats coming before he saw them. At first he thought the waves were breaking on the sand bar, because of the rhythmic noise, but he realized it was rowers, paddling.

"Deep Throat, Can I get a little light over the sand bar? Over." Greg requested some illumination from the mortar crew.

Greg heard the muffled "thump" of a mortar. A few seconds later, a parachute flare popped, right over the sand bar, perfectly silhouetting the 3 large crab-boats and/or flat-bottomed John Boats. Men were hanging over the side rowing slowly. Each boat was low in the water, with about 20 troops on them. Various makes and sizes made it difficult to get a good count. Greg didn't need a count. He aimed for the biggest one and whispered to Jen. Load HE, watch back-blast.

Jen pulled a high explosive round for the 90MM, and Greg felt the round slide into place. A click, and a slap on his ass, and he was locked and loaded.

"I'm down" whispered Jen.

Greg sighted the middle of the target boat and squeezed the trigger. WHOOOOF! The noise was loud, but, as they're named that way, the recoilless rifle barely moved. The roof, however, lit up with smoke and the flame of the rocket. Then the boat just *disappeared* in the middle. The fireball lit up the river brighter than the flare.

Greg didn't have time to enjoy his handiwork. "Load HE, Jen!" At that moment, in the relative quiet of a few enemy splashing and screaming that they couldn't swim, Greg heard Ma-Deuce open up with her distinctive Bam-Bam-Bam by the front gate. Gunny was getting some. Small arms fire opened up, and the berm area suddenly sounded like popcorn in a microwave. This was a well-coordinated attack. Luckily, the men from Dahlgren brought some counter-measures.

Jen got the second round loaded just as incoming rounds from about 50 remaining enemy started to spray the roof. Jen was hit in the leg, and luckily, dropped behind the peak of the roof – away from the bad guys. Greg ran up to take cover behind the masonry chimney.

"JEN! Jen... are you OK, baby?"

"I'm good, Cowboy, light 'em up. Those fuckers SHOT me!"

Greg took a deep breath, and sighted on the next-largest boat, and turned it into a crater in the water. About half the incoming rounds followed his smoke trail, and he ducked behind the chimney. Shards of brick and asphalt shingles sprayed all around him. At his last glance, the third boat was about 30 feet from the boat dock. Greg dropped the nose of the 90MM and said "HE" to Jennifer. She tossed him a round, which he caught after playing "Tip drill". He was also trying to stay behind the stone of the chimney. He loaded a third round, and looked over his shoulder. Jen was tying a length of para-cord around her calf. She was alert and seemed OK.

"Jen, Listen. Lay on the roof with your legs up-hill – don't go into Shock. I'll be back as soon as I can."

"Wilco, cowboy. You'll say anything to get my legs up in the air." She looked at him, smiled, and blew a kiss.

Greg got on Jen's side of the roof and ran to the edge of the house closest to the boat ramp. He sighted in the last large boat, and fired... and hit a pine tree, crashing it across the boat ramp.

"FUCK!"

Ski

A few minutes before, Ski and PFC Newman, perched comfortably in the thick foliage of a Cedar tree, equidistant from the mine-lane, 5-ton, and defensive berm watched quietly as 100- plus infantry slowly, but not quietly, made their way through the woods. Phoenix got smarter and was performing a 2-pronged attack on community, even though the thick forest made it harder.

Ski watched as the last infantry men passed him, going towards landmine alley, followed by Whip and his 20 or so 'Rangers'. He looked over at Newman, and then made the universal "cut their throat" sign. Once they were far enough away, he called in his Situation Report, or SITREP, and he slowly climbed down out of the Cedar tree, with Newman on his 6, or covering the rear.

They followed at a distance, moving like REAL Rangers and Marine Recon warriors would. Despite Ski's talk at dinner, he was convinced by Greg that each man should have an M-4, a side-arm, and whatever knife they each called "sweetness" every night before bed. Ski had his Ka-Bar, and Newman had his Gerber combat blade.

In front of them, they heard the M-2 open up, defending the peninsula. That worry of ambush gone, they moved forward for some blood. Phoenix's infantry seemed to be making their way to the mined path.

At the shrill sound of a whistle, those on the path started marching forward. They entered the path, and double-timed down it, accompanied by an occasional boom, or pop, as they detonated the mines. Phoenix was using his own men as cannon fodder! There was an occasional gurgle and screams from those trying to help as someone tripped one of the snares. Esteban was ruthless with his bent trees, and often a group of attackers would watch as a team member was yanked off the ground and shit himself as he was hung over the trail. With that many people, a buddy might be cut down before being strangled, but once again, it took a handful of men to save one, and was totally demoralizing to the attackers. Whip and his 'Rangers' didn't go on the path, but instead walked parallel to it, through the thick woods. Ski and Newman followed their prey quietly.

As the majority of the Infantry entered the kill zone in front of the bunker, the defender's small arms lit up, and it was a full-on battle. Top called in mortars, which were dropping into the middle of the bad guys at the head of the trail, creating random "crumps" and screams. Only then did the 'Rangers' enter the clearing and spread out in a defensive formation. They tried taking potshots with their little 9mm automatics, but it was truly "spray and pray". They spent longer changing their magazines than they did emptying them.

Ski tapped Newman on the shoulder and mimicked spraying his own M-4. Newman smiled and nodded, doing a parody of a dysfunctional person spraying the whole area. Ski grinned and moved forward. The 2 elite warriors leveled their M-4's into the back of the group of 'Rangers' and did their own version of Spraying. There was no praying involved, as each well-aimed, 3-round burst took out, or at least crippled a musclebound 'Ranger.' When they were done, they didn't bother to re-load, over a dozen 'Rangers' were down, and a handful were standing, looking around confused. The Marine and Ranger warriors dropped their rifles and waded into the few remaining rangers with pistols and knives. All of this was happening while the un-trained enemy infantry was being mowed down by the defenders behind the berm. The defenders were now outnumbered about 6-to-1, but seemed to be holding their own.

At that point, Top tripped the claymores in the berm, and the odds immediately went to about 4 to 1, with lots of screaming and the smell of offal coming from the poorly prepared attackers. A quick look by Ski showed that the numbers had moved to about 50 attackers against a dozen or so defenders. Ski watched as Top took a shot to the head area as he was barking orders.

Ski was rightly and fully pissed off. He looked left, found his prey. "WHIP IS MINE." Yelled Ski.

"No shit, brother, I'll bat clean-up." Said Newman. He casually double-tapped all but one of the remaining standing 'Rangers' in the face, then pointed at the last one and said, "Who said you could call yourself a Ranger? Prove it pussy."

Newman was facing, easily, a 280 lb. Gym rat. This dude was covered with tattoos and looked at the 160 lbs. (soaking wet) Newman. He was caught in the sights of Newman's Beretta, so dropped his Uzi. "I said so. Come be daddy's bitch."

Newman walked up slowly, dropped his empty pistol (not that the Thug knew it), and when the 'Ranger' rushed him, he side-stepped and stuck his Gerber combat knife into the base of his skull. There was no dance and parry, just deadly accuracy. "Check mate, Fuck-puddle. You are NOT a Ranger!" He stood over the dead Gym Rat, and yelled a victory rebel yell, as he pulled out his knife, and then proceeded to clean up the wounded 'Rangers' still twitching on the ground. He was briefly an ENT specialist, as his knife went into their eye, nose or throat, and he moved on to the next one. Then he wiped off his knife, and watched Whip and Ski circle each other.

Whip got his name because he was fast as a whip with a knife. The look in his eye was predatory as he looked Ski in the face. "I've seen you. Your brother was so proud of you. Killing both of you will be my legacy, and my mercy."

"Your legacy will be getting fed to the crabs in this harbor. I'm done talking, let's dance." Ski went silent and started to circle.

Whip moved in with a strike, faked to the right, and cut Ski on the left shoulder and jumped a few feet to the side.

"Ow." Ski said sarcastically. Then he faked throwing his Ka-Bar at Whip. When Whip moved to the side, Ski was there at his side, and shoved the Ka-Bar into his kidney. Many say that a knife to the kidney is the most painful wound anyone could experience. It's where Special Operators are trained to strike from behind, because the pain is so intense, that it renders the victim immovable, and silent.

If pain were measured by screaming, this cut would not be too bad. That said, the victim's eyes rolled up into his head. He tried to take a breath, but nothing would move into his lungs. Whip dropped to his knees, and looked like he was screaming, but no noise came out.

"That's why we sneak up on fucks like you and stab the kidney. They can't scream, bitch! Any last words? Oh, what? Can't hear you. I guess you're done then." With that, Ski grabbed Whip by the hair, and cut his throat, sawing all the way to his backbone. When he let go, Whip's head fell back, and his body fell on his own folded-under head. Even though Newman was one tough warrior, he threw up in his throat a little at the sight.

With all of the small arms noise of the battle of the berm, and the ringing of the ears that came with claymores blowing off nearby, neither Newman nor Ski could hear very well. Add to that the adrenaline of man-to-man combat, and neither of them were tuned into the motorcycles coming down the now-cleared land-mine alley. When they did hear them getting close, they turned, with knives in their hands, as Phoenix's gang of 20-plus biker cavalry came through and sprayed them both with 9mm bullets. Both men tried evasive action to get to their firearms, but there were too many men and bullets. They were both hit several times and went down hard as the motorcycles roared past.

As they lay bleeding in the dirt, Ski looked over at Newman, and gasped, "Semper Fi, Brother. We brought a knife to a gun fight." He laughed, then closed his eyes. The Marine Creed of "Always faithful" was indeed a testament to Ski's revenge of his brother's death. He reached out and grasped hands with Newman.

"Sua Sponte, friend." PFC Newman smiled as he gasped the Ranger creed, 'Of their own accord' as his last words on the planet. He did indeed choose this path, of his own accord. He also defended the honor, and name, of the US Army Rangers, admirably.

Cratering

After Hitting the tree with his poorly-aimed shot from the roof, Greg dropped flat and picked up a Flechette round as he got to the ladder. His thinking was that by the time he cleared the trees the boat was behind, they would have landed. He strapped the 90MM across his back and slid down the ladder. Dropping off the roof and running towards the bunker.

As Greg cleared the Leilani's front yard, he looked at the bunker, hoping that he could win the race, by getting there before the attackers cleared the kill zone. He saw Les in the bunker, shouting at Greg to "GET DOWN – Fire in the hole!"

Greg dropped to the ground, curled into a ball, opened his mouth, and stuck his fingers in his ears, to prevent overpressure causing ruptured ear drums. He had remembered his lesson from the first battle: Overpressure sucks. Just about then, there was a CRUMP as the cratering charge and other IED's planted around the boat ramp blew chunks of concrete and stone into the center of the group of attackers who were just coming ashore. The concussion was like a punch in the chest. Greg moved his hands to cover his head as detritus rained down all around him. He was hit in the leg by a falling chunk of stone, but he felt that it wasn't anything serious.

He got up from his protective position, and limp-sprinted to the foxhole as he heard the first line claymores detonated at the berm behind about a quarter mile behind him. He dove and slid into the foxhole, snagging himself on the end, but eventually dropped in with Les – who was on the ground with a chunk of stone imbedded in his head. Greg checked for a pulse and didn't get one. Another good man gone, another grave to dig, another reason to want revenge on Phoenix.

Greg saw Manuel sprinting through the trees, and then across the front yard of one of the empty houses on the peninsula. He was headed for Golden Bell point, on the other side of the sand bar, overlooking the inlet. Based on the intel received on the radio, he assumed it was to repel the sailboat, which had not passed the channel into Rock Harbor. Greg had more pressing needs at the moment. He had an assault force to repel.

As Greg stopped at the roadside entry to the boat ramp, he looked down and saw that the cratering charge did indeed do its job. There were four invaders, in various states of walking wounded trying to organize a defense around the crater.

Greg aimed the Flechette charge into the center rear of the crater and fired it a range of about 60 feet. The men in the crater didn't see him approach around the trees, so were not prepared. They just ceased to exist from the waist up. Flechettes create massive trauma against people, with their steel darts. 90MM worth of flechettes is much like firing 15 12-gauge shotguns at the same time. Greg set the 90MM down pulled around his M-4. A few finishing shots into the moaning bodies around the ramp, and the naval assault seemed to have been blunted.

...Except for the sailboat. Greg ran to the edge of the boat ramp, and onto the edge of the dock, as he knew he could see the inlet from there. Greg saw what had happened to the sailboat. The keel of the boat had bottomed out in the shallow inlet, as the already deeper-drafting sailboat was over-filled with men carrying guns and ammo. They were shooting in the direction of Golden Bell point. Suddenly, Greg watched a pipe bomb sail through the air, and go into the hatch of the sailboat. A muffled crump later, and the boat was foundering, with wounded men screaming for help in the water. "I can't swim!" was among the pleas for help. The fools still didn't know that they were in about 5 feet of water. They only had to stand up. Greg took the time to empty his magazine, 3 rounds at a time into the bodies around the boat, as he could see them illuminated by the burning sailboat. With that magazine empty, Greg sprinted back up the boat ramp, to check on Manuel.

Once up the ramp he ran down the road toward the last house on Golden Bell Point. Ethyl got there about 50 feet ahead of him. She was already applying a tourniquet to Manuel's bleeding leg, and he was applying pressure to the abdominal wound that he received.

Greg got there, panting, adrenaline-shaky, and asked Ethyl for a sitrep.

"This idiot disobeyed orders and took the pipe bomb to the point. He got himself shot. That's the sitrep!", she yelled with anger and sorrow in her voice. "She pulled herself together and patted his shoulder. This brave idiot better not die. You can't help with these wounds. It looks like our flank is covered. There are no more threats that I can see. Greg walked to the point and looked down into the carnage around the sailboat. The crabs would eat well tonight.

While 4 residents were successfully repelling most the naval attack, things were getting hot at the Berm. That is, if you can count 2 wounded in action, and 1 KIA as a successful defense of the flank. Greg started trotting/limping to the battle raging at the entrance, as the stone that hit his leg was starting to tell him a painful story. He looked up on the roof and saw Jennifer crawling across the roof - making her way to the ladder. She blew him a kiss, then cringed in pain, but waved him on to the front.

Top

Top and the remaining defenders had held the berm from the initial frontal assault. As they came through the mined path, he dropped 25mm grenades from Ski's M-203 into the group, and they paid the price for being first to survive the path. Top took out a few at a time while he had the distance, but there were more attackers than he could keep up with, so he switched to the M-4 and dropped them one at a time, with double-taps to the center of mass.

When the attackers overwhelmed the defenders at the berm with sheer numbers, they got close to the road opening in the berm and Top discharged the claymores, cutting down at least a dozen instantaneously. He then started calling in mortar strikes in the same pre-planned coordinates of the gap. The repeated crump of mortars taking out a handful of attackers at a time was like clockwork.

Based on the sound of the report, and the corresponding dropping attackers falling limp, or getting blown backward, Este was dropping one attacker after the other with the .308 from his roost. The Ma Deuce had exploded several, and had more laying low, but just went silent. Top figured that Gunny was either changing barrels or reloading. The M2 is usually a 2-man crew-served weapon, but could be fired by one in a stationary position, or mounted to a vehicle turret. Dealing with Jams and reloads went much slower without a second gunner to help.

Several of the attackers saw the deadly gap filling with their fellow bad-guys, so pushed the right side of the berm, across the street and as far from the mansion and its deadly fire from above as they could. They Fired an RPG at the berm, and the concussion blew Buck the firefighter back into the grass. The attackers used the crater it created in the wall as a step up and over the berm. Over 40 surviving attackers all saw the opening, and took it, as they didn't want to face any more claymores, or the ranged fire from the mortar team. Several took the opportunity to put a few rounds in Buck, who was riddled with bullets. Top saw the pressure at the gap cease, and called for another flare, so he could assess the situation.

Pop! The flare floated above the battlefield, and Top saw that the attackers were well under 50% of their strength, but most of the defender's surprises had been used up. He shouted to the defenders, "Fall back to the Mansion." He called the same message out on the radio.

As his Sheepdogs filed past him, hopping and covering in retreat, as trained, he fired as quickly as he could at the men gathering for an assault at the new hole in the berm. "Well, since the berm is breached," he said to himself, we might as well take advantage.

"Mortars, adjust fire 10 meters South, 3 East, Shot Over." As the first mortar hit on the wrong side of the berm, Top called for a minor adjustment, but the dozen or so already across rushed his position. Upon seeing the mortars move from the prior kill zone, those still on the other side of the berm rushed for the road opening. Things were going to shit quickly.

Top emptied his magazine and was hit in the right side of his chest while trying to reload. As he fell back against the berm, he hissed out his last radio call. "This is Top. Initiating Inferno One. Suggest immediate Eagles Nest retreat. At least 30 tangos coming, not all in kill zone. Sua Sponte!"

As more enemies crossed the roadside gap, Top popped the Napalm detonator buried in a plastic 55-gallon drum in front of the murder hole. A scene from hell exploded in front of the berm. This was nothing as impressive as Napalm drops seen in newsreels from Vietnam and other wars, but it was an explosion of gasoline mixed with other household chemicals to make it a gelatin-like, sticky substance. All of the enemies in front of the berm opening were covered, and ran, screaming as they burned to death. The Napalm did spray more than planned, and some came over the berm. Top's torso was covered by the angle of the berm, but he screamed as his legs were hit with a splash, and they began to burn. He quickly pushed dirt from the berm onto the fire, then looked up to see the bikers advancing out of the heat and smoke. He emptied his rifle at the bikers on his side of the berm, and then his eyes closed when he was hit again, in the side.

The remaining invaders ran past a still and smoldering Top, towards the front door of the mansion.

Gunny

The lull in the .50 Cal was because Gunny was dropping it to the ground with a rope, the planned retreat protocol. She was indeed starting to reload, and saw the battlefield situation evolving from a height, and knew that they'd need to retreat, just before Top called for it. She called up the stairs to Esteban as she ran by them, on her way down with 2 cans of .50 caliber ammunition. She heard the heavy tread of Esteban on the stairs. When they were on the ground, Este hung the .308 from Gunny's neck and picked up the .50 caliber. Soldiers from the berm were moving through the house, shooting at the attackers through the windows facing the berm. Simmons took a shot in the head and dropped down without a sound. Another part-time defender from the kitchen crew, one of the wives from Dahlgren went down, with no doubt she, too was dead.

"Retreat out the back, Sheepdogs. You know the plan! We have a surprise for these fucks. Este – set up Ma on the dock!"

Este nodded, cringing at the burns on his hands but never slowing down. Gunny followed him out with the ammo cans and the .308 still hanging around her neck. The rest of the defenders made their way along the pre-planned path of retreat along the Harbor's edge.

The attackers went from room-to-room through the mansion, looking for women, loot, and defenders that were not there. They gave rebel yells and shot their guns at nothing. Finally, 2 men came out the back door facing the dock. Gunny exploded them with the M2. There were parts all over the back entrance. Then she yelled on the radio "Fire in the hole – Blowing the mansion!" She clicked the detonator, and Rock mansion burst into flames. The brick mansion was too well-built to explode, but the windows blew out, and screams could be heard coming from most of the areas of the mansion.

As they watched the mansion burn, Gunny attended to Este's burned hands, and they cried together for their lost Sheepdogs.

Phoenix

When Greg turned off the circle towards the mansion, he saw the smoke and fires from the first Napalm blast burning out. There was no activity back-lit from his angle. It appeared that the fight was no longer at the berm.

At that moment, Greg heard the M2 pop off a dozen rounds or so. Then he heard, saw and felt the "whoosh" of Napalm going off inside of the mansion, and knew that retreat was in progress. He heard muffled screams from inside and hoped that their defensive plan was taking out most of the attackers. Seeing no movement, he decided to turn around to receive those evacuating along the pre-planned harbor retreat trail. He returned to the house, to see Jennifer sitting on the edge of the roof. "I can't get down without help, Cowboy. My leg is no good."

"OK, I'll be right up, sweetness. Keep an eye out for any of our folks emerging from the shoreline. Retreat is in progress." She aimed her .357 at the water line, although visibility wasn't good. "Sorry, I dropped the Mauser when I got shot, I think it slid into the gutter."

"No worries, Baby. We don't need any more sniping today. I'll be right up."

Greg climbed the ladder, and as he was shifting Jennifer around to get her down, the firefight in the sea grass at the water's edge started. Greg saw it happen in the flashes of the firefight about 2 houses down – halfway between the Osprey Nest and the Mansion.

Angel led the retreat from the mansion towards the Osprey Nest, their designated fallback position. Luis and Marcy followed close behind, followed by the fire fighters and a few more stragglers. As they entered a stretch of sea grass – grass that was underwater at high tide, and in the ankle-clinging mud at low-tide, the bullets started incoming. He yelled for everyone to get down, as Marcy got shot. Angel returned fire to the shadowy figures in the grass. It was dark, and muddy, and everyone was down low. It smelled bad, but mud was a good bullet-stopper.

Greg and Jennifer saw the two groups facing each other from about 50 feet away. It appeared that some of the sunken attacking "navy" boat crews had been able to swim to safety. Greg called for a flare over the harbor. A satisfying thunk and a few seconds later the harbor was illuminated in red. Greg saw a bald, tattooed head shouting orders to about 10 attackers. He aimed, and fired at Phoenix, and missed, hitting another attacker in the leg. Phoenix turned and sprayed his Automatic rifle at Greg, who ducked behind the roofline, covering Jennifer.

Greg got on the radio and called for a shift in fire, and a mortar crumped into the water about 10 yards from the attackers. Greg called in a mortar adjustment, which hit where the bad guys were – 10 seconds ago. They were retreating! Phoenix called for order and was shot at by Angel. He ducked, and low-crawled away from the defenders, towards the cover of a sea wall 2 houses up from the Osprey nest.

Greg whispered for Jen to stay low and keep quiet. He crawled to the front corner of the roof, nearest Phoenix. He aimed and pulled the trigger as the man approached. Nothing happened, as his magazine was empty. He reloaded quietly, pulled the charging handle and eased it forward quietly, this earned him a mis-feed! In his attempt to be quiet, he didn't seat the magazine properly by slapping it into the well! Clearing a mis-feed in the dark may be easy for the Special Ops guys, but for a mediocre shooter like Greg, not so much. Clearing one quietly in the dark is impossible for anyone out of practice like Greg was. Silence was his friend right now. He had the element of surprise. He reached for his hip, and his trusty .40 cal – which wasn't there. He vaguely remembered losing it in the bunker when he slid in with Les to see about his wounds. Despite reminding himself to grab it, he was focused on bringing the 90MM flechette end to the scumbags on the boat ramp.

At about this time, Tattoo-Head made his way around the sea wall and was now climbing up the stairs to the deck. Greg had not much of choice, so pulled his Gerber combat knife, and dropped the 12 feet from the roof going for a glorious killing blow. The only flaw in Greg's plan was that his empty .40 holster hooked the gutter and made a noise while changing his trajectory. Phoenix looked up and jumped back, getting a nice slash through his leather vest, and across his pectoral muscle. Greg got a more-sprained ankle, and limped backwards, as Phoenix smiled.

"You!" he growled. "Satan has delivered what he promised. I'm gonna sacrifice your bitch ass to lord of night, then take your woman with this same knife." He pulled a hideously long Bowie knife from a sheath at his back. It was right out of the "That's not a knife, this is a knife!" Movie scene.

Greg limped back along the deck towards Leilani's place, trying to get some distance, and find something to use as a shield. Having seen nothing, he dropped to the fighting stance taught by the army, and was hoping for a quick kill. The best move in a knife fight is to do a thrust horizontally across the torso, up or down, creating either edge of an 'X' from hips to opposite shoulders. In other words, disemboweling quickly is your best chance at living through a knife fight, with only one wound, if you're lucky. Only a very lucky, or superbly trained fighter survives a knife fight without at least one wound. Greg was not superbly trained, as he only had a half-day training on knife fighting in BASIC training. He was simply hoping to inflict more damage, more quickly than his opponent.

Greg saw a fishing rod, grabbed it, and threw it at Phoenix, hoping to distract him. He followed in with an upward slash, only to see Phoenix bat the rod away, move sideways quicker than Greg thought could be done, and land a slice across Greg's cheek. Greg was starting to think that maybe he should have grabbed Jennifer's sidearm, or just stayed on the roof to clear the jam. That said, being Batman and dropping on the unsuspecting prey would have been a much cooler story. He hoped his ego didn't get him killed.

With a smaller knife, and half a day's worth of hand-to-hand combat training in BASIC, Greg thought that his chances of a straight-up win in a knife fight were near zero. He had been trained in Tae-Kwon-Do when he was a kid and thought back to the One time he impressed his instructor by knocking him on his butt, with the side kick. This involved loading his hips, and then putting the weight of the body into kick at anywhere from knee to chest level.

Greg feinted with an overhand attack as he took the 2 forward steps, right toes forward, left heel forward and behind the right, load leg, hip pivot, leg punch, and CONNECTED with Phoenix's forward knee – with his doubly-sprained ankle. He thought how cool it would be if the asshole's knee bent backward, but there was no crunch. He was too tentative on the kick-through, because of the pain.

Despite his tepid kick, his weight was still significant, and Tattoo-head grimaced. Greg rejoiced in his partial success, then Phoenix buried his knife in the extended calf of Greg's leg, as he fell back. Then, with very little grace or aplomb, Greg fell to the ground in pain. In a perfect world, at least the knife would have been left in his calf, but Phoenix was good enough to pull it out quickly, and circle for a kill.

Greg fell to the deck, and crab-walked away from Phoenix with his arms behind him and his feet scuttling. Well, he did it as well as a crab with their back fin broken can crawl. He felt numerous splinters from the weather-worn deck going into his ass, and laughed out loud that one of his last thoughts were that the deck needed a good pressure-washing and refinishing.

"What's so funny, asshole? You're about to die."

"I was just thinking that revenge is a bitch, Phoenix."

"It is sweet, but not as sweet as it's going to be when I take your woman with this knife." Phoenix took 2 limping steps forward, so Greg had done some damage to him. Greg had probably broken, or at least torn muscles in his own ankle doing it, and above that, there was a 2-3" gash through his calf, bleeding profusely.

When Greg was backed up to the railing of the deck, Phoenix raised up his knife to his full height... Then he kept going higher as Leilani snuck up behind him. How someone as bulky as she was could sneak was beyond him, but she moved with grace, grabbed him by the ears, lifted and twisted. An audible snap was heard, and she dropped him into a puddle of ex-person, at Greg's feet. As he dropped his knife, she picked it up and shoved it into his heart, just to be sure, then wiped it off on his jeans.

"That's for my Bruddah. May my ancestors have peace now. I shall keep this knife as a reminder of my vengeance. She un-did Phoenix's belt and pulled off the sheath and sheathed the Bowie." She kneeled down, and evaluated Greg's wounds, then used Phoenix's belt to make a tourniquet below Greg's knee, but above his cut.

"Let's get you fixed up, Gregory. You fought well. That was an outstanding diversion." She smiled and helped him to his feet. We need to get you stitched up.

Greg smiled. "Diversion?!?! I had him right where I wanted him! Look up."

Leilani looked up, and Jennifer was leaning over the edge of the roof with her .357. She had a look of concern and love for Greg, while the blood rushed down Greg's face. He saw her look and said

"I heard chicks dig scars. I've got 2 new ones." He smiled, laughed out loud, then leaned back on the roof and passed out.

Gunny

Gunny took control of the clean-up while Greg was out. Doc and Kim were busy giving first aid to Manuel, Marcy and Greg, who were closest to them, at the circle. Greg momentarily regained consciousness, but was told to LIE STILL by Jennifer, who was also having her leg bandaged. Leilani was hovering over the wounded, who all ended up being taken to the living room of 'Greg's house' under the Osprey's nest. Greg saw that a Hawaiian was once again in charge of the house, and passed back out, thinking that all was right in the world.

The retreating wolves were chased out of the community by Gunny, Este, Luis and the firefighters plus a few other community members. Nellie stayed back at the berm and had some well-placed shotgun shots into the center of mass of the retreating bad guys. Not all killed at that distance, but each of the buckshot rounds staggered, and slowed them enough to be finished off by the community pursuers. In this way, a few more of the half-dozen or so remaining attackers were gunned down on the way to the quickest way out – the previously mined path to the road.

As the rest made it to the forest entry, they turned and shoot at their pursuers who ducked behind the berm, as bullets thunked into dirt harmlessly. Obstacles are force multipliers.

"They're going to get away!", Lindsey screamed in anger and despair. Nellie pumped a few more rounds at them, but they disappeared into the trees.

"Not if Sun Tzu has anything to do with it." With a radio call from Gunny, Bill put the final part of the plan into action. He fired up the 5-ton and drove it through the hay that was in front of it as camouflage. He plowed through it like it wasn't even there and kept driving towards the entrance/exit to landmine alley. He made a wide turn on Rock Harbor road, and pulled the 5-ton, bumper first, into the entrance to the mined lane. As the remaining wolves came around the last bend, they looked at the truck, without a gun in the mount on the roof and laughed!

"One old man, and no gun, we've got a big ride home, brothers!!!"

Bill lifted the detonator to the claymore attached to the bumper. He showed it to them, flipped them off, dropped below the windshield and detonated it. Claymores are directional explosives, with the shape of the charge set up so that the 5-ton only suffered minor charring on the bumper. They are idiot proof, not that Bill was an idiot. They do say, in big plastic letters "FRONT TOWARDS ENEMY". That was probably the last thing these ass-hats saw, before it exploded. The rest of the payload, consisting of dozens of steel ball bearings went outward from the front of the truck – into the faces and bodies of the fleeing wolves. All 5 of the remaining wolves were shredded, with blood and bits filling the woods behind them. The second battle of Rock Harbor was over, with more losses on both sides, but a victory for the residents, again. This time, it seemed there would be no bad guys left to go out and recruit, or tell stories about the

Post-Mortem

Greg came to once again, surrounded by Jennifer, Kim, and Annie. Annie was crying, with a bandaged face and holding his hand. "What's going on?"

Kim put a hand on his shoulder. "You're OK, Greg. I've got your leg patched up, and your face... well, you won't be so pretty any more, but there doesn't seem to be any major nerve damage. I've got you glued up with some Kra-Z-Glue, but I don't want you putting your weight on your leg."

"I've got to get to the front. Who's in charge? Who's hurt?" This was said with a bit of a slur, based on both his facial injury and recent unconsciousness.

"Top and Ski are both hurt pretty bad. They're in the community center with some of the other wounded from that side of the peninsula. Doc and Gunny are over there with Manuel and Marcy, who will probably make it if your fish antibiotics work – nice move! Angel has things under control. All Enemy are KIA. We made sure of that."

Jennifer kissed Greg on the lips and said "Annie was looking out the window and a stray bullet shattered it. She's got some bad cuts on her face, but she'll be OK. You're my hero! But If you had just stepped back, I could have capped that ass-hat before he cut your leg."

Greg replied, "And let you take all the glory? Hell no! Did you see my kick? A little harder and I would have busted his knee." He smiled, then got serious. "Help me up, I have to see my troops. PS – I'm glad you had my back. I love you. Let's not tell anyone about the kick, though, OK? I have a reputation as a bad ass to protect."

Jennifer laughed that throaty laugh that Greg loved so much. "OK, Cowboy. Your secret is safe with me. But you can negotiate Leilani's silence. She's a bad ass!"

Despite numerous protestations, Kim was soon walking Greg and Jennifer up Rock Harbor Drive, with each one leaning on her to take some weight off their wounded legs. Annie walked on the other side of Greg, holding his hand, and telling him stories about all the loud noises that she heard and the amazing fireworks she saw. She didn't seem to care much about the bandages on her face, but Greg could see that she would be scarred for at least her childhood.

When the 4 got within sight of the community center, Esteban, with both hands heavily bandaged, ran out and took over for Kim, who was winded. He put an arm under each of theirs, and walked, almost carried, both Greg and Jennifer into the first aid area. Angel was directing the clean-up effort out by the berm. Greg directed Este over to Top in the community center. He was bleeding, burned, and generally not looking good. He was burned badly below the waist, and bleeding in several critical places, clearly in pain.

Greg looked at Doc and asked a question with his eyes. Doc looked down, then looked at Top and said "This old Goat keeps wanting more of our Opiates. It's like they're just Aspirin to him. You stay with him – I have more work to do on Ski." Doc and Kim walked over to the table with Ski laid out on it.

"I hear you're trying to hog all of our good drugs, Top. I guess you earned it." Greg smiled a sad smile, as one of Top's eyes opened. Sorry we don't have any morphine, brother.

Top sighed, and his words croaked out. "Trying to fight the shock, Sir. Mission accomplished, enemy repelled. We have 5 wounded and 6 KIA, but we got all of the bad guys. All others present and accounted for. I'm counting you 2 love birds among the wounded, and me among the dead." Top paused, then added. "Excellent defensive plan, Sir. It's been an honor serving under you. PFC Newman and I are going to have a beer next." He paused and took a rattling breath, some more blood bubbled out of his lips on the exhale. "I'll give him your best." Top then snapped to attention, while horizontal on the table. He raised his arm painfully, and saluted Greg. He held the salute, waiting on the return.

Greg snapped to attention, and returned the salute, with tears flowing down his face. Este walked over and loomed over all of them.

Top looked over Greg's shoulder, and made eye contact with Esteban. Top smiled and said to Este, "Now you have to watch his back, big man – you can see how he clearly can't take care of himself." After another deep breath, a smile, "I've been in the revenge business for so long, now that it is over, I don't know what to do with the rest of my life." Top took one last shuddering breath, chuckled, and said, "Line 'em up. This rounds on me, Private Newman." Then he faded away, staring off into some afterlife that Greg wondered about. It gave him more faith to see the smile on Top's face.

Este, with tears dripping down his face, shuddered and said, "I knew he watched the movie." He reached around Greg's shoulder and closed Top's eyes.

Greg made his way over to Ski, who had several wounds, the worst of which appeared to be in his lung. "How's he doing, Doc?"

Well, he's strong, and we got the collapsed lung patched. He's on Fish-Mox and painkillers. We don't have x-ray's or MRI's, so all I can do is hope. I think, based on his physical condition, and sheer stubbornness, he'll make it."

"I'll make it," wheezed out Ski. "I've lived through worse."

Doc was surprised that Ski was talking, but moved past it. Doc asked, "Can you tell me where it hurts, Ski?"

"The list of where it doesn't hurt will be shorter, Doc. Heh, heh heh. My right knee has been bothering me for weeks. Today, it feels fine. Tell me the kid made it."

"Sorry, Ski. You and PFC Newman did an amazing thing, taking out the heart of the land attack. Newman didn't make it." Doc broke the news by grabbing Ski's hand.

"Some guys have all the luck," grumbled Ski. "I avenged my brother. What's there left to live for?"

"Well, there's us." Greg stated flatly. "There will be more bad guys who want our shit. You're welcome to stay here, and join the family, brother. Thanks for what you did. Top said that Newman made it to Heaven. They're having a drink right now, and frankly, I'm a little jealous at their respite. Here, we have to patch the berm, re-plant some land mines, and be ready for whatever is next."

"Well, count me among the 'sick, lame, and lazy' – at least for a while. I will heal, and plan on sticking around, Sir. With Top gone, you're going to need another asshole to boss around the troops. I'm the man for the job."

"I wish you people would stop calling me that – I'm an enlisted man! And I'm going to have to let you and Gunny argue about who's in charge!"

"Fuck that, I concede, Sir. She scares the shit outta me. You're not an enlisted man anymore. You repelled half of the invasion force, single handedly. We have a kill ratio of about 50 to 1. You're in charge, whether or not you want to be." Ski said as he laughed and fell back into unconsciousness.

"Talk to Jennifer, Les, Annie and Manuel about that 'single handed' talk, Ski.", but Greg was talking to himself and Jennifer at that point, as Ski was passed out again. "They all paid for that defense."

"You did, too, Baby. Let's go lay down, I'm starting to feel a bit light headed." Jennifer swooned, and Este caught her.

"Let's take her back home, Jefe. You need to get back in bed, too. Your cheek is bleeding again."

Jennifer

Doc gave Ski, Manuel, Marcy, Greg, Annie and Jennifer their prescribed dosage of antibiotics, and they went to their respective homes to rest, under "Doc's orders". Angel assigned Leilani and Este the task of keeping an eye on Greg and Jennifer, and playing with Annie. The mortar team, Hondurans and the remaining firefighters carried more than their load in the days after the battle, burying their dead friends and feeding bad guys to the crabs, while the wounded rested.

It seemed that everyone who was staying in the mansion had known of the "Plan C" to torch the place, so the houses on the circle had filled up with various groups. It was becoming a regular neighborhood again.

The more time passed, the more Jennifer was beating herself up for not being there when Annie got cut. She wondered if she had been in the bedroom with her daughter, would Annie be wounded now? The guilt and second-guessing about what she should have done differently were tearing her apart.

2 nights later, Greg leaned over and kissed Jennifer. He told her that her head felt hot. He asked her if she was OK, and her reply startled him. "I'm beating myself up, Greg. Looking death in the face really made me realize what Mike went through. I can't believe that I just dragged you into bed with me. What about your wife?"

Greg looked a bit confused. "Well, you know my wife probably died in Atlanta, and she cheated on me. We'll always have our years together, but I'm done with her. You didn't drag me into bed, darlin'. I came of my own free will." He smiled at the play on words.

"No, I'm serious. It feels like we rushed things, and I want to just take a little time. I need to think about this. The guilt has been killing me. What's Annie going to think?"

"Annie is good with me. You know that. Where is this coming from? We love each other. Maybe it's fast, but it's real. Don't you feel it?"

"Yes, I do, but every time I see Annie's face, I blame you. I know that's stupid, but it's my immediate instinct. When I looked off that roof, and saw you about to die, I realized the danger of getting too close to anyone. Can I just have some time to sort through my feelings, please?

"You want time now? Well, sure ", Greg replied quietly. "I don't want you to regret us, baby."

Recriminations

Greg was floored when Jennifer told him that she wanted time. He was on the tail-end of an adrenaline-flooded survival encounter, and his natural instinct was to be closer to her. Now she wanted to take time away from him? His confusion and hurt was clear, but he had no choice but to give her the space she asked for, so he nodded at her request, and a tear dripped down into his cut cheek.

"Thanks. I'm going to move back into Annie's room for a while." Jennifer got up, and limped next door, leaving Greg with his own layers of Guilt to work through. He got up, took his medicine, and went out to the chairs on the deck, looking out on the water. He asked himself "How did I fuck this up?"

Leilani was approaching the deck with Annie, who appeared to be recovering quicker and better than anyone else in the house. "Hey, you watch your mouth, Bruddah. Little babies have big ears." She set Annie down, who ran over, kissed Greg on the non-wounded cheek, then ran down the stairs to play on the dock. She cast the ultra-light rod with the spinning reel like a pro. Leilani had been busy with Annie.

"Leilani. I need your wisdom and perspective. Did Jennifer and I rush into this? What if my wife is alive? She wants some time to think about things..." Greg broke down, as some tears, manly ones, of course, rolled down his face.

"Greg, I don't know about your life or times. You said Atlanta was nuked. People come together in times of grief. Sometimes they just need someone to hold. I know the first time Esteban held me, I started to feel better."

Greg sputtered, then smiled. "That is so great! I like seeing you two together."

"Yes, we are good together, but I have to fix his ideas of breakfast. I mean, it's good, but who has burritos for breakfast? And I can't grow Poi or Breadfruit here."

Greg laughed, relieved at the change of topic. "If that's your biggest problem, you've got it made!"

"Well, our biggest problem is the queen bed next door. I think we need to scavenge for a California King!"

Greg laughed out loud again, and said, "Thank you, Leilani. I needed that. Can you go check on Jennifer? She seemed sweaty and doesn't want to talk to me right now."

Leilani went into the house and came out about 5 minutes later. "Greg, I need to go get Doc. Her leg doesn't look so good."

Doc came over, and told Greg that Jennifer wasn't responding to the fish-antibiotics. The community medicine chest didn't have anything stronger, so it was going to be up to her own immune system to win the battle, or not.

September

A long, slow painful week later, Greg went to visit Este and Leilani. "Hey, can you guys keep an eye on Annie and Jennifer?" Jennifer hasn't really been lucid at all, she's calling me 'Mike', and keeps crying. I need some time alone. It's an incoming high tide, and with the rain and the moon, it might be a huge one. I'm going to try to catch some of Jennifer's favorite – Rockfish. Maybe she'll eat something." Jennifer got even thinner, and was one hot looking, if skinny woman, but there would be no hanky panky for a while.

His neighbors, and best friends outside of the girls in his own house smiled, and Annie ran to them. Este picked her up in one lightly wrapped mitt, and flew her around the room, while Leilani smiled and told Greg "We got her, Bruddah. Get some good I'a." saying the Hawaiian word for fish.

OK. I'm going to get my stuff together. High tide is about midnight, so don't wait up. Greg went back into the house to check on Jennifer. She was still on the fish antibiotics, but her fever was so high for so many days now. She was sweaty and thrashing in the bed. Greg stripped her naked, wiped her down with a washcloth, and put his favorite Army T-shirt on her. She calmed down, and smiled when he bundled her back up in a quilt. She was out for the night. He kissed her on the forehead, which was hot.

He couldn't watch her die, but that's where he was afraid she was headed. Kim had gently prepared him for this possibility. Jennifer, when lucid, had said she wanted to have time away from him, so he was going to give it to her. He felt like she was punishing herself for her, or his perceived infidelity, or being with him when Annie got hurt by the exploding window. He'd never understand women on some days, but loved them on others.

Just before she fell asleep, Jen tapped him on the arm, and said, "Greg, why do you do it?"

"Do what, beautiful?" He kissed her on her head, which was still a little sweaty, but seemed a little cooler.

"How do you carry that load? Everyone asking you what to do?" Jennifer was semi-lucid, but at that moment wanted a real answer.

"I just make it up and hope I'm right, darling. Just get some sleep, we can talk it out later." He massaged her breast and kissed her on the lips. "Know that I love you, baby, and I do it for you and Annie, now. I pray you get to meet my kids. They would love you both. Other than that, I do it because someone has to. When people look around, and stuff's going down, somebody has to say, 'I got this!'" They don't have to be right, but they have to be confident."

The community was safe under the watchful eye of Angel and Gunny, with Ski giving orders as he recovered from his hospital bed in the community center. Gunny took the orders, even though she outranked him, because they were smart, solid orders. Greg didn't think there would be any problems there, as they got along well, and his leadership style of Socratic discussions was catching on with the formerly 'top-town' veterans. Greg figured tonight would be a good night for "fishing" alone.

After burning a bunch of energy rowing, Greg found himself in the main channel of the Nomini river. This rowing was a real workout, as he had to clear the sand bar, then row deep up the Nomini River, with help from the incoming tide. He rarely went this far, because of the distance rowing, but he needed to burn off some stress. He had been laid up for a week or so, and while his face still hurt, his leg healed better than the thought it would. It was a through-and-through knife wound that didn't hit any major blood vessels. After taking a few breaths, it was time to get down to the business of the night. His head was all twisted up, thinking about his missing daughter, likely-dead wife and son, and probably-dying Jennifer. He couldn't lose another woman. It would wreck him. Maybe he was being selfish, but after several swigs of the bourbon he brought with him, it was making more sense. He hadn't had a drink for weeks, and the Pappy Van Winkle bourbon was going straight to his head.

Greg changed the bottle in his lips to something else. He laughed out loud around the barrel of the 9mm revolver in his mouth. He thought that his last joke on the planet was pretty good, given the circumstances. "What's was the last thing to go through Greg's head on the day he died? A 9mm hollow point!" Greg laughed again at the original spin around the old joke about the last thing to go through a mosquito's head as it heads for a windshield – Its asshole. He pulled the barrel out of his mouth and took another swig of the bourbon – It was the last bottle on the peninsula, possibly the world, and what a bottle it was. He cracked it open on the day that Les lost his wife and had not touched it since. The Pappy Van Winkle Reserve – found tucked deep into the back of one of the bars of an abandoned house when he was scavenging months ago. He hadn't had a drink of alcohol in weeks, because almost all of it had already been looted and drunk, but what better way to leave the planet than with the Pappy he stashed away for a "special occasion"? He had showed more discipline than he thought he had, as he kept the bottle to toast his son and daughter's arrival, but they never showed up at the family sanctuary. Their fate was unknown to him, and he finally got to the point where he couldn't live another day without his "girls", especially with Jennifer going quickly, too. He briefly worried about Annie, but knew that Este and Leilani would take care of her, like any Hawaiian Ohana, or family, would.

Another body – probably another "floater" from Dahlgren, based on the uniform, squished against the aluminum hull of the row boat he was in. This one was pretty swollen, and Greg needed to do his duty. He was indeed clergy, and had married friends of his – to each other, at their request. He'd also given last rites, and buried too many brothers, sisters and great friends in the last year. These people he didn't even know a year ago, but adversity and hardship forge quick friendships. He took this as a sign from God that he needed to give last rites to someone else one more time. He untied the para cord noose from his ankle. It was tied to the large Hawaiian Lava stone secured with a bungee cord to the back corner of the rowboat. He went to the front of the boat, where he always kept a small supply of bricks with foot-long para-cord nooses tied to them. This trick he learned from Samuel, as Sam also had to use about one set per day to keep the harbor clear of bodies. He used a boat hook to pull the drifting corpse back toward him. He looped the noose around the ankle of the bloated stranger, and lifted the rock to the lip of the boat.

"I'm shorry for whatever you went through, you poor bashtard." He slurred. "Your pain ish done, and now you'll feed the Maryland Blue Crabs that have fed us for so long. May your spirit, or at least your protein move through the great circle of life. Hakuna Matata, my brother." Then Reverend Greg pushed the bricks off the boat, shifting the center of gravity enough that he fell against the other side, hit his head on the edge, and spilled what was left of the Pappy all over the bottom of the boat. The body was pulled to the bottom of the river, trailing a few bubbles after it. Greg would be joining the body shortly.

"Damn, Pappy, that's an un-fitting end for such a nicesh bottle.", he slurred. "Don't worry, I'll be joining you soon. Greg leaned down and sucked up as much of he could of this world-class bourbon. It was less-than-world class with the metallic taste of the boat, and the grit, sand, and general fish and foot-funk on the boat hull. Then, he went aft past the oars, and sat on the stern of the row boat again, where the outboard motor used to go when he had gasoline that wasn't bad. He looped the noose around his ankle again and tightened it. He had to get this part right, or suicide would suck. Today was a special occasion. The rock was from Grandma's garden, by way of Hawaii. For years, it decorated her garden entrance, and he splurged on this stone, hoping for it to make a connection with any of his family in Heaven. He used the last few feet of the precious para-cord from his BOB so that he could put his final plan into place.

The drunken plan was thrown together, at best. His goal was to die quickly, but not be a bother to someone else. He didn't want to be the reason that someone left alive on the peninsula had to dig another grave. He hoped to have enough time to push the rock, then pull the trigger, then fall off the back of the boat. He was pretty sure that the tide would bring the rowboat back to the harbor area when it ran back out of the Nomini, or at least beach it on the sand bar. This was his last gift to the people that he lived and suffered with for much of the last year, even if it felt like a decade. Being an officer sucked, but he hoped another would emerge in their own version of democracy. His money was on either Ski or Gunny.

Maybe the boat would drift a different direction, and he could help a stranger. He hoped that someone would at least find the boat and add to their survivability. Well, half-assed or not, it was his drunken plan, and it was time. He didn't want someone to have to give him last rites. He wanted to feed the crabs.

Greg wrapped the cord around his ankle and pulled it tight. Then he picked back up the 9mm revolver and put it in his mouth. He looked up, and said "God, I don't know what else you want from me, but I'm done. I hope I at least earned enough time with you to explain why you fed me this shit sandwich. If my wife and kids are not alive, I want to at least see their faces one last time. I hope Leigh and Jennifer don't have an eternal cat fight! I'm coming, girls." Greg then pushed the rock off the back of the boat... and heard the happy hour bell ring three times at the old homestead – as the rock started to pull him back off the boat.

Greg yelled "Wait, shit!" as he tossed the pistol towards the bow, and tried to grip the aft seat of the row boat with his ankles.

Although he was in much better shape than when this started, the rock was BIG. One of his ankles was yanked out from under the seat by Grandma's Garden Rock, and he could not hold on with his wounded leg. Anyone watching from a distance would have heard "Fuuugggghhhhhhhh!!!!" (and a large splash) as Greg's head went under water.

As Greg was being pulled to the bottom of the Nomini river – the deep part, because of the extra line, and his not wanting to be a floater – he wondered what armed force was approaching his new family. He had to go help them, but was being dragged into the deep. "Thank you, God, for at least showing me that you have a sense of humor, too." He thought. Then he remembered his ever-present Bench Made switchblade clipped to his pocket. "Funny that I didn't think to leave that for the others", he thought, as he reached in his pocket, and cut himself free.

After swimming to the surface, and wondering at the sense of Humor, and mysterious ways of God, he reached the stern of the rowboat. After dragging his now skinny (by his definition) behind back into the boat, he pointed the bow towards the Rock Harbor House Dock and started pulling on the oars. It was a long trip, but the tide had turned and helped him run back down the Nomini and up into Rock Harbor. He had spent the last 6 months rowing, so it wasn't too much of an effort, but took time. This former 300 lb. fat boy who needed blood pressure medicine to keep his heart from exploding before the dark days came had moved back through "buff" – his fighting weight of 220 lbs. at his prime when he was a soldier, and right down to the neighborhood of what he thought of as a skeleton – at 180 lbs., with his "big bones", 6'1 inch was just plain skinny. As he turned past the sandbar, which was almost blocking the inlet to Rock Harbor by now, he heard the Happy Hour bell ring again, and saw someone on the back deck.

Greg saw a strange sailboat tied to the dock. It had to come from either DC, Point Lookout, or farther down the bay, because nothing passed him as the incoming tide and his rowing took him up the Nomini river. A few minutes later, as he rowed towards the dock he yelled out "Who's that ringing my bell – you better have brought happy hour food, cuz I'm all out!" The figure on the deck moved away from the bell, and towards the deck rail. In the candlelight from the house, he saw a thin woman in silhouette with long dark hair, probably around five and a half feet tall. He watched her lean over the rail and put his binoculars from inside the back door to her eyes.

A young man came up behind her and pointed what looked like an assault rifle in the general direction of Greg, but not especially threatening him. He'd seen much, much worse in the last year, and this man wasn't really a threat, even if he did look competent enough to handle what looked like an M-16, or AR-15 type weapon. Este clamped one hand down on the front of the gun and another on the man's shoulder. Leilani stood behind the female, but was more comfortable, as they chatted. Greg's guards were cautious, but still on guard duty, as the self-appointed bodyguards didn't want to answer to Gunny or Ski for messing up. Annie was playing in the sandbox and chatting happily under the light of a torch, which was weird for the middle of the night. There was still no sign of Jennifer, who hadn't left her bed in the last 4 days.

As he pulled up to the dock, Greg realized who it was, by the light of the solar powered piling LED lights around the dock and porch. He could barely contain his emotions, as he cried out "Thank God, Maria! You finally made it!"

Greg threw a line over the dock piling, and his daughter came running down the stairs, the man under Este's watchful eye on the deck smiled and said "Dude, does your Dad always go fishing with only rocks and a pistol?"

Greg laughed out loud. The first laugh in a few weeks. As he hugged his baby – make that grown woman, as she was now 20 years old, tears of joy ran down his face. Then she asked a question that instantly turned his joy into anguish... "Dad, where's Mom and Jared?"

Greg's eyes filled with tears as he paused to gather his thoughts. "I think they're dead, but we're together again. The bad guys nuked Atlanta. Even if she lived, you know how she was so stubborn about eating her Glock if the air conditioning ever went out. I don't think we'll ever know, but I believe she's gone. Jared was even closer to the airport that blew up. Some nights I pray that they just died quickly in the blast. Other days, I hope they're still on their way."

"What?!?! Why didn't you go get her?" She demanded

"Baby, I've steeled myself to go every damn day. Then I'd plan my trip to your school. I was like a donkey between 2 bales of hay! The fact is, IF they're alive, I could walk into a nuclear dead zone and pass her on the way there, if I'm sleeping by day, and she's walking. There are a dozen routes here from there. If, against odds, they are alive, we have to wait for her here. I waited for you, and here you are."

Maria sobbed as father and daughter fell to the dock in the same spot they had taken so many happy fishing pictures in the past. Some of those pictures were mounted on the wall at home in Atlanta, and copies were in the house behind them. They were mourning and hugging each other, but at least they were together again, at last.

Jennifer limped out onto the balcony, not looking her best, but still she stole Greg's breath away. Apparently, her fever had broken while he was trying to kill himself, as she looked more human than she had in a few days. "Your dad has told me a lot about you, Maria. Let's get you some food. I, for one, am starving."

Leilani took the cue and ran into the kitchen to get started. Maria looked at Greg with a questioning glance.

"We've got a lot to get caught up on, baby girl. Let's get some food, and you can introduce me to this young man."

"And YOU can introduce me to these folks, who seem kind, but why are they living in our family house?"

"That's a long story, but we've got plenty of time. I can't tell you how many nights I've looked out over the water, hoping to see you. Tonight, you snuck right by me."

Just then, Bannon, Greg's nephew stuck his head up out of the hold. Hey, is someone gonna help me unload this big-ass Ham Radio? I told Dad we'd call when we arrive!

"Bannon! Greg bounded down the boat to his Nephew and his megawatt smile. What a fantastic Surprise. You mentioned your dad.", he paused thinking of how he might shift the mood immediately. I'll want to learn more about everyone else after we eat.

"That's OK, Unc. I know in my heart they're both still alive. Reid joined the Marines to go find Mom in Baltimore."

"Damn, a Marine? He's wanted to be Army forever."

"Yeah, but the Marines drafted him."

"Yeah, we have a lot of catching up to do. Now, Maria was called Captain? What does that make you?"

"Boat Thief." He laughed, and then handed a Ham Radio transmitter to his Uncle, making sure that Unc had both hands on it, so it didn't go swimming. "Let's go find something to eat and catch up.

"Unc, do you know how many sailboats she's wrecked in the last half of a year? All I can say is that she now knows what NOT to do with sailboats, as she has learned from her mistakes. You always said mistakes create wisdom, so she's pretty sailing-wise by now.

She said she remembered seeing others stranded on the sandbar, and laughing at them, so we waited for the tail end of incoming high tide. The wind was perfect."

"Well, let's let 'Captain Maria', eat, and you can tell me all about it."

Just then, a stunning redhead came out of the cabin of the sailboat. She smiled at Greg, and then asked Bannon to grab her pack from the boat.

"Uncle G, this is Kelly, the love of my life. She's also a hell of a warrior. Kelly, this is Crazy Uncle Greg."

Kelly smiled, curtseyed, and said "I'm so glad we're here. I couldn't stand to hear Maria whining about her daddy any more. Nice place you have here." Then she reached for his hand, and Greg pulled her across the gap. She threw her arms across Greg's waist, and kissed his cheek. I'm so glad you're here and OK. Maria, Pete and Bannon are like family to me. Now, show me around, you big hunka man.

The trio went back up the deck. Greg gave the radio to Este so he could put one arm on Maria's shoulder. They all walked them into the kitchen area, where Leilani was already preparing some sort of feast that smelled wonderful. Este was whispering into the young man's ear, with an arm clamped on his shoulder and one around the radio. Annie followed them all in, tugging on the young man Pete's sleeve.

"Hey, you pretty boy. What's your name? Wanna play Polly Pocket with me?" Pete smiled at Maria, shrugged, and winked.

"Hey Little one. My name is Pete. I'm a fireman. Who are you, beautiful?" The handsome young man smiled, handed his rifle to Este, and followed Annie to the screened in porch where the breeze was best. There, he sat on the floor in the light of the candles as the first light of false dawn lit the sky in the East and played Polly Pocket make-believe games. "Polly Pocket, huh? Maria told me all about her games with her Dad, Polly and their friend, Bug. Oh, is that Bug?"

The End?

Stay tuned for the next book in the "Rock Harbor" series, "Daddy's Home". The expected e-book publication date is at 9:04pm, sometime in the Summer of 2018. Thank you for your interest in my work, readers. And for you fellow veterans, as well as others who give some back (teachers, medical personnel, LEO, volunteers, etc.). Thank you for your service.

Here's a free preview of "Daddy's Home:

The battle of Saint Mary's

Bannon was running with his M-16 and 3 loaded magazines, but it bounced on his back, annoying him. He knew what this type of fight was going to need to be as he ran towards Sergeant Spencer.

"Sarge, if you know about the Dragons, you know I need to flank these fuckers. What's the best way out and around them?" Sarge nodded and held up his hand in the classic, "wait" signal. He yelled up to one of the snipers. "Peters! You watch that road, and when they get in the kill zone, blow it." Peters didn't even take his eyes off the road. He just gave a thumbs-up, and chambered another round in his scoped hunting rifle.

Sarge looked across to the other tower flanking the gate. "Williams, you watch the side of the road. Thin them out and make the road look like a better approach."

Williams deer rifle fired, he turned around for a second. "You mean like that, Sarge?" Then he smiled and was shot in the side of the head. His brains sprayed over Sarge and Bannon as they approached. Williams toppled off the tower, quite dead.

"God Damn it!" Spencer grabbed Bannon and spun him towards the Southeastern gate of the football stadium. "Southeast Gate. Call sign 'High Chair', response 'Red Tail'. Tell them to let you out and cover you. Flank these fucks and kill them all!" Then Sergeant

Spencer climbed the sniper tower, grabbed the deer rifle, and started shooting.

Bannon climbed up behind Sarge, dropped off 2 magazines and tapped Spencer on the leg. He handed up his M-16, too. "Here. You'll do more good with this than I will." I have my pistol and knife. Spencer took the M-16 without comment, and started shooting, one-shot, one-kill style. Bannon raced for the Eastern gate.

Upon reaching the Southeastern gate, he found the snipers there pointed Northeast, trying to help out their brothers and sisters in arms. One looked down at him and swung her rifle towards him.

"High Chair" Bannon yelled, holding his open hands up in front of his face. She swung her rifle away and back to the North, firing again. "What's the best way over the wall?"

"Come up here, it's about 12 feet down, but I don't know why you want out there."

As Bannon climbed her tower, he replied. "So that I can kill those bastards from behind. Don't shoot me, pass it on." He smiled his 1000-watt smile, and she smiled back.

"I won't shoot you, you're too cute. Come back and introduce yourself properly. Just ask for Kelly O'Keefe." She fired another round, and a man coming out of the wood line on the North dropped.

"Nice shooting, Kelly O'Keefe. I'll buy you breakfast, if you'll allow me the honor." With that, Bannon dropped over the edge, hung from the wall, and CLIMBED down it, with fingers in the mortar, or on an occasional brick edge. He dropped the last few feet, waved to Kelly, who looked suitably impressed, and ran quietly into the woods with his pistol in his left hand and his Buck knife in the right.

Bannon could tell where the cannibalistic 'Locusts' were, simply by listening. They were lousy in the woods and were yelling questions and orders to each other. He followed the edge of the noise until he was sure he was behind the last of the attackers, and then rolled up the flank, one stab at a time. He could tell when he was getting close, even to the relatively quiet ones, by the stench. These people may not have bathed since the lights went out. That said, his knife parted the crust on their clothes well enough, and he killed at least 20 of them silently, mostly by slicing their throat, or stabbing them in the kidney, then heart. He left a trail of carnage through the woods on the eastern side of the roadway entrance to the College.

When he was sure the woods on the East were clear, he darted across the road to clear out the few remaining Locusts that he could hear over there. As he was halfway across the road, Peters, the scout in the sniper tower, saw his silhouette through his scope, and blew the furthest IED from the gate. Bannon felt himself being lifted from the road, then a chunk of concrete punched him in the ribs, smashing several of them. Smaller bits of concrete hit him in the face and leg, spinning him through the air. An eternity later, he landed hard on his back, hitting his head on the road, and everything went black.

Roadside Bomb and the Off Switch

Maria, who was covering the west side of the road and gate, kept her head down low, and shot at anything that moved in the forest. As the attackers died, some as close to the wall that she could tell the color of their eyes, she noticed a slacking of activity to her right, or East. She thought to herself that Bannon was earning another group of sleepless nights. She had taken a moment about 20 minutes ago, ducking and reloading, to look East. She saw him climb a tower and go over the wall.

As the intensity of the attack slowed down, she heard a tremendous explosion on the road, but was too busy picking off the last of the strays to worry much about it. Finally, there was no more activity in the wood line, and she couldn't hear the Locusts moving or shouting orders any longer. She kept her eyes above the wall, and scanned left and right, hoping that anyone left would run away. Killing, when necessary was something she'd come to understand. Dying unnecessarily was something that she would never understand.

After several minutes of silence, she heard someone to her East outside the wire call for a medic. After the third yell of "Medic!", she recognized Sergeant Spencer's voice, and slid down the ladder, running to the field hospital. She grabbed Pete and said, "We need you outside the wire. Follow me. The 2 friends ran quickly to the gate, where Peters was keeping guard from his tower. He pointed down the road weakly and stuttered "Ou-Out there."

The two friends ran down the road to where Sergeant Spencer and a red-headed female soldier were bent over a casualty, putting pressure on wounds. When they saw Pete, they waved him over, and Sergeant Spencer got up and walked to Maria. "Maria. There was a mistake. Your cousin is fucked up, but he'll live if Pete is any good."

Maria nodded and moved past him to look at Bannon, who was indeed truly messed up. His head was bleeding, and his leg looked broken, but Pete was concentrating on his chest. Pete said "Maria, we need to prevent a collapsed lung. Help me. He was not panicking, but the look in his eye was of pure anguish.

Some shrapnel made a hole in his chest and lungs. He reached in his bag and pulled open a sterile bag. "I'm putting on this chest seal. It won't let air in but will let it out. If too much air gets between the chest wall and his lungs, his lung could collapse. I need you to watch his respiration and keep an eye on his chest to make sure one side isn't bigger than the other. Sarge, get me a stretcher while I look at his head wound. You, redhead, bind up that leg wound, it's not the worst, but we don't want him bleeding out.

"My name is Kelly, and we can't let that happen. We are supposed to have breakfast together." Kelly expertly removed her combat dressing from the belt at her waist, and wrapped the leg wound tightly. I never even learned his name."

Maria, who was checking her cousin's pulse, and looking at his chest looked up at Kelly. "He'll make your breakfast date, Kelly. He's the strongest guy I know. His name is Bannon, and he's my cousin. That is a great dressing. He's always had great taste in women. I hope your breakfast isn't tomorrow. He may need some rest first, but he'll make breakfast someday soon. I have no doubt.

Kelly moved up Bannon's body, and looked at Maria. "I've never seen anything like what he did. He rolled up the right flank by himself, and never fired a shot. He walked into the woods, and it just got quiet, from right to left. I mean, I shot a bunch, too… He's like a ghost."

"Probably not the best choice of words right now." Maria corrected sternly.

"Oh shit! I'm sorry. He's going to be OK. He climbed down the wall with his fingertips. Who does that?"

"Bannon was a rock climber before the lights went out. If anyone can make it through this, he can."

About that time, Peters came over carrying a stretcher. "Sarge sent me over with this. He says I get to carry the guy since I blew him up."

Maria stood up, and her fist followed her. It gained momentum from the ground to the 6 feet where his jaw started. She punched Peters in the "off button", as her Dad called it, and he dropped to the ground. Kelly looked at her with eyes wide open. Pete laughed, and finished bandaging Bannon. He's ready to move, Captain Maria. You girls grab a handle each on the front, and I'll take the back. I can send someone back for this ass-hat.

Kelly said, "He's not a bad guy. He was just a freshman when this happened, and he comes from California. He's not the best soldier, but he shows up on time, and in the right uniform every day. I'll come back and check on him if he's not awake in a bit. Where'd you learn to hit like that?"

"My Dad is a soldier. He taught me how to hit. I may have been a little hasty, but I couldn't stop myself. He hurt my Cuz."

"I'm sure it was an accident." Kelly said sincerely.

"I know, or he'd be dead." Maria acknowledged, patting her SOG blade. "Let's get Pete to the infirmary, then you can check on Private Ass-hat."